GW00481728

THE NICE GUY

SARAH A. DENZIL

SL HARKER

PROLOGUE

I don't believe in fate. Never have. I hate the thought of not having control over what comes next. The cynic in me thinks that it might be a lazy way of avoiding responsibility, of washing one's hands of the choices we make.

But perhaps it's comfort for broken souls.

All I know is that there often comes a time when a person must take control of their own life. No one else is going to do it. Difficult decisions will be made, and those choices will reveal the true mettle of the individual within.

When my skull collides with the wall, I know I'm facing that choice. I could give up and let it all go. There would be peace, at least. I hope so anyway. Fighting means feeling the pain. Fighting means facing the fear and doing it anyway.

So which am I going to choose?

PART I

CHAPTER 1

O n this cool September Saturday, the East River is the colour of caramel. Early-morning sunlight glints across its surface. There is a crispness in the air, though the sun's rays warm my bare neck.

I watch as men and women file into the streets, all joining as one. My fingers tighten around the cardboard sign in my left hand. It's illustrated with one image—a coat hanger.

"Can you believe how crowded it is?" Jessa's petite frame leans towards me so that I can hear her over the sea of people.

I don't like crowds, and I never have. But I'd felt it important to come out, to be a voice among the many.

"You okay?" she asks.

"Yeah, fine," I say, trying to make my smile seem genuine.

Pushing the worries out of my mind, I concentrate on the chants, the boots on the ground, Jessa's milky skin glowing golden in the Manhattan sun.

We shuffle along like a herd of cattle. Gone are the usual vendors selling street paintings of New York City's skyline or T-shirts with Big Apple logos plastered across the chest. In front of me, the double arches of the Brooklyn Bridge perch proudly beside each other. The wooden planks creak beneath my feet, but I can see through the slits that there isn't the usual traffic jam as people try to exit Brooklyn or enter Manhattan from the other side. It's instead replaced by a bottleneck of people. This women's march is important. It *feels* important. Necessary.

I reach across and clutch Jessa's slim wrist, fearing we'll be swallowed whole by the swarm. My heartbeat quickens, and my senses become overloaded. There are rowdy chants to my right. The air is filled with the heady scent of perfume mixed with body odour. Bright flags and placards are thrust into the air by the protestors. I can't catch my breath.

Jessa shields her eyes from the sun with one hand then lifts up onto her toes to get a better angle over the crowd. A tall guy with broad shoulders blocks our view up ahead.

"What's going on up there?" A line of worry creases between her eyebrows.

I follow her eyes and frown. "What do you mean? I don't see anything."

The Empire State Building is to my left, and to my right, over Jessa's head, is Lower Manhattan. The Stars and Stripes flag hanging from the bridge swishes in the wind. I've been living in New York for a while now, but I don't think I'll ever get used to the noise and the bustle. It's a love–hate thing. Most days, I love being part of this ever-evolving beast of a city. Some days, it overwhelms me.

"I think the crowd is coming to a halt," Jessa says. She stands on her tiptoes again, her silky black hair blowing in the breeze. "I think there might be a counterprotest over on the other side of the bridge. It's preventing the flow of the crowd."

"That's not good," I say.

"Don't worry. I'm sure the police will disperse them."

I hope she's right, but I also have my doubts. I've seen protests turn from peaceful to violent extremely quickly. It's one of the reasons I don't usually attend. But this felt different, so I put my doubts aside and joined my best friend.

There's a swell and a push. We take two steps back. I'm trying not to think about the fact that there's nowhere to go when you're on a bridge. We're stuck right in the centre of the crowd. I lose my grip on Jessa.

"Don't panic. Just breathe. Okay? Breathe," Jessa says, now two people away from me. "If we get separated, I'll meet you over on Washington Street."

Her voice sounds even farther away, or maybe the crowd is getting louder. It's no longer a chant but a din. The voices aren't as one; they're disparate.

The crowd swells again. This time, I'm pushed forward, and then it immediately sends me back, stumbling over my feet. I'm shoulder to shoulder with other women. A heavy boot stomps on my toe. I drop my placard and am shoved to the right as a slim girl tries to extricate herself from the swarm of people. Up ahead, bodies are being pushed down, disappearing into the crowd.

"Jessa?" I call out as more people try to squeeze past me. She's gone.

Elbows jab. Feet stumble. Voices cry out. I trip backwards, falling into the chest of the person behind me.

I'm travelling without even knowing it now. The crowd does it all on its own, and my feet no longer need me to tell them to move. When I'm lifted up about half a foot, I fixate on Washington Street. People are pouring out of the subway station there. Steam billows from the food cart across the street. If I can just reach that point and…

Someone steps on the back of my right shoe, and it slides off. It's enough to unbalance me, and I fall. With the crush of the crowd, I barely have space to protect myself as I hit the ground, landing awkwardly on my right shoulder, hitting the side of my head.

And just like that, I'm down, and the crowd is still moving, still flooding forwards, on top of me. I'm kicked in the stomach, and heels ride over my hands. Someone almost steps on my head. I'm shouting, screaming, but no one can hear me.

This is how I die.

I try to push myself up, and someone trips over my neck. They fall in front of me, and I grab onto them, hoping we can pull ourselves up together. She's young—in her twenties, maybe—though it's difficult to tell in the rush. The wood planks of the bridge shudder, and the girl in front of me pulls out of my grip, swept away by the crowd.

I'm half on my knees, covering my face with trembling hands, adrenaline pulsing through my veins. And when the strong grasp of a stranger hooks underneath my arms, it feels like one more thing to be afraid of. But this person lifts me onto their shoulder, carrying me along the bridge like a firefighter. My vision is somewhat restricted by my angle and the fact that I'm in a daze, but it seems as though the crush is finally dissipating. By the time we reach the end of the bridge, near the subway, it's easier to breathe.

The man sets me down on wobbly legs.

"Are you okay?" My saviour leans closer to examine the cut on my head. "You got a little beaten up there, I think. Do you want to go to the hospital?"

It takes me a moment to catch my breath. "No, I'm okay. I just need to find my friend."

As the fog clears from my mind and the adrenaline finally floods out of me, I realise that this man is extremely attractive. Not my usual type, though. He's all-American, classically handsome, with stubble smattering his jaw, and neatly cropped dark hair. He's far more polished than the British men I know back home.

"Let me help you," he says. "You're a little unsteady on your feet. Lean into me. That's right."

I'm starting to regain my strength when someone bumps him from behind, and we collide.

"Whoa." He chuckles, his hand bracing against my lower back to keep us both from toppling. "Easy, there. I've got you."

There's a moment when he realises he's still clinging to me and abruptly brings his hand back to his side. He smiles, and it's comforting. Maybe it's the fact that I was in this man's arms and he helped me out of the terrifying crush, but I immediately feel as though I am safe with him.

"Thank you," I say, staring deep into his brown eyes. "Thank you for saving my life."

CHAPTER 2

The handsome saviour's smile beams at me. "I'm not sure I saved your life. Anyone would have done the same thing."

"Believe me. They didn't. I think I saw at least three big guys step over me." I press my fingers to the cut on my head, and they come back red. "But I guess the crowd was pushing them forwards, so I can't really blame them. I really need to find my friend Jessa. She said to meet here, but I can't see her."

"Why don't we get you cleaned up, and you can call her? There's a bar over there. You can check out that cut and rehydrate."

It's a sensible idea. I nod.

"Oh, and I'm Ethan," he says.

"Laura."

He smiles again, and his eyes crinkle. "It's nice to meet you."

His hand rests on the small of my back as we cross the street to the bar. Normally, that much body contact with a stranger would irk me, but I know he's trying to keep me steady.

The bar is packed, but at least we're off the streets. On the road, harried groups of people hurry past, police officers cluster, and I notice the black shirts and shorts of a far-right group. Then I see a holstered gun on the hip of a stranger, and a shiver runs down my spine. I'll never get used to that.

"I'm going to go to the bathroom and check out this cut," I tell Ethan.

"Can I get you a drink while you're there?"

"A Coke would be good."

I certainly never expected to meet what my granny would have called "a nice young man" at a women's march. But then again, maybe that's exactly where I should be to meet a nice man.

It was after my divorce that I decided to come to New York. One of the busiest cities in the world is perhaps an odd choice for a woman who grew up in an old mining village in Derbyshire. But then, I'd always dreamed of leaving the green valleys behind and replacing them for somewhere with more opportunities. New York gives me that and more, though I find myself homesick from time to time.

But before New York, many years ago, I went to university in London, and that's where I met Sam. We both lived in halls of residence on a grotty side street near UCL. It'd been such a change for me, and finding Sam right away had helped me adjust. He looked out for me.

We fell in love right away. Two years after university ended, we married. While we worked internships and temp jobs in our respective fields—PR for me, publishing for Sam—we built our insular life. Just us, a few trusted friends, and our flat. But it didn't work out.

The bar bathroom is busy, but I manage to find an empty sink. There's dried blood at my temple, but the cut is thankfully small. I clean away the blood, wash the dirt from my hands, and dust down my jeans. It could've been a lot worse. I suspect I'll be bruised tomorrow, and my body is sore from the fall, but I'll live.

When I return to the table, Ethan has a Coke ready and waiting for me. I take three large gulps and wipe my mouth.

"Better?" he asks.

"Better." I smile. Then I grab my phone. "Sorry to be rude. I really need to call my friend."

"Sure," he says. "Go ahead."

I dial Jessa's number, and she answers on the second ring. "Hello?" she shouts, the hum of chatter behind her. "Laura? Where the hell are you?"

"Sorry, I almost got trampled to death, and this nice guy helped me. We came into this bar nearby to get some Cokes. We're here now."

"Oh." Jessa sounds perplexed. "Which bar?"

"I didn't get the name of it—" I grab a menu from the table, but the name has worn off.

"Wet Your Whistle," Ethan says.

I laugh. "Stop. No way is this bar called that."

Ethan points at a plaque on the wall, and sure enough, I see the bar name.

"Huh." I push my finger into my ear to hear Jessa better. "It's called Wet Your Whistle. It's right on the corner next to the bridge."

"How come I've never heard of it before?" Jessa asks, her voice ebbing with scepticism.

"I don't know. Maybe it's new?"

"All right, I'm walking that way now. I'll meet you inside."

"We're at a booth near the windows in the middle."

"Cool beans." Jessa hangs up a moment later.

I offer an apologetic smile. "She's on her way to meet us now. If that's okay."

"Excellent. I can't wait to meet her." Ethan's eyes sparkle.

An ember of interest ignites somewhere within me. This man has my attention, and he's the first in a while to get it.

I laugh. "You know, you don't have to stay. You must have lost friends in the crowd too."

"Actually, I came on my own."

"Ah. A lone protestor?"

"More of an ally," he says.

I smile. "Well, that's really admirable of you." I sip my Coke. "Tell me about yourself, Ethan. Are you from New York?"

"Born and raised."

"In Brooklyn?"

"No, Connecticut, but same difference." His laughter floats across the table, filling the space between us.

"Oh." I offer a polite smile and scratch my cheek. I feel like I've just missed an inside joke.

"I'm kidding," he says. "Actually, I was born in New York, and I live here now, but I grew up mostly in Connecticut. Which is nothing like Brooklyn at all. I was being silly." He leans into the table and plants his elbows on top. "I take it you're not from around here."

I give him a playful eye roll. "How'd you guess?"

He pretends to ponder and scratches the stubble on his chin. "The accent gives you away."

"Happens every time around you Americans." I shrug.

"British?"

"Yes," I say.

"What brings you here?"

"A job," I reply. "And my good friend Jessa. We were at the same university in London many moons ago. She dropped out after a year or so, but we always stayed in touch. And then we were roommates when I first arrived in New York. But I have my own place now, which is great."

"Well, it's nice to meet you, Laura, even under these circumstances. I'm glad I could help you." His smile fades slightly, and an intensity crosses his features. Perhaps he's remembering the swell of the crowd. It's something I know will haunt me for a long time.

But then I spot Jessa's dark hair from the other side of the bar. She lifts a hand to wave, and I beckon her over. She seems fine, if a little sweaty. I notice there's a slight tear across the neckline of her top.

"Hi." She slides into the booth and bumps her shoulder—intentionally harder than she needs to—into mine. I know this is her way of saying *nice find* about the guy sitting across from us.

"Oh, what happened to your shirt? Did you get caught?" I ask.

"Some idiot grabbed it while they were getting smushed by the crowd. What happened to your head?"

"I fell," I say. "And I lost a shoe."

"Oh, fuck." She frowns. "Want to borrow something from my apartment? It's just ten blocks from here."

"I'm good," I say, waving a hand.

Jessa turns to Ethan. "Thanks for looking out for her. It was pretty crazy in that crowd. I'm Jessa." She extends a hand to him.

"Ethan." He shakes her hand. "Pleasure to meet you."

Jessa gives him a devious smile in return. "The pleasure's all mine."

The server, having seen a new person at our table, whips into gear and asks if he can get Jessa anything to eat or drink. She wastes no time ordering a Bloody Mary.

The server turns to leave, but I stop him. "Wait. Can I get an espresso martini?"

"Sure." He nods.

"Wow." Ethan's eyebrows hook upward. "So, this just turned from a protest to a party."

"Well, it's a Bloody Mary." Jessa shrugs. "It counts as breakfast."

"It comes with a mozzarella stick and a chicken finger on it. A pickle too," the server says.

Jessa shows her pearly white teeth when she smiles at him. "Even better."

"I guess I'll have a beer. Whatever IPA is good," Ethan says.

"You've got it, sir."

"Whoa, now. Am I that old to be called 'sir'?" Ethan says with a laugh.

"That depends." Jessa applies lip gloss and checks her compact. "How old *are* you?"

"Jessa!" I swat her thigh under the table.

"What?" Her voice is fake-virtuous as she clicks the mirror closed and blots her lips together.

Ethan shrugs. "I'm actually thirty-eight."

"Well, if it helps, that bartender turned twenty-one, like, yesterday," Jessa says.

Ethan smiles, but it's not her he's looking at. It's me. And it's been a while since a man looked at me like that. Especially one as hot as Ethan. My cheeks warm. I feel the urge to fluff up my hair.

Our drinks arrive, and Ethan winces when he's called "sir" for a second time.

"Fuck the patriarchy," Ethan declares, raising his glass.

Jessa smirks. "Well, okay, then."

We clink glasses, and I give my friend a look to suggest, *He means well* so that Jessa doesn't rib him for the overenthusiasm. Once I'm a few sips into my drink, I start to relax. The alcohol makes me feel flushed and tingly in a good way. Ethan and I keep stealing glances at each other, grinning whenever our eyes meet.

"Is this your first march?" Jessa asks.

Ethan shakes his head. "Nope. I try to attend when I can."

She gives him a look like, *Am I really supposed to believe that*? But thankfully, she spares me the mortification and doesn't say it.

"That's cool that you give support like that," I say. "What do you do for work?"

Jessa bites into her pickle.

"I'm on Wall Street." He says it in a humble way with a shrug, as if he knows it sounds cliché. "What about you?"

"Oh." I rub my arm. "I'm in public relations."

"Really? And how do you like that line of work?" he asks.

"It's challenging, which is what I like," I reply.

"You know what I like?" Ethan asks.

My heart stops, and I stare at him. "What?"

"Your accent."

Beside me, Jessa inhales deeply.

"Thanks." I offer a shy smile, willing my cheeks not to turn red, but I feel them scorching anyway.

Jessa takes her drink and starts to slide out of the booth, giving me a knowing look. "I'm going to go call Bridget really quick." She makes a signal with her hand as if she's making the call and stands up.

I nod, taking her cue, appreciative of it. Bridget is Jessa's on-again-off-again "fuck buddy." Jessa's words, not mine. Jessa has a keen ability to notice when two people are hitting it off and will usually make herself scarce. She's a great wingwoman.

"Nice to meet you." She tosses Ethan an enthusiastic wave and whisks herself away.

"So…" Ethan's dark eyes glow with a mischievous glint. He drums his fingertips against the table.

"So…" I grin, nodding along, trying to pretend like my heart isn't doing somersaults inside my chest.

"A PR woman and a Wall Street guy meet at a women's march across the Brooklyn Bridge," he declares.

"It's a meet-cute," I say, shaking my head at the ridiculousness.

The server returns. "Can I get you guys another drink?"

Ethan turns from the server to regard me as he says, "How about another round at my place? I have a fantastic high-rise view of the park."

My heart patters with excitement. His gaze bores into mine. I'm barely aware of the server backing away, sensing the change in atmosphere.

Jessa always jokes that I'm the cautious one. When I meet a man on a dating app, I scope him out online first, always meet in a public place, and I never have sex on a first date. But during my student days, after a few drinks at the university nightclub, 2000s-era dance music pulsing through my veins, I never thought anything of going home with a guy I'd just met.

Maybe I want to relive that rush today of all days.

Fuck it. I'm wearing one shoe, and I'm probably bruised from head to toe under my clothes, and my blood is pumping with espresso martini before lunch. If not now, when?

I match his broad smile and say, "Sure. Why not?"

CHAPTER 3

I'm eighteen again. I'm in a cab with a man. Only this time, we aren't heading to a tiny room in university accommodation. We're going to a proper apartment in one of the most romantic cities in the world. New York passes us by in a colourful blur as we kiss until our lips are raw.

Ethan pays the driver, and we pile out. I hop across the pavement with one trainer on my foot, and then we step into a building with a doorman in a black coat and gloves.

"Good afternoon, Mr Hart," the doorman says, and Ethan returns the greeting.

I get the silly impulse to make fun of the man's lower register and formal tone, but I don't. I grin at him instead and then lower my eyes. He's no doubt seen my missing shoe. What a weirdo he must think I am.

In the elevator, we kiss again. I don't want to lose this momentum. I don't want to change my mind. I don't want to think about Sam or the divorce or the lacklustre dates I've experienced since moving here. I want to stay in this moment.

When the doors ping open and we tumble into Ethan's penthouse, I'm relieved to be away from the city. And then I see the view, and I'm pulled back to reality.

"Wow, you weren't kidding about these views of the park," I say. "Stunning."

As I gaze down at autumnal Central Park, Ethan wraps his hands around my waist and kisses my neck.

"Not as stunning as you."

Warmth floods my veins. I turn to face him, and as soon as our eyes lock, I forget all about the view.

* * *

It's warm in the apartment when I wake. The sun is rising, and the blinds are open, turning the wall into a portrait of the city below. The bed is empty, and I'm glad for the few moments alone to come to. I brush my hair out of my face and check the floor of the room for my clothes, finding them scattered across the open space. I do my best to grab them while shielding my nakedness since I'm in front of the window, though I'm not sure anyone can actually see in.

I get the first glimpse of my bruises from the crowd crush. There are three on each thigh and a couple across my abdomen, and I notice a bit of blood on the pillow from the graze across my temple. I should have applied a plaster, but once we got back to the apartment, everything else was a blur.

Yes, we'd had sex, and it was great. And then we drank a little wine in bed, ate some pizza, and fell asleep early. I hadn't meant to stay the night, but I'm quite happy I did.

I dress quickly and then call out Ethan's name.

"In here!" he responds.

I don't know where "here" is yet, but at least he's in the apartment.

"Okay…" I trail off. "Coming out in a second!"

There's no telling how bad I look after the night we had. At least I hadn't worn makeup to the march, since it would be smeared down my face right now. I nip through to the bathroom, use the toilet, and toss a fleeting glance at my reflection in the mirror.

I don't look *that* bad, but I don't look great, either. My blond hair is a little askew from sleep and sex, but it's nothing that can't be fixed with a comb-through.

I try to brush my fingers through my hair to get some of the knots out, and I readjust my T-shirt so that it doesn't look like I just haphazardly threw it over my head. I take a deep breath, pinch my cheeks to bring some colour back to them, and walk into the hallway.

I follow the smell of something syrupy, and sure enough, I find Ethan in the kitchen, standing over a bowl of pancake batter, whisking away with a happy smile lighting up his face.

"Good morning."

"Wow," I say, taking in the stack of pancakes, blueberries, and crispy bacon spread across the kitchen island. "Um, how many people are you cooking for?"

"Breakfast is the most important meal of the day." There's a frisky gleam in Ethan's eyes as he dollops batter onto the skillet. A moment later, tiny air bubbles pop out from the surface.

"Well, my breakfast usually consists of a cereal bar and a cup of coffee." I chuckle.

Ethan gestures for me to take a seat on one of the barstools. "In that case, you'll be pleasantly surprised."

"Thanks." I hug my arms around my chest, suddenly feeling out of place. Ethan's kitchen is exactly what I'd imagined a man living in a penthouse apartment would own. It's modern and bright, with marble finishes and those fancy cupboard doors without handles. The kitchen in my apartment contains a half-sized fridge and barely enough space for my pans. This is quite a contrast.

"Also, check the box on the table."

I frown, turning to the dining table a few feet from the island. It's a shoebox. "You bought me shoes? When?"

"I asked one of the doormen downstairs to go out and buy some when you were napping," he says. "He dropped them off this morning. Are they your size? Your sneaker was in British sizing, so I had to guess."

I laugh, opening the box. "Yeah, you got it spot-on."

I pull away the tissue paper and slip on the buttery-soft leather trainers. "Oh, but I can't! These are so much more expensive than mine." I'm about to remove the shoes when Ethan shakes his head.

"Hell no. Keep them. You need something to get home in. Plus, they look cute on you." He flips the pancakes. "Not to sound like a dick, but they cost, like, half as much as I usually pay for sneakers. I just wasn't too sure about which style, so I gave Kev a budget, and he picked those."

"Well, thank you," I say. "And to Kev too."

"Kev will be very happy when I tell him," Ethan says.

He serves me a hefty portion of pancakes as I make my way back to the island. He slides across the butter and syrup. I'm so hungry I get to work right away, drowning the pancakes in both.

"How is it?" Ethan asks, grabbing a plate himself and giving me an optimistic look.

"Lighter than air," I mumble around a mouthful.

He beams. "Excellent."

"Thanks for spoiling me two days in a row," I tell him.

Ethan takes my hand and squeezes it lightly. "There's more where that came from."

* * *

When I left his apartment, Ethan tried to get me a cab, but I wanted to take the subway. For one thing, it's a beautiful day, and the trees are bountiful with golden light. For another, I want to call Jessa *immediately*. I'm emerging from the subway stairs and heading down the pavement when I call her to give her all the details.

"Laauura," she says in her singsong voice. "Have you been out all night?"

"I may have," I say. "Which is in*sane*."

"For you, yeah," Jessa says. "So, tell me the gory details."

"He made me pancakes this morning," I say. "Oh, and we did it twice. He bought me new shoes, and he gave me his number, so I guess he wants to go out again."

"Awesome," she says. "He's hot, rich, and I'm a bit jealous, not gonna lie. So did you make plans before you left his place?"

"Not yet."

"Laura. Come on. He saved you from getting trampled to death. He fucked your brains out, then he fed you *breakfast* the next morning."

"Breakfast is the most important meal of the day," I say.

Jessa is quiet a moment. "Okay, you must still have sex brain to say something like that, Little Miss I-Survive-On-Coffee."

"That is my full name, by the way."

"You have it bad for him," she says.

I pause for a moment. "Yeah, you might be right about that. Which is..."

"Wonderful," she says.

"Scary," I admit.

"Don't talk yourself out of this, honey. Go with it. For one thing, I'm going to be living vicariously through you, no lie."

"I hardly think you need to," I say. "You have a great romantic life."

"I have hookups, Laura. I don't have romance. You have romance right now, coming out of your ears."

I turn a corner. "All right, I get it now. Though I'm sure you could have as much romance as you want if you really want it. Anyway, I'm almost home. I'll let you know what happens."

"I'll be hanging on the edge of my seat."

"I'm sure you will be."

As soon as I hang up with Jessa, a text notification vibrates through my phone. My stomach flips with excitement. She's right. This is the beginning of nerve-jangling, precariously balanced, new-relationship territory. I check the screen. It's from Ethan. Wow, that was fast. I appreciate a man who wears his heart on his sleeve. Dating rules have always seemed silly to me.

Hey, Laura. It's Ethan. I'd love to see you again. For a proper date this time. Let me know if you're free.

All right, now I have to admit it. This guy is almost too good to be true.

CHAPTER 4

E than chose one of the trendiest sushi restaurants in Manhattan for our date. Soft-blue light casts a neon glow across the walls, giving the place an aquatic feel. A four-tier fountain of calming, teal-tinted water gushes steadily upwards, with circles of intricately carved stone edging the water feature. This is one of those intimidating restaurants I would usually avoid. I have on my best shoes—a pair of Louboutins that cost two weeks' wages—and I just remembered how uncomfortable they are. It's like my toes are in a vice.

"You're stunning," Ethan whispers to me. His hand is on my lower back again, just like after the march. Like last time, I'm glad for its steadying presence on my body, especially in these shoes.

The hostess guides us between the tables, two menus under her arm. She pauses in front of a high-top table in the middle of the room, setting the menus down. Her smile is cheery as she gestures for me to sit. But then I see Ethan shaking his head and watch as her smile fades.

"This isn't going to work," he says abruptly. "I always feel on display sitting at these things. I'd like that booth over there." Ethan hooks his arm around my waist, holding me tight.

I freeze, embarrassed for the young hostess but also for myself. While his request isn't so unreasonable, it's Ethan's tone that surprises me. No "please" or "thank you." Maybe it's a British thing for me to expect him to be more polite to service workers. No, I don't think that's it. And he never asked me where I want to sit.

"I'm afraid that booth is reserved, sir," she says. "Perhaps I can find you an alternative."

Ethan exhales between his teeth and raises his eyebrows. "Look, I'm on a very important first date here that I want to go well." He glances at me, and I find myself smiling awkwardly at the hostess. "Now, I don't want to cause a scene, but I'm not sitting at this table."

"Understood," she says using a soft voice that's more generous than anything I could have mustered.

She collects the menus and turns on her heels towards a booth farther back, away from the centre of the room. Ethan grins at me like he's won something. Maybe this kind of behaviour is impressive to his usual dates. But as far as I'm concerned, this is not going well.

"*Much* better," Ethan says, raising his eyebrows as though to insinuate the hostess is the unreasonable one.

"Your server will be right with you," the hostess mumbles. She turns and walks away but not before flashing me a pointed look. I can't tell if it's pity or judgement.

Then, as if flipping a switch, Ethan's personality morphs again. He gives me a grin that's equally wicked and charming, gesturing for me to slide into the booth.

"After you, beautiful."

I tuck my hair behind my ear and slip into the booth, grateful to be hidden away at the back of the restaurant. Then, instead of sitting across from me on the opposite side of the table, Ethan parks himself right beside me, his thigh touching mine.

We've already been intimate, I realise that, but the presumption bothers me. Now, if I want to leave, I'll have to scooch all the way across the other side. I don't say anything because I don't want the terse Ethan to return.

He grabs a menu. "The tempura flake salmon roll is my favourite." His head swivels in my direction. "What about you?"

"California roll," I reply, my voice clipped.

He scrunches up his face in disgust. "Oh no. California rolls are awful."

I grit my teeth and force a smile. "Is everything okay, Ethan? You seem a little off."

"In what way?" he asks.

"Well, you were rather short with the hostess, and now you're insulting my taste for some bizarre reason. I feel like… like we might have to start over. Unless I leave."

He places the menu down on the table. "I'm so sorry, Laura. I've had a shitty day, and it's making me short-tempered." He waves a hand as though to erase the beginning of our date. "A start over, it is."

When he smiles, it seems genuine, so we order a bottle of wine and a tasting platter. At least this way, I'll get my California rolls. But even as the evening progresses, an unsettling sensation snakes through my body. Ethan's insistence that his bad temper came from a terrible day doesn't ring true to me. He never seemed flustered or frustrated. It was more like a show of power. Seeing him like that is making me judge our first meeting through a different lens.

He saved me, yes, and he carried me out of danger. It was brave. Or it was a display of strength. His flirtation in the bar was either cheeky or cocky, depending on how it was viewed. Inviting me back to his penthouse, buying me the trainers, making me pancakes… all of it was a display of wealth. But it had seemed so romantic at the time.

"So, tell me about your day," I say, hoping if he opens up more, I'll get to know the real Ethan. "What went wrong?"

He stiffens. "I don't want to talk about it." He shakes his head as though flustered by the question. "Let's just say someone fucked up, big-time, and a lot of money was lost."

"Ah," I say.

He stabs at a tempura roll with a chopstick. "The average person has no idea how stressful Wall Street really is. We're talking about *real* money here. Most people don't experience those kinds of consequences."

"I don't know about that," I reply. "I mean, I can't say there are too many consequences to my job, but what about all the healthcare workers out there? If they mess up, people die."

"Yeah, I guess," he says. Then he smiles and places a hand on my thigh. "How was your day, darling?"

There have been a few red flags throughout this date so far, but that hits hard. *Darling?* I almost choke on my California roll, which is delicious and much nicer than the tempura.

I edge my leg away from his hand. "I'm working on PR for a new actor. He's on Broadway and just starting out, but there's already talk of him winning—"

"There are only eleven rolls in this platter," he says, cutting me off.

"What?" I ask, incredulous.

"There were supposed to be twelve."

"How do you know? We've eaten half of them."

"I kept tabs," he says.

I blink. "You made a note of how much I eat?"

He shrugs. "Where's the waiter? We should get a refund."

"For one sushi roll? Come on, Ethan. You seem to be fixating on making everything perfect, and it's coming across as controlling and weird," I blurt out, too frustrated to be anything but bluntly honest.

"You're hot when you're angry." He grins widely.

At least the missing sushi roll is forgotten, but now his hand is on my thigh again. My eyes drift over to the bottle of wine, and I realise he drank much more than I thought and a lot more than I did. His hand journeys up my thigh. I firmly cup my hand over his and push it away. As I shake my head, I clench my teeth and utter an adamant no.

"I thought you'd like that," he murmurs.

"Excuse me?" Heat flushes across my cheeks as the couple at the next table turn to see what's going on. "Ethan, you're making me uncomfortable. We're in public, and I don't like this."

He quickly tries to backpedal. His dashing smile returns, his eyes brightening. "I'm so sorry. You just look so hot tonight. Honestly, Laura, you should take that as a compliment."

"It's not a compliment," I say. "And you're drunk. You're making me very uncomfortable, Ethan, and I'd like to leave."

"Oh, come on. Lighten up a little. I'm just trying to have fun with you. There's this great bar next door I'd love to take you to for dessert martinis."

I begin bumping my hip against his to get him to move out of the way. "Please let me out."

I half expect him to refuse to move, but he stands, giving me access out.

I throw a twenty on the table. It's the only cash I have, but it makes my point. "Thanks for dinner."

Ethan cuffs his hand around my arm as I turn to leave. His eyes search mine. There's a trace of regret in the way he looks at me, but I'm not one to be manipulated, especially by a guy I just met. I'm ready to cut my losses and move on.

"Laura, I'm sorry. I probably don't deserve it, but I'd love to get one more chance if you're willing."

"Apology accepted. I appreciate the offer, but I'm tired. I'm just going to go home."

"Can I at least call you later?" His voice is low and sad, the arrogance sapped out of him.

I remove his hand from my arm and give him a polite smile, clutching my purse under the crook of my arm. "I'm sorry. I don't think it's going to work out. I really appreciate what you did for me the other day, and we had a really special day together, but I don't think we're compatible for anything further."

I turn on my heels and swiftly walk from the restaurant, picking up my stride. It's only when I'm safely outside and around the corner, heading in the direction of the subway, that I dare to toss a glance over my shoulder. I breathe a sigh of relief. He isn't following me.

CHAPTER 5

W hen it comes to dating, I don't tend to take things personally, but last night's disaster of a date is a crushing blow. I'd really thought Ethan was a great guy.

I wake up early and head out of my apartment for a stroll. A shower isn't enough to eliminate memories of the night before. I need fresh air too. I grab a coffee and wander along the sunny streets until I stop cringing at the thought of drunk Ethan sliding his hand up my leg.

The fresh air and autumn leaves help lift my spirits, cleansing the bad taste left in my mouth from Ethan's behaviour. I can try to get on with the rest of my day without it hanging over me. Back home, I toss my keys and my bag onto the narrow table in the lounge. While it's short on space, I'm still proud of my one-bedroom apartment in a rent-controlled area of Weehawken.

Living in New Jersey isn't my forever goal, but I get stellar views of the skyline from the Hudson River. And it's better than bunking with someone in Manhattan. I've seen those glorified closet spaces that land-lords pass off as actual apartments.

I push the curtains open and sigh, glancing out at the water shimmering and tranquil below a blue sky. It's time to face the music. Jessa's going to want to know every detail about last night, and she still thinks Ethan is Mr Perfect Feminist Guy from the bridge. I hate to break it to her.

In a raspy voice, she answers on the first ring. "Hello?"

"Sorry. Did I wake you?"

She moans. "What time is it?"

I wince and chew my bottom lip. "Half past nine."

Another groan. "What sane person is up this early on a Saturday?"

I laugh. "The kind who can't sleep in. You know, morning people. We do exist. There are dozens of us."

"Ugh. I hate morning people." She pauses, catching up with the implication. "Wait. Are you at home?"

"Yeah. I'm home. Woke up in my own bed too."

"So, you didn't spend the night with the magnificent marcher?"

I sag into the couch cushions and sigh. "I'm not so sure I'd call him magnificent."

"Damn. I liked that nickname. Has a nice ring to it," she says.

"Unfortunately, it didn't go too well," I say.

"Uh-oh. Trouble in paradise already?"

"It definitely wasn't paradise. Nowhere near close to it, in fact."

Her voice is husky and soft when she replies. "Tell me everything."

I let out a harsh laugh. "I don't even know where to start. Maybe at the point where he berated a hostess or the part where he drank too much and tried to put his hand up my skirt. It was horrible, Jessa."

"Oh, sweetie. I'm so sorry."

"I don't know what changed in him. It was like something snapped. He acted like such a dick. Really arrogant, like he wanted to impress me with some alpha bullshit."

"That sucks," she says. "You know I don't tolerate that crap."

I nod. As a bar manager, Jessa has dealt with her fair share of bullies and entitled people.

"So what happened? Did you leave?" she asks.

"I did. Though to give him some credit, he did apologise before I left. And he said he was having an off night," I say.

She snorts. "Lame."

"He'd lost—or someone had lost—a lot of money on the market."

"So what?" she says. "Look, losing money doesn't make you a dick."

I laugh. "Well, at least he apologised, I guess."

"That's, like, bare minimum."

I can practically see Jessa lying sprawled out across her black futon, arms and legs dangling off the sides. She knew me through my divorce and my miscarriages and everything in between.

"I hope you're not going to see this douche again," she says.

"No, I don't think so."

"Good." She pauses. "You okay, Lor?"

"Yeah, fine."

"You deserve better, chick."

I laugh. She picked that up from me, though it brings with it bittersweet memories from when Sam used to call me chick. Thinking about what I used to have makes me realise what I want now. I want more than a night in a penthouse and some pancakes the next morning. I want a family, with a good man, someone who doesn't treat people like crap because he's had a bad day.

"Did anything else happen?" she asks.

"Nothing, really. His tone changed after I said I wanted to go home, and he asked me to give him a second chance. He said he hadn't meant to come on so strong, that he just really liked me."

"Did you believe him?"

"He seemed sincere in the moment," I said. "But it was too little too late."

"Well, I think—"

"Wait, Jessa, hold that thought a minute. I just got a text—oh my *God*."

"What? What's wrong?"

I sigh. It's so predictable I almost don't want to admit it. "Incoming wall of text from Ethan."

"Oh no," she says. "Read it to me."

I scan the message then read it aloud to Jessa. "Laura, I'm so sorry about last night. I acted like a total jerk. My behaviour is absolutely inexcusable. Unforgivable, even. But if you can find it in the kindness of your heart to forgive me anyway and let me have another chance to prove to you that I'm not a pompous asshole, I'd love another shot to turn this around. At the very least, let me take you for an apology coffee. No strings attached. Just coffee, and if you want to go home after, I'll understand. I know my limits and boundaries, and last night, well, let's just say I crossed them. I won't give you any more excuses. I'll just say I'm sorry. Let me know about the coffee."

After I finish reading, Jessa is quiet for a moment.

"Well?"

"That's… not a terrible apology."

"You're joking, right? Are you getting soft in your old age?"

"Maybe I am. Look, I would not go on that coffee date, but I do think the apology is kind of okay. He doesn't sound like a complete psycho, anyway. As always, I'll support you no matter what you decide to do."

"All right, I'll think about it," I say.

We hang up, and while I decide what to do about Ethan, I run a few errands, pick up some bread and salad for lunch, and buy some meat to make a pasta sauce with. I run a vacuum cleaner over the carpet—the one advantage of a tiny apartment is that it's done in no time—and then slump back on the sofa with my phone. I read the apology message again.

Jessa's right. I can't ignore Ethan's behaviour at the restaurant. God knows in my twenties, I would have made the terrible decision of forgiving him, but not now that I've been around the block a few times. He has to go. I text Ethan back, a polite but firm no.

I'm sorry, Ethan. I think I need some space. Water under the bridge, but I need to focus on me right now. I've decided I'm not open to a relationship at this time. But thank you for the kindness you offered me at the protest.

I drop the phone to the sofa and head over to the kitchen to pour a glass of water. I'm on edge. My muscles are pulled tight, and I don't like wondering how he's going to react to the message.

As I place the glass of water down on the kitchen counter, my phone pings. I eye the screen with trepidation, already sensing this isn't going to be an easy connection to break. His long message and the speed with which he replies indicate he's far more invested in this than I am. Yet another red flag.

I tell myself to stop being stupid and grab the phone. There are already three or four more messages by the time I unlock the phone.

I've already apologized.

It's just a cup of coffee. I'm not asking for the world…

Well, you've shown your true colors. You were more than willing to take the free shoes I bought you!

Aren't you going to reply?

I think you'll realize soon enough that you'll regret this decision.

I place my phone down on the counter and suppress the shiver working its way up my spine. Well, I'll certainly be blocking this guy.

CHAPTER 6

L ater that day, I find that Ethan Hart is still in my head. I glance at the expensive trainers he bought me and, on a whim, box them up. *Fuck him.* He can have the shoes back—if I can remember his address. He did mention it in the taxi. My phone pings as I'm wrapping parcel paper around the box.

What are you doing today? Do you want to hang out?

It's from a number I don't recognise.

I text back: *Who is this?* But there's a creeping sensation rippling over my skin that it's Ethan. I shake my head. If it is him, he's unhinged. I blocked his number.

"Good choice, Laura," I say to myself, tucking the parcel under my arm to nip to the post office. I've scribbled what I can remember of his address on the front.

And to cheer myself up, I might even pop into my favourite book-shop on the way back.

It's about a ten-minute walk to the post office. As I'm on the way there, my phone is in my bag, on silent. I keep wondering if it's him with a different phone. He could have two. One for work, perhaps? Or maybe it's someone else I haven't seen for a while. I'm hardly a socialite, so it seems unlikely.

The thought of Ethan turns my stomach. At times, I feel like he's behind me. Every now and then, I glance over my shoulder, but he's never there.

The line in the post office is long, and I wait impatiently, trying to resist the urge to check my phone.

"You don't know the zip code?" the woman at the counter asks.

I shake my head. She raises her eyebrows but takes the parcel anyway. I tap my credit card against the machine and leave feeling lighter. That's one issue sorted. Ethan can have his expensive shoes back. I wouldn't want to look at them ever again anyway.

On my way to the bookshop, I sit down on a bench by a small park and grab my phone. My heart sinks. I have more messages.

You must be too busy to talk to me. I'm not used to people ignoring me.

And then a flash of anger sweeps over my body. How dare he ruin my day like this!

I text back: *Tell me who you are, or I'll report this number to the police for harassment.*

I put the phone in my bag and carry on to the quaint, cosy book-shop on the corner, a little piece of charm tucked into a bustling city. It's my escape.

The familiar bell chimes overhead as I walk in. I breathe in the scent of paper and leather as I stroll down the aisles. I don't have anything in mind. Sometimes, I come in here just to appreciate the atmosphere. I brush my fingertips across the spines of several books, ready to pluck out one that has an interesting cover. And yet I can't relax. I need to check my phone again.

Miss me yet?

It's bizarre. I've never met a man who does this before. Does he actually think this is going to win me over?

"Can I help you find anything, ma'am?"

I jump and spin around, heart pounding. "Sor—sorry. Um…"

Her chestnut hair is trimmed across her shoulders and straight as a board. She smiles broadly then places a hand to her chest. "I'm so sorry. I didn't mean to startle you. I walk too quietly, I know."

I shove my phone into my handbag and return her friendly smile. "That's all right. No, I'm fine. I'm just browsing for now."

"Okay. Well, let me know if you need anything."

"Thanks, will do."

Ethan's persistence has had its desired effect. With every step, I sense eyes watching me. Is he in here somewhere? Does he know my neighbourhood? The store isn't *that* big, but you never know. I could have missed him somehow.

Paranoia slithers beneath my skin. Head down, bag clutched tightly to my chest, I hurry out of the shop, glancing left and right, trying to calm my pounding heart.

An older man walks a white poodle a few steps away. The dog keeps sniffing at the square box of grass around a tree. Across the street, a couple pushes a jogging pram as they run side by side next to the harbour. To my right, a woman balances a phone between her ear and shoulder, arguing loudly with someone on the other end. She laughs heartily, bagel crumbs spraying from her mouth.

They're just regular people, getting on with their daily routines, going about the hustle and bustle of their lives, and paying no attention to me whatsoever. But I still can't shake my anxiety. I quicken my stride as I notice the crosswalk sign blinking. I have only ten seconds left before the light changes at the intersection.

When I'm about a block from my house, I whisk into a bodega, remembering I need milk, tea bags, and whatever I can find that will quench my Digestive biscuit craving. Cookies are not the same no matter how many tries I give them.

I'm inspecting the cookies when my phone rings. Startled, I reach to pick it up from my bag when it abruptly stops ringing.

I look at the screen. One missed call—from the same number.

I whip around, glancing over my shoulder. My eyes skim the produce section behind me. An elderly man hobbles on a cane, carrying a cantaloupe in the crook of his free arm. There's no one else around.

A text comes through.

Keep ignoring me. See what happens.

I pick up my pace and grab everything else I need. By the time I'm at the register, loading my items onto the conveyer belt, my hands are shaking so badly the six-pack container of sparkling water I'm holding slips from my grip and plunks to the linoleum floor. One of the cans bursts open, and with a hiss, the carbonated liquid spews its fizzy stickiness all over the floor and the customer in line in front of me, who is currently paying at the counter.

"I'm so sorry," I tell him as he cuts me a scathing look.

"What's the holdup?" A woman sighs behind me, her toddler reaching at her thighs and whining.

"I—um—"

One of the staff members comes by with a mop and bucket and cleans up my mess.

"I'm really sorry." I slink back, mortified.

"Don't worry about it," the clerk says, bored.

I need to get home so I can sit down and screenshot every one of Ethan's creepy messages before I block him. Only then will I begin to feel safe. I step over the soda waters, and the woman behind the register asks me if I would like a replacement six-pack brought to the counter.

I tuck a strand of hair behind my ear and fumble to get my debit card out of my wallet. "No, that's okay. Thank you."

The clerk lifts her eyebrow. "Are you sure?"

"It's really fine."

Finally done, I link the grocery bag around my arm and scurry out of the store. The fresh air is like balm to the anxiety rattling around my body. I pull it into my lungs, finally beginning to calm, and then walk the last block to my flat.

Out of breath, hot, and frazzled, I finally pull my phone from my handbag and read a slew of emotionally conflicted texts, all from the same unknown number.

You can't hide from me forever.

I'm not the type of man who lets women get away.

You're making this harder than it has to be.

Please, just talk to me.

What the hell is your problem, anyway, Laura? I'm not this easily ignored.

I'm sorry. Can we just agree to start over? I'm a fan of clean slates. What do you say?

I lower myself into one of the bistro seats in my kitchen nook and cradle my head in my hands. Another message pops up on the screen.

I won't accept this is the end of us, Laura. There's more to our story.

I scroll through all the messages, screenshotting them. This kind of harassment needs to be documented. Then I screenshot his contact details too. After I have a record of everything I need, I scroll through to the number and tap the block button.

There. Try to bother me again, you sick freak, I think.

CHAPTER 7

I've never been so thankful for Monday morning. Getting back to work helps me draw a line after everything that happened with Ethan over the weekend, though I do occasionally find my mind wandering back to those moments. The anticipation of the text messages. The sickness in the pit of my stomach. I can only hope it's over now, but who knows with a man like him.

With a cup of tea—whatever passes for Yorkshire Tea here, it's not the same, I swear—to soothe my anxiety, I jot down a few talking points for my meeting with Ben Stemmett. He's a big client, and Anita just passed his account over to me, which is great. It's a major step up for me, a big advancement in climbing the rungs of my career ladder. And in my mid-thirties, I desperately need it. Sometimes, when I watch women younger than me start in the company, already with more experience, I can't help but worry I began my career too late. The truth is, Sam never wanted me to work after we married. I lost a lot of independence being with him. Knowing that always shakes my confidence, but I push the thoughts out of my mind and confirm with Ben's team that I'm ready to start the Zoom call.

Ben's face fills the screen. He's movie-star handsome, rare for someone carving their path on Broadway, with a row of perfect white teeth and deep-brown eyes. He's wearing his signature thick-black-rimmed glasses that enhance his eyes rather than obscure them. His black hair is soft and short, the curls haloed by the light behind him.

He's wearing a grey wool scarf and a black shirt. They're muted tones, but he looks impeccably put together, like he just walked off the set of a photo shoot.

"Hey, Ben!" I greet him with an enthusiastic grin. "How are things going?"

"They're great," he says. "Good to see you. I wish it could have been in person, but I'm stuck on the West Coast for a couple more days."

"Well, that's okay. I'm just happy we have this time to chat."

Ben's laughter floats through my laptop speakers, and he nods. "Ditto."

"I know you must be swamped right now," I say. "*Death of a Salesman* just hit the streamers, which is amazing. One of the first tele-vised plays to hit twenty million viewers. Congratulations. You must be so happy."

"Oh, thank you. That's so sweet."

I take a pause from the compliments. I never lay it on too thick with these clients. I've learned that the more famous they are, the more they need their egos stroked, but there's still a limit, an invisible boundary that you never want to cross. It might make you seem superficial or like you're trying to use them for something. It's a thin line to walk, a balance of making them feel good about themselves but not overdoing it.

But Ben is a genuine guy and one of the most down-to-earth clients I've ever had. It actually makes me want to talk him up more whenever I get the opportunity to speak to him. He doesn't have a self-centred bone in his body and always seems to want to make everyone else happy. He's also a huge Broadway star and still in his mid-twenties. We exchange a few pleasantries about our lives and how things are going— I leave out the bad date and stalking incident—and then we get right down to business.

"I think Rachel sent a schedule through to you. We can make some adjustments if you like. But *Good Morning America* is really keen to have you on the show. Then there's the media tour here in Manhattan when you get back. A piece in the *New York Times* too."

"Looks great," he says. "I think we've covered all the bases. You are by far my favourite PR rep to work with. You make everything so easy and streamlined."

I laugh and lean in close to the screen. "Can I let you in on a secret? You're my favourite too."

"You probably aren't allowed to say that." Ben laughs.

"Not even a little bit, but it's true."

"Well, I appreciate you buttering me up."

"Anytime."

Ben sighs and glances at his watch. "I need to hop off the call, but this has been great. I can't wait to dive into everything."

"I'll be in touch about that red-carpet event next week," I tell him. "The charity thing. There's some info you need about the other guests. And we can talk social media then too."

"I'll be ready," he says.

"Take care."

"Bye now."

I'm still riding the high from the Zoom call with Ben when my desk phone rings, the reception button blinking red on the keypad.

I pick up the phone and hold it to my ear. "This is Laura."

"Hey, Laura. It's Cassidy down at reception."

"Oh, hey, Cassidy." I move the phone receiver to one side and cradle it on my shoulder as I start typing up notes from the Zoom call.

"There's a guy down here waiting for you."

"A guy?" I ask. "What guy?"

"Hold on. Let me check."

I stop typing and take hold of the phone. Unless I have a delivery or a client meeting I completely forgot about, there's no guy who could be waiting for me in reception.

Her voice is muffled, like she's holding her hand over the receiver. I hear her say something, but I can't make it out. Then she laughs.

A moment later, her voice comes back crisp through the line. "He says his name is Ethan. He's holding a box of muffins. He says they're homemade." She pauses, and I hear her chewing a moment later. "And oh my *God,* they are amazing. You seriously made these?" she asks him.

I can hear Ethan's voice through the phone, and it sends an icy tremble up my spine. I lick the dryness from my lips.

"I'll be right down." I slam the phone back into its cradle before Cassidy can say anything else.

My heart is pounding, and I can't decide if it's righteous anger or fear. First the messages and now this. It's escalating behaviour, and it's creepy as fuck. I check the pocket of my blazer to make sure my mobile phone is there. I'm one step away from calling the police.

On the way to the lifts, I make a decision to ask one of the security guards to come with me when I tell Ethan where to go. One of the things I tend to forget since moving to New York is that guns exist here. Sure, this would be terrifying back in the UK, too, but the thought of Ethan owning a gun makes the hairs stand up on the back of my neck.

As the lift doors open, I clock Ethan standing next to reception with his ridiculous Tupperware box of muffins. It's another big gesture, something else he can try to make me feel guilty about later. *I'm such a nice guy! I baked you muffins! Why don't you like me?* Did I even tell him where I worked? I know I told him what I do for a living, but I don't think I ever mentioned where.

He's in a suit, one hand tucked into the pocket of his black trousers and one hand clutching the box. He's chatting to Cassidy, smiling broadly, easy charm dripping from him like golden syrup from a spoon. She has a half-eaten muffin in front of her. I don't like that. Cassidy is twenty-one, and Ethan would eat her alive.

She waves me over as soon as she sees me. "Laura, come try one of these. They are just so good."

I glance across at the security guard by the door and then nod to Cassidy. My gaze rests on Ethan, who looks like the least threatening man in the world right now. I know better, of course. I've seen his text messages. I hesitate and consider getting security but then decide that if I can end this without it becoming a big scene, I should try to go in that direction.

I paint on a smile that makes my face feel stiff before I turn to Ethan. "We should talk." I gesture to the sofas in the reception area, designed as a waiting area for clients, interviewees, and so on.

"What are you doing here?" I keep my voice low as I glare at him.

"I'm here to apologise," he says, setting the box on his knee. "I was an asshole."

"You were more than an asshole," I say. "You harassed me. Not by making those very public advances in the restaurant but by texting me the next day. Some of those messages scared me, Ethan. How do you think it makes me feel, seeing you here now at my place of work?"

"I get that," Ethan says. "The thing is, my mother always told me to own up to my mistakes, and when you returned the shoes, I knew I'd fucked up."

"Oh, *then* you knew you'd fucked up," I say, disbelief rushing through me. "Not after sending me over a dozen messages about how we weren't done? Or after I cut a date short because of your behaviour? And now you're here to do what? Frighten me some more?"

His eyes widen. "No! I would never… I didn't mean to scare you, I really didn't. I'm a really socially awkward person, and I don't always read body language well. I have some… boundary issues."

I snort. "That's an understatement."

"I'm working on it," he says, smiling.

"I hope you have a damn good therapist."

"Oh, I do," he says. "And she'll be disappointed when I tell her about all this. It's just… we had such a great connection—"

I raise a hand. "Don't even go there. That avenue is closed."

"I know," he says. "Laura, I'm so sorry for the way I behaved. I couldn't let it go at first, but now I can. And these really are just a 'sorry.' I felt like I had to do it in person. I swear I'm not stalking you."

My eyes skate to the muffins, and I stare at the box. "Okay. You've apologised, and I've accepted it. So now we can both move on with our lives."

"At least take the muffins, Laura," he says. "It's dumb, I know. Baking is a thing in my family." He shrugs.

"Thanks," I say, taking the Tupperware box. "I'll pass them around the office."

"Oh, and don't worry about the box. You don't need to return it. I won't send you the bill or anything." He smiles. "Look, I know it's crass to offer excuses, but I want you to know I'm not usually like this. I've been under a lot of pressure at work lately, and I guess the stress is starting to take its toll in the way I treat people." His eyes meet mine, and I see a flash of sincerity in them.

I sigh. "I appreciate the second apology and the muffins. But you need to leave me alone now."

"Homemade muffins," he corrects.

I bristle. "Right. Homemade. Well, is that it, then? I don't want to be rude, but I have a lot of work to do."

Ethan stands, slipping both hands into his pockets and rocking on his heels. "Yes, that's it. I promise I'll never bother you again. I'm sorry for all the trouble I've caused you. Enjoy the muffins."

He turns to leave before I can say anything else. I watch him exit the building and turn right on the sidewalk. He disappears a moment later.

On the ride back up to my floor, I replay the conversation in my head. Ethan is clearly a strange person, and I hope the therapy works so that he won't harass some other poor women. But at least he agreed to move on, finally.

I just hope he means it.

CHAPTER 8

As the week moves forward, Jessa and I coin what we call the "Ethan Watch." It's a countdown to when we think he'll start up his stalking again. The strange visit to my office felt final, but his behaviour before then suggested he doesn't let things go easily. Every now and then, I get the same stomach-churning feeling I did that day when he harassed me until I made a scene in a shop.

Work goes by in a blur until Thursday morning, when Jessa sends me an article on the women's march we attended. It feels like years ago now. *Check out the pictures*, Jessa's email says. I open it, scroll down, and click through the cycle of images at the bottom of the page.

"Oh, fuck," I say to myself and then glance over my shoulder, checking that no one else in the office heard.

The photo is clear. There I am, front and centre among the crowd at the feminist rally. I would normally be proud to see my face representing a cause I believe in. But I'm in PR, and my clients don't need to know my politics. In fact, it's in my interest that they don't, especially the Republican senator my boss, Anita, recently brought in.

My phone rings.

"Laura, you've been a busy girl."

It's Xavier, Anita's assistant. I can tell from the sarcasm that he's seen the article.

"Hey, Xav. What's the damage?"

"It's bad. Anita wants to see you right away."

"Seriously?" I say. "Because of a photo?"

"I'm just the messenger," he replies. "You'll have to speak to the boss to find out what's going on."

There's something in his tone that suggests he has more information than I do.

"All right. I'm on my way," I say.

I check my reflection in the lift, and I'm definitely paler. Not only is job security hard-won at this company, but if I lose my job, I'll probably lose my flat, and possibly my visa too.

Xavier notices the deep breath I pull in as I exit the lift.

"You'll be fine, killer," he says, moving papers around on his desk.

"Thanks," I say.

I stop in front of Anita's closed office door and rap my knuckles across it, arranging my face into something more neutral and less anxious.

"Come in," Anita calls.

With a clammy palm, I twist the knob and step into the office, trying to exude more confidence than I have. The panoramic view of Lower Manhattan stretches out behind Anita. Beyond her shoulder is the Brooklyn Bridge, where everything began.

She raises her head, shakes the curls from her shoulder, and gestures for me to come forward.

"Hey, Anita," I say, taking a seat in the chair opposite.

She folds her hands together, which is never a good sign. "We need to talk."

"It's usually a bad sign when someone tells you, 'We need to talk.'" I try to break the ice with this joke, but she just stares at me blankly with maybe a hint of disappointment. I've always been envious of her unflappability. No matter what, she's in the office, makeup applied just so, her olive-toned skin bright and clear.

"Anderson is pissed," she says flatly.

"I saw the photo this morning. I realise it's in direct opposition to his views, so I thought if I step down from the account—"

"It's too late for that," Anita says. "He gave us the axe. Just this morning."

"Shit. Over a photo?"

"No," she says. "Not over a photo. Over more than a photo, Laura. What were you thinking, talking to a journalist?"

My jaw dropped. "A journalist? I never spoke to a journalist!"

"Then why is there an article on *Medium* that attributes the following quote to you?" She clears her throat, clicks her mouse, and begins reading. "Republicans like John Anderson have no right running for president when they wish to abolish women's rights." She looks up at me. "And it says right here, Laura McAdams at Nielson and Todd PR."

"I never said that!" I place a hand over my mouth. "I have no explanation for this, but I swear I never said that." I wipe a sheen of sweat from my forehead. "What if I call him and apologise? Explain that the quote was misattributed to me. I mean, it clearly hasn't been properly sourced. Yes, I went to the march, but I got trampled on in the crowd, left early, and never spoke to anyone."

Anita sighs. "I don't think an apology is going to cut it. And there's more."

"What?"

"There's a Twitter thread talking about how John Anderson's PR company have openly stated they won't vote for him. That's you, Laura. You're his PR representative, and people on social media are talking about how you wouldn't vote for him."

"I've never publicly stated that I wouldn't vote for him. I leave my politics at the door when I step into this office, I swear."

"Do you?" She scrutinises me with her dark eyes. "Do any of us?" She leans back in her chair. "Look, the guy's an ass, but he was a client, and we need to keep the clients we have happy."

"I understand that."

Anita's eyebrows knit, and she studies me through tightly pursed lips. "John Anderson is a politician, which makes him hard to deal with in the first place. Add the fact that he's a *Republican* politician, and it creates a whole recipe for chaos, but we have a reputation to uphold."

I nod, trying to choose my words carefully. Anita's posture is rigid, and her expression offers no room for flexibility.

"Is there anything I can do to fix this?" I ask.

She shrugs. "I mean, I could fire you. That might get him back as a client."

"Right," I say, steeling myself. I didn't make those comments, but she can't possibly know that. It's bizarre to think someone would make this up just to sabotage me, but it looks like they might have. Either that, or someone wanted to sabotage John Anderson's presidential bid and grabbed my name from the website.

"Before you do, I just want to say that I understand the severity of the situation, but I never said those things. I went to the march with my friend Jessa, I got separated in the crowd on Brooklyn Bridge, and I fell down. I thought I was going to die down there. John Anderson and his politics were the last things on my mind."

Anita taps her pen on her desk and contemplates my words. A wrinkle forms between her eyebrows. "I want to believe you," she says.

I grab a second opportunity. "Look, you might not want to hear this, but maybe losing Anderson was for the best."

She tilts her head. "How so?"

I straighten my spine. "Well, think about it. If John Anderson and his team are so quick to dispose of us over a rumour that they haven't even taken the time to prove, then perhaps we're better off not associating with clients who are so quick to make snap judgements against others. Also, his politics are divisive. We risk alienating other clients by working with him. Or worse, attracting even more right-wing wackos. I know you don't want Nielson and Todd to go that way."

The reprimanding gaze in Anita's dark-brown eyes fades away, and I know I have her back on my side. Just one more reassurance will put the ball back in my court. I add, "I would never publicly shame anyone, most of all a client. It's not in my character. I care about this job and would not ever put it at risk over something as foolish as that."

Anita parts her lips and blows out a breath. She sets the pen down. "All right. I'm sold."

I try not to sound too excited when I say, "Thank you so much. I appreciate the second chance."

"Don't blow it." Anita's expression is firm as she regards me.

"I don't intend to."

The corners of Anita's lips curve upward. It's not a smile, but it's not a frown either. I'll take what I can get. "That guy is a self-righteous misogynist anyway. But you didn't hear that from me."

I make a gesture as if I'm zipping my lips. "Never."

"I'll take care of the damage control, but do me a favour and try to keep yourself out of trouble from now on."

I stand. "Thanks. I will."

As I leave her office and slide by Xavier's desk, I give him a subtle thumbs-up. He taps his fingers together in quiet applause, giving me a look as if he knew I could hold my own the whole time.

My knees tremble as I walk to the lifts. It wouldn't be the first time a journalist has made up a quote for their piece, but why would they pick me out of everyone? I hurry back to my desk and pull up the *Medium* article. Then I check the journalist. They have a website, but this seems to be their first article. Everything about this is bizarre. Either someone is trying to take me down, or they wanted to take John Anderson down. If it's me, then this is personal, and I need to watch my back.

CHAPTER 9

I'm on thin ice at work. The best thing I can do is stretch myself as far as I can. I'm the first in the office and the last to leave. I contribute to meetings, offering solutions to every problem. I research social media, keeping up with the trends. I'm on top of my clients' issues before they even notice anything is wrong, steering them back on course with carefully worded statements.

Slowly, my world tilts back into place. The Ethan problem has fixed itself—with muffins, apparently—and whoever wrote the article must have been targeting John Anderson because I've been left alone since then.

Things are good, aside from the food poisoning or whatever the hell this is.

It's approaching scarf weather in New York, but I'm sweating like a pig on my commute to work. The subway train is packed, and every carriage lurch brings on a wave of nausea. I close my eyes, willing it away. Throwing up in public has always been a social anxiety trigger of mine, and I'm spending all my energy making sure I don't do just that. Part of me wants to prise open the subway doors and make a run for it across the tracks.

The air smells like dirty laundry. I open my eyes and sit up straight. My stomach flips when I see the blackness of the subway through the plexiglass doors and windows. It's too tight, too constricting. I've never had issues with claustrophobia, but I'm being terrorised by it now.

I press my lips together and breathe through my nose, staring at the floor. Big mistake. There's a piece of chewed-up pizza crust under the seat across from me. I cover my mouth with my hand and retch. My mouth fills with saliva. The person sitting next to me stands up and moves away.

Finally, a splash of yellow colour filters in through the windows. Once the brakes stop screeching, train doors open, and I scramble off. The platform smells like rubber and urine. I hold my breath, scurrying through the crowd.

My eyes zero in on the rubbish bin by the stairs leading up to the street. I hurry to it, grab the sides of its disgusting black rim, and throw up all over a banana peel and a discarded coffee cup. When I'm done, I stand there gasping, still bent at the waist, mouth foamy with vomit.

Wiping my mouth, I sense eyes watching, most likely disgusted from what they've seen. One woman looks green at the gills, not that I blame her. I would too. I walk away, unsteady on my feet, desperate for fresh air.

A wave of a different sickness hits me—homesickness. What I wouldn't give for the clean air of my village. The silence. New York is never silent, and it isn't clean either. I'm never alone here. I'm rarely surrounded by green like I am back home. Pressure builds behind my eyes, and I feel a sharpness in my nose until I give in and let the tears fall. There's nothing to do but stand there on the pavement, letting tears roll down my cheeks. No one cares. Many of these passersby see people cry on the street every day.

I rummage through my bag, searching for tissues, and find a half-empty packet right at the bottom. I wipe away the tears and wipe my mouth too. I'll need to grab some water and mints on the way to work. Where am I? I hadn't even checked the subway station on the way here. Luckily, I realise I got off just one stop early, and it's only a few extra blocks to walk.

I actually feel okay since vomiting. My stomach seems settled now, like whatever it needed to purge is over and done with. I buy bottled water and Tic Tacs from a food stand on my way to work and chug half the bottle before I reach the building. Once inside, I hurry to the bathroom, wash my face, reapply mascara, and redo my hair. No one will know.

And then I feel ravenous. Which is weird for food poisoning or a stomach bug or whatever this is. Usually, I can't face eating for at least a couple of days after feeling sick and have to force down dry toast.

The last time I threw up when I was hungry was the last time I was pregnant.

It hits me hard. If I wasn't walking out of a public bathroom, I would find somewhere to sit. Instead, I pretend my knees aren't suddenly weak and all the blood hasn't drained from my face.

I can't be. I haven't had sex with anyone since... since Ethan.

Besides, I'm barely fertile. The last doctor I saw, back in Derbyshire, told me my chances of falling pregnant again were low, and my chances of bringing a child to term were even lower. Which means...

I push the thought out of my head and walk through the foyer. What good will it do to jump to conclusions? This is all too much of a mindfuck to allow back in my head. I don't want to think about the days I've spent in bed, tears drying on my cheeks, my husband trying desperately to join me in grief and me not quite letting him in. Resenting him, almost. Letting it push us apart.

And Ethan as the father? Someone capable of sending those messages isn't someone I would choose as my baby's father. On the other hand, could I go through this process alone? The blood. The fear. The tears. The shame. And no one to hold me?

By the time I reach the office, I've been over it all again in my mind, despite my efforts not to. My body shakes, and I'm exhausted. I hurry through to the communal kitchen and fill the kettle—one I had to buy myself—to make ginger tea. I crave a crumpet smothered in butter with a drizzle of honey on top. Or strawberry jam. The proper stuff, not the super-sweet kind they sell here.

Good, Laura. Think about food. Don't think about pregnancy or miscarriages. Catastrophising is a terrible thing. You live your pain several times over, seeing it play out in your head like it's real. My aunt always said I had a good head on my shoulders, and I believed her. But not about this. It's too raw. I can't stop my thoughts from running out of control.

Someone walks into the kitchen, and I become more British than ever, cornering this poor person into talking about the weather. I can't even remember this woman's name—Rebecca?—but I'm asking her about New York winters, even though I've lived through one, and babbling on about the biting wind this morning. She edges towards the door, and I realise I'm using her as a distraction, which isn't fair. I take my leave, rushing back to my desk, ginger tea burning my fingers.

In a few hours, it'll be lunch, and I can buy a test from the pharmacy. Maybe I'll buy ten.

No, I tell myself. I should wait until I get home. This isn't the kind of news I can dissect and then go back to my desk. I can't find out I'm pregnant and then go to a meeting.

I need to be alone.

I sip my scalding tea. *Get through the day, Laura.*

CHAPTER 10

I didn't buy ten, but I did get five. And now I'm sitting on the edge of the bath, chewing my bottom lip. Every now and then, I walk anxiously over to the sink and then back to my perch.

Two minutes has never felt so long. Last time I took a test, I watched the paper change colour and saw the cross emerge. This time, I've bought a digital test, and I'm waiting for the word—or words—to appear in the tiny box.

I rub my sweaty palms against my trousers and pull in a deep breath. Then I snatch up the plastic stick.

"Pregnant," I mutter out loud.

I'm immediately unbuttoning my trousers to take another test, but then I realise I need water. So I rush into the kitchen after bashing my arm against the bathroom door. I pour a glass of water and down it.

When I went home with Ethan that night, we'd used a condom. Even though I'd pretty much given up on the idea of becoming a mother the traditional way, I still practised safe sex for many reasons. I remember asking if he had a condom. I remember him grabbing one from a drawer in his bedside table.

How did this happen?

I drink more water. Nothing in life is one hundred per cent effective.

Pregnant.

I hurry back into the bathroom and take another test. And then I keep repeating the process until all five are lined up on the side of the bath, all saying the same thing.

Pregnant.

I have polycystic ovary syndrome. In my case, it's severe. My periods are irregular, and I had trouble with conceiving all through my marriage. When I did conceive, I could never bring the baby to term. Three years ago, I tried surgery. A surgeon lasered my ovaries in an attempt to correct the hormonal imbalance that stilted my ability to conceive.

It didn't work.

After months of pain, adhesions forming inside my body, and a second surgery to correct the first, I managed to keep my ovaries, but they haven't been in great shape since. I get three, maybe four periods a year if I'm lucky. Even conceiving is something of a miracle. But I look at these tests, and it all comes flooding back.

I curl up on the floor of my bathroom, and I start to grieve for this baby. Part of me thinks he or she is dead already and it's my fault. My body did this. My body has allowed this new life to begin, and now I don't know if my body will allow this new life to flourish or if the chance of finally giving birth to my own child will be yanked from me once more.

* * *

I wince as the doctor draws blood. The fluorescent lights blink above me. I'm leaning back in the recliner chair, trying not to look at the needle. Dr Nowak is older, in his fifties, with steel-grey hair and bright-blue eyes. I can't look at his face either, so I keep staring at the lights.

"How are you doing?" he asks. "Are you okay?"

"It's been a while since my last blood test," I say. "I guess I'm not used to it anymore."

"Try to relax," he says. "We're nearly done."

He covers it well, but I sense a hint of concern in his voice. I must be white as a sheet, and he's most likely concerned I'll faint.

"I'm okay," I say again, this time more as a pep talk to myself.

"There we go. All done." He removes the needle from my vein and places a cotton ball on the blossom of blood. A moment later, I have a plaster over the entry point, and he's organising the vial. "I did notice in your file that you've been through some fertility issues. I saw you used to be on Metformin. Have you been on it recently?"

"No," I say. "Not for several years."

"Oh." He seems surprised. "I assumed that might be the reason for your possible pregnancy."

Metformin can make a woman more fertile. It can be quite powerful. I tried it while married, and it did result in a pregnancy but, sadly, no birth.

"Then this really is a surprise," he says. He's smiling, but he's guarded, too, waiting for my reaction so he can temper his response.

"It is," I admit. I can't quite muster enthusiasm in my voice. My past pregnancies are too close to the surface, the pain still tangible.

"I'll get the results to you as soon as I can," he says. "Are you sure you're okay? Do you need a minute to recover?"

"I'm okay," I insist. "I'm just a little nervous. My last three pregnancies all resulted in miscarriage. I've never… never made it past the first trimester, and this is…" I trail off, my throat thickening with emotion.

"I understand completely," he says. "Let's take it one day at a time. Okay?"

He's being kind and gentle. Perhaps it's disingenuous of me to want to correct him. But he's also never felt a baby die inside of him before, and those words—*I understand completely*— have a power. I just nod.

"This may be a high-risk pregnancy," he says. "You're a little older too. But those words merely refer to labels and percentages that we use in medicine to inform our next steps. These are not predictions, okay? There's every chance you won't experience any issues whatsoever." He pats my hand. "Now, go home and get some rest. Someone will call you today with the results."

This time, I zone out on the subway. I have cereal bars packed in my bag to keep me from feeling hungry and sick. I ate half a bar going out of the doctor's surgery, still shaky from the blood test. Deep down, I know it's a formality. My body has told me I'm pregnant, and so have the at-home tests. So now it's all about what I do next.

There's no question in my mind that if—a huge if—I can bring this baby to term that I will keep and love this baby. This could be my last chance. It's a chance I'd never imagined I would get again. Once the ink dried on my divorce papers, I gave up the idea of ever giving birth. I did wonder if one day I might adopt, if I found the right man to parent a child with, but being pregnant again seemed like a pipe dream.

So that's decided. I'm keeping the baby. I can't afford a baby, not really. Perhaps if I moved home and had some help from Aunt Emily, things might be easier. I do love my job, but it's not so bad a sacrifice.

And then there's one last piece of the puzzle—the father, a man I would never have chosen in a million years. Someone who sent me harassing text messages and turned up at my place of work uninvited. I let out a long sigh, watching a subway station blur away as the train moves on. What am I going to do about the Ethan problem?

CHAPTER 11

I grab my phone from my bag as soon as the subway doors open. Dozens of lazy, tired commuters spill out, me among them. Every elbow seems like a weapon now. I'm protective of my stomach, one hand resting gently on my abdomen.

I climb the steps leading out to the street and dial Jessa's number.

"Hey, bitch," she says.

"Hey." I stride across the street and walk towards the crosswalk that leads into Central Park. "Please tell me you're home and you can meet me in the park."

"I'm home. I'm drying fruit."

I smile. "Of course you're drying fruit. What else would you be doing?"

"Wait," she says. "The drying-fruit trend hasn't hit the English market yet? I'm shocked."

I laugh. "Seriously, though. Do you have a few minutes to spare?"

"For you? I've got all the time in the world."

I breathe a sigh of relief. "Thanks. Can you meet me by the zoo?"

"Okay. I'll be there ASAP."

"You're the best."

An hour later, I'm sitting on a park bench with a caramel macchiato cupped in my hands. She's sitting beside me, so close our thighs touch. She pats me on the knee and smiles. I wonder if I can actually drink the coffee. I can't remember all the rules required to follow while pregnant. I place the coffee down by my feet.

"So, what's going on with you? I'm guessing this impromptu visit to the park isn't about soaking in a beautiful fall day."

I pick at a piece of hard skin by my thumbnail, avoiding her penetrating gaze. "How did you guess?"

"Please. I can read you like a book." She laughs. "Now, stop scaring me. You're so pale, Lor. What's going on?"

I clasp my hands together and take a deep breath. "I received some news recently. And I'm not sure how I feel about it. Well, I'm cautiously happy about it. But there's… it's a lot to process for many reasons."

Jessa's eyes widen. "Okay. You know you can tell me anything."

"Right," I say, my pulse quickening. And then I decide to just say it, to rip off the plaster in one quick motion. "I'm pregnant." I take in a big lungful of air. "I took five tests and went for a blood test. I haven't heard back from the doctor yet, but it seems pretty certain."

Jessa's jaw drops open. "No way. How—what—when—"

I drag a hand through my hair and rest my back against the bench, crossing my legs. I glance up at the sky. A pair of blue jays skirt from branch to branch in the tree above me. Sunshine slants through the auburn leaves, and they glint golden above, the breeze making them wink.

"It's Ethan's."

"Oh," she says. "The stalker? Ah, shit. I'm sorry. Are you sure? You didn't jump Keanu Reeves's bones at some point around the same time?"

I laugh. "It's definitely Ethan's. He's the only guy I've slept with for quite some time."

Jessa lets out a long breath. "So what are you going to do?"

"That is a good question." I lean forwards and rest my head in my hands.

Jessa slips a consoling hand across my back. "It's going to be okay, you know. Whatever you decide."

"I want to keep the baby. If… well, you know…" I trail off, scared to finish the rest of the sentence, but Jessa knows what I mean. The baby might not make it that far.

"I'm here for you. Any time." Jessa's voice is butter soft. I know she means it.

"Thank you. I'm going to need you. This is going to be quite the journey."

The corners of Jessa's lips turn up. She lets out a small laugh. "How are you not freaking out right now? I would be, I don't know, running around this park like a madwoman."

"It is turmoil in here." I tap my temple. "Nuclear meltdown."

Jessa laughs, and so do I. I let the hysteria spread through me. A group of joggers turn to stare at us, but their stares only fuel the giggles. A few moments later, the laughter fades, and we fall into a comfortable silence. I watch a flock of pigeons nipping at a discarded bag of nacho chips across the street.

"Are you going to tell him?" she asks.

"I haven't decided yet."

"Well, that's fair. Give yourself some time. I mean, you only just found out yourself."

I turn to her. "I do need some extra time to process how I'm going to handle all this. It's hard, you know? My first introduction to Ethan has not been a positive one. He's not the man I would choose to be the father of my child. I think I'm going to need to weigh it all up."

"That's smart. Nothing good ever comes from snap decisions."

I smirk at her. "Is that really you saying that, or did someone possess you?"

"Hey, now. I'm getting wiser in my mid-thirties," she jokes. "However, I will say there's nothing wrong with a little spontaneity every once in a while."

I groan and rest my elbows on my knees. "It's so hard. On the one hand, I feel like he has a right to know. He helped to make this bundle of cells, right? On the other, if everything goes right and I have this baby, do I really want this man in my child's life? Everything about him screams… *off*. You know?"

"I know," she says. "Just take it one minute at a time. You don't need to think about the big picture right now."

"I'll have to eventually, though." I rub my hands across my face. "If I don't, I'll drive myself crazy."

Jessa bumps her shoulder against mine. "You'll be fine. You're one of the most together people I know."

I smile. "Tell me what to do, Jess."

She takes my hand. "I don't know. But we can figure it out. I think you're smart to be cautious. The man had more red flags than a bull-fighter. You saved those harassing messages on your phone, right?"

I nod.

"Good. Hopefully, you'll never need to use them, but it's good you saved them in case you need to prove he harassed you at a later date."

"I hope I never need to do that."

She nods. "Me too." Then she sighs. "I guess the only thing this guy has in his favour is that he did leave you alone. Eventually."

"He did," I admit. "When he showed up at my work, I half expected him to make a scene in the lobby when I turned him down again, but instead, he cut his losses, told me he wouldn't bother me again, and left."

"And he's kept his word."

"Yes."

"Just think about it." Jessa cups her hand over my knee and gives it an endearing squeeze. "You don't have to make the decision today."

"I know," I say. "One thing I'm certain about is that I *really* want this baby. I didn't grow up with a father. He left when I was six months old. I always felt like there was something missing in my life. Do I want my child to feel the same way?"

Her eyes bloom, glinting against the late-afternoon sun. "You and your baby deserve the world. You've waited for this dream to come true for so long."

"I just thought it would be with the right guy, that's all."

Jessa shrugs and pauses before answering. "Well, it's the twenty-first century. Strong, healthy, independent women are raising children all on their own, all over this city. It's probably more common than you think." Jessa must see the worry on my face because she grabs my hand again. "It's going to be fine, Lor. You're not alone, and you can do this. And who knows? You might meet the right person to settle down with. You might find the father figure for your little bean in there in a completely different place."

I nod. I know she's right. There's a flicker of hope growing inside me. I can't forget that. This baby will save me from dark thoughts and anxieties.

Every decision can wait. Right now, I'm pregnant with hope, and I'm not alone. That's enough.

CHAPTER 12

For the second time in a month, I find myself sitting in the chair across from Anita's desk. I waited two weeks to make sure everything with the pregnancy was still moving smoothly. So far so good. I haven't experienced any spotting, and everything seems normal, though my dreams are a different story. Sometimes, I wake up and want to call Sam to tell him the news. But he's remarried now, and he wouldn't want to know. It would be selfish, me wanting to hear his voice one last time, to hear him tell me everything's going to be okay.

My boss is the only single mother I know. She's great at her job—we all know that in the office—but she's also unapologetic about taking time away from work to be with her kids. Anita might be scary at times, but a woman with a work ethic *and* a good relationship with her kids must be doing something right, and I've always admired her for it.

She's dressed in a chic tan suit that complements her olive skin tone. Her curly brown hair is swept into a sophisticated ponytail today, and gold earrings dangle from her earlobes.

"Thanks for this," I say. "I know you're busy." I wring my clammy hands.

"Sure," she says. "What did you want to talk about? You're not quitting, are you?"

"No, nothing like that."

"Okay, good," she says.

I brush the hair away from my face. "Although I'm relieved to hear you have that reaction."

Anita's smile is pleasant, friendly. "Are you okay, Laura? You look nervous. I won't bite. Too hard. Just kidding." Her laughter is like the flutter of butterfly wings.

"I'm pregnant," I say. "Six weeks. But I don't want to tell anyone in the office yet, so I'd like to keep this just between us."

She leans back in her chair. "Wow." She gives me a look of surprise. "Wow. That's—that's amazing. Congratulations."

"Thanks," I say. "It came as quite a surprise to me."

"Me too," she admits. "I didn't realise you were dating someone."

"I'm not… actually." I cross my legs, shifting my skirt. "To be honest, I came here because I wanted some advice from you. It's more than likely that I'll be raising this baby on my own."

"Oh?" Anita's eyebrows knit together.

"It's a long story." I waft a hand. "I hope it isn't too personal to ask you how you manage it. Being a single mum, I mean."

"I'm glad you came to me." She plants her palms on the desk surface. "But if we're stripping away all that veneer and going straight to the nitty-gritty candour, I'd be doing you a disservice if I didn't tell you that it's very difficult to raise a child by yourself."

"I had a feeling you'd say that." My fingers tighten around my knee.

Anita's smile is wry, as though I have no idea what I'm in for. She props one elbow up on her desk and tilts her head. "But sometimes, you have to do what you have to do, right? If the circumstances don't fit, you step into both roles because you don't have a choice."

I nod and pull in a deep breath, letting the words sink in.

"I have no doubts you'll be an amazing mom. You're strong and independent and smart. Those are all fantastic qualities."

Heat travels across my face. It has been years since my mum died, but sometimes, the grief hits me unexpectedly all over again. This is the closest I've come to compliments from a mother figure in a long time. Since I moved to New York. The power her words have on me is embarrassing but also like a warm hug. "Thank you. That means the world to me."

"And you should know I mean it. I don't hand out compliments like they're candy." Her eyes crinkle with amusement. "Can I ask you a personal question?" She pauses a beat and then quickly adds, "You don't have to answer, of course."

"Yeah, sure."

"Why isn't the father in the picture?"

I exhale and choose my words carefully, my gaze fixed on my lap. "Well, it's a little complicated—"

"I gathered that much."

I shrug, trying to give her enough information about the situation without being too specific. "I'm just not sure things are going to work out between me and the father. Early on, I noticed some troubling things about the way he treats women. I told him I wanted to part ways. He was persistent at first. It scared me, honestly."

Anita studies me hard with a frown. "Okay, that's understandable."

"Then he apologised in a gracious way. He said he's been stressed at work and that he didn't mean to be an arsehole and take it out on me. He promised to leave me alone, and to be honest, he *has* honoured that promise."

Anita nods along as I delve into the story. The whole time, I see her thinking. She twines her fingers together, tapping her fingertips on the bottom of her chin.

"Unless you think this man is dangerous, I think you should at least tell him," she says. "Give him a choice. Keeping it from him will make it worse for you in the long run. He could find out and sue for custody at a later date."

"You really think so?"

"My husband died when my daughter was a baby. She has no memory of him at all, and it kills me she didn't get to know him. I didn't have the same choice you have now. It was taken from me. I show her pictures of him, and she knows his face now that she's older, but I feel like you owe it to your baby. Fathers deserve to have a say in the matter too. I know my daughter would have wanted to grow up knowing her dad if she could have." She pauses. "But my husband was a good man, so it's easy for me to say that. He would've been a great father. It sounds like the father to your baby may be deeply flawed. That makes your decision even trickier."

Her words hit me hard. I had a similar experience to Anita's daughter, but in my case, my dad chose to leave. I've carried that rejection my entire life. It's not an easy thing to shoulder. To have a hole where a dad should be.

"He's definitely flawed," I say. "Dangerous? I don't know. I hate to write people off, because I think people can change. I was concerned by both his actions and words during our brief connection." I shake my head. "But I can't rewrite history, can I? He's the father whether I like it or not."

"If you need anything," she says, "you call me, okay? I believe in women supporting each other. My kids are in school now, and things are easier. I have time to help someone else out."

"Thank you," I say, floored by her generosity. I consider stepping around the desk for a hug, but it feels like it'd be too much.

"And about the father, you're the only one who knows what's best for your baby, and don't forget it. You don't have to take my advice, of course, but at least just think about it."

"I will absolutely do that." I stand up, still flushed and warm, my mind full of conflicting thoughts.

"And set boundaries," she says as I'm about to walk to the door. "If you don't know this man well enough to know what kind of father he'll be, you need to set boundaries right from the start. You're the mother. You're giving him this gift. Don't you forget it. By all means, communicate, talk it out, put out your feelers. Then trust your instincts."

"I will," I say.

Her advice is almost a warning. After all, like she said, I'm about to give someone who's practically a stranger to me the ultimate gift—a child. I have no idea how he's going to react to that.

* * *

I sit on Anita's advice for another week until I'm absolutely sure of what I want to do. It's a glorious sunny day at work. On my lunch break, I take a walk to a park full of auburn maple trees and find a bench to sit on. And then I work up the courage to dial the number of the company where Ethan works. I had to do some investigating to find him, since I'd blocked his number. But luckily, I'd remembered the name of the finance company he talked about. I press the call button on my phone before placing it against my ear.

As it rings, I watch an adorable older couple eating sandwiches together in the park. Maybe Ethan and I won't be close like that, but perhaps we can raise a baby together as a responsible, cordial team.

"Chase Bank," says a chirpy female voice. "How may I direct your call?"

"Ethan—" I clear the raspy frog from my unused voice. "Sorry. Ethan Hart. Can I be connected to Ethan Hart?"

There's a beat of silence on the other end, and the woman comes back saying, "One moment, please."

I'm put on hold with symphony music playing on the line. A moment later, it clicks through, and I hear Ethan's voice.

"Ethan Hart." He sounds professional and unassuming.

I can do this. "Ethan."

"Yes?" His voice lifts. He's curious.

"Hey. It's—it's Laura. Laura McAdams. From the bridge march." I cringe inside. Like he wouldn't remember me. It hasn't been *that* long.

He's quiet for a moment. "Laura? Hey. Is—what's going on?" He sounds confused to hear from me. "Why are you calling my office?"

"I didn't have your phone number anymore. Sorry." I flush with the heat of embarrassment. The happy couple on the bench have balled up their empty sandwich wrappers and pushed them into a brown recycling bag.

"Oh." He sounds disappointed for a moment, but then a cheeriness returns to his voice. "Well, it's nice to hear from you."

"Right." I take a deep breath. On to the hard part. "I was wondering if you might want to have lunch with me. Say, tomorrow, if you're free. Sorry it's last-minute—"

"No, that's all right. I can do lunch tomorrow. I might have to get my assistant to move some things around on my calendar, but let's see. Hmm…" He trails off a moment, I assume to glance at his schedule. "I can do one o'clock. Or is that too late?"

"I can do one," I confirm.

"Great."

"There's this place I like to go to sometimes. An Italian restaurant. I need to stay close to work. It's in Midtown, near Hell's Kitchen." I wipe a bead of sweat from my brow.

"What's the name?" he asks.

"Tavola."

"Oh, I've heard of it," he says. "Never been. Excited to try it now."

"Great." I blow a sigh of relief through parted lips. The sun warms my back. "Thank you. I'll see you tomorrow at one."

"I'll be there."

I hang up, my heart pattering. I can do this. One step at a time.

CHAPTER 13

When I round the corner onto Ninth Avenue, I spot Ethan sitting at one of the outdoor bistro tables. It's a pleasant October day, and the table umbrella shades him from the sun, blocking his expression from my view. Ice water beads condensation on the two glasses, one in front of him, one in front of the empty seat—the one waiting for me.

I take a deep breath, plaster on a friendly smile, and toss him a wave as I approach. He immediately stands. He's wearing a black suit and a sky-blue tie. He looks fresh and handsome and smells faintly of citrus aftershave. As wary as I am of him, I can't deny that he's extremely attractive. It makes his behaviour more mind-boggling. Ethan has the world at his feet with his looks and money, and yet he isolates people so readily.

"Hi," he says, his eyes moving across me. "You look fantastic."

When he tries to hug me, I step away and shake my head, offering my hand instead. "It's nice to see you, Ethan."

He gestures at the empty seat, and I sit, clasping my hands together. The heating lamp underneath the umbrella hums low in the background. My heart jumps around in my chest. I pull in a deep breath, calming myself, and a question crosses Ethan's face. He can see I'm nervous, and it seems to be something he didn't expect.

"So, to what do I owe the pleasure of your company for lunch today?" He presses his tie to his chest then adjusts a cuff.

The server approaches the table before I can answer. I order a Sprite to help ward off the morning sickness. Ethan asks for a Coke. I'm relieved he doesn't pick something with alcohol in it. Maybe this lunch encounter will go smoother than I'd hoped.

The waiter leaves, and I open my mouth to speak, but Ethan takes control again. He pushes the bread basket in my direction. "Would you like some bread?"

I pluck a piece out and pick up my knife before spreading butter across the bread. Ethan does the same. The whole time, his expression indicates that he's weighing me up. There's a smile playing at the corners of his mouth, and I imagine him beginning to feel like I want him back.

It bugs me.

"I actually wanted to have lunch with you for a specific reason," I say. I take a quick sip of soda, relieving my dry throat. "There's something I need to tell you, and it isn't going to be easy to say. So I suppose I should just come out with it." I wipe my clammy palms against my thighs.

Ethan frowns, sets his bread down, and knits his eyebrows. "Okay, what is it?"

The words blurt from my mouth on the tail end of a large sigh. "I'm pregnant. I had a positive home test—well, I took five, actually—and then I went to the doctor to confirm it with a blood test." I force myself to move my eyes from my plate to him. "I found out a few weeks ago. I have an ultrasound scheduled at the end of the month."

Ethan's eyebrows shoot up his forehead. He's silent for a moment, and then a smile spreads across his face. His eyes brighten, and he sits up straighter. "You're—you're really pregnant?"

"Yes."

"And it's mine? You know this for sure?"

I break his gaze, pressing my palms together under the white linen tablecloth. "You're the only person I've…been with in that time frame, so yes. If you want to have a test to confirm—"

Ethan reaches across the table, shaking his head, his eyes glistening beneath the glow of the table heaters. A siren blares in the distance. A car honks. A bicyclist breezes past us in the bike lane on the street. Life is in motion all around us, but I've stopped spinning. I'm concreted into my seat at this restaurant, under this umbrella, at this table.

"This is the best news I could ever get," he says. He leans back in his seat. "I'm going to be a dad? A dad?"

I can't help but smile. "You're going to be a dad."

This is not the reaction I was expecting to get from him, although I must say, it's the best-case scenario playing out. He's not making a scene. He hasn't snapped at anyone or lost his temper. He seems over the moon about this pregnancy announcement, even though we went on only one official date. We don't even know the simplest things about each other, like each other's middle names or each other's favourite colour. Yet here he is, elation written across his face as though nothing else in the world matters.

"Yes," he exclaims. "This is the best gift anyone has ever given me. Ever. Wow. Laura, I know this is an accident, but thank you so much."

I shake my head. "I really thought you were going to be upset."

"Are you kidding me?" Ethan reaches for the hand that I've now exposed from under the table, and he laces his fingers through mine. He gives my hand a gentle squeeze. "I'm thrilled."

The server returns to the table, carrying our hot pasta dishes. Ethan beams at him. "I'm going to be a father."

The server glances between us, setting the food down and offering a polite smile. "Congratulations. I can bring out a slice of tiramisu on the house for you if you like at the end of your meal."

Ethan looks at me, allowing me to decide.

"Sure." I shrug. "Why not?"

Ethan lifts his glass of Coke, and I do the same with my Sprite. "Cheers to new beginnings," he says.

"Cheers." I realise I'm still gawking at him.

"Can I go to your first ultrasound with you?" he asks.

"I was going to ask you if you wanted to go," I admit.

"Yes, of course," he almost shouts, still grinning a mile wide. "I would love to attend if you'll let me."

If you'll let me.

Another good sign. Ethan has seemingly learned where he went wrong with me. I still want to take this slowly, one step at a time, but he's on his best behaviour, at least for now.

I choose my words carefully, hoping to set some boundaries early on. "I'd like that. I do want to take things slowly, but if you want to be in the baby's life, I think we can work as a team to make that happen."

Ethan reaches across the table so quickly he almost spills his drink in the process. He readjusts it, apologises for his overzealous response, and starts giddily asking me a million questions about the pregnancy. He asks me how I've been feeling. I tell him, honestly, that I've been feeling horrible, and that's what prompted me to get a test.

He picks up a fork. "You can call me any time of the day or night. If you want ice cream at three a.m., I'll get it. If you want deli soup, I'll bring some over. I can pay for prenatal care classes too."

"Maybe we can try a couple together," I suggest. "But I do need to lay out some ground rules, if you're willing to listen." I dab the corners of my mouth with my napkin.

Ethan nods. "Sure. Of course."

I hold his gaze. "Ethan, I meant what I said back in my office lobby when you brought me those muffins. We have nothing but a platonic relationship. I would like to be the one who determines just how frequently we meet. Right now, I'd prefer it if we start by attending doctor's visits together, and then we'll see what happens from there. You don't need to pay for anything or buy me ice cream in the middle of the night. We're not a couple. We won't be doing anything like that."

"I'm willing to do whatever it takes." Ethan doesn't miss a beat. "If you want me to back off, then all you have to do is tell me. I'll let you make the rules. You can call me if you want me to go with you to the doctor. I won't bother you until then, and I won't call you first. I'll let you be the one to initiate the conversations and the calls or texts."

I breathe out through parted lips and relax my shoulders. "Thank you, Ethan, really. You are being so cool about all this, and I appreciate it."

Ethan's eyes crinkle with warmth, and I recognise some of the same charm that captured my attention from the beginning.

"I told you, I'm really not a bad guy. You just happened to meet me while I was in the middle of a bad week."

Maybe it's the hormones, but I find myself empathising with him. It took two of us to make this baby, and I would like us both to bring him or her into the world as a cohesive team. I want us to be a strong parental unit that will bring structure and love into our child's life.

Ethan's enthusiasm is making me happy that I took Anita's advice. I made the right decision to involve him. I'm not too proud to admit that I'll need help and that my baby will need a father figure.

Ethan can't stop smiling, and it's rubbing off on me. I can't believe this is happening, but hope blooms in my heart. I can't bring myself to tell him about my history. I don't want to cast any shadows over this moment. We can have this, can't we? This one moment of happiness.

CHAPTER 14

E than meets me in the lobby of the doctor's office, a takeaway cup in his hand.

"I thought you might want some mint tea for the nausea," he says, handing it to me.

"Thanks. That's so nice of you." I take a sip, letting the hot liquid warm my throat. It'd been a tough morning, and I'd already thrown up before leaving my apartment. Nerves tickle my stomach in preparation for this scan.

"Are you all right?" he asks. "You look a bit pale."

"I'm fine. It's just morning sickness."

We make our way up in the lift together and then take a seat in the waiting room.

"I want you to be comfortable," he says. "So make sure you tell me if you need anything. I want to make sure you are getting the things you need and even sometimes the things you want." He pauses and smiles. "Within the boundaries, of course."

I give him a thankful smile over the rim of my tea. "Of course."

A nurse in scrubs opens the door and calls, "Laura McAdams?"

I rise from my seat. "That's me."

I'm escorted to a brightly lit examination room, and I undress from the waist down in preparation for the scan. Once I'm settled with the paper sheet over my lower half, Ethan and Dr Nowak enter the room together. There's a sweet, hopeful look on Ethan's face, like a puppy about to play fetch. But all I feel is dread. I'm so sure something will be wrong. I can feel it.

Dr Nowak moves to my front while Ethan comes to stand by my waist. When I look up at him, I still can't believe this is happening, that a man who once sent me creepy text messages is now the father of my baby. I pull in a deep breath. The ultrasound monitor is wheeled up right beside us, and all of a sudden, there is my uterus. Ethan grins, pointing at the screen, but the doctor is quiet, checking everything over, and I'm anxiously waiting for bad news.

"May I?" Ethan whispers, reaching his hand to mine.

Distracted, I let him hold my hand. My heart rattles my rib cage, but I have to admit, the gesture is comforting. I'd considered changing my mind about Ethan coming with me today. I almost called him to say I would prefer Jessa with me. But now that I'm lying here, waiting for the doctor to speak, even Ethan's presence is a good one.

"All right. The baby looks happy and healthy," the doctor says finally.

"Are you sure?" I ask.

"Absolutely. Congratulations to you both."

Ethan and I exchange relieved glances. He sighs, propping his shoulders against the wall behind him. He weaves his fingers through his hair, and I notice his hand is shaking. "This is great news."

All of the relief seeps out of me in happy tears, and the doctor grabs a box of tissues for me. I pluck one out and dab it under my damp eyes. When I glance over at Ethan, even his eyes are red-rimmed and watery. He stares at the screen, a broad smile plastered across his face. There is our baby. I can hardly believe it. A tiny baby, resembling a potato, flipping around in its amniotic sac without a care in the world, blissfully unaware of anything scary that exists outside of its fluid-filled cocoon.

An unbelievable surge of love for this unborn child washes over me. I make a silent vow to it, through our connection and bond, the blood and the cells and the arteries we currently share, to protect him or her every day of their life.

A look of wonder and excitement flares across Ethan's eyes. That's when the magic of happiness tingles all over me, starting in my stomach and rushing warm endorphins through my veins.

"Everything looks good so far," Dr Nowak continues, his fingers moving across the keyboard underneath the ultrasound screen. "I'm just going to check the crown-to-rump length to make sure we're measuring at eight weeks like we're supposed to." He pauses for a moment and regards me. "If the baby measures a little over or under the estimate, don't worry. That's perfectly normal."

I suck in a deep breath and nod. "Okay, good."

I can handle this. Once I hear the heartbeat, I'll be more reassured.

The arrows and line go across the baby's tiny body from top to bottom as the doctor does his measurements.

"More good news to share," he says. "Everything is measuring on target."

I sink into the back of the examination table, riding on the crest of this wave, elated. I sniff and brush the tears from my wet cheeks with the back of my hand.

"Let's see if we can pick out the heartbeat." Dr Nowak moves the wand around inside me. He presses another button on the keypad, and the three of us pause a moment, dead silence in the room as we wait expectantly for the sound.

And then it happens. It's music to my ears, the clomping of what sounds like horse hooves galloping through the monitor speakers.

Ethan's posture straightens. "That's the heartbeat?"

The doctor nods. "Indeed, it is."

"Wow." Ethan covers his mouth with a hand, his face crinkling with emotion. "It's wonderful."

Dr Nowak takes some screenshots of the heartbeat.

"Is it fast enough?" I ask.

"It's perfect. It's at one sixty-five, which is well within the healthy range."

I blow out another sigh of relief through parted lips and gaze at the ceiling. My baby has a beating heart. A *healthy* beating heart.

Dr Nowak asks if we would like to take some pictures home, and of course we both jump at the chance. I can't wait to show Jessa. I can send pictures to Aunt Emily too. Even Ethan asks if he can have a set of pictures to take home for himself, and a sprig of hope takes root inside me and immediately starts to blossom.

"I can't wait to show these to Mom," he says. "She's going to be ecstatic."

I smile. Today, he's a regular guy excited to be a dad, looking forward to telling the grandma all about it. And then sadness washes over me. There'll be no grandparents on my side of the family. But my Aunt Emily will make up for that. I know she will.

I get dressed and check out, and when I meet Ethan a few minutes later in the lobby, he places his hand on my lower back and escorts me out the door. This time, it seems more chivalric than possessive, and I let him do it, still lost in that warm, fuzzy feeling of knowing everything is going to be okay.

"How about you let me take you to lunch to celebrate? My treat. Then I promise I'll leave you alone so you can get back to work or whatever else you have planned for the rest of your day."

I rest my hand on my stomach, which is still flat for now. "I'll let you treat me to a bowl of soup from Alli's. I haven't been eating heavy foods recently."

"Soup sounds excellent," he says.

"Great."

One step at a time with him. He's scoring points, but the cynical side of me won't let me forget how atrocious he was in the beginning.

It's puzzling how his personality has seemingly flipped a switch. The arrogant, impatient jerk has all but vanished, replaced by this charming and sweet version of Ethan. What's the catch? Maybe there isn't one, and like he keeps saying, I just met him in the middle of a bad week. I'm happy it's going well for now, but in the back of my mind, something is warning me to be cautious all the same.

CHAPTER 15

I t's a bright and sunny Monday, and I've taken a personal day. The weather is cooler, and I'm in a thick, comfortable cardigan as I make myself toast and jam at the kitchen counter. I hear the street noise down below, but mostly, the flat is quiet and peaceful.

I'm just past the twelve-week milestone, and when I look in the mirror, naked, I can see the slight curve of roundness in my lower abdomen. I sit at the table with my toast and a cup of tea then dial Ethan's number.

He answers on the first ring, a smile in his voice. "Hey, you."

Things are going better than expected with Ethan, and I'm starting to warm a bit more to him. It helps that he has stuck to his word, not overstepping or trying to control my pregnancy. All in all, I've appreciated having a partner going through this with me, even if Ethan isn't the teammate I would have chosen.

"Hi." I sink my teeth into the toast. It's smeared with damson jam sent by Aunt Emily, and I make a satisfied groaning sound. "Wow."

Ethan pauses then begins to laugh. "Everything okay over there?"

"Amazing." Through my chewing, the word comes out garbled.

"Are you eating something?"

"Yes, toast with proper British jam."

"Oh, I'm sorry. Did I catch you at a bad time? Should I leave you and the jam alone?"

I laugh. "Sorry. I can't stop eating at the moment, so I'm in a constant state of multitasking. But that was rude of me."

"It's okay," he says. "You are growing my baby inside of you."

"I just called to tell you that I've officially crossed the twelve-week milestone." It's wonderful to say the words aloud, to step across that threshold. Each week I make it with this miracle baby is one week closer to making it to full term.

"That's great!" he says. "How are you feeling? Well, I know your appetite is coming back."

"Yeah. It's getting better. Sorry if I sound like a slopping pig." I laugh. "But yes, I'm hungry today. The baby wanted jam."

"A baby after my own heart."

"But to answer your question, I'm starting to feel better, although sometimes, the queasiness will hit me out of nowhere."

"I hope you're not overdoing it," he says.

"I'm trying not to."

"But knowing you, you're still exercising like it's your religion and working yourself to the bone at your job," he says.

"How'd you guess?" I smile to myself. I much prefer this playful banter that has developed between us over the last few weeks. I glance at my watch. "Oh, crap. I forgot I need to call my aunt Emily today. Sometimes, the time difference slips my mind. I can use the excuse of having pregnancy brain, though."

"That's just my baby taking all your smarts for himself," Ethan says.

I chuckle, but something about what he said throws me off. Is it because he referred to the baby as *his* and not *ours*, or is it the fact that he's assuming the baby will be a boy? Neither of us know the sex of the baby yet.

I decide to brush it off for now. I can't suspect every little thing he says or does of being ill-intended. I remind myself to relax before I drive myself crazy.

"At this rate, you might be right. I couldn't find my sunglasses yesterday, and it took me a full minute to realize they were on my face."

"Wow."

"Yeah. That bad."

"Okay. I won't keep you any longer. Have a good chat with your aunt." He sounds breezy and unbothered. A good sign, I hope.

I hang up and swiftly dial Emily's number.

Nerves flutter in the pit of my stomach. Emily isn't just an aunt to me. She's much more. And yet I haven't told her about Ethan or the baby. I think I might have mentioned going on a bad date to her back when Ethan and I first met, but once I found out I was pregnant, I never mentioned it. I didn't want to get her hopes up. But now I've reached my twelve-week mark, and I feel much better about spreading the news. My eyes drift over to the damson jam made with fruit picked from the wild garden that stretches behind her old house, the one with my initials carved into the magnolia tree. Nostalgia hits me with a pang.

"Good evening, darling," she says. "You have thirty minutes until *University Challenge.*"

I smile at the sound of her voice. "Oh dear. I wouldn't want to get in the way of your date with Paxman."

"He's retiring, darling."

"What?" I say. "I must return to England immediately. You'll need comfort in this terrible time."

"Oh, you must," she replies. "When are you coming home? Isn't this American jaunt over with yet? I miss your face."

"Em," I say. I never called her aunty, only ever Em or Emily. "There's something I need to tell you."

"Laura, dear, do spit it out. You know I don't cope well with suspense."

"I'm pregnant," I say. "I just made it past the twelve-week milestone. I wanted to tell you sooner, but given everything that happened before… I decided to wait a bit longer. I hope you won't be upset."

"You're pregnant?" she exclaims. "Darling, that's *wonderful.* I'm so happy for you!"

"Thank you." I stand up and start pacing around the small living room. I have too much energy and need to burn it off.

"I didn't even realise there was a man," she says, albeit without judgement.

"Yeah, about that," I say. "It's a bit complicated.

"Well," she says, "I suppose I can record *University Challenge.* Go on."

I tell her everything, from the way Ethan scooped me up at the women's march to his bizarre date behaviour to his elation about being a father. Her first reaction surprises me.

"So he's a *Wall Street* banker? Hmm. I'm not sure I like that."

I can't help but laugh. "*That's* the part you don't like."

I can hear her moving around the house. She must be stress-tidying. That's the only time she does any cleaning at all. "No, Laura, you already know what I'm going to say. Keep cautious with this one. I don't like the way he treated you."

"He's been kind ever since."

She lets out a derisive snort. "Now you have something he wants. He has to be nice to you."

I touch my stomach. She's right. I know she is, but I don't want to believe it.

"You can always come home," she says, a note of hope in her voice. "I can help you."

"The baby needs a father," I say.

"The baby needs you," she says. "If there's a stable father in the picture, then all the better, but this man…" She sighs. "I'm concerned."

"I swear I have it under control."

"I hope so," she replies.

I wish I could see her face. Her brown eyes and greying hair. Dimpled cheeks and crinkly eyes. She was always more beautiful than my mother, and yet Emily has been single for over two decades now. Her ex-husband was, as she always puts it, "a wrong 'un." She may be overly cautious because of that experience, but I also know she's right.

"Is there anything I can do for you?" she asks. "Anything you need?"

"You can always FaceTime me," I say.

"I hate that thing. I'd rather you were here, with me, so I could reach out and touch you."

"I swear I'll visit soon," I say. "I wish you were here to experience this happy time with me."

There's a pause and a sigh before she says, "That would be lovely in theory."

Emily doesn't travel. She loves her house too much.

"I know your mum would be happy for you," she says. We pause a moment, letting her absence sink in all over again.

"Thank you," I say. "Love you, Em."

"Love you, darling," she says.

I hear tears in her voice as I hang up. It's like someone has popped my balloon, and part of me resents Emily for doing that. And yet it was what I needed to hear.

Careful, Laura. Remember those screenshotted text messages from the man who is now your baby's father…

CHAPTER 16

I duck into the restaurant, shrugging out of my waterlogged raincoat. Droplets of water spray across the floor, and the damp ends of my hair cling to my shirt, leaving two wet patches just below my collarbone. There's something nostalgic to me about a good downpour. It makes me think of puddles on the pavement, gum boots in the countryside and umbrellas turned inside out by the wind.

Maybe I should have googled this place before agreeing to meet Ethan here. This time, he got to pick, and yet again, it's much swankier than my taste, especially just for lunch on a random weekday afternoon.

The restaurant is crowded, so the hostess escorts me to the table. Chandeliers hang from the ceiling, and a pianist sits perched at a baby grand, his fingers brushing the keys. Soft jazz blends with the sound of polite conversation emanating from full tables.

As we approach, Ethan stands to greet me, his eyes lively, his smile too bright. Warning bells chime in my head because he's not alone, and he didn't tell me he was bringing anyone. His guest, an older woman with long dark hair, stands to greet me too. She's beautiful, with the slim, angular face of a model and striking eyes just as lively as Ethan's. I see the resemblance immediately.

She's wearing a vibrant long-sleeved maxi dress that hugs her slender figure. Her long hair hangs loose on top of the geometric pattern. An elder flower child. A seventies goddess grown up.

"Hello," I say and offer a polite smile, clutching my handbag strap against my shoulder while I turn to Ethan for an explanation—or an introduction.

"Laura." He steps behind me and plants a hand on my lower back. I try not to stiffen. "This is my mother, Alice."

Hopefully, the smile I give her doesn't appear as forced as it feels to me. "Hello." I offer a hand. "It's lovely to meet you."

Alice's eyes roam across me curiously, and I immediately regret the blouse and comfy jeans I threw on this morning. Neither Ethan nor Alice appear to have been caught in the downpour. There's not a single splash of water on either of them.

"Sorry. It started pouring about a block before I got here," I explain.

Ethan gestures for me to fill the empty seat behind him. "It's no problem at all."

Sure it's not, for him. He's dry as a bone.

"Your accent is absolutely divine," Alice says. "I just love meeting English people. I lived in London for a time. I think it was the… let's see, the late eighties. Around eighty-nine."

"How lovely," I say, taking my seat. "Did you live there long?"

"Oh, six months or so. I worked as a model for a while, and London was a good base. And a great time, if you know what I mean." She waggles her eyebrows. "The men are just as divine as your accent."

"Mother, really. Before we order?" Ethan says, exasperated.

Alice leans over and strokes her son's face. "Oh, don't mind him. He thinks I'm awfully tacky."

"Oh, you're not…" I mumble.

The server arrives to take our orders, and I panic order a sandwich. My eyes kept lingering on the wine menu. He brought his mother without any warning, and now I'm on the backfoot. I assumed I would be meeting her at some point—I am carrying her grandchild, after all— but Ethan and I haven't even discussed his mother yet.

Alice places her napkin in her lap and straightens her posture. It's not surprising at all that she used to be a model. I look at her and then Ethan and back again. They could be twins, they're so alike. The same sharp jaw and russet eyes. The same dark shiny hair.

"It's wonderful to meet you, Laura," she says. "Ethan talks about you nonstop. He's so excited about the baby."

I sip my lemonade. "We both are. I know it's not a conventional way to have a child, but I'm thrilled. I really am. My ex-husband and I tried for a long time, and to be honest, I never thought this would happen for me."

"You and I have something in common, then," Alice says. "I had many disappointments before Ethan. And after. It never quite leaves you, does it?"

I find myself gazing into her warm eyes and knowing exactly what she means. A surprise lump forms in my throat. I swallow it away and nod.

"Mom came into the city this morning, and I thought it would be a great opportunity for you both to meet," Ethan says. "I hope you don't mind."

"Well, I would've dressed better if I'd known," I say, trying to be diplomatic. "But this baby is going to be part of all our lives, so I'm glad to meet you, Alice."

Alice places one hand on my stomach. The sudden body contact makes me jolt, but I allow her to keep her hand there.

"It's so wonderful. I can't wait to be a grandmother. Of course, no one is allowed to even utter the word *grandmother* in my presence." She removes her hand. "Perhaps I'll be a mee-maw." She shudders. "Oh no, I think that's worse. Alice, it is."

I laugh. Despite the shock, I'm warming up to Ethan's mother. Then the food arrives, and we all tuck in.

"Laura's in PR," Ethan says, helping the conversation along. "She represents that Broadway actor you like. What's his name?"

"Ben Stemmett," I reply.

"Oh, he's a dish," Alice says. "He's got a little Marlon Brando in him. I met Marlon once. Of course, he'd lost his looks by then. Though I must admit, I was tempted." She grins.

"Mother!" Ethan warns. "Not the ex-lover stories so soon."

Alice pops an olive into her mouth. "Of course not, darling. We'll be here all night if I start on them. Besides, I'm sure Laura isn't interested in Mick Jagger's lovemaking abilities."

"You bet I am," I say, laughing at Ethan's discomfort.

Ethan's eye rolls are mostly good-humoured, and I begin to love Alice. After modelling for years in London, Paris, and New York, she settled with Ethan's father and focused on being a wife. She's been an artist for three decades now and loves to craft erotic sculptures.

"Tits are very in right now," she blurts out. "The younger generation are particularly admiring of all kinds of tits, which I think is rather wonderful."

"I'll have to come and see these sculptures some time," I say, almost forgetting that Ethan and I have a deal to maintain our boundaries.

"Please do." She places her fork down on a half-empty plate. "I have so much to show you. Like photo albums! Oh, you should see Ethan as a child. He was such a beautiful toddler. And do you know, he was very interested in my makeup as a boy." She laughs.

"Mother, please," Ethan says, his voice taking on a whiny quality I've never heard before.

"Did you *really* sleep with Mick Jagger?" I ask, changing the subject.

"Don't mind my mother and her obnoxious stories to get attention." Ethan sighs and leans back, stretching his arm out across the back of my seat. It's a possessive move, but I don't want to seem uptight in front of the free-spirited Alice. He's acting almost jealous that his mother is getting more attention from me than he is.

"Oh, darling, stop being a buzzkill." Alice takes a sip of her chardonnay then smiles. Her eyes twinkle. "Yes, I did spend a night with him, and other rock stars if I'm honest. He was on tour, and a few of the other models got backstage passes from the agency. We partied hard with the entire band well into the night. Nothing heavy, of course. Pot and vodka, mostly. It was amazing." She bats her hand through the air as if it's no big deal and that was everyday life for her back then.

"Wow."

Alice beams. "I've got a million stories just like it." She leans across the table. "I even dated Bruce Springsteen for a while."

"You're kidding!"

"I left him because he was too boring."

"Bruce Springsteen? Boring?"

Alice shrugs. "He didn't want to go out much."

"It sounds like you've had a fun modelling career."

"I've slowed down quite a bit," she admits, her eyes steering to Ethan. "After I had him."

"Yeah, right," Ethan scoffs, but he's smiling. "You've always been a socialite, Mother."

Alice plants on a fake sheepish smile as if to say, "Guilty as charged."

"The seventies and eighties were good to me. What can I say? I did slow down a bit to focus on my art after Ethan was born. The parties I attended were tamer affairs after that."

"Sounds like it was a really amazing time," I say.

"Well, I think *you* are really amazing." Her eyes sparkle. "Any woman who can get my son to slow down and who steals his heart, like you have, has to have something special."

I toss a fleeting glance at Ethan. He's smiling politely, but I can tell by his stiff jaw that he's equally as uncomfortable as I am. I don't know what he's told her about the nature of our relationship, but something tells me now isn't the time or the place to correct or clarify things for her.

She's sweet and lighthearted, and I'm comfortable around her. I don't want to spoil that before it's begun.

"If I could give you one piece of advice, it's to try not to take things too seriously. Go with the flow and never take any moments of your life for granted. Live them as if they are your last." She casts me a zesty wink and brings her wineglass to her lips.

I nod and laugh. "Well, I don't have nearly as many exciting stories as you, but I will take that advice to heart, thank you."

"Yes, thank you for your wisdom, Mother," Ethan says, his voice dripping with sarcasm.

Alice grabs his cheeks, smooshing his lips together. I'm momentarily shocked. Her red fingernails dig into his skin, and it's almost like she wants to hurt him.

"What's the matter, Ethan? Aren't you getting enough attention?" She laughs, releasing him, and then drains the rest of her glass. "He's a wonderful man, Laura. Don't get me wrong. Successful, handsome, bright, and everything a mother could wish for. But he does take himself rather seriously, a trait he did not inherit from me."

"And on that note," Ethan says, "I think it might be time to get the bill."

I gape a little after that odd exchange, but then Alice starts telling me about the time she fell over on the catwalk in the early nineties and knocked Naomi Campbell clean off her feet. I'm soon so distracted I barely think about it. After we finish lunch and say goodbye, Ethan departs with his mum, and I head back to work, walking instead of taking the subway because I need time to process what just happened.

At least it's not raining anymore, although the clouds are grey and threatening.

Once I arrive at my building, I pause right outside the lobby before typing out a quick message to Ethan while I still have the nerve.

Hey! I enjoyed lunch. Your mother is wonderful. Truly. It was great to meet her, but I would appreciate it if for next time, you would run these things by me beforehand so I have time to prepare or at least expect it. No big deal or anything, but that would be great!

I end it with a smile emoji and hit Send. I go back to work, focusing on my tasks. But a few hours later, as I'm packing up to leave for the day, I start to experience the prickly needles of frustration that I've had before with Ethan. He never responded to my text.

CHAPTER 17

Someone whistles behind me as I'm grabbing a pack of cheese crackers and an apple juice from the break room. It's just over a week since the lunch with Ethan and his mother. I'm starting to show, and everyone in the office knows the news. It's been a quiet week but a nice one. Ethan has stayed silent, choosing not to reply to my last text. Confused by the wolf whistle, I turn around, finding Xavier waltzing into the room. He starts clapping when he sees me.

I laugh and prop my hands on the counter behind me. "What's with the applause?"

"It's a standing ovation, not applause."

"For me?" I point at my chest.

"Yep." Xavier is wearing a blue-and-yellow knit sweater with black skinny jeans. "You are glowing."

"You think so?" I ask.

"One thousand percent."

I push off the counter and pick up my snack and drink. "Thanks for the confidence boost. I feel like a beached whale."

"You look like a goddess," Xavier says.

I laugh. "You're so kind, thanks. It's all hormones, though. I'm sure it'll be downhill from here on out." I smile, pleasantly surprised by the compliment. Xavier isn't the type to sugarcoat anything. If I looked like I had the world's worst hangover, he would tell me.

He opens the fridge and pulls out a takeaway container with some sort of pasta inside then makes his way over to the microwave. "Can I ask you something?"

I pause. "Sure."

"How many people are asking if they can touch your belly?"

I arch a playful eyebrow. "Is this your roundabout way of asking me if you can touch my belly?"

Xavier crinkles his face and shakes his head. "Oh, hell no. I'm not one of those types who invades people's personal space."

"Thank God for that."

"Does it bother you when people ask you?"

I shrug. "Not really. I like being pregnant now that the morning sickness has tapered off a bit."

He grimaces. "I could not be a woman. But I'm happy you're living your best life." He tosses his container, lid still on, into the microwave and shuts the door before punching buttons on the panel. The microwave whirls to life.

"Thanks. I suppose I am. I'd best get back to the grind," I say, turning around to trek back to my desk.

"See you later, Momma." He gives me a wave.

Now that I'm starting to show, I'm noticing that I'm getting more attention, but I don't mind it. I'm proud to show off a budding baby bump.

I pass Anita coming out of the bathroom as I round the corner of the hallway. Her eyes light up when she sees me.

"You look so cute," she says.

"Thanks."

"How are you feeling these days?" she asks.

"Much better, actually." I hold up my apple juice and crackers. "Food helps ward off most of the nausea."

"That's good to hear. Enjoy the snack," Anita says, passing in the opposite direction.

When I sit back down at my desk, I wiggle the mouse to wake my computer screen and discover that Ethan has sent me an email.

The subject line reads, *Articles about pregnancy—read these —important!*

I breathe in deep and drag the breath back out. Against my better judgement, I click on the email. It's more out of curiosity than anything.

When I open the email, there are several links to articles in the body of the text.

Hey, just some information for you to study up on. Talk to you soon! Ethan.

I frown. "Study up on?" Does he think there's going to be a final exam? Well, I guess it's a practical rather than written test, what with the blood and screaming and so on. The first link is all about eating healthy and organic foods during pregnancy, especially in the first trimester. The second article is about ways you can rest and relax your body and slow down your mind to keep you and your baby calm. The third article is about home-birth deliveries.

I wince. Home-birth deliveries? That is never going to happen. He knows my pregnancy is a high-risk one. I need a hospital, trained professionals, and medication on standby. He won't be pushing this baby out of his body, so why he's muscling in on how I do it, I don't know.

I decide I've had enough, so I don't click the rest of the links. Maybe I'll look at them later, but I'm not holding my breath.

Ethan has already taken up enough of my time today. Work is much more interesting. I dive back into my inbox, happily munching on crackers and without a care in the world. The hours breeze by because I have so much to do. There are conference calls to join, meetings to attend, and clients who need attention.

Tiredness hits me as I almost drop off on the commute home. The subway train gently sways beneath me. These days, my energy drains a lot faster than it would normally. Slowly, my eyelids close, and I almost miss my stop, miraculously stirred awake by a man's boisterous laughter beside me.

Forcing my body to move, I head over to the doors just in time. My phone rings as I'm on my way up the subway steps.

"Hello?"

"Why didn't you answer my call before?" Ethan asks.

"What call?" I ask.

He huffs then pauses. "Laura, I've called you three times in a row. It went straight to voicemail until now."

"Okay, well, I've been on the subway. My phone doesn't work underground."

He calms down and sighs. "Sorry. I was just freaked out that something might have happened to you or the baby."

"You don't need to worry. I'm just on my way home from work. You know I commute at this time of day."

He pauses again. "It's over an hour later than normal. Why aren't you home yet?"

His tone makes my hackles rise. "There's a lot of work to do, and someone kept sending me articles to read while I was doing it. I fell asleep on the train because I'm so exhausted."

I make my way around the corner to my apartment block.

"That leads me to my next point," he says.

There's a note of smugness in his voice that sets my teeth on edge.

"I emailed you those articles earlier, and I never heard back from you."

Angrily, I jab my finger at the keypad, pushing in the code for my building. "Ethan, like I told you a moment ago, I was very busy at work today. I didn't have time to respond to your email." My shoes click across the tiled lobby, echoing through the space. I'm alone, and a prickling sensation travels across the back of my neck.

"Did you at least read the articles?" he insists.

This guy really has the audacity to call me out for not responding to an email when he never responded to me about his mother being at lunch. I'm the one setting the boundaries here. I push the lift button, and it lights up immediately.

"Laura? Are you there?"

"I'm here."

"So? What about the articles?" he demands. "You read them, right?"

"I haven't had the chance."

He scoffs. "Wow."

"I will get to them. Just calm down." The lift stops on the floor below mine, and a confused elderly woman blinks back at me when the doors open.

"Sorry, going up." I point my finger upward.

She nods and backs away.

The doors close again. The lift moves up one level and stops. I get out and walk to my door, keys in hand.

"Who were you just talking to?" Ethan asks, his voice laced with suspicion.

"A woman in the elevator." *Not that it's any of your business,* I think.

"Oh." He sounds disappointed, as if he's looking for a fight. Then he hammers on and gets one anyway. "Laura, it's important to me that you read those articles. I took time out of my own busy day to send them to you."

"You know what, Ethan? I need you to back off. You're starting to do that thing again where you suffocate me. I said I would read the articles, and I was going to until you started pestering me about them. Now, I think I'll just delete the email altogether, because I'm not interested in eating organic food and giving birth in a fucking bath."

"No one said you had to give birth in a bath*tub,*" he snaps.

"Well, no home births for me, thanks," I say.

"You're being a bitch for no reason."

I open my mouth to give him hell for that, but he hangs up before I can. *Coward.* Shoving open my door, I let out the last wave of frustration by flinging my phone across the room. It falls onto the couch and bounces off the cushion, hitting the floor. Rather than pick it up, I stalk to my bathroom sink and splash cold water on my burning face, trying to tame my thumping heart.

Having a baby with Ethan is like being connected to Jekyll and Hyde, only one is a clinging whiny baby and the other is sweet and caring. His mood swings are giving me whiplash. Maybe Ethan should be more worried about the stress *he's* causing me rather than getting me on a celery-and-avocado-smoothie diet.

My phone buzzes as I'm on my way back to my living room.

"Great." I groan. Reluctantly, I plop down on the couch and pick it up.

The message is from Ethan, of course.

You will not disrespect me again. I am this baby's father, which means I have a say in what happens to him.

Again, he's referring to the baby as a "him" without confirmation of the gender. I swallow hard and keep reading.

I want my baby to be born healthy and to be cared for during this pregnancy. You need to eat properly and exercise right but not too much, just enough to ensure you stay fit and trim.

Why is he commenting on my body? I'm not his property. A rush of anger worms its way through me, followed by something else—a tickle of shame. *Fuck him for making me feel like this.*

I read on. *I'm entitled to be in this baby's life. You can't stop me from offering my opinions on how he will be raised. I'm just trying to help you better yourself, Laura. Can't you understand that?*

What stands out to me the most is how manipulative his language is. It's clear he's trying to control me. In fact, this escalation could all be because he *can't* control me. I'm not his wife. I'm not in his life twenty-four hours a day, seven days a week, and I think that terrifies him. He has no idea what I'm doing when he's not around.

"Jesus," I whisper, placing the phone down.

All the anger has faded from my body now. I'm more perplexed than anything. There was always a chance Ethan would go this way. Emily warned me, but I knew before, by how he reacted to my first rejection.

You have something he wants, Emily had said to me. That's a potentially dangerous place to be with a controlling man. Now I need to figure out how I'm going to manage this.

I place a hand on my stomach. "It's okay, jellybean. We'll figure this out."

CHAPTER 18

I'm cautious for the next week, not wanting to upset the apple cart. In what I'm detecting is his usual pattern, Ethan calls me to apologise for his outburst, and we agree to move on. There's not much else I can do, but I sense the fact that I'm losing some of the control I thought I had. Or maybe I never had control at all, and it was an illusion. Ethan lulled me into a false sense of security with his sudden maturity.

It's early evening, and I'm making my way home after work, my head still busy with small jobs I need to organise tomorrow. Exhaustion creeps over me, and I stifle a yawn as I hop into the lift.

As soon as I get to my apartment door, I know there's something wrong. It rests open a fraction of an inch, revealing the quiet stillness inside my home. My fingers lightly brush the lock, where my door has been ripped open, wood splinters protruding from the doorframe. I grab my phone and dial the emergency services. For my first go, I forget myself and dial 999 then cancel the call and ring 911. I head back down to the lobby of the building while on the call, one hand protectively on my bump. It all happens quickly. I make sure to let the superintendent know so that the other residents on my floor can be warned, and then I wait for the police to arrive.

Someone has been in my home. Maybe they're still there. They could be hiding behind the door, waiting. An itch works its way up my skin, like goose bumps but pricklier.

The police arrive impressively fast, and two officers introduce themselves to me. Officer Striker is in his fifties, sporting a salt-and-pepper moustache, and Officer Daniels is younger and clean-shaven.

"You British?" Daniels asks as we travel up to my floor.

"Yeah," I say.

He nods. "I've got some family in Leicestershire." He pronounces it Less-est-er-shy-er, which coaxes a smile out of me despite the circumstances.

"It's a nice area."

"Oh, good," he says. "Maybe I'll visit."

We reach my apartment, and the officers enter, eyes scanning the space with curiosity. Striker keeps one hand hovering just above his gun at all times.

"Looks like they took my TV," I say.

This is my first glimpse at my newly tainted home. It's been ransacked, stuff thrown everywhere. A lacy thong lies on the back of the sofa. I internally cringe.

"Take an inventory of what was stolen," Striker suggests. "Then we'll file a report. Whoever did this is gone. So we'll search the area, see if we can find any witnesses, and check out the CCTV in the building. Okay?"

"Yeah, thanks," I say in something of a daze.

I wander through the small space, picking up underwear, shoes, and bags. Then I head into the bedroom and realise my jewellery box is open with some of my rings gone. My stomach sinks when I realise they took Mum's emerald solitaire ring. It's just an item, and it doesn't matter, but tears fill my eyes, and I'm forced to sniff the tears away.

This apartment is supposed to be the sanctuary I'll bring my baby into. Yes, it's small, but I had a spot reserved for the crib. That spot is now covered in junk—my yoga mat on top of a raincoat with random bits of cutlery thrown over them.

"Whoever did this really went to town," Daniels says. "Feels personal."

I turn to him. "You think so?"

"Have you had any issues with anyone recently?" he asks.

The one name that pops into my head is, of course, Ethan. But why would he want to do this to me? What would he gain? And would he really risk his reputation to break into my apartment and scare me?

"It could be kids messing around," Striker suggests with a shrug.

"We get a lot of break-ins that look like this. Especially in women's apartments. They're teenagers. Immature. They like to look at bras."

Daniels glares at him.

"What?" Striker says. "I'm just saying in my experience, that sort of thing happens."

Officer Striker's fingers thread through the belt loops of his pants, and he rocks back on his heels. Daniels straightens up my tiny table and chairs, and we sit down so I can file a report. Striker must see the pallor of my skin because he comes back with a glass of orange juice, perhaps feeling guilty for his dismissive comment.

"Here," he says. "You look like you need the sugar."

I nod gratefully and sip slowly, not wanting to give myself a head rush.

"Can you get a locksmith out here to fix your door?" he asks.

I nod. "I'll call someone."

Daniels disappears from the apartment as I list off the items missing from the apartment—my television, my laptop, and my jewellery. None of them were new or worth much. They took about a hundred dollars I keep in my apartment for emergencies. The only item of value was my mother's ring. I already miss it. For years I've kept it in my room not daring to wear it in case I lose it. And now it's gone.

"Why me?" I ask. "There are three apartments on this floor alone. Why not break into the other apartments?"

"I'd imagine that whoever did this knew you lived alone. They may have been watching you for a while, tracking your movements. They figured out when you'd be at work. They also know, and don't take this the wrong way, that they won't be walking into the apartment of a burly fella with a rifle. A pregnant woman living alone is a lot easier to deal with."

I shiver. The thought of being watched… There's enough on my plate as it is without all this.

Daniels returns to the apartment, his skin flushed as though he ran up the stairs. "I spoke to the building manager about surveillance."

"And?" I blink at him.

"Unfortunately, somebody smashed the CCTV camera in the hall and used a crowbar to wrench the door open."

"But you need a code to get into the building," I say. "And for the elevator."

"Someone might have let them in," he says. "It happens a lot. People assume someone's a guest when really, they're up to no good."

"Damn it," I say. "All this for my old Samsung TV?" Though I have to admit, the ring is worth much more.

The officers exchange glances, and Striker asks, "Is there anyone you can stay with in the meantime, until you get that door fixed? They really did a number on it with the crowbar."

"I have someone," I say, immediately thinking of Jessa.

They tell me to call them if anything else comes up, day or night. I promise to do so, and they leave. I'm able to shut my door, but I can't lock it, so before contacting Jessa, I call a locksmith to come out. Luckily, they can send someone out within the hour since it's an emergency. I prop a chair up against the door as a fail-safe and grab a knife from the block. Even though I know Striker and Daniels searched my apartment, I can't shake the feeling that someone is here, watching me.

I dial Jessa's number and hear my trembling voice tell her the whole story, suddenly aware of how much this break-in has hit me.

"I don't know if I'm going to be able to get over this," I say. "How can I bring the baby home knowing someone did this to me? I… I think I may have to start apartment hunting. I'm afraid that I'll stay paranoid that it might happen again, or worse, I'll be home next time, and they'll try to hurt me or the baby."

"Want to come and stay with me for a couple days?"

"Do you mind? I hate to burden you like this but—"

"You are my best friend," she says. "You'd do the same thing for me. Right?"

"Of course."

"Then it's settled," she says. "What time is the locksmith coming?"

I glance at my watch. "Should be soon."

"Do you want some company while you wait for him?"

"That would be amazing," I say. "I don't feel safe here on my own."

"I'm setting off right now."

We hang up. I gaze at my ransacked apartment and a shiver of freezing-cold fear works its way down my spine.

CHAPTER 19

After staying with Jessa for almost a week, I didn't want to leave. We entertain ourselves with board games and Chinese food when Jessa isn't working at the bar. But eventually, I had to face up to the fact that I can't live with her forever, and I have a perfectly good apartment with a new lock. So we tidy up my apartment together, watch a few rom-coms, and attempt to make it feel like home again. Sure, it's different here, but it's not as bad as I thought it would be.

I've been back in the apartment for a few days now, and I'm slowly beginning to feel safe. I'm dozing on the sofa with the afternoon sun filtering through the window, warming my skin. It's November, and while the weather is cold, the late-autumn sunshine hits my windows midafternoon.

A knock on the door pulls me from my slumber, and my body instantly tenses. I sit up, alert. Perhaps it's the police returning to give me an update. I've heard nothing so far.

"Just a minute," I call.

Before I open the door, I peer through the peephole just to be sure. When I see Ethan, I'm not sure whether to be pleased or disappointed.

I swing the door open. "Ethan, this is a... surprise."

"Sorry to just drop by." He bends and picks up what looks like a large TV box.

I back away, allowing him into the apartment. In a moment of weakness, I called and let him know about the break-in. I wasn't sure if I would need his help at some point. Ethan is obviously a difficult person to deal with, but he is the baby's father, so if I was ever desperate, I wanted him on standby.

"Well, it looks like your new door lock works well," he says, resting the box down by the wall.

I nod. "Yes. Um, Ethan, what's that?"

He pats the top, giving me a proud smile. "I know yours was stolen, so I bought you the latest model. Do you like it?"

"I… I don't know what to say. I have insurance that would take care of a new TV," I say, somewhat floored.

"Yeah, but that'll take forever to sort out," he says. "I figured you must be bored. Look, sorry if I overstepped again, but I wanted to do something for you. There's more too." He pulls a second box out of a bag. "I heard your laptop was taken and figured you'd be lost without it." He takes in my gobsmacked expression. "Oh no. I've overstepped again, haven't I? I swear, this is all about keeping the mother of my baby happy and nothing bad."

I lift a hand, placating him before anything escalates. "I get it. Thank you. This is a really generous gesture. I appreciate it. Really."

He beams. "Great! Do you want me to set up the TV for you?"

"That would be amazing, thanks. I'll get you some scissors. Hold on." As I'm rummaging around in the kitchen, I call over my shoulder, "Do you need a hand? I know these TVs are heavy."

"Absolutely not," he says. "Rest up."

I sense he wants to say more. Probably something about "his" baby or son, unless I'm jumping to conclusions. Sometimes, I'm not sure which Ethan I'm going to get.

"I bought a new hanging stand too," he says. "Since your old one got messed up in the robbery. I'll set the new one back in the same spot."

"Honestly, you didn't have to go to so much trouble."

"I'm the type who likes to go the extra mile." He doesn't say it smugly. It's clear the calmer version of Ethan has shown up today. "Laura, I have so much to apologise to you for."

"Ethan, you really don't have to do this—"

"No, I need to. If not for you then for myself. I've been a jerk most of the time we've known each other, which isn't that long. If I could take back all the things I've done wrong with you, I would. I just want a chance to start over. Just wipe the slate clean and fresh. I can't tell you how beyond thrilled I am that you're carrying my baby. I want to protect you both for the rest of my life, and I intend to treat you and the baby with the utmost respect and care."

"That's really sweet." My words fall short of what I want to say. Maybe because I'm not entirely sure *what* I want to say to him. That I'm sceptical. That there is a pattern to his behaviour, and this apology falls flat considering everything else that has already happened.

He laughs. "Am I selling any of this to you?'

"Well, I'm not complaining about the new TV." I laugh. "I know you've offered to pay for things in the past, and I've always said no. I try to make my own way through life, you know? I wouldn't usually accept anything so generous, but I've been worrying about how to replace all this stuff." I sigh. "And the flat feels sort of empty."

"You should accept more," he says. "I would if the roles were reversed." He waggles a screwdriver in my direction. "My mother always told me to accept whatever leg up I can get in life."

"Yeah, but there's no such thing as a free lunch, right?" I reply.

He smiles at that but doesn't say anything more.

I make coffee as he drills the new stand into the wall, and I watch as he mounts the new TV. It's not an easy job, and several times, I find myself walking out of the room rather than watch him struggle. When he's finished, he's breathing harder than normal. He turns around, hands planted on either side of his waist. "Want to take her for a spin?" He reaches for the remote and hands it over to me.

"I do, but it might take some time, setting all my apps up and trying to remember all my streaming-service passwords."

Ethan gives me a commiserative laugh. "I hear you on that one." He starts tossing all the packaging debris into the empty box. "Okay, I'll wrap up here and get out of your hair so you can tend to the pass-words. I hope you enjoy the new TV. It's a gift, no strings attached, I promise." He holds his hands out by his sides, giving the impression that he has every intention of at least trying to keep that promise. "Maybe there is such a thing as a free lunch."

"I hope it wasn't too expensive."

"Nah." He swats his hand through the air. "It's the least I can do after what you've been through. I mean it when I say that I'm trying to do better. Even if it seems like I don't hear you, I take everything you say to me to heart, and I'm working on myself."

"Thank you again. For that and the new TV. It's amazing. Really. I can't wait to binge-watch true crime."

He lifts a curious eyebrow. "True crime, eh?"

I shrug. "Guilty pleasure."

"I think that's across the board for all females."

"Oh, and you were doing so well," I reply. "Females? Really?"

"Sorry," he says. "Women."

I walk him to the door. "That's much better."

He smiles, standing in the open doorway for a beat too long, and there's an awkward silence between us. He tucks the empty box under his arm. "I guess I'll take off, then."

"Have a great rest of your day."

"Let me know how that TV works out."

"Maybe I'll send you a picture later."

His eyes brighten. "I'd like that."

I close the door and lock it behind me. Through the peephole, I see him trekking down the hall with the TV box.

I sigh and lean against the door. When the police were in this apartment just a few days ago, a fleeting, horrible thought had popped into my head—what if Ethan broke into my apartment? It could be some sort of punishment for me chastising him about the articles. But yet again, his personality flipped. I felt almost… safe with him today. *Safe? Is that the right word?* I don't know what to think anymore.

* * *

The next morning, I'm flustered and running late for work. I shove past a cluster of other drowsy commuters in the subway and hurry down the block towards my office. I'm cursing myself for oversleeping this morning, but there's nothing I can do about it now.

When I finally skid to a grinding halt in front of my desk, out of breath and far too sweaty for my liking, I notice there's an empty packing box on top of it. Confused and trying to remember if I'd left it there for some reason, I hear someone clear their throat behind me.

I spin around, cheeks still warm from the journey here, sweat making my dress cling to my lower back.

"Anita," I say, breathless, struggling to calm my racing heart. "Sorry. I didn't see you there."

Anita doesn't smile. Her lips are stretched into a thin line, and she has dark circles under her eyes. She beckons me with a roll of her hand towards her office. "Laura, I need to speak to you alone."

Alarmed, I just stare at her for a moment. "Sorry I'm late. I overslept and—"

"It's fine. Just come with me." Her voice is clipped.

"Sure, I'll be right there," I say, turning away.

I dump my bag on my desk, next to the box. *What the fuck?* I know exactly what it means when a box is placed on a desk. Before I force my body to keep moving, I sweep a tear from the corner of my eye, sensing the entire office staring at me. Then, like a dead man walking, I make my way to Anita's office.

CHAPTER 20

I arrange my skirt, take a seat, and examine Anita's expression as she settles into her chair. Fear nestles in the pit of my stomach because I already know what's about to happen. But what I don't understand is why.

She lets out a heavy sigh. A shadow falls across her eyes, and it turns my blood cold. Some motherly instinct prompts me to place a hand on my baby bump. I want to either shield the baby or comfort myself, I'm not sure which.

"Unfortunately, this isn't going to be a good meeting." Anita rolls her chair forwards a few inches. She seems fidgety, almost nervous, and that isn't like the Anita I know.

"What's going on?" There's a hard edge to my voice. I try to temper it, concerned a defensive tone might make things worse. "Are there going to be cutbacks? Redundancies? Only, this is a really shitty time for that." I gesture at my stomach.

"No," she says. "That's not it at all." She grabs her phone and types something in. Then her thumb swipes the screen before she holds it out for me to see.

"Did you write this?" she asks, revealing another *Medium* article.

I notice my name underneath the heading of the article. Below that is my Broadway client's name, Ben Stemmett. Quickly, I scan the first few sentences. The blood drains from my face.

"I… don't understand," I say.

"Did you write this?" she asks.

"No, I certainly did not," I reply, hoping there's enough force in my voice to convince her. "Ben isn't just a client. He's a friend. I'm a *fan* of his, for God's sake. I wouldn't trash him in a *Medium* article. Why would I do that?"

"So this is the first time you've seen this article?" she asks.

"Yes. Absolutely. I wouldn't have known about it until you showed me."

"Then you're not keeping on top of things, Laura," she chastises. "PR is your job, and somehow, another article attached to *your name* calls our client 'an insipid, talentless ape with no charisma.' How could this happen?"

"Jesus," I mumble. I'm ashamed now because she's right. Even though I didn't write the article, I should have Google Alerts set up for Ben so I can keep on top of things. I thought I did. This one must have slipped through.

"Ben's agent called me this morning, and I have to say…" Anita trails off, shaking her head. "Let me put it this way. I got an earful, and I didn't even write it." She pauses for effect, her eyes boring into mine. "Laura, this is a serious matter. I'm the face of this firm, and this makes me look bad. It makes our entire firm look bad. I can't sugarcoat this. I'm pissed. I'm the one who ends up having to clean up the mess in the end. But this mess is unfixable." She frowns, still shaking her head. "We lost him as a client."

She sets her phone down on the desk and crosses her arms. Her eyes still hold me, scrutinising me. She's searching for the truth, for proof that I might have had something to do with this.

"I'm—I'm completely blindsided right now." I touch my fingers to my temples. "I have a close relationship with Ben. I would never hurt him in this way."

Anita leans forward, her eyes narrowing. "Close? In what capacity?"

"Nothing inappropriate, of course."

Anita is quiet for a moment. Her probing eyes never waver from mine. "If you didn't write this article, then why is your name attached to it?"

"I honestly don't know," I say. "The same reason my name cropped up in the press about John Anderson, I suppose. Someone is going after our clients, and for some reason, they've homed in on me."

"Did you piss someone off? Well, other than me?" She lifts her eyebrows.

"I can't think of anyone who would be out to get me enough to write this article and pose as me."

That's the problem with *Medium*. Anyone can write and publish on it. You don't have to even be official. It's dangerous territory, and it's coming around to bite me now.

"Laura, I'm sorry, but even if I believed you—which I want to—I can't sweep this one under the rug. This is the second offense linked to you."

"Anita, I swear on my life, on my baby's life, that I did not write this article. Why would I do anything to jeopardise my job when I've been working so hard and I have a child on the way? It doesn't make any sense."

Anita chews her bottom lip, contemplating. She sighs. "I'm sorry, Laura, but the board is breathing down my neck about this. Unfortunately, I'm going to have to let you go. We have a reputation to uphold, and if we can't get this article taken down or calm Ben's people down enough not to bad-mouth us all over town, then we are ultimately screwed six ways from Sunday."

I know she's right, but a flash of anger surges through me. From Anita's perspective, I'm either a loose cannon who likes to sabotage the company, or I've pissed off the wrong person, and they're coming at me with full force. Either way, my employment at the company is damaging to the business.

But I'm also an employee being targeted, and they're hanging me out to dry. Not just that, but I'm a pregnant, soon-to-be single mother who needs this job.

"Why not investigate this first?" I ask. "Find out who keeps pinning this stuff on me and why. I'm your employee—"

"We don't have the resources," she says.

I get to my feet. "So much for women supporting women. So much for all that bullshit you spouted about being here for me."

"I still mean that," she says.

I scoff. "No you don't. At the end of the day, you have your own back, and that's what matters, isn't it? Maybe you wrote that article."

"Laura!" she says in surprise.

"Maybe I'm a threat to you." My eyes prick with tears.

"You're not a threat to me and never have been." She stands, her eyes trailing over to the office door. "Norman is going to escort you from the building now."

"That won't be necessary—"

"It's protocol," she interjects with an apologetic shrug. "It has nothing to do with you."

My body is completely numb as she walks me through the office. I keep my head down. I can't even look at Xavier when I pass his desk.

I'll probably never see him again, and I won't get a proper chance to say goodbye, not with Anita here beside me. I'll never be able to give my side of the story. They're watching me leave, thinking I deserve this. And then there's Ben, who no doubt believes I betrayed and insulted him. I wish I could tell him I didn't do this.

As we round the corner to my desk, I see Norman already waiting for me. His stoic eyes point down at the floor. He doesn't even have the decency to look me in the eye.

I turn to Anita for one last-ditch effort to save my job. "Anita, this was not me. You know it wasn't."

She holds up a hand and shakes her head. "I'm sorry, Laura, but it's just the way it has to be. Either somebody is out to get you, or you might want to get yourself checked out for a mental health issue. Either way, I can't prove it, which means I have to let you go."

She turns and walks away without so much as a goodbye. The rest of the office sits there staring as I throw a few of my belongings into a box. My hands are shaking. My knees tremble. The anger and disappointment slowly seep out of me and are replaced by a horrible sense of self-pity. *How am I going to pay my rent? How am I going to eat? Buy baby clothes?* This can't be happening.

I clutch the box close to my chest, resting it just above my baby bump, then Norman and I take a silent elevator ride to the lobby. I leave through the revolving doors in the ground-floor lobby, knowing he's watching me walk along the pavement before he heads back upstairs.

Finally, the tears come. As I make my way down a busy New York street, carrying my sad little box, the tears streak across my face. Somewhere before I reach the subway station, I find a dumpster and throw the box in. *What the fuck do I need that for anyway?* I wipe the tears away, watch the sun glint across the cabs, and buy a pretzel. First the break-in and now this. Surely something isn't right here. The two could be linked, but then again, I might be paranoid. I am living in New York. It's tough here. Still, all of these misfortunes in the space of a few weeks?

I take my pretzel on the subway train and try not to let all the conflicting thoughts flood my head. Right now, I'm exhausted, but tomorrow, I'll figure this out. Someone wanted me gone from Nielson and Todd, and I'm going to find out who it was.

CHAPTER 21

By the time I reach my apartment, I feel like I've been hollowed out. I collapse on the bed and gently touch my bump just to be sure the baby is still in there. The jellybean kicks, letting me know everything is okay. But then, when I close my eyes, I see the judgemental stares of my colleagues. They probably think I'm unhinged by now. Why else would these *Medium* articles keep occurring?

I sit, grab my phone, and pull up the article. There it is in black and white with my name underneath the title. Ben Stemmett needs to quit, the article claims. It's a scathing takedown of a talented young man who doesn't deserve it. *Poor Ben.* I read through it quickly, shaking my head. And then I notice something interesting. The article is written in American English, not British English. I sit up straight.

While I do tend to try to use American spellings in my work emails, my old habits usually slip through. However, if I was going to write an article, I would probably use the language and spelling I was comfortable with. Maybe this could clear me of any involvement. But then I shake my head. At this point, Anita doesn't care whether I wrote it or not. She has already decided I'm more trouble than I'm worth.

I click on my name. There's a profile set up using a photograph taken from our workplace website. It's so blatant. Someone obviously did all this just to make me lose my job. And the worst part is how little time and effort it took.

Shaking my head with anger, I copy and paste the help desk's email address into a new message and send a strongly worded email to them explaining the situation. I ask for the article to be taken down. If that doesn't work, I might need to get a lawyer, and I definitely can't afford that. Perhaps it's best to cut my losses and move on. The damage is done. Mud sticks, and rumours fly. I wouldn't blame Ben if he told the world about his experience with our company.

It's not even ten o'clock, but I need to talk to someone. Emily would be sweet about this but not fully grasp the situation. I dial Jessa's number, feeling a little guilty about her being at work. I know she's working an early shift today, dealing with the brunch crowd.

"Hey, Lor. Everything okay?"

I never call her at work, so she immediately knows something has happened.

"I got fired today," I say.

There's a sharp gasp on the other end. "Fired? *Fired*? But... you're pregnant. They can't do that!"

"They did."

"But why?"

I let out a long sigh and explain the situation. More than once, I fight back tears until the frustration and anger returns, putting some fire in my guts.

"Wow, Laura, I don't know what to say."

I can almost hear Jessa shaking her head in disbelief.

"I don't get it. Why would anyone want to do this to you?"

"I don't get it either. The only thing I can think of is that someone is poaching our clients and using me to do it. But why me? I..." I trail off, my head full of conflicting thoughts. "Part of me wonders if this is Ethan."

She pauses then says, "Really?"

"Everything that's happened recently puts me in a more vulnerable position. The robbery, me losing my job. It forces me to rely on him, doesn't it? And then if I take his money, I *owe* him. You know?"

"Wow," she says. "Wow." Her voice deepens and becomes cautious. "I'm worried. If you think he's capable of something like that, then what else is he capable of?" I hear someone talking in a muffled voice behind her, then Jessa responds with "I haven't seen it. It may be on the counter over there" before she comes back on the line with me. "Sorry. Work stuff."

"I should go. Let you get back to work," I say.

"No! Tell me what's been going on with Ethan recently. What's making you suspect him?"

When she puts it like that, I flounder. "Nothing… concrete. I guess it's just a feeling. I… I can't know for sure that he's this conniving, but all of this happened not long after we had a huge fight about him interfering." I rub a palm over my face, wiping away sweat. "If he *is* behind this, what am I going to do? I'm connected to this man for eighteen years."

"Fuck," she says.

"Yep. I'm completely fucked."

"I'll come over later, okay? We'll talk about this. I'm not saying you're wrong or that I don't believe you, but there could be an explanation behind it all. This is big if it is him. This is changing-your-number-and-moving-out-of-state big."

"I know," I admit.

"I don't want you to move," she says.

I laugh. "Me neither. I like it here."

Jessa gets back to work, and I head through to the kitchen to pour a cup of tea, hoping I might have some of Emily's damson jam left. I know why I'm avoiding calling her—because she'll think I'm right about Ethan sabotaging my life. She'll have me booked on the first flight to Manchester airport. I smile to myself, grabbing the jar from the fridge. Aunt Em always has my back.

But Jessa is more cautious. She has actually met Ethan, and she's seen him be good to me as well as heard all about his more batshit-crazy moments. My mind flips back and forth between feeling sure the father of my child is a psycho and worrying I'm reading too much into a series of unfortunate coincidences.

As I'm sitting down with a plate of toast and jam, my phone lights up. Speaking of the devil, I have a text from Ethan, asking if the TV is working okay and whether I would like to meet for a catch-up soon. I leave it on read for a moment. Perhaps if I gauge his reaction to my not replying straightaway, it'll give me some insight into where his headspace is.

I'm partway through my second piece of toast when my phone

lights up again. Expecting it to be Ethan asking why I haven't replied, I steel myself for an argument. But instead, it's an email. I frown. The subject heading is *PR representative needed.* Curious, I open it.

Hello, Laura.

My name is Charles Hampshire, and I am one of the PR consultants heading a team at Indigo Industries. We've been informed about your little hiccup with the Broadway star Ben Stemmett.

My heart sinks. News travels fast. I continue reading.

I just want to say that we have had our eye on you for quite some time now. We'd love it if you'd come join our team. We've been waiting for our moment to make a move, and now that this article has been published, we'd love to offer you an opportunity to come in for an official interview this afternoon.

I drop the toast to my plate, floored by the audacity of this email. Before I do anything, I type Indigo Industries into the search bar and wait for the results. Sure enough, there's a website. It's a clean design, professional and to the point. However, it's somewhat vague. There's no list of clients, but there is a staff page and a picture of Charles Hampshire. God, what a fake-British name that is.

Something is off. The email sort of implies that they were behind the article. *We've had our eye on you for quite some time now.* That's creepy as fuck. I want to reply back and accuse them of sabotaging my career, but something stops me from doing that. I don't know what is going on right now, so keeping things vague is my best option.

I'm sorry, I start typing back to him. *I'm not looking for a job right now. I need to get my bearings, although I do appreciate the offer for an interview and any opportunity to be considered. Sincerely, Laura*

I screenshot his email and my reply in case I need a backup. Then I spend some time poking around on the website. It doesn't take long since the website is very basic. So I move on to Charles Hampshire's social media pages. He has accounts, but they're all set to private. I rest against the sofa and weigh up all the options. If Charles Hampshire and Indigo Industries are fake, someone went to a lot of trouble to get me fired and then cover their tracks. If Indigo Industries is real, then either Charles set this whole thing up as a way to poach me from Anita, or he genuinely heard about the article and decided I was still worth employing. If it's the former, then I wouldn't want to work for a company like that anyway. But if it's the latter, I just turned down a chance at a decent job.

And now I'm left alone in my apartment with many of my belongings missing—and no job. Soon, I'll have no visa either. I'm running out of options.

CHAPTER 22

As I walk along Brooklyn Bridge, I can't help but think about the moment I first met Ethan. My bump is coming along nicely now, protruding from my coat. The cold early-December wind nips at my nose and ears, but I still stop for a moment, staring at the spot where I collapsed under the crowd. He'd felt like my saviour.

I have much more complicated feelings about Ethan now. It's been two weeks since I lost my job, and now that I've cooled off, I've lost the conviction that he orchestrated the entire thing. It seems much too far-fetched. Plus, he's been relatively quiet about it all. There's been no swooping in with a solution to my problems. He's backed off. For now, anyway. Who knows what today might bring.

We're meeting at a restaurant about a block away from the pub I'd limped into with one shoe on the day of the march. There's news to share with him. I had a doctor's appointment a few days ago, and everything went well. I won't have any more appointments for a while, even with my high-risk pregnancy. Everything seems fine. But that isn't the only thing on the agenda, and I'm not sure he'll be pleased with what else I need to say.

Ethan stands and waves me over to a table near the back of the restaurant. He's smiling, which is a good sign, and wearing his work suit. He kisses me on the cheek. "You're glowing, Laura," he says.

I unwrap a scarf and place it on the chair between us. "I'm not sure about that."

My stomach tickles with nerves as I look at him, because I'm about to broach a subject I'm not sure he'll like. The waiter comes over to fill our glasses with water, and I fiddle around with my coat and hat, not wanting to look at him.

"So, everything went well at the doctor's," I say, explaining my last checkup.

"That's great news," he says. "And how's the job hunting going?"

"It's not," I admit. "It's on hold."

He sips his water and raises his eyebrows. "It is? How come?"

"Well," I say, "I'm not sure I want to stay in New York."

He doesn't react for a moment. Instead, he clears his throat and places his hands in his lap. "Wow. Really?"

"Don't get me wrong. I do love this city, but the job market is tough, and I'm probably going to run out of money sooner rather than later. Not to mention my visa. It's dependent on my job, so—"

"Don't worry about that," he says suddenly. "I'll just ask Mother to take care of it. She has some friends in high places, if you know what I mean." He chuckles. "Unless you want to get married."

I let out a nervous laugh, not wanting to entertain that notion. "The other stuff, though... I... I miss the place I grew up. I miss my aunt. I miss so much about back home. Fields, trees, gardens, good cheese." I sigh. "I'm sorry. I know this might feel like a shock for you. I want to reassure you that you'll still have a huge part in our baby's life—"

"You want to go back to England?" he asks. "But there'll be an ocean between us! How could I possibly have a part in his life? I'd miss his first steps, his first words, his first haircut." Ethan sighs.

"I know it's a lot," I say. "But so is the thought of staying in New York without a job and raising this baby with someone I hardly know. Sorry if that's blunt, but—"

"I get it," he says. "But we do know each other, Laura."

The waiter comes over to take our orders, and I find it difficult to look Ethan in the eye again. This lunch is going to be extremely awkward.

"Look, I understand how you feel," he says. "You've had a horrible month. I get that. But I have a proposition for you. And I don't want you to dismiss it right away, okay? Because I want to show you that you do have family here. Things can work out."

His words make every muscle in my body tense. While he seems on his best behaviour today, being charming and kind, I get the feeling I'm about to be manipulated, and I brace myself for what might come next. "What is this proposition?"

"How about you spend a day out in the Hamptons at my mother's house with me before you make your final decision? I know it's December, so the weather isn't great, but you'll love it there. I promise. And it's somewhere I'd like our child to visit a lot. I think you should see it before you make any final decisions."

"Does your mother know the reality of our relationship now?" I ask. "Only the first time we met, she seemed to believe we were a couple. I hope you put the record straight."

"I did," he reassures me. "And it was just a misunderstanding. I didn't lead her down that path, if that's what you're worried about."

I'm relieved to hear he put things right in that regard. Visiting his mum does seem like a reasonable idea, though I can't help but wonder what the endgame is. Perhaps he's going to try to persuade me to move in with his mother. And while I do like her, that would be too much. On the other hand, if I move back in with Emily, it would be nice to have an opportunity to say goodbye to Alice.

"Okay," I say.

"I can drive you over this weekend if you like."

"That's okay. I have a car."

"You do?" he seems surprised.

"I don't use it often," I admit. Truthfully, it's old, and I don't particularly like driving it, but I also don't like the thought of not having an escape plan when I visit Ethan's mum.

"Are you sure?" he asks.

I nod, and the food arrives—a club sandwich for me, a tuna salad for Ethan.

"My mother is going to be so thrilled. I'll call her after lunch and let her know."

He seems optimistic that a day with him and Alice can win me around. I have my doubts, obviously. But he's right about the fact that our child will most likely be visiting him and his mother every now and then. I do need to see what that place is going to be like. My appetite soon diminishes when I think about what the future holds.

Ethan will always be a tricky person to deal with, and I'm never going to shift the worry in the pit of my stomach. This baby unites us indefinitely, putting me on a constant knife edge. Conflicted as always, I watch Ethan smiling as he eats.

CHAPTER 23

It takes me about an hour and a half to get out to Bridgehampton, but the stretches of sprawling grass and sand dunes make the journey worth it. Even in winter, with the stark-blue sky and low sun, the sea appears inviting but awe-inducing at the same time. Choppy waves break across the rocks. I have to remind myself to keep an eye on the road because the sea is so hypnotic.

Ethan had told me to arrive at eleven and that his mother would have brunch served for us. His exact words were that Alice would have her housekeeper "whip us up something scrumptious." According to the GPS, I'm only five minutes away. I let out a slow breath, forcing my heart to calm down. I've been concentrating on staying on the right side of the road all morning and only now feel the prickly nerves about the visit.

I almost miss the driveway because it's set off the highway, and it's covered by a cluster of trees and scrub bushes. The car judders as I make the turn onto a long, unpaved driveway. Dirt and pebbles crackle under my car's new snow tyres.

The baby kicks, and I smile. "Oh, you want to meet Grandma, do you? Well, okay. I'm doing this for you. I could be on the sofa watching *Real Housewives* right now, so I hope you appreciate this."

I consider the fluttery kicks inside my uterus to be a good omen as I park the car. Ethan's black Audi is already here. He'll be on his best behaviour today. Anything to stop me going back to England. Of course he'll be charming and sweet, but it won't work. I'm already thinking about Christmas with Emily—the two of us in her beautiful house, waking on Christmas morning. We'll have mince pies for breakfast with a dollop of crème fraiche. My stomach rumbles.

The house is perched atop a perfectly manicured lawn next to a section of the Long Island Sound. As soon as I open my door, I can hear the ocean waves crashing in the distance. The salty sea air hits me, and the breeze tickles my skin. Something about being near the ocean has always soothed my soul.

The house is a two-story building. It's large but not overly pretentious. The exterior siding is a walnut colour, a lovely contrast to the vanilla-white trim that spans every corner and edge. The tips of the slated roof point towards a perfect cobalt sky without a cloud in sight. It reminds me of a gingerbread house, put together with icing at the seams.

It could be a summer day if it wasn't for the biting-cold wind. I grab my bag and sling the strap over my shoulder. My legs are as heavy as lead as I clear the distance between my car and the wraparound porch. Before I even get a chance to knock, the door swings open.

Alice stands there looking like an eccentric fairy. Her silky hair billows behind her, wispy strands caught in the breeze. Her slender arms wrap around me before I can blink.

"Laura, darling, it's *wonderful* to see you. Thank you so much for coming to visit me at my home." She plants her hand against her chest. "It truly means the world to me. You and the baby are my honoured guests today."

"Oh, thank you. That's so sweet."

Ethan walks up behind his mother, and she gives me one more possessive squeeze before letting me go. Maybe it's the baby hormones, but Alice's maternal vibes warm up the icy centre at my core.

The two of them wave me in, and Alice scoops me by the arm as soon as my coat is off.

"You must get the tour." Alice directs me through the hall.

Ethan sighs. "Mother, she needs to rest after the drive."

"I'm fine," I say. "I'd love a tour."

My eyes lock with his, but he quickly backs down with a nonchalant shrug. "Okay. You're the boss."

The rooms are amazing. Each one reveals more of Alice's personality. She clearly adores colour and travel. The art on the walls is provocative and sensual. The eyes of many nude women look down at us. Her living room shelves are full of odd little knickknacks. She pulls down a few ornaments and tells me stories of charming markets in exotic locations, of haggling the vendors down to a good price. Other pieces turn out to be gifts from extremely famous people. Not just rock stars but politicians and artists too.

We pass a gallery wall offering panoramic views of the beach. Shimmering sand dunes bob and weave between the house and the water. In between huge windows is a cluster of framed erotic paintings Alice proudly declares to be her own work.

I'll admit, they're impressive. The vivid colour schemes, the textures, the detail on the bodies—they're beautiful. They're the kind that display nudity from a different, nonjudgmental perspective. The paintings embody an openness of sexuality that seems pure and innocent, natural.

Alice points at a piece where a woman is floating on a lily pad, her naked breasts exposed and voluptuous. Her nipples are pink and erect. She's posing in an erotic way with her legs tucked up, and her finger lightly touches her bottom lip.

"I painted this one in the back of Studio 54 while Donna Summer smoked a joint behind me." Alice laughs. She taps a fingertip against her chin. "In fact, I'm pretty sure I smoked that joint with her, and that's what inspired this painting you stand before right now. A time capsule into the eighties, if you will."

"Not these stories again, Mother." Ethan's cheeks turn beetroot red.

Alice ruffles his hair. "Are you embarrassed, Binky?"

"Binky?" I ask.

"My nickname as a child," he says. "Laura didn't need to know that."

"He doesn't appreciate the art because he's not of creative mind," Alice says. "But maybe my grandson will inherit a bit more of me and a lot less of Ethan's father." She lifts her eyebrows and pointedly looks at her son.

I watch Ethan carefully, beginning to feel sorry for him now. She's clearly trying to embarrass him in front of me.

"That's not true," he says quietly.

But while he's speaking, Alice whisks me away to another room. She glides to the back of the house with me in tow, her long dress swishing along behind her. She opens a set of French doors leading into a heated conservatory.

A short red-haired woman in a maid uniform hurries over to us, carrying a tray with drinks. "For you and your guests."

I sip the sweet lemonade. "Thank you. That's delicious... um..."

"Rosie," the maid says.

I give her a friendly smile. "Nice to meet you. I'm Laura."

"Brunch will be served soon," Rosie says, glancing at Alice before she leaves.

We sit down on the garden furniture, and a few moments later, Ethan swaggers in, his face set in a harder expression that gives me pause. It's clear his mother's comments have upset him. I have to say, even though I worry about Ethan's ever-changing mood, I find the interactions between him and Alice to be fascinating. It explains a lot about him.

"How are you, dear?" Alice asks, suddenly directing the attention to me. "You've had a rough month, Ethan tells me."

He sits down on a floral sofa and puts his feet up on a footstool. "Her boss is an idiot."

"I did lose my job," I admit. I try not to look at Ethan as I explain what happened.

"Oh, how ridiculous," Alice says. "So this mysterious other company wanted to hire you? But why attempt to headhunt someone by getting them fired first?"

"My industry is competitive, but it was..." I shrug, not knowing how to describe the strange turn of events. "I don't know. Maybe I'm better suited to a different job."

"You want to give up PR completely?" Ethan asks, and there's almost a hint of hope in his voice.

"I don't know, exactly. I'm not sure what else I could do, but at least I can have a think about it. I have some savings, though not a lot. I can take a little time."

Alice grabs hold of my knee. "That's right. You're young. Take your time."

I laugh. "I'm thirty-five. I'm not young."

"Yes you are," she says. "I'm still young, which means you're a child."

Rosie enters the conservatory with quiche, fruit tarts, and croissants. And as we eat, Alice tells me stories about how she used to attend feminist marches too. She thinks it's amazing that I'll be raising my baby as a single mother but appreciates that I'm willing to let her son have his shared time too.

I notice how Ethan is watching me interact with his mother, and I can tell by the glint in his eyes and the smile on his face that he's pleased with the bond we're forming.

After the food, Alice takes me upstairs, which is full of guest rooms and bathrooms. She leads me into a gorgeous red-and-pink room with roses all over the walls and pink velvet curtains draping to the patterned carpet.

"When you stay, this is your room. I thought you'd like it."

It reminds me of my aunt's garden. I nod, staring up at the pretty ceiling rose above my head. "I do love it."

Alice takes hold of my hand and leads me through to a small room that shares a door with the bedroom. "And this is for your baby."

My jaw drops, and I turn to Ethan. He smiles sheepishly, glancing away.

"This is beautiful," I whisper. My eyes fill with tears. I haven't seen a furnished nursery since I found out I was pregnant, and this one is stunning.

There is no room like this in my apartment. The baby will be sleeping in my bedroom in a crib I haven't put together yet. But this is a real nursery. The walls are bright yellow. There's an enormous wooden crib in the centre and a baby-changing area with nappies piled high, ready to go. A small wardrobe for the baby's clothes stands next to a toy chest and a bookcase. I walk over to the crib, place my hands on the wooden railing, and finger the planets mobile dangling above it.

"What do you think?" Ethan asks.

"It's stunning."

Alice walks up behind me and wraps an arm over my shoulder. "Ethan told me you were thinking of moving back to your aunt's house in England. But we would love for you to stay here. You'd be most welcome."

I shake my head, tears clouding my vision. "I… I can't."

"At least stay in New York. You have family here, and you are loved. Your baby has a place here, with us," she says.

I glance up at Ethan. His dark eyes burn with intensity, waiting for me to answer.

I turn away and reach down into the crib before lifting a soft, cream blanket. "Okay. I'll stay in New York. For now."

PART II

CHAPTER 24

There's a June heat wave in New York, and my fan is barely working. I've already thrown the windows wide open, and there's no air-conditioning in my apartment. I'm close to my due date, huge, and sweating constantly, even when I don't move.

I lean forwards with a grimace and a grunt, trying to peel my back off the sofa. My laptop needs a charge, and I don't have the charger in the room with me. Every step is an annoyance. I wipe damp hair from my forehead and trudge into the bedroom to plug in the laptop. Then I remember the cooling patches Alice sent me and waddle into the bathroom to put them in the fridge.

Ethan and Alice wanted me to move into her Hamptons home, and I have to say, it was tempting. If I trusted Ethan even a tiny bit more, I might have agreed, but I've seen too many ugly sides of him to want to spend twenty-four seven with him and his family.

But dare I say it about Alice? She's like a second mum, or even a stand-in aunt while I'm away from Emily. I talk to Emily all the time, but I also talk to Alice almost daily. And it was she who convinced me to write a memoir about my troubles with infertility. So, for the last five months, while my bump has grown and grown until I thought I might pop, I've written about those experiences, and it's been cathartic to say the least. It's not easy when you need to wee every ten minutes, but it's been rewarding nonetheless.

Right now, it feels like the baby's feet are wedged in my rib cage, and my heartburn keeps me awake half the night, along with leg cramps. Every time the baby stretches and punches my bladder, it sends excruciating pain shooting through my pelvic area.

Not that I'm complaining, because I did it. I made it to this point. I'm about to meet my baby. And after everything, I never thought I would be here.

I make my way back to my bed and reach for my phone. When I see that the screen is filled with text messages from Ethan, I let out a soft sigh.

What are you doing?

Hello?

Laura?

Why haven't you answered me?

Is everything all right?

You're not in labor, are you?

Okay, this isn't funny anymore. If you don't call me back within the next half hour, I'm calling the police to have a wellness check done on you.

After months of dealing with Ethan, I've gradually come to the conclusion that his overzealousness is annoying, and there's a side to him that definitely wants more control than I let him have, but he's more or less harmless.

I'm fine, Ethan. Stop worrying so much. No need for a wellness check. I just had my phone in the other room, and it's a lot for me to get up and around these last few days. You understand.

The more my pregnancy progresses, the more overbearing he gets. I'm trying my best to deal with it because he really is taking care of me, and when I tell him to back off and give me space, he usually complies, apologising profusely. It's the same song and dance I've had to deal with for the last forty weeks. I've learned to pick and choose my battles.

My phone dings again. I suppress a frustrated scream, but when I notice it's Jessa inviting me down to Central Park for lunch, I happily oblige. I need to get out of this apartment. Some sunshine and fresh air will do me—and the baby—a world of good.

* * *

The park is loud in the heat. There's a family enthusiastically playing with a Frisbee, and a golden retriever leaps around their feet. Jessa and

I have found a bench under an elm. I stab a piece of lettuce onto my fork, enjoying the salad I picked up from a deli on the way.

"He's been better lately, but today, he offered to arrange a wellness check for me." I roll my eyes. "I never know with him. One minute, it seems like he's on the verge of a mental collapse, and then it's like the slate is wiped clean, and he's a normal person again."

"He's definitely intense," she says. "Maybe you need to cut down contact again."

I take a sip of my Sprite as I think about that. "Sometimes, that makes it worse."

A couple skates past on rollerblades, hand in hand. There's an ache inside me. I want that. But whoever I next let into my life will need to deal with not only my baby but also with Ethan and his controlling ways.

"I can't wait to be able to do more physical activity once I pop this baby out," I tell Jessa.

She lifts an eyebrow. "Like rollerblading and Frisbee? I've never seen you do either of those things."

I laugh. "No, but maybe jogging and stuff like that."

"Take it one step at a time, sister." Jessa sinks her teeth into her turkey sandwich and groans with delight. "So good."

I stand up to throw my salad container away after I take the last bite. The moment I stand up, I feel an explosion of hot wetness in my underwear. It streams down my legs, and I stand there, mouth wide open, salad container clutched in one hand, legs shoulder-width apart. I meet Jessa's gaze for a moment. Her hand flies to her mouth, and she stares at the puddle forming between my shoes.

"Um—"

"I think my water just broke." I drop the salad box.

Jessa springs into action almost immediately. Luckily, she picked me up in her car, and it's parked in a parallel spot less than a block away.

"Can you make it to the car?" She takes my hands and guides me with one arm roped around my waist for support.

"I—I think so."

A sharp cramp jolts through my abdomen, and I wince, sucking in a sharp breath through my teeth.

Jessa stiffens. "What's wrong? Are you hurt?"

"I—think—cramp—probably a contraction…"

Jessa tries to hurry with me, but there's a throbbing between my legs that makes me feel like I've been punched repeatedly in the crotch.

"Sorry, this is as fast as I can walk," I tell her.

"It's okay, sweetie. You're doing amazing. Just take your time."

"You sound like Kris Jenner," I mumble. "God, this is so embarrassing." I let out a low groan as more people begin to stare.

"We're almost there," Jessa says. "Look." She points at the car up ahead.

"Finally," I whisper.

Jessa helps me into the passenger seat. I lean forwards and place my head against the dashboard as another contraction threatens to take me out. The pain makes my vision blur.

"Just practice your breathing," she says, shoving the car in gear and flooring it out of the parking space. "We'll be at the hospital in no time. There's no reason to worry."

Her eyes are wide, and there's a layer of perspiration beading on her forehead that says otherwise, but I do my best to breathe through the intense pain. "Do you want me to call Ethan on the way?" she asks.

"Not yet," I tell her.

I know I should let her, but I don't want him at the hospital. Not yet.

CHAPTER 25

Of course, we end up stuck in traffic, but Jessa manages to slip down a few side streets, and the journey ends up not being as long as I'd worried. We arrive at the hospital, and I'm wheeled in. I'm a lot calmer, getting into the rhythm of the contractions, bracing myself for the pain. A nurse hooks me up an IV and helps me change into a hospital gown. I settle into the bed, and Dr Nowak arrives.

"Laura, we're a little too far along for an epidural," he says. "But we're going to make you as comfortable as we can."

"Jessa!" I say, alarmed.

"It's going to be okay. Look at me and grab my hand." She holds out her hand.

The contractions are still coming three minutes apart, excruciating pain tearing through me. I squeeze poor Jessa's hand, and she turns very pale.

"Sorry," I say.

"That's okay, warrior woman." She grins. "Do you want me to call Ethan?"

I shake my head. "I don't want him here yet." I lean into my pillow, enjoying a moment of respite between contractions. "Once he gets here, he's just going to be making demands to the nurses and trying to bark orders. He wants to be in control of everything, especially during a crisis."

"Okay," she says. "You're the boss today. Whatever you want, okay?"

"I want this baby out of me right now. Can I have that?"

"Sorry, sweetie," she says.

Time blurs as I work through contractions. The pressure gradually builds to an unbearable level, and I feel like I need to push. As soon as the nurse returns, I tell her. She calls for the doctor to come check how far I'm dilated, and sure enough, it's time.

"*Now* you can call Ethan." I dig my nails into Jessa's hand between breaths.

Jessa scurries to the other side of the room and dials Ethan's number. Soon, the doctor is in position between my legs with a nurse to assist. Jessa stays right by my side, holding my hand.

"We're going to push for ten seconds and rest for five," the nurse says. "I'll help you. I'll tell you when, okay? Here we go, Mommy."

With all the pain and anxiety, I don't mean to say it out loud, but I do. "I'm not a fucking mommy. Don't call me that."

"Breathe with me, Laura," someone else says. I don't even know who it is.

I breathe. I push. I look at Jessa, and I tell her I can't do this.

"Yes, you fucking can," Jessa says.

The pressure mounts, and the pain tears through me. There's some chatter between my legs, and Jessa stares at them in horror.

"What's going on?" I ask.

"Honey, it's best I never tell you what I just saw," she says.

"Poop!" The nurse doesn't sugarcoat it.

I start to laugh, and so does Jessa.

"Concentrate," Dr Nowak warns. He has his hands inside me now.

I push. I breathe. The pressure builds again. I push. I breathe. I sweat. I bleed. And then there's a release. I see a gloppy, wet, tiny ball of baby. Adrenaline and love rush through me. I did it. I never, ever thought I could, and yet I did.

"Jessa, you should cut the umbilical cord," I say, nodding towards Dr Nowak.

"Me?" she turns to me with tears in her eyes.

I nod. "Thank you for being with me."

One of the nurses clamps the cord, and Jessa cuts through it. Then she turns to me and grins.

Dr Nowak holds up the baby. "Congratulations, Mummy. It's a boy!"

A moment later, the nurses are handing me the baby, instructing me to place him on my chest so he gets immediate skin-on-skin contact, and the bond can be made.

I'm crying. Jessa's crying. The baby is crying. It's music to my ears. He has a healthy pair of lungs, and he's wailing, but as I tuck him under my gown, he begins to calm down and tries to suck on his tiny fist.

"We'll get a lactation specialist to you soon," says the nurse. "Then you can try breastfeeding."

I nod. "Sorry for shouting."

She smiles. "I've heard worse."

They don't take him away to clean him and weigh him for several minutes, and when they do, it rips me apart because I want to hold him forever. My heart bursts with enormous love for him already. My heart now lives outside my body and inside that tiny baby.

"Are you ready for the placenta?" the doctor asks.

"No, I'm ready for a nap," I say.

There's no joy in passing it, and the contractions take me by surprise, but a few minutes later, everything that needed to come out of me has.

While they are swaddling my baby boy in a blanket and placing a tiny hat on his head, Ethan and his mother rush into the room, red-faced and breathing hard.

Jessa helps me sit up, and the nurse hands the baby over to me. I'm exhausted, sweaty, and sticky. I'm freezing now, so Jessa is wrapping me up in a blanket one of the nurses brought over.

"Should I be this cold?" I ask, teeth chattering.

"Don't worry. It's normal," the nurse reassures me.

I make a mental note to get all of the names of the nurses popping in and out before I leave. Everything happened much faster than I expected. These women were with me during the most amazing and stressful moment of my life, and I want to remember them.

Ethan marches over to the side of the bed, his eyes raging. His lips are twisted in anger. A darkness overshadows the room. Even the nurses, who know nothing about him, slink quietly away.

I look quickly between him, Alice, and Jessa.

"You already had the baby?" he asks.

"Jessa called you as soon as she could—"

"You should have called me *immediately*." Ethan's fists are balled at his sides, and his teeth are clenched. His pink gums are exposed through his curled upper lip.

Thank goodness Alice steps in to defuse her son's mood.

She plants a hand on his shoulder and strokes his back a moment. "Look, Ethan. You're a daddy now. Look at Laura! She did this all by herself. You should be encouraging her and praising her. Tell her what a good job she did and how proud you are of her." She nudges him in the back.

Ethan stares at the baby as he's yawning, and some of the storm clouds in his eyes start to break. He unclenches his fists, and his shoulders relax. A smile spreads across his face, and his expression lightens.

"You did amazing, Laura. I'm so proud of you." He leans down and plants a tender kiss on my sweaty forehead.

He looks at our baby with what I believe to be genuine love.

"May I?" he asks, reaching for the baby before I can say yes or no. His eyes gleam with tears.

"Of course." I help him make the exchange. "Just support the neck with the crook of your arm."

He flashes his eyes at me as if he wants to say something snarky, but he doesn't.

"A boy?" he asks hopefully.

I nod. "Yes, a boy."

CHAPTER 26

E than holds our blanket-swaddled baby in his arms, gently swaying him. In my head, my baby boy is already called Christopher, after my mother, Christine. It feels right. As I watch Ethan with our son, I find my fingers twitching, aching to have my baby back. But Ethan beams down at Christopher, who makes gentle squeaking sounds that are so cute they melt my heart.

With Jessa's help, I shimmy myself further up on the pillows, into a sitting position. I'm still in a lot of pain, but it's getting better. Alice stands beside Ethan, gazing down adoringly at her brand-new grandson.

"He's so cute," Alice says. "Darling, he looks just like you." She squeezes Ethan's arm and smiles.

"I've decided to name him Christopher James," I say.

Both Ethan's and Alice's eyes shoot up at me.

"Christopher James?" Ethan says. "Why? I thought we talked about Ethan Junior?"

I press my lips together. Not once has Ethan ever told me he wanted to name the baby Ethan Jr.

I glance up at Jessa, but she's staring at her phone, pretending not to be paying attention.

"Christopher is in honour of my mother, whose name was Christine. James is for my grandfather, Jim. Both names are important to me," I say.

A dark cloud crosses Ethan's face, one that makes my body tense. It reminds me of our first date. His temper is brewing again.

"What's more significant than naming the baby after his own father?" Ethan asks.

Alice takes a deep breath beside him and removes her hand from his arm. At first, I assume she's going to come to my rescue and tell Ethan he's being unreasonable, that I just endured the labour and pushed the baby out after nine challenging months. Or maybe that he should be more considerate of my wishes and agree that Christopher James is a beautiful name for her grandson.

But she doesn't. Instead, she says, "I think Ethan Junior has a nice ring to it. Perhaps we could consider it." She holds her hands up. "We don't have to decide right now… But it's an option, isn't it?"

Ethan nods.

"Ethan," I say. "Forgive me, but we never discussed baby names. I just assumed you would let me handle it—"

"And why wouldn't you think I'd want a say on what to name my son?" His eyes narrow.

"Because you never mentioned it!" I snap.

Jessa immediately gets up from her chair and moves towards the bed. She heard it too. She heard his change in tone. She grabs my hand protectively.

"Ethan, you told me from the beginning that you would respect my boundaries," I remind him.

He scoffs, and my heart drops when his arms slacken as if he's forgotten he's holding our baby. Alice quickly scoops the baby from his arms. She cuddles him, whispering to him, her voice soothing. I place one hand on my chest, my heart thumping. My eyes never move from Christopher's tiny form.

"This is my *son* we're talking about. Not some bullshit rules you want to impose on *our* relationship. The two have nothing to do with each other," he says.

I choose my words carefully, nearly choking them out. "Ethan, I'm just saying that we both agreed that you would let me do the child rearing—"

"So, that means I don't get a choice on what his name is?" he snaps.

"I've made the decision, and it's final." I give him a firm look that leaves no room for debate.

He stares at me, waiting to see if I fold, but I don't budge. I notice his jaw tighten, and it starts to twitch. No one is saying anything. The tension is like a balloon ready to pop.

"Ethan," Alice says in a nervous voice as she hands Christopher back to me. "It's getting late. Why don't we let Laura get some rest, and we'll come back later?"

Ethan's eyes bore into mine, full of rage. The heat of his stare makes my cheeks flush.

"All right." He takes a step back towards the door. His eyes are still rooted to mine.

I release an audible sigh of relief when he finally complies. Alice cuffs a stiff hand around his wrist and tugs him away from the bed.

"I'll be back tomorrow to visit my baby," he says.

Alice cuts me a look as if to question what's wrong with me and shakes her head briefly, and they step out into the hallway.

My head collapses on the pillow, and I stare at the ceiling.

"Well, that was fucking weird," Jessa says as soon as we're alone again.

I wipe sweat from my forehead. "Sorry you had to witness that."

"So, I guess you weren't exaggerating about him," she says. "He's every bit as Jekyll and Hyde as you said."

I narrow my eyes. "Wait. All this time, you thought I was exaggerating?"

"No, not exactly," she says. "I guess part of me figured he couldn't be quite as crazy as you said."

I almost laugh. "Jessa, you keep forgetting I'm British. If anything, we play things down, not exaggerate. It's in my blood." I sigh. "I'm so glad he's gone."

"Me too," she says. "I mean, you just had his baby. He has a son. You'd think he wouldn't care that much if he had the same name as him. The gift is the baby himself, right?"

"I've never been a fan of giving sons the same name as their father," I admit. "It feels narcissistic. Plus, we don't really do the 'junior' in England. The whole tradition is strange to me. You'd think he'd get that."

Jessa glances at her watch just as a nurse comes in to check on us. "Damn. I gotta get going. I have a shift at work. Are you going to be okay here by yourself?"

I stroke my baby's cheek and gaze down at him with a smile. "I'm not alone. I have a buddy. Plus, I need to call my aunt. I sent her a photo on WhatsApp, but we haven't spoken yet."

"Right. I'll come by and pick you up tomorrow. Just call me when they discharge you." She leans down and kisses my forehead and the top of Christopher's. "Wow, I love the smell of newborn head."

"It's like a drug."

After a quick, gushing video call to my favourite aunt, I fall asleep with Christopher sleeping in a bassinet beside me.

* * *

The next morning, I expect Jessa here around nine, but it's ten, and she still hasn't turned up. Ethan is sitting on the chair in my hospital room, holding Christopher and stroking his head. I can't help but notice his inexperience and roughness with the baby.

"Be careful with his soft spot," I say.

Ethan shoots me a glare. "I'm not going to hurt him, Laura."

"Can we talk about yesterday?" I ask.

He sighs. "I guess so."

"You completely blindsided me about the name Junior. I think you know that. You also know I'm British, and we don't call our children Junior. But I'm willing to compromise," I say. "How about Christopher James Ethan McAdams."

He looks up at me. "Christopher Ethan James McAdams, and we have a deal."

"Okay, I can do that," I say. "Look, I really don't want to freeze you out. It's just, you're a tad controlling, Ethan, and I need to…" I want to say, *I need to protect myself from you*, but I don't. I choose my words carefully. "I just need to make sure we find a middle ground that feels comfortable for us both."

The words are true. It's what I've been doing from the very beginning. I've known for a long time that I'm in dangerous waters with Ethan, and I don't want to let my head dip below the surface. No matter what, we're linked together by the child in his arms, and I'm well aware that legally, he has rights. The more I push, the more he might pull in the other direction, and I don't want to find myself in a court with Ethan, his mother, and all of his money, because I'm not completely sure I would win. Talking to Ethan is so often about placating him while holding back a little of the power for myself. It's exhausting but necessary.

"That's fine," he says, but he seems distracted by Christopher's tiny burps and hiccups.

I text Jessa for the fourth time this morning. This is so unlike her. But perhaps she's tired from the long day yesterday.

"Why are you so glued to your phone?" Ethan asks.

"I'm trying to get in touch with Jessa." An unsettled sensation burrows in my stomach. "She's not responding to my calls or texts."

Ethan frowns and stops stroking Christopher's head. "Maybe she's just busy."

"It's not like her. Especially since she told me she'd pick me up and take me home."

"I can take you home," he offers. "I have my car with me."

I chew my bottom lip, debating.

Where are you? I text her one more time. *Is everything okay?*

When Jessa doesn't respond after another five minutes, I look at Ethan. "All right. You can take us home."

A look of satisfaction spreads across his face. It seems as though he feels like he's won one over me, and I hate that thought. It's like he hasn't listened to a thing I've said, and every part of raising this baby together will be one battle after another.

CHAPTER 27

"I just don't know about raising Christopher in this apartment, Laura." Ethan's hands are on his hips. With disapproval, his eyes inspect every corner of the admittedly small space.

It's been two days since I came home from the hospital, and I'm sitting on the sofa with Christopher, trying to get him to latch. He's fussy and red-faced. His lips curl over his gums as he wails. It's been a struggle to get him to nurse, but I'm not giving up. My lactation consultant, Allie, gave me a few techniques to make it easier. I'm hoping those might work.

"Laura?" he says. "Are you listening."

I'm not shy about breastfeeding in his presence anymore. On the first day in the hospital, it was weird, then I got past it. Seeing as Ethan barely wants to leave my side, I haven't had much of a choice. On the other hand, Christopher is not an easy baby, and it does help having Ethan around. I can see he's trying as he soothes our son, but he's not a natural with babies.

"Yes, I'm listening," I snap. "No, I'm not moving in with you and your mother. Yes, I'm incredibly grateful for the offer."

He raises his eyebrows.

"We've been over all of this before. I promise you, we're absolutely fine here."

"But look at this coffee table, for instance." He kicks the corner with the tip of his shoe. "It's sharp."

"Christopher is a newborn," I remind him. "He can't crawl or walk yet. When the time comes, I'll babyproof."

Ethan's eyes scan the room for something else to complain about. He wants to pick a fight, but I'm too exhausted to deal with it.

"Look at the kitchen, Laura. The dishes from breakfast are still on the table." He throws his hands up in exasperation.

A fly buzzes around a discarded piece of cream cheese bagel that I'd abandoned after Christopher started screaming earlier.

I cringe but hold my ground. "I need to tend to the baby, Ethan. The dishes can wait."

Ethan rolls his eyes and turns his back to me. "What about the nursery? Or lack thereof, I should say."

Christopher squirms. I know he's hungry. He's rooting for my nipple, but he won't latch.

"I only have a one-bedroom apartment, Ethan. Where do you suggest I put the nursery?"

"He needs his own space."

"Plenty of newborns sleep in bassinets next to their parents' beds," I point out.

"He'll eventually need a crib," Ethan counters.

"I'll cross that bridge when I come to it."

"I hope you aren't falling asleep in the bed with him. He could die, you know. You could smother him. They say that most of the babies who die from SIDS are—"

"Ethan, enough!" I shout.

"Excuse me?" He swivels and takes a step closer.

I stiffen and hug a crying Christopher closer to my chest. He finally latches onto my nipple. The room goes silent aside from Christopher's sniffles and the sounds of him feeding.

I lower my voice. "I'm just having a hard time right now, and I don't need you in here criticising everything I do or nitpicking every detail of what you think is wrong with my apartment. Christopher and I are happy here. We're cosy and healthy. There's nothing to worry about."

To my relief, Ethan's surprised expression softens. He slumps onto the sofa next to me then reaches for my knee and gives it a quick squeeze. It's supposed to be an apology, I think, but I move my knee away slightly.

"I'm sorry I'm being so hard on you," he says. "I just want the best for him. That's all."

"And I don't?" I ask.

"That's not what I meant." He lets out a long breath. "This is not where I pictured my first-born son living." He turns to me. "This isn't how I imagined it would be with the mother of my child."

Despite his mood swings, I can relate. None of this is how I imagined it either. "Why not be grateful and enjoy this, okay? Accept that I'm not moving in with you, and accept that the situation with Christopher is going to be very different to a regular family. It doesn't mean we don't love him, does it?"

"I know," he says.

I can tell there's more he wants to say, but instead, he gestures to Christopher. "Can I hold him after he finishes eating? Maybe that will give you a chance to tidy up a bit and maybe…" He trails off, his eyes scanning me up and down. "Take a shower?"

My cheeks flush, but I know he's now trying to help, not criticise, then I wonder if perhaps the state of the apartment is alarming. Maybe, for once, Ethan isn't trying to start a fight. He's concerned. Plus, I haven't had a proper shower in two days.

"I've had a couple rough nights," I murmur.

"It's starting to show. You know you could move in with my mother alone if that would make you more comfortable. I'd stay in the city and come over most evenings. It really would be better for you. You could wake up to the sound of the ocean right outside your window every morning. Wouldn't that be a dream?" His eyes dazzle as he tries to sell it to me.

I would rather live in a cardboard box than with either of them. Alice lost my trust after the name issue. The house would be amazing, but the strings that come with it would be unbearable.

"No, I like being in my own space," I say. "It's familiar to me, and that's what I need right now. I need a place I love."

"But for how long, Laura? How long?" he asks.

He's right, and I know it, but I don't want him badgering me into doing something I don't want to do, so I pass him Christopher and head to the bathroom for a quick shower. Every moment I'm under the water, I can't stop thinking about him in there alone with my son. It's as though every part of my body tells me it's a bad idea to leave that man alone with such precious cargo. But he is my baby's father, whether I like it or not.

While I rinse my hair, my thoughts drift back to Jessa, who has been completely silent for two days now. And that's even more worrying. Jessa sometimes does go AWOL, but she would never fail to pick me up from the hospital. Something is wrong, and it's been nagging at the back of my mind since Ethan brought me home.

"Better?" he asks.

I nod. Christopher squirms in his arms and begins to cry. Ethan quickly hands him to me, and I settle on the sofa. He stands up with a sigh and a stretch then leans over me to kiss Christopher's tiny head.

"I'll see you tomorrow," he says. "Think about it, at least. Won't you?"

"I will," I lie.

As soon as he's gone, the tension in the room dissolves. Even the baby seems happier.

Once Christopher drops off, I settle him in the bassinet for a nap and make a start on cleaning up. It's not easy. I'm going slowly, still sore, still exhausted. About five minutes in, he starts crying, so I waddle to the bedroom to soothe him. Then I lose motivation to tidy and lie down on the bed for a moment. I wake about thirty minutes later to the buzzer going off.

Christopher is soon screaming at the top of his lungs. I pick him up, wincing as I carry him carefully across the apartment to answer the buzzer.

"Hey, it's Jessa. Can I come up?"

"Yes, of course!" I buzz her in, relieved.

With dismay, I realise I have no time to clean up the rest of the mess but quickly stuff the leftover bagel in the bin, at least. Jessa enters as I'm hastily throwing dirty dishes in the sink.

"Sorry it's a—oh my God, Jessa!"

"It's not as bad as it looks," she says. "Don't panic."

There's a deep-blue bruise across one eye, which is also swollen to twice its normal size. Her right wrist is in a bright-pink cast.

"What happened?"

We move over to the sofa, and Jessa wiggles her fingers at Christopher. He begins to settle, cooing sweetly again.

"I'm so sorry I didn't pick you up from the hospital," she says. "I've had the worst couple of days. First, I lost my phone. That's why I haven't called. Then I was pulling across a junction, and this car came out of nowhere. Some idiot ran a red light, smashed into me, and drove off."

"Jesus! Have the police caught them?"

"They're working on it, apparently," Jessa says. "They think it might have been a stolen car. So now I need a new phone *and* a new car. Insurance is coming through for me, but it sucks. This little guy is cheering me up, though. Hey, sweetie."

"Is your wrist broken?" I ask, still shocked by her revelation.

"Yep. Which means I get to sport this fashion accessory for the next six weeks." She lifts her arm.

I wince. "I'm so sorry."

She shrugs. "Don't worry about it. I'm tough."

"I'm just relieved it wasn't worse," I say.

"You and me both. And I don't recommend car accidents to anyone. Not a fan."

Jessa reaches for the baby, and we arrange him carefully so that holding him doesn't hurt her wrist.

"I guess it was bad luck," she says. "Losing my phone and having the accident in one day. I hated letting you down like that."

"God, Jessa, don't be silly! I'm just glad you're okay."

"How did you get home?"

"Ethan brought me."

Her smile thins. "I guess it worked out okay for him that day."

There's a note in her voice that catches my attention. It's not exactly bitterness but frustration perhaps—or suspicion.

"I meant to call your mum and check you were okay, but things have been hectic here," I say.

"That's okay," she says. "I had a trip to the hospital and felt pretty out of it with painkillers. They kept me in overnight to check for a concussion."

"I'm so sorry. I can't believe this happened to you." I rub her shoulders. It's clear Jessa is on the verge of tears, and that rarely happens. She's always so bubbly.

"It really threw me, Laura," she says. "I keep having these awful nightmares about the accident and…"

Her expression sharpens when she turns to me.

"What is it?" I prompt.

She sniffs. Her eyes drift from me to Christopher and back to me. "I dream that Ethan was driving the car."

CHAPTER 28

Jessa's words play in my mind for the next few days. But I know for a fact Ethan could not have been driving the car. He was in the hospital with me when Jessa had her accident. I don't blame her for feeling suspicious. It was perfect timing for Ethan to swoop in and take me home from the hospital. If I hadn't been with him, I'd be thinking the exact same thing.

Still, there's a cloud hanging over me as I go about my days. With every nappy change and feed, my thoughts are darker. Jessa's news left me shaken. I can't put my finger on why, but it seems to trigger the same feelings I had after the apartment was burgled.

It's around ten a.m., and through Christopher's screaming, I barely hear the knock on my door. When he gets colicky, his cries drown out everything else, and I'm sure that by this point, my neighbours must hate me.

"Coming!" I shout, setting Christopher down in his swing and strapping him in. I programme it to the song that seems to soothe him the most and switch the motion setting to low.

Relief floods me when I see my lactation consultant, Allie, standing in the hallway.

"Thank you so much for coming." I open the door wide so she can step in.

"Of course. You sounded frantic on the phone." She glances over at Christopher, who is still crying in his swing.

"I'm losing my mind," I admit. "It's been like this for hours."

"It will get better. I promise." She pats my upper arm and makes her way over to the baby.

Embarrassed, I quickly brush away a few tears as I follow her in. Allie is polite, but even she can't help but stare at the place. There's a mountain of clean, unfolded laundry on the sofa. A stack of unwashed dishes peeks over the edge of my kitchen sink. Dust collects on every surface, something I'm just now noticing. I should have a better handle on things, but I don't. I can never sleep long enough to be rested. And when I'm not rested, I have only enough energy to take care of Christopher, not to focus on housework.

Allie stops in front of Christopher's swing. He's still crying but not wailing like before.

"You probably think I'm an unfit mother when you come in here and see this." I let out a humourless laugh. "I'm trying. I swear I am. But he wants to eat every hour on the hour, and only half the time am I successful in getting him to latch. The rest of the time, he's screaming. I'm surprised I haven't had any neighbour complaints so far."

"It's not you, Laura. None of this is your fault," she says. "It takes every new mother time to establish a routine with their baby."

"I swear I am normally a tidy person. I know my apartment is small. It worked when it was just me, but babies have so much… *stuff*. I'm trying to figure out a solution."

"Laura, it's okay. You don't have to explain yourself to me. I'm not judging you. I'm here because I'm concerned for you, and I want to help you."

"Thank you," I say. "Sorry. I just get so embarrassed by…" My mind searches for the right word.

"By not being perfect?" she suggests.

"No… I… I don't know. None of this has been easy. Christopher's father's family are very rich and overbearing, and they want to control everything. I've been a mess since I found out I was pregnant. I lost my job, and now I can't even keep my apartment clean. I'm a failure, and I can feel them circling me, waiting for an opportunity…" I drift off, overwhelmed by the emotions flooding my body.

"An opportunity for what?" she asks gently.

"To take my baby away from me." The words come out barely louder than a whisper. I've finally said it out loud.

Allie shakes her head. "That would never happen over a messy apartment. You're a good mother. And Christopher is still breastfeeding. No judge would ever separate a breastfeeding baby and mother unless that child was in grave danger. Trust me. You're safe. And you're doing a good job. Now, come on. Let's figure out why he isn't latching."

I nod. I look at my baby boy, now much calmer but still awake. His eyes are wide open and scanning the ceiling.

"Do you want to try to nurse him while I'm here so that we can see what the problem is?" she offers.

"Yes, please."

When I pick him up, he stretches and yawns, pumping his arms and feet. Despite all the stress, I can't help but smile.

"He loves to be held and normally can't stand it when I put him down. Which is half the reason why I'm unshowered and my home is messy."

"He loves you," Allie says. "Stop beating yourself up over the trivial things."

She helps me get him latched and tells me what to do next time he gets fussy and doesn't seem to want to do it. But the whole time she's there, whenever her gaze moves to another part of the flat, it makes me paranoid that maybe she is judging me.

After Christopher is asleep, I'm so self-conscious about her curious stares that I tell her I need to sleep, too, and escort her to the door with the promise I'll call her if I need her help again. Maybe it's all in my head. I'm extra vulnerable right now because I'm exhausted, and I could be imagining things, but after I step into a much-needed hot shower, I finally allow myself to cry.

* * *

For the rest of the afternoon, while Christopher naps for a change, I potter around the apartment, finally putting away his tiny babygrows and socks. It makes me sad that there's no real cabinet for his belongings. Instead, I have a small shelving unit that I bought from Ikea. If I'd taken Ethan up on his offer, there would be a perfect little wardrobe waiting for him. But no, I made the right decision. I know I did.

Then we FaceTime Emily for a while. She walks me around the garden, through the roses and the lavender, and it's like I can smell the flowers. My stomach aches for home. Ethan and I have an agreement, but the temptation to break it grows stronger with every day I struggle in this tiny apartment. But I can't shake the feeling that it would be cruel to separate Christopher from his father and grandmother. I never had a dad. Could I do that to my son?

Once I'm done on the phone with Emily, Christopher decides it's time for a feed again, and I follow Allie's advice. It takes a while, and he certainly shows me the power of his lungs again, but we get there. I clip him back in his swing and dial Ethan's number. The birth certificate came this morning, and I want to let him know.

"You registered his birth without me. That means I'm not on the birth certificate," he says. "Laura, how could you? And his name is Christopher James?"

"Christopher *Ethan* James," I say. "That's what we agreed on, remember?"

"I agreed to no such thing," he says. "I wanted Ethan Junior. You know that. I wanted everyone to know he's my son. Which includes being on the birth certificate."

"But we're not a couple, Ethan. I just thought I should register his birth now, and maybe we can add you onto the certificate at a later date," I say.

"Well, whatever you do, just remember I have rights. You're trying to take them away from me by changing his name and not including my name, but I still have them. I can get the courts to request a DNA test at any time."

My skin itches. I stay calm when I respond, "Is that something you want to do?"

"It's something I'm considering," he says. "I still can't believe you lied to me about the name."

I stare at the beige wall of my apartment, completely gobsmacked. And then my baby brain makes me wonder if I imagined the entire conversation we had about baby names. "No, we talked. It was a compromise, remember?"

"You lied to me." His voice is malicious enough to send icy shivers through my bones.

"I didn't lie to you."

"You told me you were considering Christopher but that you hadn't made up your mind," he says.

My pulse races. Either Ethan is remembering wrong, or he's deliberately trying to gaslight me into believing I said something I never did.

"That's not true, and you know it. We talked it through, and this was the compromise. Stop doing this—"

"No, you stop doing this. Stop being such a bitch about everything."

"I gave birth to your son. Remember that?" I snap. "You can't talk to me that way."

"You betrayed me," he says, doubling down. "You went behind my back."

I hang up. He's acting crazy, and I don't want to indulge him. Then I step over to my door and check every lock. I don't really want the live version of his insanity. What excuse will he come up with this time? He lost some money at work? His goldfish died, and he decided to berate the mother of his child?

How could Ethan completely forget an entire conversation? It's bizarre. Unless it was me who forgot the conversation. Or invented it. No, I realise I'm exhausted and wrapped up in breastfeeding and nappy changes, but I would never forget something like that. I remember the grateful expression on Ethan's face. He seemed happy to find a decent compromise.

It's as I'm ensuring the chain is in place across my door that I realise how afraid I am of Ethan. Over the last ten months, I've gone back and forth with my feelings for him. Sometimes, he scares me. Other times, he convinces me he's a good person with some personal issues. Most of the time, I'm sure I can handle him, tantrums and all, and then he does something so out of left field that it unbalances me again. Today was supposed to be a happy day for both of us. Christopher is official. He's here, and he has a name and an identity. He has a mother and a father.

And yet, this apartment doesn't feel like a home anymore, and it certainly doesn't feel safe. There's another rift between me and his father. Dread lies low in my belly. A negative voice inside my head tells me I can't do this. I'm a terrible mother, and I'm going to fail to keep my baby safe.

CHAPTER 29

A s usual, after the altercation with Ethan, I don't hear from him for a few days. It leaves me grateful for the time it gives me to decompress after our fight. But it also leaves me annoyed that he can't be mature enough to talk things through. The more I get to know Ethan, the more I realise he considers our son to be his possession. An extension of him. Something to control.

Ethan is a man used to getting his own way, one who throws tantrums when he doesn't and then apologises later. He's never been violent with me, but I've been unnerved by him many times. The thought of him wanting Christopher for himself scares me more than any threat to me.

I want to truly unpack my feelings about Ethan, but Christopher is still colicky and fussy. My thoughts are scattered from exhaustion. The problems with the apartment aren't going away, and I find myself unable to sleep, scrolling through articles on postnatal depression.

When Christopher naps, I write. It's my one reprieve and possibly what's holding me together right now. As I sit cross-legged on the bed, sheets tangled, my fingers fly across the keyboard, every moment of elation and sorrow pouring out onto the pages. I can let it all out, even my concerns. Every fragmented thought comes out in those moments.

Some thoughts frighten me with their darkness, and when Jessa invites me to her apartment for lunch, I find myself on the brink of letting them all spill out.

"Your eye looks so much better," I say as she passes me a mug of hot peppermint tea.

"And I can pick up Christopher properly now, look," she says, moving her arm in a way she wasn't able to last week.

"Is it still painful?" I ask.

She shakes her head. "Not really, but the cast stays on for another month. Anyway, I didn't invite you here to talk about me. I wanted to talk about *you*. I'm worried about you, Laura. You're barely leaving the apartment. That's why I insisted you come here today. I thought you might need a change of scenery."

I wave a hand. "It's a bit of a nightmare with the pram and the lift and Christopher crying all the time. Sometimes, it's easier to just stay in."

"Yeah, but you need a break from the same four walls. Can I take him for a couple of hours? Let you get some rest?"

I immediately tense up at the thought of not being around him. But it's also tempting. Still, I shake my head. Then I begin to cry. Then it all comes out.

"We're not bonding… I don't know what I'm doing wrong. I can't even breastfeed properly, so I've had to use the bottle… and… I just…"

Jessa leans over and rubs my shoulder. "Oh, hon. Let it all out."

I wipe my nose and pull in a deep breath. "He's my miracle baby, Jess. I never thought I'd even bring a child to term. But it's like he *hates* me for dragging him into this world. I can't even provide a decent home for him. He doesn't have a proper family. It's just me and his nutcase of a father."

Jessa starts to laugh, and I find myself laughing with her.

"Then I take it Ethan's not helping things?" she asks.

"He's helping me reach new levels of insanity." I laugh again, but even to my ears, it's tinged with sadness. "He's so overbearing and critical." I sigh. "But he is right about my apartment. I'm drowning there. The walls are closing in on me."

"I had no idea things had gotten that bad." Jessa taps her fingertips against the table. "Why don't you move in with me? As of last week, I have a free bedroom."

"Seriously?"

"Yup. She got a job in Colorado," Jessa says.

"I'm such a bad friend. I didn't even know," I say. "I probably didn't ask. I'm so sorry."

Jessa just shrugs. "I didn't even like her, if I'm honest. She used to steal my oat milk and leave wet towels on the floor."

I laugh. "Well, Christopher is too young to leave towels everywhere. But I can't put you through this. He's a colicky baby, and you have a job. You don't need a screaming baby waking you up at three in the morning."

"It won't bother me, I swear. Your mental health is more important to me."

Her expression is so sincere that I can't help but contemplate her offer. My lease is currently on a month-to-month plan, so I wouldn't have to break a contract.

"Are you sure?" I ask.

Jessa nods and stands up. She walks to a door at the end of the small hallway that separates the two bedrooms.

She opens it and switches on a light. "Look, this is a supply closet, and it's by no means perfect. There's no window in here, but it could work for the time being as a makeshift nursery. It could fit a crib and maybe a small dresser."

I join her at the closet, allowing my gaze to roam across the small space. She's right. It isn't perfect, but it's big enough for a baby.

"Jessa, this is an incredibly generous offer."

"Does that mean you're going to take it?" she asks.

The thought of living with someone I love and of having a space for myself is overwhelming. With Jessa's help, I won't have to rely on Ethan as much, and I'll have room to breathe.

"Of course I am! But only if you're sure about this. Have you thought it through? Because neither of us are much fun to live with," I warn.

Jessa ropes her arms around me and plants a big kiss on my cheek. "The three of us are going to have a blast." She slaps both hands on my cheeks. "Say it with me. We're going to have a blast."

"We're going to have a blast." I begin to laugh, and she pulls me into the closet so that we can do a little jig around the tiny space.

Then we head back to the pram, and I take Christopher out and bounce him in my arms.

"I'll help you pack all your stuff," Jessa says.

"I'll support you with half the rent."

Jessa makes a face. "No." She holds her arms out for the baby, and I pass him to her.

"Come on," I say. "You have to let me contribute. It's not fair otherwise."

Jessa shrugs, debating. "You can pay the utilities but only after you get settled in." She leans down to Christopher and strokes his fine hair.

"You are the best. Seriously. You just tossed me a lifeline," I say. And I mean every word.

* * *

On my walk home from the subway station, Christopher starts screaming just before we roll up to our apartment. I have trouble navigating the pram in and out of passersby. But despite all that, I'm walking on air. His cries are no longer stressful because I know I'll soon be getting help.

The phone ringing, on the other hand… I dig it out from the bottom of my handbag and swear when I see the name on the screen. It's Ethan, probably ready to rain on my parade. But ignoring him will only cause more friction, so I answer.

"Hey, I'm a little busy here—" I start.

"That's why I'm calling." He sounds furious already.

Balancing the phone between my ear and shoulder, I manage to wheel the pram into the building and talk at the same time. "What do you mean?"

"I went to your apartment and rang the doorbell and knocked a bunch of times. You never came to the door."

I grit my teeth. "Well, that's because I wasn't home. I'm just getting back from Jessa's. Why didn't you call ahead?"

"If you take my baby somewhere, I deserve to know where it is!" he snaps.

I stop dead in the centre of the lobby. Christopher quiets, and the place goes still. "We're not going to get very far if you carry on like that. I'm Christopher's mother, and I can take him wherever I like."

He's acting like I took Christopher to an Ebola lab and rubbed his face on the petri dishes.

Ethan sighs. "Sorry, I'm a bit anxious. It was a shock getting to the apartment and not seeing you. It's just you're always there, so I pictured you on a plane back to England or something."

"I wouldn't do that," I say. "Ethan, you can't keep tabs on me like this. It's suffocating."

"I'm just worried about you and the baby."

It strikes me then that he always says "the baby." I'm not sure I've ever heard him say the name Christopher when referring to our child.

"Please," he says in a less aggressive tone this time. "I just want to spend some time with my baby boy. I haven't seen him all week. I miss him."

"Christopher misses you too," I say, and perhaps it's the good mood that I'm in, but as soon as the idea pops into my head, I decide to roll with it. "Why don't we go out to your mum's house in the Hamptons this weekend?"

At least I won't be alone with Ethan there. His mother can act as buffer. Plus, I would like to patch things up with her after the name debacle. Alice has, at times, felt like a mother figure to me. She's one of the reasons I put up with her son's bullshit.

"Are you sure?" he asks. "Oh, Laura, that would be awesome. Thank you. I know things have been rocky recently, but I'd like to put things right with you and… Christopher."

"Good," I reply.

After the phone call, I place a hand on Christopher's warm forehead and let out a long sigh. "One step at a time with your daddy." I can only hope Ethan manages to curb his controlling tendencies long enough to let us breathe.

CHAPTER 30

The countryside blurs across the window like a paint smear while Ethan talks as fast as he drives. In the rearview mirror, Christopher is fast asleep, not aware of his father's chatter or the speed he's travelling. I'm trying to tune Ethan out because he won't stop harping on about the best schools for Christopher's education, and I don't quite know what to say. For all I know, Ethan and Alice have applied to the schools already.

My mind drifts back to my rural comprehensive school. Buses full of kids travelling from village to village. Running the cross-country track through the woods. Bumping into teachers in the local pubs. Maybe that's what I want, not some redbrick building in Connecticut or upstate New York.

"Hey, could you slow down a bit, please?" My fingers grip the handrest.

Ethan frowns and looks at the dash. His knuckles tighten around the steering wheel. "I'm maintaining the speed limit."

I peer over the centre console so I can see if he's lying. He is—he's going over seventy.

"The speed limit is fifty-five, Ethan."

He smirks. "What are you, the road police? Stop telling me how to drive."

Ethan's raised voice wakes Christopher, and he starts to fuss. I flash

Ethan an irked glance and reach behind me to put the pacifier back in his mouth.

"He shouldn't suck on that thing," he says.

"It soothes him."

"He's going to get an overbite," he warns.

"No, he's not."

"Whatever." Ethan rolls his eyes. "Anyway, before I was so *rudely* interrupted, back to the schools—"

"It's too soon," I say, sighing. "He's one month old!"

"We have to get on waiting lists for the good ones." He waves a hand, and I internally scream at him to put it back on the steering wheel. "But you haven't been on top of it. That's why I always need to pick up the slack where you fall short."

"Fall short?"

"I'm not criticising," he says. "I know you're busy. I don't get to be there for the day-to-day, do I? I'm on the sidelines, watching. So this is what I can do. I can get Christopher's name on all the waiting lists for the best schools."

"Okay, fine," I say. Anything to shut him up. A waiting list isn't an enrolment. Christopher isn't at a fancy school until the day he walks through the doors. And as much as I hate to admit it, there's a chance I could change my mind at a later date and regret not doing it.

We finally pull into Alice's driveway, and my shoulders relax. The journey has, quite frankly, been exhausting. Every minute, I've regretted allowing Ethan to pick me up. Now, I have a budding migraine pressing on the edge of my skull.

Ethan removes the car seat and carries Christopher up the front steps to the door. He's every bit the proud parent, ready to show off his baby. The door opens, and an equally proud grandmother comes into view.

"There's my little boo-bear," Alice coos, her arms open wide to receive her grandson.

I note that Alice avoids using the name Christopher too. While Ethan has relented recently, she still finds nicknames to use instead. Does she think I'm going to change my son's name again?

Ethan sets the baby seat down next to the kitchen table, and Alice begins unstrapping him from the harness.

"I just got him to sleep—"

"Oh, but he's my grandson, and I want to hold him," she interrupts.

"Yes, but—"

"No buts," she says, her voice firmer. "I haven't seen him for a week. I'm going to hold him."

She turns back to my baby, a beaming smile plastered across her face. It occurs to me then that she hasn't even welcomed me here or even said hello.

Sure enough, as soon as she picks him up, he starts crying. The words "I told you so" are on the tip of my tongue, but I don't dare say them aloud.

Alice bounces Christopher in her arms and saunters into the living room, singing him a nursery rhyme. Ethan follows his mother as I pick up my bag. Hovering by the living room door, I'm unsure whether to sit down on a sofa or take my bag upstairs.

Alice puts her hand on Ethan's arm. "What's wrong, Binky? You look upset."

Slowly, Ethan turns to me, and Alice follows his gaze.

"What's going on?" she asks.

"She is being defiant about boarding schools," Ethan says, nodding in my direction.

"What?" I blurt out. "I just said we could put Christopher on a waiting—"

"Oh, that terrible name." Alice rolls her eyes.

"That is my son's name," I remind her, shocked to be faced with such rudeness from both of them. "Ethan, I haven't been defiant. I just think that it's too premature to discuss schools. But sure, put his name on some lists. What does it matter? We can decide later, right?"

She frowns. "In what way is being prepared for your child's education premature?" She scoffs. "We need to decide on a clear path to an Ivy League college now."

"He's a baby, Alice," I say. "When Christopher is older, he'll decide which college he wants to go to. Maybe he won't want to go to college."

She rounds on Ethan. "This is your responsibility. I told you to talk to her about the schools. She obviously doesn't care at all."

"Mommy, I did talk to her," he says.

"But you didn't convince her, clearly," she replies, her voice icy.

Ethan wanders closer to his mother and places a hand on Christopher's forehead. "I'm working on it. I swear I am."

They're discussing me as though I'm not even in the room. Moving my weight from one foot to the other, I don't know what to do. If Christopher was in my arms at this moment, I would be tempted to walk straight out of that door, get the bus, and never come back here again. Hell, maybe I'd go straight to the airport and get the nearest flight back to the UK. Fuck these rich arseholes.

But what actually happens is that Alice sighs and hands the baby to Ethan after Rosie the maid hurries into the room to declare lunch is ready.

"We're eating outside," Alice says.

Maybe it's the understatement of the year, but something is off about her today. It's not so much of a mood swing but a personality swing. Yet again, spending time with Alice reveals more about why Ethan is the way he is.

We walk through the conservatory and out onto a patio near the pool. A large table is set with salad, cooked chicken, and bread rolls. Ethan places Christopher in his car seat and keeps him close to him and Alice on the other side of the table. My heart beats harder now. It's like they're trying to isolate me from my son. But Christopher will soon need a feed, so it won't last long.

Throughout the lunch, they continue to discuss ways in which to raise Christopher, ignoring all of my suggestions.

"There needs to be a good art department at the school," Alice says.

"He's going to be a businessman, not an artist, Mother," Ethan replies. "No son of mine is hawking his gaudy paintings around art festivals."

"Maybe Christopher can decide that," I say, but neither of them respond to me.

Rosie returns to the table sometime later and points at Alice's plate. "Would you like me to take that for you, madam?"

Alice glares at her. "Does it look like I'm finished?"

Rosie licks her lips and backs away. There's no surprise on her face, which makes me realise this is how Alice treats her staff regularly. I stare at her, trying to peel back the layers, but she's just like Ethan, keeping that poker face.

After lunch, Christopher begins to cry, and I take him through to the kitchen to feed. I find Rosie there washing dishes, and I smile shyly at her, arranging the cape across my shoulders to be discreet. We have a hard time. I'm tense, and Christopher doesn't want to latch. It takes a few minutes, but finally, we get it, and I begin to relax.

Then Ethan walks into the room, and my muscles clench again.

"Mom wants to know what's happening with your apartment." He leans against the counter, eyes lazily observing the maid cleaning up after lunch. He sips his beer, waiting for a response. I don't give him one.

Alice saunters in, clicking her fingers. "Rosie. Is it Rosie? Marie? Whatever your name is, you need to be careful with that wineglass." She regards me. "What are you both talking about?"

"Laura's apartment and how unsuitable it is," Ethan says. "It's time for her to move in with one of us."

"Actually, I'm moving in with Jessa," I say. "Her roommate moved out, and she has the extra space. I'll get my own room, and Christopher will have his own space too—"

"What?" Ethan's eyes burn through me. He slams the half-empty beer bottle onto the counter, and Rosie jumps in surprise.

"Ethan…" Alice trails off, her voice guarded. "Calm down."

He rounds on her, his eyes blazing. "Calm *down*? You want me to calm *down*?" He points an accusatory finger at me as though I'm on trial for murder. "She is moving in with that friend of hers. The bartender or waitress or whatever." He says it in a degrading way that makes it sound like any service-industry job is beneath him.

"Jessa is a bar manager. She has a steady job and a nice apartment. She's my best friend, and I need her."

"How many times have I asked you to move in with one of us?" Ethan shouts. "*We* are his family. Not Jessa."

"Ethan, I just would feel more comfortable at Jessa's. And she's like family to me," I say.

The atmosphere in the kitchen freezes. Ethan isn't just having a tantrum. As usual, he's livid, and adrenaline rushes through me. My body stills. All my attention focuses on placating him so I can get out of this situation.

"What's wrong with living with me, the baby's father?"

"You…" I trail off. The words get tangled in my mouth. I want to tell him he's overbearing, quick-tempered, and scary, but my gut instinct tells me to stay quiet.

Ethan shakes his head. He grabs a plate from the drying rack and smashes it against the tiled floor. The maid yelps and hurries out of the kitchen. Christopher startles, and milk spills down his cheeks and onto my dress. I pull him out from under the cape, carry him into the hallway, and load him into his car seat.

"What are you doing?" Ethan is right behind me, his breath tickling the nape of my neck.

I ignore him, fixing the strap of my nursing bra. After yanking the cape from my neck, I stuff it into my bag.

Alice appears in the hallway, somewhere in my peripheral vision. She places an arm on her son's shoulder. "Calm down. You're scaring them. Laura, stop. We've both had a little too much to drink. That's all."

But I'm shaking my head. She had opportunities throughout the lunch to allow me to speak, and she rejected me at every stage. Ethan blocks my way when I pick up the car seat and try to leave the house.

I turn to Alice. "You could have calmed him, but you didn't. You're behind him at almost every step, emboldening him to be like this. Ethan, get out of my way. I'll be in touch once I'm back in New York. However, it's clear that we cannot continue like this."

"Like what?" he asks, his voice dripping with a seething rage.

"It's not safe to be around you anymore," I say.

Ethan lifts a hand as though to slap me, but Alice catches it before he strikes. I quickly squeeze past them both and hurry out of the house. Thankfully, Alice never locked the door.

I know there's a bus station a few blocks from Alice's house. Both Christopher and my bag are heavy, weighing me down, but I need to get there as fast as I can. When I glance over my shoulder, I'm relieved to see that neither of them are following me.

After a few minutes, I start to relax. Alice must have convinced him to stay put. The intersection comes into view. There's a supermarket with a stop nearby, and the bus is already parked there. I pick up my pace, hurry up the three steps, and swipe my metro card at the last second before the driver closes the doors. There's just enough room to place the car seat down next to me, and I run a finger across Christopher's soft cheek. Thankfully, he's already fast asleep. The bus pulls away from the stop, and I exhale. We're free. For now.

CHAPTER 31

Three days pass without so much as a text message from Ethan or Alice. He's gone silent many times after an argument, but part of me did expect some grovelling this time. What happened at his mother's house felt different. Like a shift had occurred. I thought Ethan might sense that and try his best to cling on as I pull away from him.

During the three days of silence, I'm too busy moving to give the situation much thought. It's a welcome break from the constant worry of what Ethan might do next.

Jessa holds up a pale-blue lamp. "Where do you want this?"

Hands on my hips and a sheen of sweat across my forehead, I regard the bedroom and shake my head. "Oh, that goes on my night-stand, which the movers haven't brought yet."

"Oh." She frowns.

"Just put it in the corner for now."

"Cool." Jessa shrugs and sets it down.

"This place is so great, Jessa," I say. "Thank you so much."

"Thank my granny," she says. "I inherited it from her. Otherwise, I'd never be able to afford an apartment this size."

I look up at the ceiling, pressing my palms together. "Thank you, Granny Chen."

Jessa bats my arm and laughs. "What else do you need help with?"

"Why don't we take a break? I'm exhausted." There's a box of unpacked books at my feet, and we've been doing this for hours. Every muscle in my body aches. But it's a good ache. Moving in with Jessa is the best decision I've made in a long time. "Christopher's napping. If you keep an eye on him, I'll order us some sandwiches from downstairs."

"Fantastic." Jessa stretches out her back. "Don't you just love the convenience of the city?"

"Yes, and the fact that you have a deli on the bottom floor of your apartment building helps too. I don't know why I didn't move here sooner."

Twenty minutes later, I return with a toasted bagel with avocado for me and a turkey-and-cream-cheese one for her. We plop down in front of her TV, and Jessa clicks on a true crime show. Soon, we settle in, forgetting all about the unpacking. Of course, the husband of the murder victim turns out to be a controlling man her family warned her about, and something about him begins to remind me of Ethan.

I look at Christopher and his precious pink cheeks. His eyes move under the closed lids, and I wonder what his dreams involve. The purple bunny, maybe, or his planets mobile. "Christopher deserves better than this mess."

Jessa's forehead creases. "Has something happened?"

"I ran away from Alice's house in the Hamptons."

"You ran away? What the hell?"

"Yeah, I was putting off telling you about it because it's so bizarre. I thought you might judge me." I scratch the back of my head.

"I would never!" she insists.

"Maybe 'judge' is the wrong word. I just didn't want to keep going on about my situation because it must be annoying for you." I pull in a deep breath and tell her all about the lunch.

Jessa picks at a piece of lettuce, avoiding my eyes. "What are we going to do about him? Because I'm getting scared of where this is going. What's his endgame?"

"To completely take over my life and Christopher's life." I pause and rub my fingers across my lips. "If it was just me, I'd get as far away from him as I possibly can. But it isn't just me, and even if I move, it won't stop him. Can you imagine? Ethan would never let me live. If I moved back in with Emily, he'd follow me. If I disappeared, he'd track me down. Besides, wouldn't that be kidnapping now? Legally, he has rights to his son. Even without his name on the birth certificate, he has a right to custody of Christopher. He even threatened to have a court ask for a DNA test." I shake my head. "I'm losing sleep over this. Every time I try to set boundaries, he smashes through them. But he's never hurt me or Christopher. The worst thing he's ever done is smash a plate. Do you think the screenshots I kept are enough to get a restraining order?"

"You won't know until you try," Jessa says.

"That would be the final nail in the coffin, wouldn't it? The days of Ethan being on his best behaviour would soon be over."

"Yeah, but he was never being his true self in those moments, was he?" Jessa says. "It's all part of the manipulation. Don't you think?"

"I don't know what to think anymore. I thought I could handle him. I thought he was just a whiny, entitled baby. I thought I could stay in control of this." I pull the sleeve of my top over my hand and worry the hem. "I grew up without a dad, and I didn't want that for my child. And in my head, it became more important for him to have a dad than a good dad. Now I'm beginning to think it's more important to have a good dad than any dad at all."

"I'm so sorry, Laura," Jessa says, pulling me into her shoulder. "Want me to kick his ass?"

The laugh is much needed.

Sitting up, I gaze at my son one more time. He's still fast asleep, blissfully unaware of my stress, and I thank God for that.

"I have an idea of what I want to do, but I need to know what you think first," I say.

Jessa pushes her foot against the floor to get the recliner to rock. "Go on."

"I want to tell Ethan that after his outburst at his mother's house, I'd prefer it, at least for a while, to have supervised visits. Tell him that he can't see Christopher on his own."

Jessa sucks in a sharp breath and wedges her hands between her thighs.

Her reaction isn't one I expected. "You don't think it will work."

"Honestly, I'm thinking it's time to go no-contact. Get that restraining order pushed through. Kick him out of your life."

"That feels nuclear," I say. "I'm not sure I'm ready for nuclear because I'm scared of Ethan's retaliation. Did you know his mother pulled some strings and got me a visa to stay in the country?"

She sits up straight. "What?"

I nod. "What other strings can she pull? Especially in the family courts. But maybe supervised visitation that I arrange through proper legal channels could work. Though I don't have a clue about any of that. And I have no money." I sigh. "I have to do *something*. I can't just carry on like this. And I don't trust either of them anymore."

Jessa hugs her arms around her chest. "You're right to be worried. I've seen Ethan's controlling nature firsthand at the hospital. The way he reacted about the baby's name was…" She raises an eyebrow. "Unhinged. So, if you need me to be there when you propose the idea, I will. Maybe it'd defuse some of the tension."

I stare at the ceiling. "Maybe I can word it to where it comes across as in his favour, to make it sound like he's getting the better end of the deal. He likes to get his way. I'll just start by offering him a definitive schedule of when he can see Christopher. I'll make it often enough that he won't think to question me. It gives me time to find a lawyer to help with restricting his access altogether."

"It's probably for the best right now."

I turn to see Christopher stirring in his swing. The one thing I know about Ethan is that I can't underestimate him. Every step matters when I need to keep my son safe.

CHAPTER 32

Ethan and I share some terse messages that are mostly businesslike. I often send him photos of Christopher between his visits, and I carry on doing that. Then I suggest he come to Jessa's flat on Saturday one week after the disastrous visit to the Hamptons. Christopher can be difficult in public spaces, and I feel more comfortable at home. Plus, Jessa will be here too. He agrees. Every one of his messages is cautious, almost formal, though he doesn't apologise this time. That catches my attention. Ethan has a tendency to apologise profusely after we have an altercation.

He agrees to the visitation schedule without the need for lawyers, which I'm thankful for. I'd had a horrible feeling I would end up begging Emily for a loan to pay for it all.

It's two p.m., and Ethan is cradling a sleeping Christopher. The room is quiet except for Jessa's large wall clock ticking away. Traffic noise filters in through the open window. Jessa appears as stressed as I feel, her posture rigid in her purple armchair. Alice is the only one who moves, constantly pacing back and forth, staring out of the windows, glancing at the sofa and coffee table. I feel like she's searching for something to criticise.

"Well, this place is much better than your last apartment," Alice says.

"Jessa has been so generous." I smile but sense it freeze on my face.

"Let me hold him," Alice says, reaching her arms out to lift Christopher.

Ethan's arms tense around the baby, and he shakes his head. There appears to be a rift between them today. Alice rolls her eyes.

"You're hogging him," she declares like a child not getting a turn with a toy.

"He's my *son.*" There's bitterness in Ethan's sharp gaze when he regards me. "And apparently, I can only see him on certain days, like I'm some kind of convict."

I open my mouth and close it again, choosing not to cause an argument. Jessa glances at me, her mouth tight with concern. Even though no one has raised a voice, every ion of my being wants to walk over to Ethan, take my son, and never let him touch Christopher ever again.

"How's the shacking up going between you two?" Ethan asks.

There's a hint of resentment and an innuendo there.

"We're not shacking up," I tell him. "But it's going very well, thank you."

"No?" Ethan smirks. "So, you're not plotting against me every chance you get?"

"Stop being so irrational, Ethan. Just enjoy the visit with your son," Alice says.

She's certainly in the mood to criticise her son today. Yet again, I find myself analysing their dynamic. She either infantilises him to the point of making him think he's a prince, or she tears him apart. Against my will, I pity him.

"It would be better if I weren't sitting in this stranger's house being watched like a hawk every time I move a single muscle," he says.

"Jessa isn't a stranger," I remind him.

Ethan glares at me. "She is to me."

"She's like Christopher's aunt, so you'll have to get used to it," I say.

"That's because you only care about what's best for you and not the baby!" he snaps.

"Keep snapping at me, and this visitation is over," I say.

Alice steps over to Ethan again. "Be careful with his neck, darling." She reaches for Christopher.

Ethan stands abruptly, and I flinch. He turns to his mother with a callous expression. "Don't tell me how to hold my own baby."

She changes tack. "Binky, you're a *wonderful* father. Babies just have soft necks. You have to do exercises to help them strengthen those muscles." She looks at me. "Are you doing those exercises, Laura?"

"Yes, I give him 'tummy time,'" I say.

"Hmm." Alice narrows her eyes as if she doesn't believe me but doesn't comment further.

Ethan plops back down on the sofa, and Jessa eyeballs me, just as shocked as I am.

"Please be gentle, dear," Alice says.

"Actually, I'd like you to be gentle too," I say. "Moving around like that can't be good for him."

Ethan draws out an exaggerated sigh.

"He looks *just* like you." Alice gives him a beaming smile. It at least breaks the tension.

I don't think he looks anything like Ethan, and I'm thankful for that, but I don't dare say otherwise.

After another agonising thirty minutes, they finally hand over the baby and leave. Ethan tells me he'll call me later to make more arrangements for scheduled visits, and I agree. He doesn't want to leave before he has confirmed dates for the next few days, which I also agree to. It's going to be a hard road, but at least we're coming to a solution to ensure my baby has a father, but Ethan can't continue overstepping boundaries.

"That went well, I think." Jessa closes the door behind them.

My jaw unclenches, and I rub it, realising how hard it's aching. "It could have been worse," I admit.

"You weren't kidding about Alice, though." Jessa clicks her tongue and shakes her head. "Wow."

I laugh. "I know. She's a piece of work."

"They both are. Did you hear the comment—"

"Shacking up." I nod.

"Asshole."

She takes Christopher for a snuggle, and I'm infinitely calmer watching my son in her arms than his father's. My body relaxes, like someone just loosened the strings pulling me tight.

* * *

"You know, I don't think you're going to need me anymore," Allie says, making her way to the door.

"I don't know about that. We still have our difficult days."

The consultant shakes her head. "It's like I'm visiting a completely different mother and baby. You have so much more confidence, Laura. You're going to be just fine."

There's a prickling sensation in my nose like I'm going to cry, but it's from relief, not sadness.

"But you can still give me a call if you need me," she says.

I open the door for her and wave her off into the hallway. Just as I'm about to close it and head back to Christopher, a man wearing a delivery uniform waves to me.

"Are you Laura McAdams?"

"Yes…" I trail off, apprehensive, too caught off guard to ask him who wants to know first.

"I have a delivery from an Ethan Hart," he declares and holds out the papers for me to take.

"Oh." I frown. "Okay."

"I'll need your signature here," he says, passing me a clipboard and a pen. I notice that the document says *Notice of Service, delivery, and recipient confirmation signature.*

"What is this?" I ask.

"Court papers, ma'am." His lips pinch together as though he has to deal with difficult people all the time and he's preparing for an argument.

"For what?"

He shakes his head. "I'm just the messenger."

"What if I don't sign them?" I ask.

"I can still confirm they were hand delivered, so it won't make much difference." He shrugs.

I shove the pen and clipboard back at his chest. "Well, I'm not signing them."

My heart is pounding as I close the door and hurry over to the sofa. Before I rip open the envelope, I make sure to check on Christopher, but he's wriggling around in his floor gym.

"Please don't let this be what I think it is," I say quietly to myself.

My fingers tremble as I tear open the envelope. At the top-right section of the first page is a civil lawsuit docket number, then my and Ethan's names are printed in the top-left corner. I skim quickly through the rest of the document.

Ethan is suing me for custody of Christopher.

CHAPTER 33

My mind drifts to my many lunchtime meetings with Ethan as I scan the restaurant. We're at a place chosen by him, so it's a long subway ride from Jessa's apartment and fancier than I would like. Ethan is stabbing away at his chicken salad. It surprised me that he agreed to this, and it's definitely my last-ditch attempt at reaching a compromise. The truth is I'm afraid to go up against him. We've reached the point I've been afraid of since this whole thing started. While I have many advantages on my side—I'm the primary caregiver, I'm still breastfeeding, and I've provided a decent home for Christopher—Ethan has advantages too. He's rich, he has connections, and I feel like he's going to keep dragging me through the system until he gets what he wants.

Unless I can get him back on my side. Is that even possible? There's only one way to find out.

"Thanks for agreeing to meet me for lunch to talk things over." I smile, hoping it might soothe some of the hostility between us.

"Why wouldn't I?" He places his fork down on the plate and shrugs nonchalantly.

"Well, I didn't know what to think when I got served those papers."

He leans back in his chair and adjusts a shirt sleeve. Today, he strikes me as a man completely in control, someone about to confidently take over a business meeting. "That was nothing against you,

Laura. It's just how the court system works. I aim to make sure I get what I want, and it's a surefire way to ensure I do exactly that."

His cocksure attitude makes my stomach flip. I gaze down at the soup in front of me, my appetite completely gone. "Wouldn't you rather we sort this out together than in the courts?"

"We're talking in person now, are we not?" Ethan grabs his fork.

Before I can answer, my phone dings, and I see that Jessa has sent me a selfie of her and Christopher. She's beaming into the camera while Christopher sleeps bundled in her arms.

"Can I see?" Ethan asks, noticing me looking at the picture.

I slide the phone to him, and he grins. "Our boy is so cute, isn't he?"

"He is," I agree. "And that's why I want to keep this civil, Ethan. Because of Christopher. Because there's so much at stake. If we can reach an agreement here today, would you be willing to drop the custody suit?"

He's quiet as though he's contemplating this.

"We both know you would never win full custody," I tell him. "I met with a lawyer, and he told me it's incredibly rare for a baby less than six months old to be removed from the mother. I'm still breast-feeding, Ethan."

"I'm aware," he says. "It's not what I want either. But at least this way, I get to request a paternity test and can at least prove in the eyes of the law that I'm the father. You not putting me on the birth certificate denies me that."

"But I'm already agreeing to joint custody. Why do you need to drag me through the courts and drain my money to prove that? It makes no sense."

"I don't think I'm being unreasonable," he says.

I soften my voice again, pandering to him in the same way his mother does. "I understand. You have a right to spend time with him. I'm not trying to take that away from you. I thought things were going well with our arrangement."

Ethan's eyes narrow. "How could you possibly think that? You won't even let me be alone with him."

I choose my next words carefully. "Well, there are reasons for that."

"Not legitimate ones."

"Ethan, you have shown signs of an aggressive temper. You have a controlling nature. These are all factors that brought me to this decision. I'm just trying to look out for Christopher's safety."

"And you think I'm not capable of keeping my own flesh and blood safe?" He jabs the fork at me then throws it down on the plate.

"I didn't say that—"

"You didn't have to. You just went behind my back and made up these asinine rules about when and where I can see my son, and never by myself. How are we supposed to bond if you're always hovering over my shoulder, wincing if I pick him up wrong? You say *I'm* the controlling one. Laura, I think it's time for you to take a cold, hard look in the mirror."

The words sting. I flex my hand and clench it, keeping my emotions in check. "I'm reacting to your behaviour, not setting the tone. You did that the morning after we first met—"

"And you'll never forgive me for it, will you?" He shakes his head, turning away.

"No," I say. "I won't. Because you harassed me, and now you're the father of my child, and I have to deal with that. Nothing about this situation is going to change, and all I can do is stop you from controlling me and my son." My voice wobbles, and shame washes over me. So much for keeping my emotions in check.

Ethan reaches down to lift something out of his briefcase. It's a printout of a Google search. He hands it over to me as if he's just won the lottery and wants to rub it in my face.

"What's this?" I take the sheets of paper and spread them out on the table.

On the paper, in the search bar, is a postnatal depression search I googled recently. The date is there, as are the search results that popped up after I hit the search button. The pages after that all are from links I clicked, doing my research on the topic.

When I raise my gaze to Ethan's, he's smiling.

Frost creeps across my skin. "How did you get this?"

He's silently smirking, back in control, back where he wants to be.

"You can't present this in court," I say. "You obviously obtained it through illegal means."

"I can, and I will." He pauses, debating. "If I have to."

"I didn't give you permission to access my computer like this. It's a breach of privacy."

Ethan snatches the pages from my hands and places them back in his briefcase. "Laura, you brought this on yourself. Everything was going fine until you told me I can't see my son alone. I'm not some dog you need to watch over. I'm a grown man. I don't require a babysitter."

"Yes, but it's different when it comes to—"

He brings up a hand to shush me. Frustratingly, it works. I shut up, embarrassed.

"This was a mistake," I mutter. "I have to go." The restaurant feels unbearably hot. My knees wobble as I rise. When did he go through my internet search history? Have I ever left him alone long enough? Maybe that time in the shower, but I was ten minutes at most.

Ethan glances at my plate of unfinished food then back at me. "You didn't eat the rest of your chicken—"

"I've lost my appetite," I say.

Before I lose my nerve, I march out of the restaurant. I don't bother to pay my half either. Let him foot the bill if he wants to be in charge of everything.

Once I'm on the street, I take a deep breath and round the corner. I need to put some distance between me and Ethan. Walking fast helps me burn off some of this pulsing adrenaline. Somewhere between the restaurant and the subway station, I remember my own contingency plan. I hurry over to a bench to sit for a few moments, checking around me to make sure Ethan hasn't followed me here. Then I scroll through the screenshots on my phone.

I go all the way to the beginning, through recipes and saved Tweets and a hundred other inconsequential files. *What the hell?* Every time Ethan has harassed me via text or email, I've saved a screenshot. None of them are in my phone. I scroll desperately through my messages, searching for the originals, taking my chat with Ethan all the way back to when we first met. They're gone.

He got to my phone too.

I'm on that bench for about thirty minutes, checking every possible storage option, my inbox, my files, my Dropbox folder, and my spam folder, and I find nothing. Every time I've left him alone with my phone, he's tampered with it. And now he has dirt on me, and I have nothing to prove his controlling, possessive nature. Nothing.

CHAPTER 34

On a train that smells like urine, I reach my lowest point. Whatever comes next isn't going to be easy. It's going to be harder than anything I've experienced before. There's a half-finished manuscript on my laptop, waiting for an ending, but right now, I couldn't say what it will be. Ethan has money and some dodgy evidence he obtained illegally, whereas I have nothing.

I lean back against the seat, resting my head against a window. The one source of comfort is knowing that babies as young as Christopher are almost never taken away from their mothers. He needs me. The subway brakes screech to a grinding halt. This is my stop. My legs wobble as I pull myself up and step onto the platform.

People swarm me, and the stench of the subway is cloying at the back of my throat. It's too hot down here. I desperately need the feel of a cool breeze on my skin. Once I hurry up the steps, I finally find myself breathing in fresh air.

There's an ache in my chest, like my ribs are slowly impacting. Ethan has accessed my computer and phone somehow. I left him alone when I was in the shower, and that may have given him time to do one of those things. I can't imagine he had the time to do both. But he gave me my new laptop. My blood runs cold. He gave me a new laptop, and that means there could be software installed to track my Google searches—keystroke software.

I feel sick. He's been ahead of me this whole time because he's been playing dirty. He knows everything I've searched for online since he gave me that computer. Every time I've checked flights to Manchester when daydreaming of leaving New York. Every lawyer I've researched. He must know how much money is in my bank account and the fact I can't afford the best. I can't even afford the mediocre.

He knows everything. He's been spying on me.

What if he arranged the break-in? Everything bad that has happened to me has benefitted him. Losing my job. Being robbed. Both things destabilise my life so that he's one step closer to controlling me. I need to get home and hug my baby. I need to see him.

I fire off a message to Jessa, letting her know I'm on the way back. By the time I round the corner to her apartment building five minutes later, she still hasn't responded to my text. My heart starts to pound.

This is ridiculous, I remind myself. There's no reason to feel anxious. Jessa is great with the baby, and I have nothing to worry about. She could be changing his diaper or making herself a snack. Her phone might have run out of battery.

I head into the lobby of the building, and worry blooms in the pit of my stomach, unfurling slowly, poisoning my blood. It gets worse as I travel up to her floor. I'm so nauseated I think I might throw up. There's one question circling around my head—why did Ethan agree to meet me? If he's the kind of man who broke into my apartment, installed tracking software on my new computer, and deleted files from my phone, then there's no way in hell he would agree to a compromise.

So why did he agree to meet with me?

I unlock the door and step into a silent apartment.

"Jessa?" I call out. "I'm back."

I step into the room with feet like concrete weights. There's no sign of her or Christopher, but his soft-blue blanket has been abandoned halfway across the lounge carpet. A half-empty bottle of milk sits on the coffee table next to it.

"Jessa!" My voice is urgent now, insistent. Instinct takes over, forcing me through the apartment as quickly as my pulse pounds.

Christopher's room is empty. My bedroom is empty. The lounge is empty.

"Jessa, please answer me!"

Adrenaline spiking my blood, I turn to the one bedroom I haven't checked yet, Jessa's room at the end of the hallway. The door is open a crack. There's a large window in her room, and it extends across one wall, making it one of the brightest in the house. Silvery light filters out into the dark hallway. I push the door open with my palm, and the door drags across the thick carpet.

I gasp. Jessa lies facedown on the floor, her legs sprawled out, with her arms tucked underneath her chest.

I run over to her and drop to my knees. "Jessa! Can you hear me?"

Before I try moving her, I call 911, and while I wait for them to answer, I push two fingers beneath her chin, searching for a pulse. She's alive. Relief floods through me.

The operator tells me not to move her but to keep an eye on her pulse.

"Do you know if she collapsed or whether she was hurt?"

I lean over my friend, examining the sticky, matted mess of her hair. Blood. "I think… I think she's been hit."

Before the operator can say another word, I'm on my feet, running through the apartment.

"Talk to me," the voice on the line says. "What's happening? Is there an intruder in your apartment?"

I don't answer. I'm rushing through every room, searching the floor, under beds, in cupboards, showers, anything and everything. Then I hurry back to Jessa's room once more to check.

"My baby is gone!" I scream. "They took my baby!" *They*. The word falls from my mouth before I understand the meaning. Ethan and Alice took him. They planned this. I was never going to win, and they were never going to compromise. It was always going to end like this.

PART III

CHAPTER 35

The salmon-coloured office walls remind me of undercooked scrambled eggs. I blink away from them, repulsed. Beneath the woollen jumper I'm wearing, my stomach complains. The jumper hangs from me, no longer snug against my skin. There's no fat on my bones anymore. Grief wore it all away.

Lucas scratches his forehead with the top of his pen. This is our first meeting, and I worry I've made a mistake, that he's too young and inexperienced to find my son. But there's comfort in his calming brown eyes, and on the phone, he expressed an enthusiasm for the case, unlike the last guy I hired. That old codger had lost the love of the job long ago and clearly seemed to be going through the motions.

Behind Lucas is a large diploma encased in an expensive-looking frame. *University of Miami, bachelor's in criminal justice.* On his desk is a half-empty coffee mug reading, *Private Detective life is a mood forever.*

He catches me looking at the mug and grins. "A gift from my niece."

"Ah." I nod, offering a polite smile.

"So..." Lucas trails off, leaning into the back of his roller chair. It emits a squeak as he rocks back and forth. "The purpose of this meeting is for me to obtain as much information as possible and figure out where we are and where we need to be."

My spine straightens, and I cross my legs before clasping my hands over my knees. "Okay, I can do that."

"I aim to make myself familiar with each client's case that I take on." He holds eye contact, which I appreciate. "The more background I have, the better I can be of service to you."

"Right." I draw in a deep breath. "Like I mentioned over the phone, the father of my son disappeared with my baby, Christopher, six months ago, and so far, the police have no leads." A familiar anger surges through my veins. Fuck Ethan. Fuck Alice. Once I have Christopher back, they can rot in hell.

"I'm so sorry," he says. "I lost a daughter two years ago. There's no pain like it."

I wasn't expecting that. The sudden sense of torment emanates from him in the tensed jawline and downcast eyes. It thuds into my chest, sending a wrecking ball into my ribs.

"I'm so sorry," I say. "How did your daughter die?"

"Leukaemia," he says. "She held on as long as she could, but it… it ravaged through her."

"May I see a picture of her?" I ask.

His face lights up. He grabs his wallet from his trouser pocket and pulls out a photograph of a sweet brown-haired child sitting on a rainbow bedspread. She's wearing pyjamas covered in penguins.

"She was lovely," I say, wincing at the past tense. Lucas takes it in stride.

"She was," he replies. He smiles fondly at the photograph and places it back in his wallet. "Can I see Christopher?"

I grab my phone and scroll through my pictures, searching for a good one. "I want to get some printed out but…" I trail off, my voice breaking.

"I understand," he says.

The thought of printing out pictures of Christopher makes me feel as though he's never coming back or that I've given up hope he'll ever come back. I shake the thought away and show Lucas an image of Christopher laughing in his swing. His red, wet lips are pulled back to reveal gums, his eyes crinkled, his soft hair fluffed up from play.

"Beautiful. And now that I know him, this is personal." He meets my gaze. "Laura, I will find your son. You and him will be reunited. Now, tell me everything you know."

I explain what it was like returning home from that lunch to find Christopher gone. Ethan was never seen after the lunch, aside from sightings on a few New York streets by eyewitnesses. Alice was not at her house in the Hamptons. She'd grabbed supplies from her house and run—with my baby.

Poor Jessa never saw it coming. Alice turned up to her apartment with a lie about how I was hurt, and she needed to make an urgent phone call. Jessa never expected Alice to whack her over the head with a wrench she'd brought from her own house. The police found it tossed in the bins at the back of the apartment building, with Jessa's blood on one end and Alice's fingerprints on the other. They had no intention of covering this up. They grabbed my son and got out as fast as they could.

The whole thing was frenzied. As though they had limited time to do what they needed to do. I've often thought that and wondered why they didn't take their time to plan the kidnapping.

"The police looked into security and surveillance footage from around where I lived at the time. They checked airport security cameras and pulled CCTV tapes from gas stations along the route that Ethan would likely take to the airport, but so far, there's been nothing. They looked at JFK, Newark, LaGuardia, even went as far up as the county airport in White Plains. They checked interstate toll cameras, too, just in case they went to another airport in Philadelphia or Washington. Nothing. They came back empty-handed."

Lucas's forehead wrinkles, and his eyebrows knit, bridging together. "No footage of them at all?"

I shake my head. "It's like they just vanished."

I stare at my hands cradled in my lap. "It's been an exhausting six months. I haven't been able to sleep or eat much. I have no energy. My bones are tired. All the life has been sucked out of them. My muscles ache all the time. I'm such a mess that I'm on medication now."

"Hey, if you're a mess, me too. I've taken pills for anxiety for years. And yet I'm still the best private detective in this city." He smiles.

"You'd better be," I say, letting out a small laugh. It feels good. "My best friend has memory-loss issues after this. Plus, she's traumatised. One moment, she was babysitting a sweet baby. The next, his grand-mother is knocking her out with a wrench."

"Jesus, these people," Lucas says.

I shake my head. "You have no idea."

"What else can you tell me?" he asks.

I think about that for a moment. "Well, they must have tossed their mobile phones and bought new ones because the police are having a hard time tracing the originals."

"Did they leave everything behind?"

"Mostly, yes. They took essentials for Christopher, like onesies, diapers, and so on."

"What about cell phone records? I didn't see that part when I checked through your file. It was kind of bare, but I'll do my best to get what documents I can if I take your case."

"They pulled the records, but they can only show when calls and texts were sent and received. They can't delve into a deeper forensic analysis of the phones until they find them. And all their phone contact ceased two days before they stole Christopher."

"You were at a meeting with the father at the time, correct?"

"Yes. I was having lunch with him to see if we could come to an agreement on custody. Ethan was at the point where he'd filed a petition for custody."

Lucas lifts an eyebrow. "Well, I can understand why you didn't want these two around your child."

I nod. "I left the lunch prematurely because I became upset with Ethan. He turned up to the lunch with a printout of my Google searches."

"He what?"

"Before I gave birth, I was robbed. My laptop was stolen. Ethan very generously gave me a new laptop."

"Shit," Lucas says, his eyes drifting towards the window. "Did he install something on it?"

"Keystroke-tracking software."

He shakes his head. "Go on."

"After I left the lunch, I also realised he'd deleted screenshots from my phone. I'd kept some of his unpleasant text messages from him. In case…" My voice cracks. "In case I had problems with him down the line. The thing is, I knew… I knew he wasn't a good person, but I never thought he was this dangerous."

"It's okay," he says. "He did this to you. It's all his fault, and you're not to blame."

I let out a humourless laugh. There's no way I won't blame myself for the rest of my life if I never see Christopher again. "After that, I went home and... Well, you know what I found."

Lucas reaches for a box of tissues and hands them over to me. I take one and give him a sheepish thank-you.

"And Jessa, can she remember anything that happened from that day?"

"She remembers Alice coming to the door, panicked, insisting that there'd been an accident and I was in hospital. She wanted my aunt's phone number to contact her. Of course Jessa let her in. She wouldn't have if it hadn't sounded like an emergency, but neither of us had any idea what they were capable of. I think Jessa went into her bedroom to get her address book with my aunt's details, and that's when Alice hit her from behind." I cover my mouth with my hand. "Jessa could have been killed. It was awful."

Lucas frowns and taps the edge of his pen against the surface of his desk. "What else have the police said?"

"Not much." I shrug. "I tried to get the media to put pressure on the police, but it went nowhere. Ethan's family have connections. They're rich. When the news outlets reported on this, they made it come across as though Ethan had been forced to take the baby away from me. They never mentioned Jessa's violent attack. Instead, they called him "the father of the child" and mentioned him disappearing. That's about it." I blink my damp eyelashes up at him and dab the tissue under my eyes. "I'm so fucking sick of it. They have my *son*."

He nods. "Let's find him and bring him home."

I want to believe him. The prospect of touching Christopher's warm, round cheeks. Seeing his sweet smile and his eyes light up... It makes the hope inside me gleam brighter until it's practically glittering.

Christopher, I'm out here, and I'm searching for you. I love you. I will never give up on you. I will never stop until I'm breathing in your scent, my fingertips curling through your hair.

CHAPTER 36

The burger tastes like cardboard, and it isn't because I bought it from a drive-through. These days, all food tastes beige to me. But at least I'm eating. Sometimes, I forget. The ache in my stomach doesn't crave food. It wants nothing but my son.

I set my half-eaten burger on the wrapper, put it on the passenger seat, and place the Diet Coke in my cupholder. Then, through the binoculars I bought from Target, I watch the family inside the house. The lights are on, giving me an excellent view. A tall man with broad shoulders and dark hair jogs upstairs with his back turned to me so that I can't make out his face. Soon after, a woman, petite with long brown hair, glides up to the second floor with a baby on her hip.

My heart skips a beat. How old is the baby? Seven months, like Christopher? I lean forward, towards the windscreen of my car. *Christopher? Is that you?* But no. This baby looks close to Christopher's age, but aside from common baby features, there's no likeness. Their baby has a dusting of fine red hair across the scalp. I take the binoculars away from my face and lean back, sighing hard. For a moment there, I thought all of this would be over, just like that. As easy as that.

I swallow hard, thinking about what it would be like if I did see him in a house or on the street. That's if I recognise him at all. Six months is a long time for children. They change so quickly. The thought of me passing by my own baby boy makes my stomach roil.

I take a deep breath and shove the binoculars up against my eye sockets again, scanning the house windows. There's no movement. The family must have gone upstairs. I pan the higher windows, but the blinds are all shut. They're probably reading a book to their sweet baby or singing him or her a lullaby.

Alice owns this house. The family inside rent it from her. I'm in Connecticut, desperate for information. I've already tried talking to the family renting the property, but they wouldn't help me. I can't shake the feeling that they know something. They could be hiding the Harts inside that house, keeping my baby from me.

I place the binoculars in my lap and take another bite of my tasteless food. It's not lost on me that camping outside of a house is desperate. But this is the only lead I have, and I need to do something.

Moving the binoculars back to my eyes, I check the windows again. A shadowy figure stands in one of the upstairs windows and then disappears into the dark. I sink down into my seat. The person looked right at me, like they saw me. But even with the binoculars, I couldn't make out their features. The room was too dark.

There's a chance they saw me, though. Perhaps I didn't park far enough away from the house. The curtains close abruptly, blocking my view. Whoever it was—maybe the father of the family—saw me watching and reacted.

I run a hand through my hair, tired, bloated from the burger, and ready to give up for the night. But as I'm about to turn on the ignition, a dark, hooded figure appears by my window. A pale fist beats against the glass. My elbow hits the steering wheel as my body starts.

"Laura?" a muffled male voice asks.

I pause, my finger hovering over the ignition switch.

"It's Detective Bill Henderson." He presses his gold-plated badge against the window.

I sigh and brush shaking fingers against my sweaty forehead. When I roll the window down, Detective Henderson clamps a hand over the door and gives me a disapproving look through the shadows.

"We've talked about this," he says. "You shouldn't be here."

"Then arrest me."

Bill Henderson has salt and pepper in his beard, and whenever he's forced to speak with me, he sounds weary. "You can't be spying on Alice Hart's rental properties anymore. I thought we had an understanding."

I wipe my hands with my napkin, unable to look him in the eye. "I know they've got a baby in there."

He shakes his head. "And you know it's not Christopher in there."

He's right, but I don't feel like admitting it. "How can we be sure of that?"

"Because neither Ethan nor Alice is stupid enough to abduct a baby and then leave him with the renters."

"Isn't hiding in plain sight smart?" I shift closer to the detective. "Look, I know you think I'm crazy, but no one saw them leave the country, right? They haven't used their passports, been in an airport, or driven across any borders. So how are they living without being seen?" I glance at the house. "What if there's some sort of secret room in one of these rentals? What if Alice and Ethan are holding these people hostage?"

"We've questioned all the renters at all the properties. We've searched all the houses too. These are things you know. They aren't hiding anything, your baby included."

"Yes, but things could have changed between then and now..." I trail off, the argument dissolving on my tongue.

Bill stands up straight, removing his hand from the door. He's shaking his head, his expression adamant. "Why don't you let us do our jobs, okay?" His voice is gentle, but his face means business.

"Can you at least perform an updated sweep of the properties? Just to make sure?"

"I can't without cause. Not without a warrant."

"You had one before," I point out.

"Yes, but to request another one, we need more cause, a lead, something to give the judge a reason to grant another warrant. There have been no leads or suspicious activity to prove this. We can't use the same warrant. We'd have to get another one."

It's so frustrating that I want to scream. But it's not Bill Henderson I want to scream at. It's Ethan and Alice and anyone who has helped them steal my son.

"Can't you walk up and talk to them? See if they're acting strange? Just see if they've talked to Ethan or Alice?"

Bill thinks a moment. "I can do that."

I sigh with relief.

He watches me for a moment. "But you have to promise me something."

"What?"

"That you'll stop stalking these rental properties. You're going to get yourself in trouble."

"Okay," I say. "I'll stop doing this." The words come easy to me because I don't take them seriously. I'll do whatever it takes to get my son back, and if that includes "getting into trouble," then so be it. Even with Lucas Garcia helping me, there've been no leads for months. Why should I trust these men to find my baby?

"Go home, Laura," Bill says.

"How will I know you've spoken to the renters?"

"You have my word," he says.

It's the best I'm going to get.

I start my car and put it in Drive. Another wasted night. I'm no better than the detectives. I have no leads, and despite how much I've tried to find new information over the last few months, I've come up empty. Alice, Ethan, and Christopher vanished without a trace.

CHAPTER 37

Before I know it, the next day has come and gone. Last night, when I snuck back into the apartment, Jessa emerged from her room, rubbing tired eyes, her shorts and T-shirt rumpled. It became my second lecture of the night and my second promise to not do this anymore. I collapsed on my bed, exhausted, emotionally drained, and didn't get up until long into the afternoon.

As soon as the sun begins to set, I make the two-hour trip up I-95 to Connecticut. These days, I don't even need GPS to help me find my way. It's second nature to me.

The fighter in me can't let go. I can't turn off being a mother just because my baby isn't here. This isn't a shift I can clock off from.

Here I am, breaking promises to Bill Henderson and my best friend. Promises I never had any intention of keeping. I park deliberately in the patch of darkness in between the streetlamps to conceal myself better in the shadows. I wait for movement inside or outside the house.

The engine is off, and the car is cold. It's quiet after eleven on a freezing January night. Most of the lights in the windows have been turned off. The occasional car creeps past, and I sink deeper into my seat like a recluse. I blend in well in my black Nissan Sentra. I upgraded after Christopher went missing. It's a lease but still out of my budget. It killed me to borrow money from Emily, but I needed to be able to get around better.

I don't usually come so late, but I want to know what happens after midnight. In the past, I've been too afraid to stay overnight in fear of being arrested, but just once, I want to keep an eye on this place long into the early hours of the morning. But I'm already exhausted. Fatigue makes my eyelids heavy. My neck lolls to the side. I straighten up and wind the window down, hoping the biting wind will keep me awake.

Eventually, my stinging eyes succumb to the exhaustion, and I doze off. I don't know how much time has passed when a hooded figure dressed in all black snaps me out of the trenches of sleep. A thunderous knock bangs against the side of my door.

"Bill, I'm sorry I—"

But it isn't Bill this time. Before I have time to react, a man dressed in all black reaches inside the car. Pitching my weight away from him, I try to escape my attacker's grip. But gloved fingers yank a cluster of my hair, tearing it from the scalp.

I scream, fumbling with the ignition button, but he yanks me back towards the window. Pain sears through my scalp like a spreading wildfire. The car door opens. I'm being dragged out. My legs skid across gritty pavement. I'm trying to scream, but he has one hand clamped over my mouth. I part my lips and bite down as hard as I can into his gloved hand. The man curses, releasing his hand, but his arm reaches back, and a moment later, it's crashing down on the side of my jaw.

The world turns upside down. Air leaves my lungs as a stinging pain vibrates through my jaw, pulsing to the back of my skull. Huge hands lock around my wrists, pinning me down. When I open my mouth to scream, he seizes my throat before the sound has time to leave my body. Tighter, harder, he squeezes and squeezes. I can't draw in any air. My lungs are starved. Fire spreads through my chest. I feel my eyes bulging from their sockets.

Christopher.

His name is a talisman, bringing me home. Refocusing myself, I kick out at the man, but he's using his knees to dig into my sides, keeping me immobilised. I raise my hands, attempting to claw his face, fingers digging beneath the balaclava he wears. I break skin. His DNA, whoever he is, is now embedded underneath my fingernails. If he kills me, at least the police have this.

He swats my hands away and zigzags his head to prevent me from lifting his mask. The world goes fuzzy for a moment. He tightens his grip again, and the fight starts to leave my body. I'm too weak. My muscles go slack, and my arms fall limp to my sides. The sound of my own choking voice will haunt my nightmares.

Behind him, there's a whirl of movement. Dark hair. Arms like tree stumps. Someone collides into my attacker like a bowling ball knocking down its last-standing pin. Finally, my attacker crumples to the ground with a grunt. I gasp for air, gulping greedily.

I sit up, watching the two men fight. My first thought is that someone walking by saw me being attacked and intervened, but when the streetlight illuminates my saviour's face, I see that it's Lucas. The attacker rises from the tarmac. Lucas attempts to rugby-tackle him to the ground, but whoever it is remains light on his feet, dodging the attack and disappearing into the shadows. The masked man finally ducks behind a house, melting into the shadows.

Panting hard, Lucas doesn't follow. He helps me to the pavement and lowers me gently to the curved ledge.

"Are you okay?" he asks, frowning.

I try to speak, but my throat is too raw. Lucas notices and uses the torch function on his phone to examine the wounds.

"I'm going to call an ambulance," he says. "What the fuck was that?"

I'd like to know myself, I think. Whoever it was wanted me dead. My first thought is obviously of Ethan. But I would have recognised his eyes and the shape of his body. The man attacking me was much taller and broader than Ethan.

Lucas removes his coat and places it over my shoulders. I hadn't even realised I was shivering.

"Take it easy," he says. "Everything's going to be okay. You're going to be just fine."

I'm not so sure. Ethan and Alice want my son, and they also want me dead.

CHAPTER 38

It's too cold in the interview room. I rub my hands across my arms as goose bumps prickle there.

After I had a quick checkup in the hospital, the doctor recorded the bruises on my neck and my two bloodshot eyes, and I insisted on discharging myself. I'll need to monitor myself and check for changes in my throat in case there are neck lesions the doctors didn't find. Ever since Mum died, I've hated hospitals, but I certainly couldn't bear being in the same hospital where I gave birth to Christopher. So instead, Lucas drove me to the police station to give my statement regarding the attack.

Beside me, Lucas reaches for his Styrofoam cup of coffee and takes a long sip. I do the same. It's been a draining experience, and I need the caffeine. But I have difficulty swallowing and almost cough it up onto the table.

"Laura? Are you okay?" Lucas asks gently.

I nod, placing the cup down.

Detective Henderson blinks at us from across the table. "I thought you were going to leave those houses alone."

"Well, I lied," I croak.

"Clearly." He lets out a whistling breath. "I hate that this happened to you, but I hope the reality of the situation is beginning to sink in, at least. The people who stole your child are not good people. And there are plenty of other bad people who may notice a woman sitting alone in her car at one in the morning." He sighs.

"I understand all that," I whisper. "But I'll take whatever risk I need to take in order to get my son back."

"That isn't really a statement you want to say to a police officer," Henderson says. "But I do appreciate this is hell for you. On the other hand, we don't want to leave your baby without a mother, now, do we?" He leans across the table. "Listen to me carefully, Laura. Your son isn't in any of those rental properties, and by staking out the place in front of them, you're doing nothing but putting yourself in danger."

"But there has to be a connection," I protest, glancing at Lucas for support. "Someone else doesn't want me watching those houses. The attack makes that abundantly clear."

The detective pushes a toothpick between his teeth and studies me. "How long were you out there watching the house before you got attacked?"

"I don't know," I admit. "I dozed off. I heard someone approaching the car. I thought it was going to be you giving me another reprimand."

Henderson's upper lip twitches as if it wants to curl into a smile, but his mouth won't let it happen.

"If it makes you feel any better, I'm not sure I want to go back to that place now," I say. "So you don't have to worry about me anymore." This time, I mean it.

I shudder at the memory of my assailant's gloved fingers pressing into my neck, squeezing the life from me. For the first time in my life, I genuinely thought I was going to die and never see my son's face again.

The detective swipes his hand across his chin and jaw. He leans back in his seat, sighing and giving me a look that says, "What am I going to do with you?"

"It does seem unlikely that a man dressed in all black and a mask would randomly come out of nowhere in the middle of a quiet residential neighbourhood and start attacking a random woman sitting in her car," Lucas adds.

"I'm aware of that," the detective says. "Something does feel off about what happened tonight." He turns to me. "Do you think Ethan Hart is capable of hiring someone to keep tabs on you? Watch your movements?"

"I wouldn't put it past him. He has the means," I say. "Honestly, it was my first thought, other than the fact I might die."

"Do you think that whoever attacked you meant to kill you? Or were they trying to scare you?" he asks.

My hand rises to my neck. I'd been shocked by the bruises, not because they were terrible to look at but for the opposite reason. I'd imagined myself black and blue, but strangulation doesn't always result in dramatic bruising. Instead, there are a few red marks but not much else.

"I thought I was going to die," I say. "I started to pass out, and he kept going. And it certainly wasn't sexual. He wasn't—look, he didn't want to take his time. He wanted it over and done with. It happened within minutes. He grabbed me, pulled me out of the car, pinned me down, and strangled me. There was no sense of enjoyment or anything like that. It was… businesslike."

Henderson swallows hard, squirms in his seat, and glances at Lucas. "What about you? How did you happen to get there so fast?"

"I'm trying to look out for her." Lucas's eyes pan to me, and he shrugs. "When I heard what she was doing, I decided to check up on her."

Even though it's slightly creepy that the private investigator I hired was watching me in the dead of night, I still give him an appreciative smile and nod.

"Thank God you showed up when you did," is all I allow myself to say.

There's no way I'm going to let myself cry in this room with one detective and one former detective watching me, but I'm close. It's almost dawn, and I'm exhausted, already worrying about collecting my car from the place I was assaulted.

I turn back to Henderson. "What are you going to do next?"

The detective sighs and rubs his fingers over his forehead. "I'll perform a neighbourhood sweep. I'll see if anyone has cameras they'll let us view. If the guy ran in front of the houses back there, we might get lucky with doorbell cameras and CCTV. I'll have my team search the area for clues and do interviews with neighbours who might become potential witnesses. But for now, I have your statement, we have the DNA from under your fingernails, and we have something to work with. If Ethan Hart did hire this motherfucker, chances are he messed up somewhere, and that could reveal another clue."

Lucas is first to stand, reaching across the table to shake hands with Detective Henderson. "Thanks so much, Bill. We'll be in touch if we hear anything or see anything suspicious. I suspect you'll do the same for us?"

Henderson gives one quick nod of his chin. "Absolutely."

A few minutes later, as we're stepping out of the station into a misty night, Lucas turns towards me. "How about we go get some real coffee? That stuff in there tasted like dirt water."

"Sure," I say. "Who needs sleep?"

He grins. "Not me. And by God, I don't think I could anyway. I'm still running on adrenaline. How about you?"

"I'm somewhere in between, about ready to crash," I say. "Every now and then, what happened hits me. But there's no way I could sleep."

He drives around until we find a diner that's open and order two coffees. Sitting across from me under the low-slung lights, with the laminated menus in front of us and the candy-apple-red plastic-encased seats at our backs, Lucas regards me with a hint of steel in his eyes.

"I think what we talked about at the station is right. Ethan hired a thug to scare you," he says.

The waitress wipes down an empty table. In the background, a sad country tune drawls from a jukebox in the corner. For some reason, I start to laugh. It's croaky and high-pitched, which makes it even funnier to me.

"What's funny?" he asks, frowning.

"Well, I'll take your postulation that he hired a thug to scare me, and I'll raise you. Ethan hired that man to *kill* me."

"That's not really funny, Laura," he says.

"No. It's ridiculous and terrifying, and I'm starting to lose it." All the laughter fades away, and I'm left with the terror of what happened to me. "Why would they want to just scare me? It seems more likely that they would want to finish me off completely." I run a finger along the rim of my coffee cup. "Lucas, that man was waiting for the last breath to leave my lips. He squeezed my throat with every intention of killing me."

"I know," he says, shaking his head.

"They want me dead. They want me out of the picture so they don't have to worry about me coming after Christopher. I feel it in every fibre of my body."

CHAPTER 39

J essa is upset with me. I can see it in the hollowed, darkened circles
under her eyes. I slip my keys in my purse and slowly pad to the
living room, where she's sitting, motionless, staring at the wall. A
halo of yellow light hovers over her head from the floor lamp.

I break the silence. "Hey."

Her gaze slowly turns to me. "Hey," she says flatly.

"Are you okay?" I sit across from her on the sofa and push my
hands between my thighs, taking a deep breath. The air between us is
tense and heavy.

Jessa's eyes flare. "I don't know. You tell me. Where have you
been?"

I don't say anything, and she rolls her eyes.

"I told you not to go to those houses, Laura. And now you're hurt?
Jesus! Did someone strangle you?"

My fingers flutter up to my neck. "You sound just like Detective
Henderson."

Jessa peels away from the recliner, straightening her body. "Yeah,
well, maybe that's for good reason. Maybe it's a sign that you should
listen to the people who care about you and don't want to see you get
hurt."

"I know," I say. "But none of that matters. He's my baby, Jessa. My
only child. And he's gone. And I don't know if they're looking after
him. I know nothing."

"Laura, listen to me. You're going to get yourself killed. Just like I nearly died because of being in your life. And now I have to sit back and watch you put yourself and me in danger again?" She sighs. "Look, you need to see this from my perspective. I wish you wouldn't be so stubborn about this."

"Stubborn about what?" I ask. I'm still wincing at her bringing up the attack. The thought that Jessa might have lifelong complications because she was helping me makes me feel sick to my stomach. It's one of the reasons why her cutting words make me immediately defensive.

She shakes her head. "Why can't you just let the police do their job?"

"Because they're not doing their job. You know that. I mean, do you see my baby son in my arms? Because I don't. My arms are empty. Fuck this. I'm going for a shower. We can talk about this later."

"No," she snaps. "I'm sorry, Laura, but if you're going to continue playing amateur sleuth, then I want you to move out."

"What?" I regard my best friend with complete shock. "Are you serious?"

She nods. "I've never been so scared in all my life. Every day, I forget things. Stupid things, like my mom's birthday or what time my doctor's appointment is or the name of my favourite bagel place near work. I forget these things because your baby's grandmother whacked me over the head with a wrench. It's because of you, Laura."

"Jessa, I'm so sorry—"

"I know," she says. "And I don't blame you for what happened." She gives me a tearful smile. "I love you like a sister and always will. But I can't keep living in fear because of what you're doing."

I wipe tears from my eyes and pull her into a hug. "I'm sorry. You're right. I should move out. I've put you through enough."

"You mean you won't give it up? The private detective and the house stalking?" She regards me, her eyes wide open in shock.

"I can't. I have to find him. I don't care what it takes."

She backs up a step. "Okay. Well, I hope it works out for you." She starts walking towards her bedroom, her movements slow, as though she's still in shock at my reaction. "There's no rush. For you moving out, I mean. Take your time."

"Thanks," I say.

As soon as I head into my bedroom and close the door, I know that a fundamental part of my friendship with Jessa just died. I also know that I won't be able to mourn that part of our friendship until everything with Christopher, Ethan, and Alice is resolved. I lie down on the bed, gazing at the ceiling fan as it whirls around, over and over. Exhaustion, fear, and sadness creep into every ion of my body.

Before I can worry about where I'm going to live, I fall asleep, still in my clothes. My sleep is thankfully dreamless, but when I wake, it's with a start. My stomach growls, and I head to the kitchen to make breakfast, noticing on the way that it's actually afternoon. The apartment is empty with Jessa at work.

I pour some cereal, make a cup of tea, and check my emails and messages for any news. It's what I do every time I wake up and usually all throughout the day too. There's nothing, not even a text from Lucas. After eating my cereal, I call Emily's number, craving her comforting voice.

"Hi, love," she says. "Any news?"

"Nothing," I say.

"What's wrong? Your voice sounds different."

"Oh, I just have a cold," I say.

"Are you okay? It sounds like more than a cold. Have you been crying, darling?"

"Actually, Jessa and I had a fight, and she wants me to move out."

"Oh," she says. "Well, I'm sorry to hear that. I always liked Jessa. What happened?"

I tap the side of the phone, suddenly realizing I might be about to receive the same lecture from my aunt that I did from my best friend. "Ever since Alice attacked her, Jessa has been scared of it happening again. And honestly, I don't blame her."

There's no answer on the other end of the line, just the sound of Emily's quiet breaths. Then she asks, "Are you in danger, Laura?"

"No," I lie.

"Do you need anything?"

I let out a long, sad sigh. "I hate to ask this…"

"Go on," she says.

"I'm running low on money. I was wondering if you'd be willing to help me out again."

She sighs. She doesn't answer right away. My pulse thunders in my temples.

"I think you should come home now, Laura. Back to England. I'd be able to help you and take better care of you from here."

"Do you think Christopher is in England?" I snap.

"No, but—"

"Then I'll stay where I am. And I can take care of myself."

"That's not what it sounds like to me." Her voice is gentle. "Do the police have any leads?"

"The police are useless."

"I may be able to send you a little bit of extra money if you're in a pinch," she says.

"I'm so sorry, Em," I say. "I know I'm letting everyone down—"

"What are you talking about?" she says. "There's no one at blame here except the two people who stole my nephew before I could even see him in the flesh." Her voice cracks.

"Thank you," I say. "I'm going to visit you, and when I do, I'll have Christopher in my arms. I swear it."

"I can't wait," she says. There's a long sniff on the other end of the line.

We tearfully say our goodbyes, and I hang up. I want to keep that promise, but the energy is draining from me. It's like I'm treading water, and the undercurrent is pulling me deeper, deeper down. How long until I drown?

CHAPTER 40

I force myself to lie low for at least a week. Jessa is right that I'm being reckless, and my throat needs to heal before I put myself out there again. The man who attacked me hasn't been found yet. He's still out there, waiting to hurt me. My dreams are dark, full of violent promises and the wail of a baby in pain. In one, I'm drowning in my car as snakes slither in through the open windows, wrapping around me, squeezing the air out of my lungs. I can hear Christopher screaming for me, but I can't get to him.

When not experiencing excruciating nightmares, I spend my time apartment hunting. It's looking unlikely that I'll find a place to live in alone. Not without a job. While I desperately want to spend all of my time looking for Christopher, I may need to pick up some work with flexible hours. Bartending or waitressing, perhaps.

I'm deep into an online search when my phone rings. I snatch it up immediately. "Hello?"

"Hey, Laura. It's Lucas."

I close my laptop lid. "Lucas, please don't take this the wrong way, but every time you call me, my heart explodes. Do you have any good news for me?"

"I definitely have news. You could call it a step in the right direction, perhaps."

"Oh?" As predicted, my heart thumps harder.

"I've met with some of Ethan's friends. The ones willing to cooperate and talk to me, at least."

"Okay," I say, cautiously optimistic based on his tone. "What did you find out?"

"He's got a few ex-girlfriends who were able to shed some light on his behaviour."

"Bitter ones?"

"Bitter enough that they didn't immediately hang up on me when I told them I just needed to ask a few questions about him."

"What did they say?" I grab my mug of tea from the coffee table.

"Collectively? They tell me he's a real jerk. Controlling. Manipulative. Always wanting to get his way."

"That sounds like Ethan. Does it help us, though?"

"It confirms it wasn't just you that had a problem with him," Lucas says. "I know it's a small thing, but it's better than nothing."

"Did any of them know Ethan had a son? Do they know where he might have taken Christopher?"

"Yes, some did know Ethan had a child. It sounds like the gossip about Ethan's son had spread through their world, which is that of the very privileged. But no. None of them had any idea about where he might have taken Christopher."

I sigh. "Can you give me any of their names?"

"Absolutely. Got a pen handy?"

"Hold on." I walk into the kitchen and snatch open the drawer beside the fridge. My shaking fingers fumble under a candle, a battery, a lighter, and a box of tape before I find a few neon sticky notes and a blue ink pen. "I'm ready."

Lucas lists names as I jot them down.

"What about Alice?"

"I spoke to some of her associates, but those leads didn't really get me anywhere. Either she kept her nasty side in check around them, or they are trying to protect her. Either way, it was a dead end for now, but I'm still working on finding out more about her. There's a tennis club Ethan attended in Connecticut if you want the name. I think it's members only, but you could try to scope it out. Perhaps get a day pass or something."

My pen hovers over the Post-it note, ready to jot down the information.

"And what about the man who attacked me?" I ask.

"Nothing yet, Laura. Sorry."

We say our goodbyes and hang up. My hand lifts to my neck, no longer ringed with red finger marks. I feel like a shell of my former self. But I have to keep going.

* * *

The Seaside Golf Resort in Greenwich, Connecticut, is awash in white, from the lilies planted outside the door to the shorts and polo shirts worn by almost every single person there, including the staff. The women wear strings of pearls and bright trainers. High, immaculate ponytails pull the skin around their eyes tight. They walk with their shoulders pulled back, bouncing on the soles of pristine tennis shoes. I try not to compare myself with them since I'm dressed in black leggings and scuffed trainers, sticking out like a sore thumb.

It's the middle of the day on Saturday, and the tennis club is packed. The women chatter as they stroll past me, not paying me a single ounce of attention. I'm surprised they don't stare. I thought I would attract attention, wearing the wrong outfit. But in a way, their obvious attempt to ignore me is as blatant as if they'd turned and looked right at my face.

The men are a different matter. I notice their eyes flick over to me, but the look is fleeting. I'm judged "not hot enough." Fine by me.

"Here's your day pass, ma'am." A bubbly woman with chestnut hair, also in a ponytail, smiles broadly as she hands over the lanyard that reads *Day-guest pass.*

"Thanks." I return her polite gaze and take the lanyard before slinging it over my neck like an ornament. "My fiancé is Ethan Hart. I plan on getting a membership, but I just want to try it out and see how I like it first."

The receptionist's eyes widen with recognition. "You're Ethan's fiancée? But… isn't he…"

She has obviously heard the news about Ethan's disappearance, but she doesn't want to say anything in case she has it wrong. I maintain my poise. I want her to think I might be sticking around for a while.

"Congratulations," she says, smiling thinly.

"Thanks. I'm in the middle of wedding planning now, and I'm *so* excited."

"Pardon me? You're Ethan's fiancée?"

Wow, he sure is popular around here, I think. I turn from the desk in response to the voice behind me.

Two women circle me like sharks on a blood trail. Their curious eyes size me up. They're quite obviously wondering who I am and why I claim to be Ethan Hart's fiancée. I'm looking for one specific ex-girlfriend Lucas told me about. Her name is Cynthia. He was with Cynthia for much longer than the others, so if there's anyone who knows him, really knows him, she's the one to try. Lucas told me her description and her routine at the tennis club. If she's a creature of habit like Lucas claims, I'm bound to find her around here somewhere.

I come face-to-face with a blond bombshell whose golden locks layer over her shoulders, flowing down across her collarbone like a waterfall of fresh-spun silk. Her eyes are radiant blue. But her fake tan is a bit overkill, making the straight row of white teeth between glossy lips even brighter.

Beside her is a woman with an ivory complexion and black hair that fans across one shoulder in waves. Both women look at me as if they want to eat me alive but not before they get all the juicy details about me first.

"I am." I nod.

"Wow." The women exchange a less-than-subtle look of surprise.

"Is there something I should be worried about?" I plant a mock-nervous expression on my face, giving them an anxious laugh.

"Well…" The dark-haired woman twirls a single strand of hair around her finger. "Not *really*."

"Why aren't you with him right now?" The other woman's platinum eyebrows knit in suspicion.

"What do you mean?" I maintain my breeziness, acting as if it's not out of the ordinary to play tennis without him.

"Isn't he on vacation?" the blonde asks. "I'm sure I heard something to that effect. I figured if you were his fiancée, you'd be with him." She purses her lips together into a "gotcha" smirk, but I'm already one step ahead of her.

"Oh, that's a business trip. Significant others weren't invited." I wave a dismissive hand, but inside, I'm dizzy, hoping she'll buy it.

She lets out a tinkling laugh. "Well, that's too bad for you, isn't it? I've heard Cabo is wonderful this time of year." She begins walking away, but not before I see her glance pointedly at my left hand, no doubt noticing I'm not wearing an engagement ring. She smirks to herself.

"I thought he was in France," the dark-haired one leans in and whispers to the blonde. "That's what I heard him telling Stefan. But then I read in the news…" She trails off, casting me a backwards glance.

I find the interaction with them both extremely illuminating. It doesn't matter to me whether they think I'm Ethan's fiancée or not. I just want to listen in on as much gossip about him as I can. Now I know that Alice and Ethan laid the foundation of their "vacation," no doubt spreading rumours about where they were going. France. Cabo. Wherever else they could throw the police off the right track.

I think about both options for a moment. Cabo is one of those places I heard about from TV shows like *90210* and *The O.C.* I believe it's in Mexico. Could that really be where he is? Or is that woman just full of it? Maybe she was lying, trying to catch *me* in a lie or trying to figure out how much I know.

The tennis racket I borrowed from Jessa slips around in my clammy hands as I make my way towards the courts. Low early-February sun casts a strong glow, and I squint. Cynthia plays on court three every Saturday throughout the winter. It's one of the indoor courts. My trainers squeak against the polished surface as I make my way through the main doors. There's one woman sitting alone on a bench, tying her shoelaces.

When I'm a few steps away, she looks at me and frowns. "You're not Mallory."

"Are you Cynthia Johnson?" I ask.

Her strawberry-blond curls bounce around her face, framing her chin. Her eyebrows bridge in confusion. "Yes."

I cut to the chase. "Do you know Ethan Hart?"

She slowly stands up, and I realise she's taller than I first realised. I lift my chin to maintain her gaze.

"I'm sorry. Do I know you?" she asks, grabbing her racket from the bench.

"No, but I heard you used to date Ethan. I'm in a relationship with him now, and I'd love to go to coffee with you and pick your brain about him."

The pink tinge to Cynthia's cheeks evaporates, and her gaze darkens. She tries to brush past me. "Excuse me. My partner is just arriving."

As if on cue, an older woman in a bob walks in carrying a bag.

"Cynthia, you ready?" she shouts from across the court.

"Yes!" Cynthia shouts, curls bobbing along on her shoulders as she walks away.

"Wait, please." The urgency in my voice seems to work. She stops in her tracks.

"What do you want from me?" she says. "I'm not the gossiping type, but if you are dating Ethan, then good luck to you. That's all I'll say." She turns her back to me again.

"I'm not dating him," I blurt out. "I had his baby. I'm the mother of his child. The child he kidnapped from me. Please, I need help. I don't know what else to do."

I narrow the space between us in an instant. I'm standing so close I can smell her perfume.

"His name is Christopher. He's just over seven months old now. Ethan took him from me because he didn't like the custody agreement we had."

"You…are the one he had a child with?" Cynthia looks thrown off now. But her expression softens.

I nod. "We weren't in a serious relationship. I became pregnant after a one-night stand with Ethan. He was nothing but difficult to deal with right from the start. His controlling behaviour kept escalating bit by bit until he stole my child. Does that sound familiar to you? Please. I just want my baby back. Whatever you can tell me about Ethan could help."

She turns towards the other player and then back to me. "I don't want to get into any trouble. There's really not much I can help you with. It's not like I know where he took your baby."

"I know," I say. "I don't expect you to know. But it seems as though you were in a relationship with Ethan for much longer than any of his other exes. That means you know him better. You might know more than you think. Please. The police aren't getting anywhere. I'm doing everything I can. All I ask is that you let me treat you to coffee—and that you tell me about who Ethan really is."

Cynthia holds up one finger to her tennis partner. The flush has returned to her cheeks, and she's still giving me that sceptical frown, but after I wait half a heartbeat, she relents.

"All right, one coffee. But I have to finish my game first. And not here. We have to go somewhere else."

I nod and step back towards the bench. "Thank you. That's fair. I'll wait. You can pick the place."

I've already been waiting for six months. I can wait another half hour. I just hope she has some of the answers I so desperately need.

CHAPTER 41

By the time Cynthia and I reach the café, it's almost four o'clock. Cynthia dons a pink cardigan that she pulls over her tennis outfit. Her posture is straight and rigid. She's not the friendliest woman in the world and regards me with caution. But I did see the sympathy in her eyes when I explained my situation.

"I'm sorry to turn up at your sports club. It's not a polite thing to do. I understand that," I say. "But I'm sure you can appreciate that this situation is desperate. And time sensitive." I'm trying to keep my voice calm. Cynthia says nothing, but her green eyes peer at me with curiosity. She's listening. She lifts her coffee cup and takes a sip.

"Basically, I'm at a loss about what to do. I don't know how to find Ethan."

"I'm assuming he changed his number?" she asks.

"Yes, and Alice too."

She gives a slight bristle, I notice, at the mention of Ethan's mother's name, but Cynthia keeps her poise.

"I'm sorry. I can't help you with that. I don't have their contact information," she says.

I can't help but smile. "I feel like we had a similar experience with Alice."

She sighs. "Well, she is one of a kind."

I raise my eyebrows. "She certainly is. I think being around his mother told me more about Ethan than he ever did."

She nods. "They had a toxic relationship."

"Right?" Something lifts inside my body. This is the first time I've had the opportunity to talk to someone who knows Ethan. "The way she mothered him. It was creepy. Sycophantic one moment, overly critical the next."

"She shaped that man into the spoiled misogynist he is." Cynthia's expression tightens.

"You've no idea how good it feels to hear someone else say that." I lean back in my chair. "Guess where I met him."

She shrugs.

"I met him at a women's march."

A bark of laughter emits from Cynthia. It's chest deep and genuine. She leans over her coffee, and I find myself doing the same, joining in her laughter.

"I'm sorry," she says, straightening up. "That's not funny. This man stole your child."

"He did," I say. "But it's still funny. Fucking terrifying too. Ethan Hart is a manipulator. He's so good at pretending he isn't a threat. He even threw me off with a box of homemade muffins, for God's sake. This is exactly why I wanted to meet with you. I need to get inside his head."

"I don't know what I can tell you except for the fact I can't stand the man or his hippy-bitch mother." Her hands flex. "What about the police?"

"They are doing all they can, which isn't much when they don't have a clue where he is."

Cynthia's forehead wrinkles. "What about a private investigator?"

"I have one. Within my budget anyway. I'm not from your world."

"Well," she says, "Ethan is smart. He knows what he wants out of life. He's the driven type. Always has been."

"Cynthia?"

"Yes?" Her big green eyes meet mine.

"I know about the surface stuff with Ethan already. I know how taxing he can be on a person, emotionally and mentally. I need you to dig deeper."

Cynthia swallows and clasps her hands, averting her eyes from the table. Her gaze won't meet mine. She's tense, looking anywhere but at me. Then I realise she's traumatised.

I try a different tactic. "All right, how about I tell you some character traits he exhibited around me, and you can tell me if you recognise any of them from when you knew him?"

Cynthia continues avoiding eye contact. "I don't know if I want to talk about this. I—"

"It's okay," I say. "Let's take it slow." I start listing all the red-flag evidence on each finger. "Ethan was prone to meltdowns whenever something didn't go his way. Ethan didn't understand boundaries, but when you forced him to look inside himself, he would ease up. He would apologise, become a different person entirely, a perfect gentleman. It was like night and day. A switch being flipped. I never knew from minute to minute when his temper might flare up. I was constantly walking on eggshells with him."

Finally, Cynthia lifts her chin and meets my gaze. A flicker of understanding warms her eyes. I'm getting through to her.

"His mood swings weren't the only problem," I explain. "Weird things started happening in my personal life."

"What kind of weird things?"

"Well, for instance, my character was called into question at my job." I went on to tell her about how someone wrote the terrible review about my client, posing as me. "I was fired for that."

"Oh, that's terrible." She places her head in her hands.

"My apartment was burgled. Ethan bought me a new television and laptop. Volunteered to set them up and everything. He liked being my knight in shining armour. The new laptop had keystroke-tracking software installed on it. He used it to see what I was searching online."

Cynthia squirms in her seat, her hands tightening over each other.

"After I had my baby, I told Ethan I wanted my best friend to take us home from the hospital. Then she was in a car accident and broke her wrist." I sigh. "There's no doubt more. All strange coincidences. Apart, they don't seem that suspicious. Tied together, they start to feel connected."

"Maybe." Cynthia blinks down at her coffee.

"He deleted files from my phone. He told me he would use the information stolen from my computer in court after he filed for custody of my son. I told him I would back off if he dropped the petition. That's when he took Christopher." My voice breaks on my son's name. "I think he was afraid I'd move back to England with his son.

He never had any intention of sharing him with me, of being a co-parent."

Cynthia's eyes flash with sympathy. Her posture softens. She reaches a hand across the table and clasps it over mine.

"I'm sorry you are going through this. I can't imagine how horrible it's been to not know where your child is."

"It's a nightmare," I say. "I'm in pain all the time."

Cynthia exhales slowly, thinking. "There were… things about Ethan. Unfavourable things." She pauses to trace the rim of her coffee mug. "He was controlling with me too. In the beginning, I didn't notice it as much. It was more like dropping hints."

"Like what?"

Cynthia winces as though she hates to talk about this subject. "He would buy me clothes. Saying things like, 'This will make you look thinner,' or 'I think your hair would look better like this,' and he would pull up a picture of a model or something on his phone." Cynthia grimaces as though she's reliving it. "It wasn't just my physical appearance he would criticise. He'd complain about the charity work I was involved in or how much time and effort I put into my interior design business. He'd make me feel guilty about putting anything other than *him* first."

"That… sounds… painfully familiar." Now I'm the one who can't look her in the eye.

"I left him after he hit me."

I raise my head. "He was physical with you?"

"More than once," Cynthia admits. "The first time was a slap. Short and sharp. Easy to ignore when you're in the middle of all his games." She sighs. "But when he pushed me down the stairs and kicked me, I finally got out."

"I'm so sorry." This time, I reach for her hand. "I'm surprised he let you leave without a fuss."

She leans back. "I wouldn't put it like that. There were… odd coincidences, like the ones you mentioned."

"What were they?"

She raised an eyebrow. "My computer was hacked, and a few private files and pictures were stolen. Those photos were later found leaked onto porn sites." Her eyes screw shut.

This is the part she didn't want to talk about. I understand now. "Oh, Cynthia, I'm so sorry."

"It was a horrible time. I went to the police, but they never found evidence it was Ethan."

"Of course not."

"I always suspected it, though."

I roll my eyes. "Perfect Ethan, always getting away with his crimes. His mother probably had a hand in it."

"Eventually, the strange things stopped happening. Maybe he got bored. I didn't care. I just wanted to move on with my life." She glances out of the window, her features pensive. "I stopped going to the tennis club for a while too. I was only brave enough to return once I'd had confirmation from a friend that Ethan was pursuing someone else."

I swallow the dread knotted in my throat. "Maybe that someone was me."

Cynthia clenches and unclenches her fingers. "I couldn't have known."

I can't hold her gaze, so I look at the table. "I know."

"I heard something, though," Cynthia says. "Something that might help you. Or at least point you in the right direction."

My heart pauses. "What is it?"

Her eyes flash. "You didn't hear it from me. I ask that this conversation, all of it, stays confidential."

"Of course."

She breathes in deeply. "This is word of mouth, but a friend of mine's husband told her that he overheard Ethan bragging about taking his son to Greece for a vacation. Then my friend called me and told me. I swear that's all I know." She raises her hands defensively as if she expects me to start yelling at her.

"Greece?" I ask.

Cynthia gives me one slow nod. Her expression is clouded with pity. "That's what I heard."

I'm quiet for a moment, thinking. I sip my lukewarm tea. "Are you sure he mentioned his son?"

"Positive," she says. "I'd heard rumblings of Ethan having a child but nothing concrete. No one knew who the mother was, except we knew there hadn't been a wedding. My friend Joanne is married to Nick, who plays tennis with Ethan every week. Nick loves Ethan, thinks he's the best guy ever, and Ethan tends to brag to Nick. It's all about money, as it always is in our world. Ethan has more of it than Nick, and Nick bows down to those who have it." She taps her coffee mug. "Which makes me think Ethan might have let something real slip. You know?"

"I get it," I say. "So far, I've heard that he's in Cabo and France. Though I think a lot of these people have read the newspapers and are just stirring the pot."

She nods. "Word has spread. Unfortunately, most people here think you're the crazy one."

"Of course they do. But you think this Nick guy might be the one with the real info?"

"Maybe," she says.

"Should I talk to him?"

She bites her lip. "All right. Let me get you his number."

CHAPTER 42

I'm tempted to call Ethan's friend Nick when I return to my car, but instead, I drive back to Jessa's apartment first. And then, by the time I'm home, I'm exhausted. Fearing that I might not be able to form cohesive sentences, I decide to wait until morning.

Jessa and I have been avoiding each other since our fight, and she has already left when I get up the next day. I pour a cup of coffee and decide to try Ethan's Nick.

I make the call on the way to the sofa, nerves jangling through my body. When he answers, I almost forget to speak. But as soon as I explain who I am, he hangs up. Feeling deflated, I scope him out on social media instead. It doesn't surprise me that Nick is a carbon copy of Ethan, down to the polished brogues and side parting. I pass his number on to Lucas rather than try again. There's no way Nick is going to speak to me.

Which leaves me with nothing left to try for the time being. I fire off a quick message to Lucas including Nick's number. Maybe he can get something out of this guy.

Later in the day, I head out to New Jersey to look at a new apartment. Living there involves sharing a room with someone else. Unfortunately, that might be my only hope of being able to afford somewhere right now. This place is a hellhole. The "bedroom" is just a section of an already tiny room, partitioned by a curtain. I would be sharing that room with a terse man called Gerald. I thank the Realtor and make my way back to Jessa's.

Maybe it's guilt or the fact I can't sit still anymore, but I clean the apartment and then make us both soup. But she stays late at work again, so I end up taking a bowl into my bedroom. I'm dunking a slice of sourdough into it when I get a call.

I glance at the number on my phone—Lucas. Carefully, I place the soup on my bedside table and answer.

"Laura," he says. "I have news."

"What?" My heart leaps up to my throat.

"The police found the man who attacked you. Laura, this is huge. He confirmed that Alice and Ethan hired him to kill you."

It's amazing news, but I'm still disappointed. Every time Lucas calls, I hope to hear about Christopher, and every time, it's something completely different. "Seriously? How did they find him? How did they get him to confess?"

"I have to give it to the police this time. They did a thorough job. An officer posed as Ethan on the dark net and lured him in. They had to cut the man a deal to get him to talk. It turns out this guy has been at a few crime scenes in his time and left behind some incriminating DNA. They have him pinned for six murders and counting. Turning over his clients will help with his sentencing."

"Oh my God," I say. "Six murders? Then I got off easy."

"Yes, you did," he says. "Which is why I thought I should call you myself. You need to know how serious this is."

"What else did you find out?" Since his news, the light in my room seems too dark. I want to get out of bed and check all the locks. One hit man is behind bars, but there are others available for hire. I don't know how much money the Harts have to keep hiring these thugs, but it's beginning to feel like a never-ending supply.

"There's more," Lucas says. "According to Bill Henderson, the hit man broke down his last bank statement when turning in some of his clients. Ethan Hart wired money to him from a Greek bank account."

I sit up straight. "Greece. Are you sure?"

"Yes," he says. "Does that mean something to you?"

"Remember how I passed on the number for that Nick guy?"

"Yeah, he wouldn't talk to you."

"Right, well, Nick and Ethan are good friends. Ethan told Nick he was taking his son to Greece. At first, I thought it was a long shot. Ethan planted a load of seeds about going on vacation before disappearing, probably to throw me off. But along with the bank info… Lucas, he's in Greece. He has to be. Can you trace that bank's location?"

"Yes, but—"

"I'm getting on the next plane flying out," I interrupt. "I'm going to Greece. I just need you to tell me where the bank is. Maybe he's still there." I jump out of bed, ready to pack. There's energy in my limbs again. I keep picturing my son's eyes, his smile, the curve of his forehead.

"Wait a minute, Laura," Lucas says. "You can't do that."

"Why the fuck not?"

"It's not safe," he says.

"Oh, okay, then I won't go there to get my son. I'll stay here in the place where Ethan knows I live. That's much safer."

"Well, fuck. I guess I'm going with you, then," he says.

"What?"

"It's not safe in Greece, but you're right, it isn't safe where you are, either. Now, I can trace the bank's information, but it still won't lead me directly to Ethan. He's careful. He might not even *be* in Greece. It might just be an account he's using to throw the authorities off his scent. But Henderson already tipped off the police in Greece. They'll get involved on their end and will hopefully keep us in the loop."

"Listen, Lucas. I… I can't pay you," I say. "I'm so sorry. I'm almost out of money, and I'll be maxing out my credit cards for this trip. I had to borrow some money and—"

"Laura, at this point, I don't even care about the money. I'm invested now. You're a good person, and you don't deserve to be going through this hell. All I want now is to help you reunite with your baby."

I sit down on the bed. "Are you sure? This is a big favour to ask of anyone."

"I've got nothing better to do," he says with a laugh.

"What about… I don't know, your home life? Wife or whatever?"

"What wife?" he says, almost bitterly. "Look, don't feel bad. Just know I'm not making any promises. We'll be dealing with a different police department as well as Greek law. Now, I know nothing about either, but I'm happy to help the best I can."

"Okay," I say.

"Unfortunately, Christopher is Ethan's biological son, and for all we know, Ethan may have rights there too. But I swear to you I'll do everything I can."

"I believe you," I say. The thought brings me a sense of calm. I really do believe him.

"Good."

"What are my chances of seeing him again?" I ask.

Lucas doesn't answer.

CHAPTER 43

Within hours, the plane tickets are bought, I've fired off messages to Emily and Jessa, and I'm on my way to JFK airport. It's a nine-hour flight, and I doubt I'll sleep on the way. We have a *lead*—an actual bona fide lead—that could result in me finding my baby. This nightmare could be over soon.

Messages return to me.

Jessa: *What the fuck are you doing?*

Emily: *Be careful, sweetheart. Don't take any risks, and listen to the police.* She sends a follow-up three minutes later: *Don't take any shit either. Know your rights.*

I briefly wonder if the British police could get involved. I'm a British citizen, after all. Christopher was snatched in New York and possibly taken to Greece, but the British police intervened in the case of Madeleine McCann when she disappeared in Portugal. No one has given me that suggestion. I make a mental note to raise it with Lucas.

I meet him outside the airport doors, and we go through security together. While I'm spaced out, he gently takes my bags and places them on the appropriate conveyor belts. He's not talkative, which I like. There's nothing worse than the kind of person who tries to "cheer you up" because they can't stand sadness. He knows when to be calm and quiet. I'm coming to rely on him, and that worries me. With everything that has happened recently, I'm not sure throwing all my trust into another person's hands is a good idea.

We find our seats and settle in. As someone who always carried weight on her hips, I used to hate restrictive plane seats, but now I notice there's room to spare. It's a shock.

"How are you doing?" Lucas asks. "Would you like a drink? A glass of wine? Shot of vodka?"

"I'm okay," I say. "I want to sleep so I'm refreshed when we get there, but I don't think I can."

"Well, I'm sorry to abandon you, but I need a nap. The jet lag is going to be a killer, and I need to be on top of it. So if you don't mind, I'm going to order a whisky and put in my AirPods."

I smile. "Do you have some relaxing music to help you drop off?"

"A sleepcast," he says. "One of those meditation wind-downs."

I chuckle to myself. I can't picture Lucas meditating.

When he closes his eyes and begins to snore softly, I try to nap. But the passenger in the window seat is fidgety. At least they aren't chatty. That, I couldn't deal with right now.

Every time my eyelids drift, I see Ethan. I see him angry, eyes wild, smashing a plate at Alice's expensive Hamptons home. He hit Cynthia. He hired a murderer to take me out. I'll not rest until he's either behind bars or dead.

I realise then... I want him dead. Prison isn't enough. He should die for what he's done to me, my family, and the string of traumatised women he left behind him.

* * *

When the wheels touch down in Athens, Lucas wakes with a start. He's immediately alert, checking the area around him, making sure there's no danger. Once he has assessed that there isn't, he gets up and grabs our bags.

This time, he's more agitated as we make our way off the plane and through customs. There's a herd of people clogging the exits. It's busier than expected for an out-of-season trip. I'm used to it, however, and use my special skills as a British woman to queue correctly.

"You ready for this?" Lucas asks as we make our way through the airport.

"No," I say. "Would anyone be? I mean, I'm ready to get Christopher back, of course, but everything else... I... don't know what to expect."

He nods. "That's good. Stay on your toes. Expect anything. We have absolutely no idea what will happen from here on, and the less expectation you carry, the better."

Jesus, I think. He makes it sound like I might not even find my baby alive.

I push that thought down before it bubbles up, and I sling the rucksack over my shoulder. *No, that is impossible.* Ethan is many things—and I certainly wouldn't rule out murder—but killing his own son would be counterproductive. Ethan views Christopher as an extension of him. He's a narcissist. Killing my son—his son—would be like killing part of himself. Unless he wanted to do it just to devastate me.

"First stop is going to be the Ministry of Citizen Protection," Lucas says, throwing our luggage into the boot of a taxi.

"Okay."

I climb into the taxi, and Lucas gives the driver the address. Laiko music blasts from the speakers. Even in February, the breeze is pleasantly warm—compared to New York, anyway—and I'm glad I packed linen trousers and light cotton blouses. My hair whips around my face. I pluck an elastic band from my wrist and tie my hair back.

The downtown streets of Athens are crowded. I'm overcome with irrational envy. Gorgeous bronzed-skinned people stroll leisurely, window shopping, laughing over mimosas while perched under umbrellas, and dining on delicious Greek food. They can afford to laugh and take a walk. They don't have a missing child to find.

My mouth waters when I look at the stacks of baklava perched in bags on the counters of food stands. Even through the stress and emotional turmoil, I find hunger gnawing at my stomach. I ate next to nothing on the plane.

After a short drive, the cab driver pulls up against the curb of the Ministry of Citizen Protection. It's a tall building, a high-rise like a large hotel. The shadow of it looms across the road. My stomach tickles with nerves, and I pray that the Hellenic police will be helpful.

We pay the driver, grab our bags, and exit the vehicle. If Lucas is nervous, he doesn't show it. His eyes lift towards the skyscraper.

"What time is our meeting again?" I glance at my phone.

"In ten minutes," he says. "We'd better get moving."

We're meeting with a representative from the International Parental Child Abduction Centre, a branch of the US Embassy and Consulate of Greece. I'm trying not to feel intimidated by the official-sounding departments. But as we step inside the lobby and enter the lift, a sense of dread washes over me.

Twenty-two floors whizz by. My stomach is in knots. Half a dozen people get in and out of the lift, and it takes a few minutes to reach our floor. I'm sweating by the time we exit. From there, we're greeted by a receptionist who politely asks us to take a seat in one of the waiting room chairs.

Lucas sits first. I pace, unable to pacify my fraying nerves.

"Are you okay?" he asks.

"I think you should do the talking," I say. "You're calmer than I am. You'll make a better case."

"That's fine," he says. "But you also need to show them what this is doing to you."

"I might come across as hysterical."

He shakes his head. "Determined. Not hysterical."

The senior constable emerges from a set of double doors. The constable, I am pleasantly surprised to note, is a woman. I let out a relieved exhale. She'll understand. She has to.

Fortyish, tall, and broad shouldered, she introduces herself as Elena Pappas and leads us to a corner office at the end of a hallway lit by fluorescent lights. Along the way, we pass office cubicles fronted by glass doors. I hear phones faintly ringing. Soft-talking voices flutter through the space.

Once we reach Elena's office, she closes the door. "Please, sit." She motions to two green leather chairs.

The light filters in through the slits in the window blinds, casting a warm yellow tone over the environment. Her desk is surprisingly cluttered, with stacks of papers tossed haphazardly along the mahogany surface. It could be either a good or a bad thing. She's clearly busy, but she obviously makes an effort to work through her mounting pile. On the other hand, she's so busy she doesn't have time to tidy her desk.

Lucas dives straight in, explaining why we're here. While he's talking, Elena nods, her expression personable. To her credit, she appears invested. She maintains eye contact.

When Lucas finishes, she opens the file resting on top of the others.

My heart skips when I see my name, and the blood rushes to my face when I see Christopher's photograph. There's a picture created by the New York Police Department, augmented to show what he might look like at his current age. Even in the imagined depiction of him just over seven months old, he's tiny. I can't bear it. He should be with me, not *them*.

"Yes, I have all your information here." Elena's eyes skim over the contents of the documents, and she moves a manicured nail over the words on the page. She lifts her head, and my heart plummets when I notice she's frowning.

"I am working with the Hellenic authorities to resolve this case. I'm uncertain as to why you came here from…" She trails off, her eyes landing back on the papers. "America?"

I slide to the tip of my seat and meet her gaze, trying to find a balance between passionate and psychotic. "We think Ethan brought Christopher to Greece. The trail has gone cold in the US. He's obviously not there. But he used a bank account here."

Elena shrugs, her frown revealing the fine lines around her mouth. "Well, we have no leads here to go on, but we are working on it."

"You got the details of the bank account, didn't you?" I ask.

"That's right," she says. "But I'm afraid it doesn't mean your son and his father are physically here."

"Don't call him that," I say. "Ethan is not my baby's father. He's the monster who donated sperm."

"I apologise," Elena says, lifting her palms in contrition.

Every hair stands up on the backs of my arms. I can feel it. We're already facing a losing battle. I can't trust this woman.

"I've come this far." My voice sounds like shattering glass. "I'm not going home without my son."

She nods. Her expression softens, but I don't see a woman determined to reunite me with my baby. She turns to Lucas. "Do you have lodging here in Athens? We'll contact you as soon as there is a development in the case."

Lucas gives her our contact details.

Elena's eyes skirt between us. "I'm sorry this seems like a dead end for now or a wasted trip."

Lucas swats a hand, unfazed. "No, that's all right. We'll investigate what we can while we're here."

Elena stands and extends a hand across her desk. The conversation is over.

* * *

It's a cheap hotel, but at least it's comfortable. We booked adjoining rooms, so we have easy access when needed. Right now, we're in my room. Lucas sits at the desk and opens his laptop.

Despite the exhausting nine hours on a plane followed by half an hour in a stuffy office, I can't stop pacing up and down. I find myself staring out of the window, watching people walk up and down the busy streets.

"I should be out there, looking for him," I say.

"That would be a waste of time. He could be anywhere, Laura." Lucas types a password into the keyboard. "I'm going to do some research."

"Yeah, but this hotel is in a convenient location. What if Ethan and Alice booked a room here? I think I might head down to the lobby and show pictures of Ethan and Christopher to the hotel staff. Maybe someone will recognise them."

Lucas shrugs. "Go for it. Just take your phone, and don't leave the hotel."

"Sure." I head out the door with my room key and phone in hand. I should really take a shower first, but I don't want to kick Lucas out of the room.

The lobby is quiet, and I get the impression that the hotel isn't busy this time of year. I plaster on a smile and chat with the concierge and a couple of bellboys hanging around. No one recognises Ethan, Alice, or Christopher. It seems like a dead end, so I jump back in the lift and hope Lucas has had a more fruitful time.

When I open our room door, he immediately beckons me over to the laptop.

"What did you find?" I ask, senses sharpening.

Lucas's dark eyes flare. "You're never going to believe it."

"Don't make me guess. I'm tired."

"Look," he says, pointing at some sort of chart. "There was a private flight to Crete the day Christopher went missing. From New York."

"Okay—"

"And guess who owns the private jet."

I sit on the bed, elbows leaning on my knees. "Who?"

"Have you ever heard of Gary Michaels?"

"The guy who created that shopping app? Of course I know who he is. He's a billionaire."

"Did you know that he and Alice Hart dated in the 2010s?"

"What?" I gasp.

Lucas nods. "Gary Michaels—tech billionaire and Alice's ex-boyfriend—chartered a flight the day Christopher went missing. And it landed in Crete."

CHAPTER 44

We book the overnight ferry from Athens to Chania, and I sleep for the full eight-hour journey. Lucas wakes me gently as the other passengers are disembarking. Confused and still half asleep, I wipe away the accumulation of drool in the corner of my mouth, hoping he didn't see it.

I've been to Crete before. Emily and I went, back when she would actually leave the country. I was a teenager, about fifteen, I think, and bored out of my brain. It wasn't long after Mum died, and I had a lot of personal demons to work through. It's a beautiful island, surrounded by the teal waters, the cliffs higher and craggier than I'd expected. But we stayed at an all-inclusive hotel without much nightlife around it. It meant I was forced to spend every evening dining with my aunt, going slightly insane and wishing I was back home with my friends.

Bored is not the emotion I feel as I step onto Cretan land. I'm wired, every muscle pulled tight, every sense on high alert.

Before we left, Lucas called the Hellenic police and explained the situation to them. But Crete is a large island. Finding Ethan and Alice is not going to be easy, even with their help.

"I want to talk to the port authority staff," I say. "Maybe if I show them the pictures, it might jog someone's memory."

Lucas nods. "Good plan."

It's a long shot. After all, they did fly here. But at the same time, if they've caught a ferry to a different island at some point, they might have spent time here at the port. I clench my phone tightly inside my sweaty fist, wondering how close we are to finding my baby.

The ferry workers aren't the friendliest, but they politely glance at the pictures and shake their heads. No one recognises Christopher. Or Ethan. Or Alice. I'm met with blinking, confused faces. It's a little past dawn, and no one has the patience for it.

After an hour or so, we decide to head to our hotel. Another cheap one hastily booked after paying for the ferry tickets. I'm almost completely out of money, but I can't think about that. Not now. We're so close.

We check into the hotel and book adjoining rooms again. After a power nap, shower, and breakfast, we're back out under the cool February sun. I send photos of Christopher to Lucas, and we split up, speaking to receptionists in all the local hotels. After going through half a dozen places in the Chania region, we meet at a seaside restaurant for lunch.

I almost collapse into my chair. "It's useless."

Lucas sits down next to me and releases a heavy sigh. "Come on now. At least here, we have a better shot of nailing down their whereabouts."

"Thanks for trying to make me feel better," I say.

"Is it working?"

I tilt my head. "Do you really want the answer to that?"

Lucas smiles, dips his head down, and nods. "All right."

I reach over and clasp my hand over his. His chin lifts to meet my gaze.

"Thank you," I whisper, my voice cracking with emotion. "You're doing everything you can, and I appreciate it more than I can express."

Suddenly embarrassed, I move my hand away and turn my head to gaze out at the sea. A waitress takes our order, and I choose a Greek salad. I'm overtaken by the feeling that this is wrong. It's like I'm on holiday, sitting here at this table with the sea view. But I have to eat. When the waitress returns, I show her the pictures of Christopher.

"Oh, what a beautiful baby," she says, not understanding at first.

"He's missing," I say, taking no pleasure in the way the smile disappears from her face.

She's chatty, and as she's in the process of serving us food, I've told her pretty much the entire story. She has tears in her eyes by the time our coffees arrive.

"Send me the pictures," she says. "I'll ask everyone."

"Really? Thank you so much."

We swap numbers, and I find out her name is Katerina. Lucas is grinning as we drink our coffees.

"What?" I ask.

"Carry on making allies like that, and we'll find them in no time. That was great, Laura. This is a busy restaurant. I'm sure she sees many people every day."

I shake my head because it doesn't feel like enough. If only the police here would let me film an appeal. Christopher's image should be on television.

"So, we think Gary Michaels flew Alice, Ethan, and Christopher here. What would they do once they arrived?" I ask.

"Well, babies aren't easy," he says. "They need a crib, clothes, food, and diapers. If I was kidnapping a newborn, I'd want to rent a place, not stay in a hotel."

"Right," I say. "Hotels are noisy, and people will ask questions. They might have stayed in one temporarily, but an apartment or a villa would be better." I pause. "They must have fake passports. Surely they'd need to show ID to rent somewhere."

"Unless they paid cash. Or they know a friend."

"Can we talk to Gary Michaels?" I ask.

Lucas exhales a whistle through his nose. "Somehow, I doubt it."

"What about the police? Can they question him? He lives in New York, right?"

He sips his coffee. "I mean, we can try. Men like him are protected."

"I know." My fingers curl around the hot cup. "Trust me. I know."

"Don't lose hope," he says. "Investigations like this are always about taking two steps forward and one step back."

* * *

For the rest of the afternoon, I keep hoping Katerina is going to call me with a lead. She doesn't. Lucas and I hit the streets, checking off hotels on our map. The people are friendly, making the process slightly easier. But as the sun begins to set, we know we aren't going to find any information today. What we need to do next is head back to the hotel and do some research.

"The police might be able to obtain CCTV footage at Chania and Heraklion airports," he says.

I nod. "That's good. If we manage to get footage of them leaving with Gary Michaels, then surely, it'd be enough evidence to force him in for questioning. What if Gary set them up somewhere? Have we checked to see if he owns property on Crete?"

Lucas's eyes light up. "You're good at this. Fancy coming on board after we find Christopher?"

I laugh. In all honesty, it feels good to be out doing something. I have ideas and a place to start. For six months, I waited in limbo, watching as the bureaucratic process prevented overworked police officers from finding my son. Now I'm here, with someone who listens to me, and I'm close. I can feel it.

Lucas grabs us some food from a gyros van and returns to the hotel. We huddle around the laptop, eating, hopeful. Lucas asks his New York colleagues to run checks on Gary Michaels and his listed properties. I sit on the bed, picking at my kebab.

"There's nothing else we can do until morning," he says. "I'm going to turn in."

"Okay." I nod, licking the grease from my fingertips.

He hesitates by the door, looking back at me. Something passes between our eyes. It's unspoken, and it's new, like the bud of a plant slowly unfurling. As soon as the door closes, I realise that I wanted him to stay with me. And then the food turns sour in my stomach. How can I even think that at a time like this?

CHAPTER 45

We meet for breakfast the next morning. As I pick at a pastry and sip black coffee, I try not to think about the feelings that crept up in my mind last night.

Lucas places a napkin on his lap. "Well, we can rule out Gary Michaels giving Alice a villa. There's no record of him owning property in Greece. He has houses in New York, LA, London, Sydney, and Rome. Nothing in Greece, though."

"Fuck." I sigh.

"I'm going to call the Hellenic police today and see what's happening on their end."

"Okay…" I trail off, momentarily distracted by a young woman tugging a little boy along into the hotel restaurant. The boy digs his heels into the road, a stubborn look crossing his face. I want nothing more than to see the evolution of Christopher's stubborn expressions.

"My buddy at the embassy is going to make some calls, see if we can get any surveillance footage at all the Greek airports," Lucas says. "You might call it a hunch, but I'm convinced that Ethan and Alice have left Crete. Whether that's by plane or boat, I'm still trying to figure that out. Surveillance cameras, wherever they might be planted, will certainly assist with that."

"That sounds good."

"Hang in there. We're close. I can feel it," he says.

But I feel unconvinced. Lucas sounds worried, no matter what he says. It's clear he feels like we've hit a brick wall.

* * *

Rather than wallow in self-pity, I spend the morning walking around the harbour, holding out my phone, chatting to tourists and locals. One woman shoos me away, and I realise I've approached her before. My stomach growls, and I make my way over to a small café, order a salad and a coffee, then gaze out at the sea. My feet are full of blisters, and my hair is sticky with sweat.

When I show the waiter my photograph, he informs me in a deadpan voice that I've already asked him. Then he warns me that if I ask his customers again, he'll throw me out.

By the time my salad arrives, I'm holding back tears. After the awkward encounter with the waiter, I can stomach only half of the food. But I do drain the coffee for extra energy. Then I head back out as a yacht approaches the harbour. It isn't one I've seen before, so I make my way down to the dock, hoping to catch the people on board.

A man hops off the boat and begins walking away. He's wearing expensive taupe slacks and a tight-fitting black T-shirt that hugs his muscular torso. He looks to be in his mid-fifties.

"Excuse me," I call out, trying to attract his attention.

He turns around and gives me a curious frown, his forehead creasing.

"Sorry to bother you," I begin, jogging to quickly close the distance between us. "But I was wondering if you are familiar with this area. Perhaps you could let me show you a picture of—"

The man shakes his head, waving his hands in front of me. He starts talking fast in a language I can't understand, which I assume to be Greek.

My heart sinks. He can't understand me. This is the first time since landing in Greece that I'm encountering this problem. Many of the locals, especially in these tourist spots, know how to speak fluent English, but this man doesn't seem to be following a single word I'm saying.

With everything going on, I haven't had a chance to learn much

Greek. Only "please" and "thank you." But I show him the picture anyway.

"You—you know this man?" I tap my finger on the screen, in the centre of Ethan's face. "You've seen him before?"

The man nods with a spark of enthusiasm. He says something chatty in Greek.

"You know him? Oh my God."

I glance around, combing the dock for anyone else around who might be able to translate for us. The man points towards a row of boats anchored at the harbour. There's just one woman nearby. I quickly approach.

"Excuse me!" I shout. "Do you speak English?"

"Yes," she says, a wary expression on her face.

"Can you translate for us?" I point at the man beside me. "I need to talk to him."

The woman gazes at the man for the first time. She says something to him. He nods, smiling.

She turns her focus back to me. "Yes, I can help you."

"Can you ask him if he recognises this man?" I point at the screen again.

She asks the man. He says something back.

"He's seen him before, yes."

My pulse is flying. "Can he tell me where he's seen him?"

The man explains, using animated hand gestures, every now and then glancing back at the dock, pointing.

"He says he saw the man in the photo with a baby and another woman," the woman says.

The world is suddenly too blinding white, and I feel the deck sway beneath my feet. I blink, pulling myself together. "You—you saw a man, a baby, and a woman?"

"He says the three of them were living on a yacht beside his boat. He noticed them coming and going frequently but thought it was strange because the baby seemed too young to be living on the yacht. The woman looked too old to be the mother. And they are out here in winter, which is very odd."

"Is this her?" I swipe to a picture of Alice.

The man regards the picture, turns to the translator, then to me before he slowly nods.

He says something else. The woman begins to speak.

"He says he saw them sail out one day. He can't remember when, but they have not returned since then."

My heart drops to my knees. *They were here.*

CHAPTER 46

"This man"—I tap the screen with the photo of Ethan and Alice for reference—"and this woman, they abducted my baby. I'm his mother."

I scroll to another picture of me holding Christopher. In this photo, we're sitting in the recliner in Jessa's living room. I'm holding him up and grinning from ear to ear. Christopher is wearing a powder-blue onesie with dinosaurs printed on the front.

The woman translates to the man. Then she turns to me. "I'm sorry to hear about your trouble."

I swallow hard. My mouth and throat are suddenly too dry. "Will you help me with something else? Would you be willing to give a statement to the local police? An official statement from a witness will go a long way."

I wring my hands together and wait for the woman to translate. "I'll even pay your fare to the station. I'll do anything." I flash him a pleading glance.

The woman translates. He says something to her in a low and solemn voice.

The woman meets my eye. "He has children himself. He says as a father, he can hear the pain in your voice. He wants to help you. He'll agree to give a witness statement to the police for you."

I exhale loudly. I want to hug the man, but I stop myself. "Thank you. You have no idea how much this will help me."

We make plans to head over to the police headquarters together. I call Lucas to inform him, and he tells me with excitement brimming in his voice that he'll meet me there.

* * *

Elena Pappas meets us in a cluttered office space at a local police station. We're with the man from the dock—Yiannis—who is down from Athens to spend time on his yacht. Elena works as the translator this time, and Lucas records the conversation on his phone, for his personal notes, after obtaining the man's permission as well as Elena's.

"The detective on the case will take this information right away," she says. "I'll call you with any further details as soon as I can."

"Is there anything else we can do?" I ask.

"Not right now." She begins shuffling papers, dismissing us. We take the hint and leave.

Lucas and I stand outside on the street. My body is taut with adrenaline. The blood pumps hard through my veins. I feel like I could run a marathon and still have energy left to spare. Lucas is the opposite. He's calm as he pulls up a map on his phone and starts inspecting it.

"What are you looking into?"

"I'm trying to figure out where they might have gone on the yacht." He points at the map on the screen. "It looks like there are a few possibilities."

"Like what?"

"If Ethan's going for convenience and the closest destination, Karpathos is a good contender. Or Santorini."

"How do we know which to choose? And how do we know whether they suspect anything? Maybe they went farther afield to Italy or even North Africa."

"I can't say for sure," he says. "It depends on the size of the yacht and whether they have a captain or are sailing themselves. We know the Harts are rich, but they're not billionaires. They have limits. My gut is telling me they haven't gone far. My bet is Santorini. It's a popular destination, and my instinct says Alice needs her creature comforts. She'll gravitate towards the best hotels and villas. They'll be tired of being on the yacht. Maybe they don't know we're closing in. Maybe they need a more permanent abode."

"Then I'm going to Santorini," I say.

"Laura, wait." Lucas pushes the phone into his back pocket. "We need to talk about this first."

"What's there to talk about?"

"We can't just keep jumping from place to place like this."

"We came to Crete, and we got the biggest lead of all."

"That was different. We had an actual lead that Ethan had been here." Lucas puts his hand on my lower back. "We need to let the police handle it from here. I know the waiting is hard for you, but I promise you, they're going to do everything they can to solve this. We can't just take a guess at where Ethan is—"

"You just did," I say, moving away from him. "Don't do that if you don't want to follow the trail."

"I know," he says. "I was just thinking out loud. Look, if we find them, we need the police on our side. The officials know what they're doing, and they can properly, and safely, bring Ethan into custody without violence. There's no telling what he might do if he sees you. He's already defensive, being on the run."

I shake my head. I know he's right, but I can't stand by and watch. Nothing terrifies me more than the thought of the police botching this. "Can't we at least go to Santorini on our own? Find a place to stay there? I promise I won't get involved. I just want to be there if—*when* —they find Christopher."

Lucas shakes his head.

"He's going to need his mother right away," I say. "I… well, I guess I can't breastfeed him anymore. But he'll need me. And I'll need to hold him."

"All right," he says. "If the police decide to check out Santorini first, we'll follow them."

I grab his hand. I'm not sure why. It's not for support or even thanks. I just want to touch him. Idly, Lucas's thumb strokes the inside of my palm. His dark eyes lock onto mine. We stand there like that for a long time. I don't think either of us dare to move.

CHAPTER 47

S antorini is one of those bucket-list places I've always wanted to visit. But I never expected to come for this reason. As I gaze out of the window of our clifftop hotel, the azure sea stretches for miles. The white roofs of hotels and steep roads slope down to a jagged coastline.

After the Greek police received a tip-off about a man matching Ethan's description leaving a yacht at the Athinios harbour, we hopped on a ferry. After another four hours on a boat, my stomach churning, we booked into the cheapest hotel we could find in the area. I used my overdraft to do it.

We arrived yesterday. So far, there has been no news.

I pace the room for a few minutes and then head next door to see Lucas. After a brief knock, he opens the door and lets me in. I notice the dark shadows beneath his eyes. The last few days have taken a toll.

"How are you doing?" he asks. "Do you want to get some lunch?"

I shake my head. The media have finally jumped on the story, and when I leave the hotel, I notice journalists and photographers invading my space. Even though I want this kind of pressure on Ethan, part of me misses the independence I had before the press got involved.

"I take it you haven't heard anything?" I ask.

"You know I'd tell you if I had," he says.

We order room service more as something to do rather than because either of us are hungry. Lucas keeps his laptop on, refreshing news articles while checking his phone for texts or calls.

I bite into an apple. "I'm going stir-crazy in here."

"Me too," he admits.

"I'm so glad you're here with me," I say. "I... I could never have made it this far without you. But I doubt I'll ever be able to pay you what I owe. You could've gone back to New York and taken on a rich client, but you didn't."

"I didn't." When he turns to me, his gaze is intense. It's as though he challenges me to guess his intentions.

"Christopher is my priority," I mumble. It's more to myself than to Lucas. A reminder to stay focused.

"Mine too," he says.

"Sorry, I didn't mean to imply—"

"I know. It's fine." He smiles. Then he turns away and stares out of the window. "But you should know I'm here for you too." His gaze comes back to me, dark and intense.

Something flutters in the pit of my stomach. I don't want to be feeling this way about a man, not now. Not until I have my son back. And yet my body ignores the plea and heats from my toes to my forehead.

When my phone rings, I start. My fingertips fumble as I answer. "Hello?"

"My name is Detective Papadakis. Is this Ms McAdams?"

"Yes," I say, my heart pounding.

I recognise the name. Papadakis was assigned to our case from the Ministry of Citizen Protection division of the Hellenic police. He has a bellowing, assertive voice. I put it on speaker as he goes through the updates with me.

"We have combed through the main port of Athinios," he declares. "We've searched ferry boats, port boats, yachts, even container ships."

I lift a hand to my chest. "And?"

The detective lets out a long, resigned sigh. "And there is nothing to report as of yet."

Slowly, I sink onto the mattress. "Oh."

"We still have further ground to cover," he says. "But I wanted to let you know where we are. Okay?"

"Okay," I say, disappointment evident in my voice.

"We'll keep you updated."

"All right. I appreciate the call."

After I hang up, I stare at the floor for a long time. The mattress dips as Lucas sits next to me. He puts a hand on my thigh. "They know what they're doing. If Ethan is out there, they'll find him."

But I can't stand the pity. I can't stand the pain. I need to be alone. Without saying a word, I pick up my phone and leave the room. I head back to my own and stare out at the sea, wondering where the fuck my son is. It can't be safe for a baby out there on the water. If they're at sea, how are they going to buy him formula?

* * *

For three more days, I sit in this hotel room. Waiting for information. Praying. Fretting. Pacing.

On the afternoon on the third day, my phone rings again. My voice croaks when I snatch it from the bedside table.

"We've found an empty yacht," Papadakis says, "with discarded baby clothes left inside. We need you to come and identify the clothes."

I burst through to Lucas's room, and he springs into action. Together, we hurry out of the hotel and stride down to the harbour. My heart thunders against my chest, close to bursting. I close my hands into fists, clenching the wiry muscles along my arms.

Papadakis greets me and shows me through to the abandoned yacht now moored on the harbour. As I move through the small space, it's clear Ethan and Alice left in a hurry. I find a pair of heeled shoes in Alice's size and some dirty shorts and tops big enough for an eight-month-old baby. I notice the beige stain on one from where he spit up.

Numbness spreads through my body. A coping mechanism, I think. If I feel every emotion right now, I'll never get through this. Instead, I push it all down and focus on the task at hand.

I find empty packets of diapers and baby formula discarded in the living area. That must mean they haven't transitioned him to food yet. He'll need those vitamins and minerals if he's going to grow. But these are people who put a baby on a boat. How do they even keep him safe? Lock him in the rooms below deck? I notice the room with the most discarded baby items locks from the outside. I struggle to keep my breakfast down.

I must let out a small audible sound because the detective turns to me.

"I apologise," Papadakis says. "I know this is hard. But I must ask if you can identify any of these things."

I shake my head. "Everything is the right size and the right style, but it's all new." I point at the shoes. "Alice would wear those, and they are in her shoe size. But they still have the label attached."

He nods. "Okay, thank you, Ms McAdams."

Before I leave, I lift the soiled baby T-shirt and hold it close to my face, inhaling the scent of him. And then I'm gone. I'm lost to memories of my son. Someone has to pick me up off the floor and help me out. Lucas.

I manage to compose myself only once we're back on the street.

I turn to Lucas. "Now what?"

He doesn't have an answer.

CHAPTER 48

A week goes by like a blink, and Lucas and I don't meet in his room to discuss plans anymore. I shuffle along the streets of Santorini with no purpose, no destination. I'm aimlessly searching, mainly for answers. I rub the heels of my hands into my groggy eyes, attempting to rub away some of the haze. The afternoon shade crawls across the white-walled buildings, inching its way closer to the water as if it's trying to reach the ocean before the sun sets.

I hold up pictures of Ethan and Alice, even Christopher, even though I know he won't look the same.

"Have you seen this man and woman with a baby?" I halt in front of a flower shop where a young couple is inspecting the floral arrangements on display on the sidewalk in front of the business. They shake their heads.

A camera clicks. A journalist takes my photograph then scuttles away. When I'm alone, I see myself in the reflection of the shop. My hair is greasy. I haven't showered today, and there are armpit stains on my shirt. It's the perfect photo for a sensational headline. I can see it now: *Mother of missing baby has a breakdown.*

Lucas is as lost as I am. Every day, he turns on his laptop and stares at it. Nothing else has happened since the abandoned yacht was found. The Hellenic police have no more leads. CCTV at Athens airport had mysteriously vanished, meaning there was nothing connecting Gary

Michaels to the case. Aside from the yacht and that one sighting in Santorini, no one has seen Ethan or Alice.

Tomorrow, there'll be a horrible photograph of me looking like an unfit mother. There won't be any sympathy for me. People will pick up the newspaper and ask themselves if I even deserve my son back. I've seen the rumblings already. I've read the comments underneath the online articles.

Well, she wouldn't give him custody. What other choice did the dad have?

The mother sounds like a piece of work tbh.

I'm not being funny, but the mother lost her job because she was so terrible at it. There's something off here. I don't trust her.

I walk down to the shore and remove my shoes before tucking my socks into them. Then I carry them as I trudge through the white sand that is still warm under the tapering heat of the day. I stop to watch a middle-aged couple strolling hand in hand at the lapping water, ankles submerged. I'd kill to be that happy and have zero problems.

It's alarming how quickly those comments get into your head. Even though I know I'm a good mother who loves her son, who tried her best given the circumstances, the words get under my skin. I begin to feel like the worst person in the world.

The sun disappears behind the sea, the remnants of its vibrant colour splashed across the canvas of the sky. I stare at the pastel hues, in awe of the breathtaking beauty around me, wishing I could enjoy it.

My gaze travels across the beach, searching for photographers. This would make another great picture to build their story—the mother crying on the beach alone. But there's no one here except for a group of young Greek teenagers playing Frisbee.

This is it, I think. *This is me giving in.*

The sea is so blue it almost seems warm. I gaze out at the red buoys marking the safe and unsafe areas to swim, watching them bob up and down with the tide. I wonder how long it would take me to drown. Long enough to feel pain? But then the pain would subside, and I would no longer exist in a world where my child is lost to me. I exhale slowly.

And then my phone begins to ring. At first, I ignore it. Lucas probably wants me back at the hotel. I can tell he's worried about me. On the third ring, I grope into my pocket. The number on the screen isn't one I recognise, but I answer it anyway.

"Hello?"

"Laura?" It's a woman's voice.

I drop my knees to the sand, pitching my body forwards. "Yes. Yes, this is Laura."

My heart pounds. *I know this voice. I know this voice.*

"It's Alice," she says.

CHAPTER 49

"Don't hang up," she says.

"I'm not, Alice." I climb to my feet. "I'm not hanging up. I'm right here, ready to talk."

I spin around, plagued by the sense that someone is watching me. The group of teenagers continue to throw their Frisbee. The old couple are making their way back to the road on the other side of the beach. There are no other shadows lingering on the beach as the sun begins to set.

"This isn't working," she says. "It's not… it's not what I imagined it would be."

She sounds agitated. I imagine her pacing somewhere. The desire to ask her a million questions washes over me, but I know I need to go slowly. Instead, I concentrate on the sound of her voice, turning up the volume on my phone. There has to be a clue in the background somewhere.

"Where's Christopher?" I ask. "I can't hear him crying. Where is he? Is he safe?"

"Yes, yes, he's fine," she says, almost flippantly. "He's asleep. Ethan is watching him. For a change."

She sounds resentful. So, she's been saddled with looking after Christopher during the abduction. And now it sounds as though she's had enough of it. My God. I might actually get my son back because Alice can't be bothered to babysit her grandson.

"I really miss him, Alice," I say. "You have no idea how much I want to hold him in my arms again. I'd love to take care of him, even for an hour."

She's quiet for a moment. I hear a car in the background. So she has stepped out of wherever they're staying to make this call.

"That's why I'm calling," she says. "I can't live on the run like this. It's ridiculous. I'm too old for all this."

I bite my bottom lip. I want to ask her what she expected. Perhaps she thought her billionaire ex would prop up her lifestyle somewhere more fabulous than a small yacht outside Santorini.

"What are you proposing?" I ask.

"Are you alone?"

"Yes."

"Where are you?" she demands.

"I'm in Santorini." I don't give her my exact location, just in case.

Alice releases a long and heavy sigh. She's quiet for a moment. "All right." I hear another car. "I've tried to talk sense into Ethan, but he won't listen to reason."

"What do you mean?" My tongue moves like sandpaper inside my dry mouth.

"He won't give up," she says. "I told him to just give the kid back, but he won't do it. I can't cope with a baby that cries all day and night. I can't keep looking over my shoulder, wondering if the authorities are right behind me everywhere I go. I need freedom."

"Wait, why is Christopher crying?" I ask.

"How should I know?" she snaps.

"Does he have a fever? A rash?"

"He was a little warm earlier," she says. "But I think he's fine."

That doesn't fill me with confidence.

"Alice, I can take Christopher to the hospital and have him checked out. He needs me. You know that, don't you? He needs his mother. Let me take him home. Please. Please, Alice."

She's silent another moment, debating. My stomach knots.

"Where are you staying?" she asks.

I tell her.

She's quiet for a moment. "There's a hill above your hotel, and at the top, there's a small church. Meet me there at two a.m. I'll need to sneak out while Ethan is asleep. And come alone. If you don't come alone, you won't get Ethan Junior." She sighs heavily. "I can't do this anymore. I want it to be over. I want to be left alone. I know the only way to do that is to give you your son." She pauses. "I'm no criminal. And I'm not going to behave like one anymore."

She hangs up before I can ask her anything else. My face is hot. My ears are hot. My chest is burning. That slimy cow has been calling him Ethan Jr. Well, they can call him whatever they want, but it's not his legal name, and it never will be.

I watch the kids playing Frisbee, trying to process everything that just happened. Before I make any decisions, I need to slow down and unpack every word of that call. I don't see how calling me would benefit her unless she was telling the truth. A colicky baby on a yacht can't be much fun, and Ethan was never a natural father. Jesus, neither of them are natural parents.

Then there's the issue about who I tell. Surely I would be an idiot not to involve the police. But part of me thinks I'd also be an idiot to tell them. I don't know what resources Alice has available to her. If she has an informant, she may find out before I meet her—I check the time—in seven hours. *Seven.* How am I going to wait that long?

I decide to try calling the number back. I want more details from her. I want to know where they've been and some assurance that Christopher is well. Right now, I'm terrified that he's feverish and she hasn't taken him to the hospital because she'll be caught. I get a message saying the line has been disconnected. Alice must have called me from a burner phone and destroyed it immediately after.

The teenagers are packing up their bags, laughing and joking as they shove the Frisbee in a backpack. Now someone is walking their dog along the shore.

I chew on a thumbnail. Ethan, and possibly Alice, hired a hit man to have me killed. Turning up alone to meet one of them could be a similar trap. *Fuck.* I walk a few paces towards the sea, purely as something to do with my body. In that case, Alice could be lying about wanting to give Christopher back. There's no way for me to know for sure.

Detective Papadakis has been helpful so far. He's certainly kept me in the loop. And yet Ethan and Alice have been one step ahead of the Hellenic police ever since we arrived.

My trust in the police is almost as low as my trust in Alice. How do

I know they'll make the right choices? They may head up to the church with guns blazing, signalling from a mile off that I'm not alone.

Lucas would never want me to do something like this alone. He would insist on coming with me, if for no other reason than to keep me safe. But I have to take Alice's warning seriously. She could have hired guards who are watching, lurking, waiting in the shadows to see what I'll do. Lucas becomes a liability in that situation.

Then it dawns on me. I know what I need to do. I pick up my phone and dial.

CHAPTER 50

The concrete steps unspool like winding yarn beneath my feet as I make my way up the steep incline. I feel like I'm being lifted into the night sky. A handful of stars twinkle and glitter above. It's peaceful and quiet, but inside my chest, a bouncing heart pumps adrenaline around my body. The skin on my palms itches. Both my knees are weak. Sweat tracks down my spine despite the cool edge to the night.

The church comes into view. My gaze travels across the area, searching for signs of Alice, but I see nothing in the shadows. Here, the road flattens out, and I have reached the summit.

Every one of my senses is on high alert. I'm focused. Ready. And when I hear the quiet sound of a gurgling baby, I rush towards it.

"Alice," I hiss. "Alice, come out. I'm alone."

She emerges from the side of the building. Her black hair shimmers under the moonlight. A sob escapes my throat when I see Christopher on her hip. It's the first time I've seen him for over seven months, and part of me feels like I'm dreaming. But I'm not. He's real. I take in every part of him. His complexion is the colour of cream, with two rosy patches in the centre of his cheeks. His eyes are two blinking pennies. His soft, dark hair curls at the end in a wavy wisp.

I reach out for him, tears clouding my vision. "Christopher."

His face scrunches up, turning bright red almost immediately. Something is wrong. As Alice moves towards a streetlight, I see the light sheen of sweat budding across my son's forehead.

"Does he have a fever?" I ask, tracking her movements.

But Alice ignores me. She walks away from the church towards the edge of the cliff. I'm so startled I freeze.

"What are you doing?" I take a step towards her.

As soon as she sees me move, she lifts my crying son and dangles him over the edge. "Don't come any closer."

"No!" I scream.

She shushes me. "Keep your voice down."

I hold out my hands. "Okay. I'll do everything you say. I promise. But please, back away from the cliff. Don't hurt him. I won't move until you tell me to, I swear."

Alice stares at me, her pupils dilated, the whites of her eyes bloodshot. She makes no effort to move in any direction. Christopher wriggles in her arms, and I gasp. Finally, she lifts him back over the edge and rests him on her hip again. His cries die down, and he looks up at his grandmother. I see trust in my baby's eyes, like he's comfortable with her and knows her. He's calm, blissfully unaware of his current danger.

"Where's Ethan?" I ask.

Alice's lips twist into a grimace. "I drugged him and left him in our brand-new yacht on the other side of the island. You'll never find him. He doesn't know I'm doing this."

"What do you want me to do, Alice?" I ask.

"I want you to take this baby back, if you want him so bad," she says. "I just need to know if I can trust you."

Christopher lets out a gurgling sound and clutches her arm with a dimpled fist. My heart breaks. I'm so desperate to hold him and feel his soft, warm skin.

I offer out my arms again. "Look, I'm here alone like you asked. I'm standing a few feet away from you. I've done everything you asked. Hand him over to me."

Alice shakes her head. "First, we need to talk about what's going to happen after."

"Okay, that's fine," I say. "Whatever you want to do."

Alice squeezes her lips together and regards me through narrowed, suspicious eyes. "Ethan is not going to be a problem. You can trust me on that," she says.

"How do I know that?" I ask.

"Well, you'll have to trust me. I'll give you the baby if you promise to give us a head start." She sighs. "Look, I'm not an idiot. People will notice you have your baby back. And I suppose we can't do anything about that. But I have a friend who will help set me up a long way from here. I need to get to that friend before you go to the police."

"Okay," I say. "I promise to give you both a head start."

"Ethan and I will disappear. You'll never have to worry about us resurfacing again. I don't want to raise this baby on the run, on a yacht. It's been an utter nightmare."

"May I…" I take a cautious step in her direction. She stiffens but allows me to come closer.

I take another guarded step then another. I'm not breathing. I don't want to frighten her away. She's tentative about this arrangement, I can tell.

My arms reach out. They find purchase on Christopher's tiny body. I lift him from Alice, and I press his warm body against mine, inhaling his scent.

"My darling boy," I murmur.

He's here. He's finally in my arms.

And then I check him. I feel his forehead and examine his arms for any marks. He seems fine, if a little on the warm side, and there's some mucus under his nostrils as though he might have had a cold.

"I told you he was all right," Alice says.

When Christopher hears her voice, he cries and reaches out for his grandmother. Alice looks sharply away then but not quick enough for me to miss the tears in her eyes. He wants her. He knows her. He doesn't know me anymore. He doesn't want me. His pink cheeks grow redder. He squirms, trying to get away from me and go back to her—to what's familiar. I hug him close and whisper to him, trying to soothe him. He's crying, and I'm crying—but mine are tears of joy. I press my lips to his forehead and kiss him.

I turn back to Alice to assure her we'll be okay. Despite everything, she cares for him in her own limited way, and I think she knew he needed a normal life with me, not a chaotic one with her and Ethan. As I'm about to thank her, the words die in my throat. Alice's hand flies up to her face. Her eyes stare over my head at something behind me, terror reflecting back at me.

Afraid, I move away, ready to run. But a heavy object crashes against my skull. Pain sears through my scalp, spreading across my neck and shoulders. The breath knocks from my lungs. My arms go limp, and Christopher slides from my grip.

In a whirl, Alice snatches Christopher back. A male voice shouts my name, but my eardrums are woozy, and the sound is muffled.

The ground is moving. Footsteps thunder behind me. Alice backs into the shadows, clutching Christopher possessively to her chest. Then a blurry shape comes into focus. A large man looms over me, his face in shadow.

I lift my hand to the back of my head and feel the warm, sticky wetness of blood. The man takes a step forwards, his face coming into the light.

"Did you miss me?" he asks.

Ethan's eyes. Ethan's nose. Ethan's jaw. His dark, wavy hair. His broad shoulders. He smiles. I back away from him, but he continues to approach.

There's a shift in atmosphere. Another sound close by. We spin towards the clatter of footsteps on tarmac—Lucas. I asked him to find a place to watch the exchange in case anything happened to me.

"Laura!" Lucas shouts.

"Get Christopher!" I scream.

Ethan's eyes are fierce, his teeth bared like a predator's. He lunges at me to keep me from moving, but at the last second, I duck away from his swinging arm. He reaches for any part of my body he can grab, successfully clutching my elbow with his strong fingers. He yanks me in his direction, but he's wobbly on his feet.

It's then I realise Alice wasn't lying about drugging her son. He's not himself. He's groggy. Then again, so am I from the head injury he just gave me.

I slam my weight into his body, and he lands against the road barrier. Beyond it, the cliff drops down into the dark, churning sea below. I want him gone. I want his head bashed against the rocks below. But my shove wasn't enough to tip him over. He turns, stretching out for me, and I throw my weight against him one more time.

This time, he pulls me with him. We both barrel forwards together, teetering at the edge. The darkness yawns below.

If he topples over the side, he's taking me with him. His grip on my arms is cold and sturdy. I open my mouth, lean into his face, and sink my teeth into the tip of his nose.

Ethan wails in pain, eyes huge with shock. His strong fingers lose their grip on me, and I watch coldly as his arms flail. I'm not myself when my palms press into his chest and push. At least, I don't think I am. Intentionally taking a life is not something I thought I would ever be capable of. But I do it, and I mean it. I want him dead.

Ethan's heels rock back on the uneven surface beneath his feet. He yelps, and his eyes trail over to where I assume his mother stands behind me. I take a step forwards when my balance falters, and he tips over the barrier. One more shove, and his shoes stumble against the rocks. He slips. The rocks skid and slide under him, yielding to his weight, sending him plunging into the open vastness of darkness.

I turn away, my jaw slack. It doesn't stop me from hearing his screech of terror followed by a *thump*.

Another scream tears through the silence—Alice. I watch as Lucas removes Christopher from Alice's arms, and she sinks to the ground outside the church. I hurry over to them, and Lucas hands me my son.

Christopher is upset now, tears streaming down his face. Perhaps he senses the tension in my body and the grief coming from his grandmother. I glance down at Alice, almost feeling sorry for her.

"I'll call the police," Lucas says. "What you did was self-defence. Ethan almost dragged you over that cliff with him."

I nod. It was, and it wasn't. After all, I pushed him more than once.

But I had to end this. Alice might have been telling the truth about wanting a fresh start without Christopher, but there was no way Ethan would ever allow me to live a happy, carefree life with my son. For as long as he lived, he would be chasing me.

And that's why he had to die.

PART IV

CHAPTER 51

"Tea, darling? It's chamomile and honey." Emily saunters onto the patio with a mug.

I take it and smile. "Thanks."

"I see he's found the petunia bushes." She chuckles, pointing at my toddling, pink-cheeked, adventurous boy.

"And before that, it was the fennel plant that fascinated him." I point at the impressive row of herbs my aunt has growing in her back garden. It's early September, but the summer weather clings on. We're in light cardigans and jeans, gazing up at the rust-coloured leaves of the old oak tree at the bottom of the garden.

"He's a boy after my own heart." Emily brings her hand to her chest.

"I think he stole your heart." I laugh.

"There's no question about it."

She walks over to him and scoops him into her arms. He giggles and squeals as she plants sloppy wet kisses on his cheek. His chestnut-brown hair looks almost auburn gold under the afternoon sun.

Christopher is now a precocious four-year-old who runs around shouting "Mummy, look at me!" as he pretends to be Spider-Man or kicks a ball around the garden. We've come a long way since the horrifying first eight months of his life. But every time I remember the pain during those months, I'm reminded of how lucky I am to have him back.

I stand up and stretch, needing to move and flex my muscles. I never knew how much running around it would take to keep up with a four-year-old. But having Emily around to help has been an enormous bonus as I navigate the wonderful and messy trials of parenthood.

As soon as I arrived back in England, I revisited my partial memoir and readjusted the ending based on everything that happened with Christopher's abduction. Of course, I landed a publishing deal for my autobiography, though I'll forever wonder if it was solely due to Christopher's abduction and the press attention it garnered during the last week of his disappearance. I spent another few months working on the book, determined to get all the pieces just right.

Since its release, I've had to navigate the choppy waters of fame—or rather, infamy. It wasn't plain sailing. I turned down most offers for a book tour and instead chose to do one daytime television interview that, thankfully, went well enough to ensure the book was a success. Now my agent is asking for a follow-up, but I feel contented that my story—my horror story—is finally over.

Emily glances at her phone for the second time in an hour.

"Another text? Wow, he's keen!" I say.

She shrugs. "Well, we're both old, so we have no time to waste." Her secret smile brings me joy.

She places the phone in her pocket and wanders across the lawn to Christopher. She crouches down with him, pointing at a robin playing on a low limb of the oak. The robin puffs out its brilliant red chest, and I can hear her telling him about the different kinds of birds and flowers and trees.

I love him so much it hurts.

The sun beats down, and I sense my skin beginning to burn. So I wave at them both and make my way back to the house.

"There's some post for you on the table," Emily calls.

"Anything from…her?" I bristle.

The expression on her face tells me everything I need to know.

I sigh and turn towards the glass door. There, sitting on the kitchen table, is another letter from the penitentiary in New York where Alice is currently serving her sentence for child abduction. She was extradited back to the United States from Greece for the trial. There, she was sentenced for the aggravated assault of Jessa Chen and the abduction of

Christopher James McAdams. I removed the "Ethan" from his name as soon as I had him home.

I'd given my witness statements remotely, with no desire to be in the same courtroom as her ever again. Lucas went every day. It was a stressful time. The pilot from Gary Michaels's private plane gave a statement that he had seen Ethan, Alice, and Christopher on the flight. It forced her billionaire ex's hand, and in exchange for a suspended sentence, he confessed to helping them escape. The scandal went wild, trending on Twitter. He lost his place on the board of most of his tech companies.

The way I'd been treated by the media came up as a topic in many articles. There were discussions about Alice's money and how it protected her and Ethan and how the media trod lightly about the abduction, some places even leaning into the justice-for-dads narrative, despite there being clear evidence that Ethan was a controlling and abusive man. Often, these articles completely ignored Jessa's life-changing injuries caused by Alice Hart.

Then Ethan's exes came forward, detailing how he'd keep them in line. His constant tantrums over his girlfriends not wearing the outfits chosen by him or them staying out longer than agreed. Hearing their stories made me nauseated. These women were guilted into sex with him, isolated from their friends, and in some cases, even hit by him.

Before I pick up the letter, I pull in a deep breath. Every month, Alice writes to me. At first, I sent the letters back unopened. But that was before she appealed the sentence. Now I read them all, because I want to know where her headspace is. If Alice ever gets out of prison, I need to know if she poses a threat to me. I tear into the envelope, almost ripping the thin paper of the letter itself. Then I scan the contents to see if she has anything new to say.

Please send a picture of my grandson. She never calls him Christopher. It's always "my grandson." *I miss my grandson. Why are you keeping him from me?* Not once has she owned up to or taken any responsibility for her part in the kidnapping. Not once has she said outright the words "I'm sorry." It's always some variation like, *I wish things could have turned out differently*, or *How long are you going to keep punishing me for this? I gave him back to you, didn't I?*

I ignore all her attempts at manipulation. Every time I read a letter from Alice, the insincerity and the flatness of her words on the page leave me annoyed and baffled. It's like she's only writing out what she thinks I want to hear. I don't have the energy or the patience for any of it. But she has good lawyers, and I'm afraid of the appeal. In court, Alice was seen as Ethan's victim, as a woman under the influence of her violent son. After all, she did give Christopher back to me. The jury sympathised with her at times, especially when she turned on the charm while giving her evidence.

I'm bracing myself for her return.

CHAPTER 52

"Hey, sweetie! Oh, sorry, did I catch you at a bad time?"

Shopping bags fall down my wrist as I balance a whingey Christopher on my hip and lift the phone at the same time. Jessa's smiling face fills the screen, and she wiggles her fingers at Christopher.

"No, I'm good. I'm just on my way back to the car," I say. "I swear I buy new clothes and shoes for him every day. He won't stop growing!"

"Aww, I miss his face. When can I next visit?"

"Whenever you want, Jess. You know Emily and I love having you here."

It's a warm day, and I'm starting to sweat. I'm in Derby, and pavements are dusty from the Indian summer we've just had.

"You're probably going to regret that invitation because I'll never leave."

"That's fine by me." I cross the road towards the car park. "So tell me all about everything you've got going on. How was the latest appointment?"

"So much better. My short-term memory has improved so much they can hardly believe it. And I made a pretty big decision."

"Tell me." I lower Christopher to the ground as I unlock the car.

"As you know, I can't really manage the bar anymore. Even with the improvements, it's just too fast. I can't keep up like I used to. And I've been feeling bad about relying on my parents so much as an adult. You're going to be shocked when I tell you I'm finally growing up."

I laugh. "You're way more mature than you think you are, Jess. Anyway, stop stalling. Tell me!"

"I've decided to retrain. I want to help people who have gone through the same kind of injuries as me."

"Jessa, that is amazing." I pause. "But I'm sorry you've been through hell because of me."

"It wasn't your fault. It was…" She lowers her voice. "That witch's fault."

I glance at Christopher to make sure he's not listening. He's taken a Spider-Man figure out of his pocket and is playing with it on the car door. "Yeah, speaking of the witch…"

Jessa's expression changes. Fear darkens her eyes. "She won't get out. She can't. She's only served three years of her sentence. They can't deny the injuries she caused me."

I smile, trying not to let my worry show. "You're right. The appeal isn't for what she did to you. It's for the abduction."

Jessa sighs. "Like that woman has ever been a victim of anything. The abduction added several years onto her sentence. I want to feel like she's never getting out, but…"

I nod, understanding. I'm even less optimistic than Jessa. Alice has served more than half of her sentence for aggravated assault. That means if she wins her appeal against the abduction charges, she could be out very soon. But I don't say that.

"The thought of her being free makes me want to puke," Jessa says.

"Mummy, I want an ice cream," Christopher says.

"Yeah, Mummy," Jessa adds. "Get the boy an ice cream!" She laughs.

"Jessa says I can have one," Christopher says.

"All right. How about we get one on the way back?"

He throws his hands in the air and celebrates, and Jessa cracks up.

"You'd better go, Mummy," Jessa says. She puts on a fake English accent. "Toodle-oo."

I roll my eyes. "Speak to you soon, Jess."

I hang up, wishing we had more time to talk about Alice's appeal. I know how much it must be killing her to know Alice could be back in New York by the end of the year. It's killing me too. I've been considering asking Jessa to come and join me here, but she has family in New York. She loves it there. Why should she have to move?

I want to believe that Alice will move on from all of this. But she hasn't. Her letters still fixate on Christopher. I can never go to New York while she's there. The best I can do is file for a restraining order to try to stop her tracking me down. At least the home office should stop her from legally coming into the country. I'm going to have my MP's number on speed dial if the appeal goes through.

Pulling myself away from thoughts of Alice, I open the car door and place the bags in the back seat. Christopher just started at school, and I updated his uniform with another pair of trousers and two more jumpers. He already has a hole at the knee in one pair, and my darning skills just made it look even worse. It's going to be an expensive year if he keeps enacting superhero stunts with his friends at break time.

When I turn around to tell him to get in the car, I notice that he's wandered over to an older man a few cars down. He has his Spider-Man figure out and is waving it in the air as the man laughs.

"Christopher!" I yell, not meaning to sound so panicked. My heart is pounding, and I have to pull in a deep breath to calm myself down. "It's time to go."

He waves at the man and runs back to me, his cheeks flushed. The man nods before walking away with a cane and a slight limp.

"Christopher, don't wander off like that," I say.

"I was just showing him my toy," he protests.

"Come on. Let's get you that ice cream." I open the passenger door for him, feeling guilty about shouting. Then I climb in the driver's side.

"Yes!" Christopher says. "Chocolate, please."

I nod, still distracted. No matter how much time passes since Ethan died, I still feel the need to check over my shoulder. And I especially hate it when Christopher wanders away from me. Still, I can't help but feel like I was rude to not go over to the man and chat with him for a while. After all, Christopher did go over to him and bother him with his Spider-Man toy.

It's Alice's appeal that has me spooked. Her being in prison gives me a sense that justice has been served. Ethan is dead. Alice is behind bars. If she's free to walk the streets, to go back to her life of privilege, then that sense of justice is shattered. It's not a world I want to believe exists.

CHAPTER 53

We stop at an ice cream parlour Christopher loves and order big bowls of chocolate ice cream. I ping a text to Emily to make sure she knows not to make a big meal for dinner. It's a Saturday, and she likes to cook. I usually do the Sunday roast, though.

As I wipe ice cream from Christopher's face, I can't help but think about the future. We can't live with Emily forever. My book sales have been good enough for me to afford a very nice house in the same area, but we've lived with my aunt for this long because it feels safe in her house. When my mum died, Emily made me feel protected there, and now she's done the same thing again. But I can't keep relying on her.

I need to forge my own future. I haven't had a long-term relationship for years. Lucas and I FaceTime, too, and I still feel that magnetic draw to him that I felt in Greece, but we're in different countries now, living completely different lives. I'm stuck in limbo. Most of my friends are in New York, not Derbyshire. And now with the threat of Alice's appeal, I feel even more stuck.

"You look sad, Mummy," Christopher says.

He catches me off guard. "I'm not sad."

"Who is Alice?"

My back straightens. "What makes you ask that, buddy?"

"You keep talking about her. You and Em-em and Jessa. Who is she?"

My fingers tighten around my spoon. When it became apparent that

Christopher didn't remember being on the yacht, I had never been so relieved. He doesn't remember Alice or Ethan at all. As far as he's concerned, his life started with me and Emily, safely back in England.

"She's someone who hurt Aunt Jessa. And now she might be moving back to New York, and I don't want her to be around Jessa."

Christopher nods. "I don't want that either."

"Well, it's not going to happen. I've been talking to Lucas, and he doesn't think it's going to happen either. Which is good." I keep my voice bright. "How's the ice cream, sweet pea?"

He grins. "So good. Can I have another scoop?"

I check my watch. It's almost five in the afternoon now. We have another hour on the road, and I don't want to be late for dinner with Emily. "No. Come on. Let's get back."

As we're getting out of our seats, a man walks over. He's tall, broad-shouldered, and dark-haired. There's something about his smile that freezes my blood. But of course, I'm imprinting Ethan's face onto his. It's been an annoying phenomenon that dozens of hours of therapy still hasn't corrected.

"I'm so sorry to bother you. I just wanted to let you know that my wife loves your book."

"Thank you," I say.

The man seems perfectly nice and has a daughter with him. But I'm still shaking as he moves away from the table. I raise my eyebrows, more to myself, at my overreaction. If I keep seeing Ethan's face on every single man, how am I ever going to have another relationship?

Christopher slips his hand into mine as we leave. It's one of those moments where I'm aware of how quickly he's had to grow up. He knows when to comfort me, and that makes my heart hurt. I need to get better at covering up my anxiety for him. Or the damn therapy needs to start working. Soon, I'll be seeing Alice's face imprinted on every sixty-year-old woman I see.

We get in the car, and I send Emily another text to let her know we're on our way back.

We have a visitor for dinner. Is that okay? she asks.

For a moment, I'm confused. But then I realise it must be the mystery man. *Is it Max?*

Yes. He just turned up. I'm a bit frazzled, to be honest. But at least you can meet him.

I can't wait.

"It's been a long day," I say half to myself, putting the car in gear.

"I got new trousers!" Christopher declares.

"Yes, you did, buddy."

The drive goes by quickly, though we hit a bit of traffic while leaving the city. Christopher dozes in his seat, tired from all the walking around the shops. I begin to decompress, relieved to be going home. A full day out always drains me.

The display screen on the dashboard tells me my phone is ringing, and I note that it's Lucas. While I want to talk to him, I'm worried he might have bad news about Alice's appeal, so I decide not to answer.

My fingers tighten against the steering wheel, and I concentrate on the road. It begins to rain, coming down fast and hard. The windscreen wipers squeak their way over the glass. Soon, the main roads narrow and twist into the rural lanes around Emily's house. I've never liked driving down these skinny tracks in bad weather. I take it steady, pulling into the side of the road when a car comes in the opposite direction. Christopher softly snores in the seat next to me. I feel bad about giving him ice cream. Emily has a guest for dinner, and Christopher isn't going to want any food at all. Still, at least he can nap while we eat.

The tension uncoils from my body as I pull into the driveway. We're home and safe. The rain soaks me as I run around to Christopher's side to let him out. He stirs as I gently place him against my shoulder, shielding him from the rain with the umbrella. I decide to take him in first and come back for the bags later. Maybe tomorrow morning if it carries on like this.

Rain patters against the stone path. I hurry, not wanting to trip and fall with Christopher in my arms.

"Phew, it's raining cats and dogs out there," I say, stepping into the hallway.

I take Christopher straight through to the lounge and place him down on the sofa. Then I straighten up, smoothing my wet hair away from my face.

"Oh, hello. You must be Max." I take a step towards the stranger standing in the living room doorway. And then I stop.

"Hello, Laura."

He has a soft, northern accent. He leans on a cane, waiting for me to approach. But I don't take another step. In fact, I move away from him.

"You were in the car park," I say.

The man must be in his late sixties. He rests on a wooden cane with a dark handle. His greying hair is covered by a beaten-up trilby hat, and he wears a smart wax jacket over a shirt.

"Yes. I met Christopher."

"What are you… What are you doing here?"

"I'm Max," he says.

Something isn't right. This is too much of a coincidence. Why doesn't he walk into the room? Why is he standing there in the shadows?

"Christopher was showing me his Spider-Man toy. He's a sweet boy."

The man smiles. He has straight white teeth.

I take another step towards my son. "Who are you?"

Suddenly, Christopher jumps up from the sofa and runs towards the man. I reach out, but he's too quick for me to grab hold of him.

"Hello again," Max says, lifting my son up. He hoists him onto his hip and holds him there.

I find the whole thing bizarre to watch. It's like witnessing an older man perform a physical movement too young for his age. The cane drops to the floor, unneeded. I reach into my jeans pocket for my phone.

"He's a good boy, your kid."

The man's voice is changing. The northern accent melts away.

"Junior, wasn't it?"

I pull the phone from my pocket. Then I pause. "What?"

"His name. Wasn't it Ethan Junior?"

Every hair prickles across my scalp, moving from the nape of my neck to my forehead. *That voice.* I would know that voice anywhere. It's the one that comes to me in my nightmares. And then he says the words that have terrified me for years.

"Have you missed me, Laura?"

CHAPTER 54

"Ethan," I say.

He smiles. "What's the matter? Didn't you recognise me? Mother taught me a thing or two when it comes to makeup. And you should see the things that can be done with latex these days." He peels a fake nose from his face, and Christopher squirms, terrified.

His real nose is scarred from where my teeth sank into his flesh. Ethan clutches my son tighter, his fingers digging into Christopher's arm.

"Please don't hurt him!" I cry.

I stare down at the phone and squeeze the edges to quickly call the emergency service.

"Laura!" he shouts in a deep, commanding voice.

When I look up, he has one hand wrapped around Christopher's neck. I sprint across the room, but Ethan squeezes his hand, and Christopher lets out a whimper. I stop, one arm stretched out, begging him to stop.

"Call the police, and I will snap his neck."

I shake my head. "You won't. You haven't come all this way for your son only to murder him."

"Won't I? I have nothing left to lose, Laura. You made sure of that. If I let you call the police, I'll be going back to a life of nothingness, won't I? I may as well take you all with me. Now, be a good girl and put your phone in my pocket. Come on. Don't try anything, or I will kill Junior here."

There are tears running down my face as I inch towards him. Christopher's red, crying face stares at me as I place the phone in Ethan's pocket before moving away again.

"See. Now wasn't that easy?" He removes his hand from Christopher's neck. "Why couldn't you be like that when we were co-parenting? I only ever wanted you to do what I told you to do because it was for the best." He sighs.

"You sabotaged my career, broke into my apartment, installed keystroke-tracking software on my laptop, and abducted my child. Nothing you did was for me. It was all for you."

He just smiles.

"Where is Emily?" I ask.

"She's safe," he says. "For now."

I hate him so much. More than I've ever hated anyone or anything in my entire life. It's like an infection spreading around my body. I flex my hands, longing to claw at his face like a wild animal. The *fight* reflex is a strong one, calling to me, but while he has Christopher, I can't. Maybe if it was just me, I would risk it, but I can't. Both Emily's and Christopher's lives are in my hands. I'm well aware of how many women have been killed trying to defend themselves against violent men. I'm smaller than him, and even if I use a weapon, statistically, he's more likely to take that weapon from me and use it on me.

Nausea creeps through my stomach. It pains me to admit that the best thing I can do is fawn until I can put a plan into action. I can pretend to be the woman he wants me to be. Maybe he'll let his guard down that way.

"Would you like a drink?" I ask sweetly.

"What, and have you drug me? I don't think so. Why don't we all sit down on the sofa so we can have a chat?" he says.

"Okay," I say. "But maybe you can let me know where Aunt Emily is as I sit down." I make my way over to the sofa. My knees tremble with every step. As I slowly lower myself onto the beige cushion, I realise my teeth are starting to chatter, and I'm not even cold. I rest my chin on my palm so that Ethan won't notice.

"All you need to know is that I'm going to kill her unless you do everything I tell you to do." His eyes bore into me, cold and calculated.

Christopher's quiet crying turns into sobs.

"It's okay, buddy," I say, tears pricking at my eyes. "Everything is going to be okay."

"Daddy's here, Junior," Ethan says, bouncing Christopher like he's still a baby. "What has Mommy told you about me? Nothing good, I expect."

"I haven't told him anything," I say quietly. "He doesn't remember you."

"And whose fault is that?" he asks.

I flinch. His voice is like a snarl, the hatred dripping from every word. The room goes quiet aside from the sound of Christopher crying. Ethan removes his hat and jacket, pulls away a wig, and begins tearing at the latex makeup on his face. I turn away. Somehow, seeing his real face makes it even harder. That moment in the ice cream parlour terrified me, as has every other moment where I've conjured Ethan's face, bringing him back from the dead. Well, here he is. Alive.

"How did you do it?" I ask. "How did you get away?"

He turns to me, and I see the other scars on his face now. He must have incurred them during the fall.

"You mean after you tried to kill me?" He smiles. "Well, I didn't fall as far as you wanted me to. There was a ledge about a quarter of the way down. As you can see, I still faced a few challenges. A dislocated shoulder, cuts and bruises all over me. But I managed to steal a boat and get away."

"And you made it all the way to England. Impressive."

"Yes, it is, isn't it? Luckily, Mother and I always kept a few friends in low places. There was one willing to provide a place for me to stay for a while." He shrugs. "As you know, Mother had a lot of lovers over the years. All were rich, but some were bad people. I made sure to stay friendly with them in case I needed things."

"Is that how you knew where to hire a hit man?" I ask.

He readjusts Christopher. "Perhaps."

"And whoever drove into Jessa's car that day."

He smiles. "I was hoping that would result in something more than a broken wrist. How is Jessa?"

"She's fine. She moved to Florida," I lie. If anything bad happens to me, I don't want him going after her.

Ethan turns his attention to Christopher. "He looks like me. Ethan

Junior. That's going to be your name from now on. Now that I'm done playing your mommy's games. That's right. Mommy is going to play my game."

"I've always been playing your game, Ethan," I say, my voice devoid of emotion. "Right from the first moment I clapped eyes on you."

He ignores me. "Mommy is going to do everything I tell her to do because if she doesn't, I'll kill her aunty. Maybe I'll slit Emily's throat and watch all the blood drain out of her body. Wouldn't that be fun?"

My body goes cold. This is Ethan with the mask off. Every pretence gone. He's a complete and utter psychopath.

"Mommy is going to give me a big kiss."

Revulsion shudders through me. "No."

He turns his head so I can see only his profile. He taps an impatient finger against his cheek. "Kiss me here and tell me you love me."

I close my hands into tight fists and suppress a shiver. My lips press against his flushed and fevered skin. It takes everything I have not to throw up. I make it quick, and my lips barely skid across his skin. Afterwards, I control the urge to wipe my mouth.

He doesn't make me do it again, but he does turn to me, his eyes narrowed and malicious. "You forgot to tell me you love me."

"I love you," I mumble.

"Huh?" He cups a hand over his ear and tilts his head closer to me. "What's that? I couldn't hear you. *Speak up*."

My voice is deadpan but louder. "I love you."

He starts to laugh. "Oh, what a wonderful family I have. I'm so happy to be back in the arms of my loving wife. And to have the son I always wanted in my arms. I always knew we'd get here eventually. Whatever the cost."

CHAPTER 55

"Now. I want you to make me supper." He tilts his head again, studying me. "What kind of host are you? You don't have dinner ready on the table for your loving husband?"

"Okay… I… I'll need to go into the kitchen."

"Why don't we all go?" Ethan lifts Christopher onto the ground and clasps his hand.

I watch, my heart in my mouth, constantly hoping for an opportunity to take my son back. Christopher's gaze meets mine, fear and tears gathered in his eyes. Ethan lifts himself to his feet and gestures for me to follow.

"Mommy has to hold my other hand."

"No," I whisper.

"Come on! The Hart family love each other. We're all going to walk through the house together. Isn't that right, Junior?" He reaches out his free hand.

Reluctantly, I take it, my fingers limp inside his grip. I can't stand the feel of him, but I'm surprised to see there's latex makeup on the backs of his hands, too, to make his skin appear more mottled. The planning he's put into this is shocking.

He lets me go as we enter the kitchen. I see the remnants of Emily's meal—a casserole dish abandoned on the kitchen counter, the ingredients not yet cooked. He must have caught her as she was putting it in the oven, and my eyes prick with tears. I try to figure out how long he had to subdue her. It depends on whether Emily wrote those text messages to me or not. If she did, he had only an hour to hide her. Surely that means she's somewhere inside the house. But if he had longer, he could have taken her to another location.

But he was at the car park at the same time as me. And with an hour of driving, that definitely suggests he had around two hours at the most. Could he have hidden her somewhere away from the house? I'm not sure.

"Hey!" Ethan calls. "Concentrate on making me food, not on moping around. I want spaghetti. Now."

"We don't have it," I say. "How about a sandwich?"

"Fine. Make a sandwich, then. But if it's bad, I'm going to chew it up and spit it out and make *you* eat it."

I grab a loaf of bread from the cupboard and butter and cheese from the fridge. He rests a hip against the counter, practically breathing down my neck. My eyes drift over to the knife block, but Ethan is watching me like a hawk. He lifts a hand to Christopher's throat and gently encircles his slim neck.

"If you try anything with those knives, I'll strangle the life out of him. Can you kill me before I kill our son?" There's no trace of the smug smile on his face. There's no life in his eyes.

Trying to shake all the fear out of my body, I decide to keep him talking. "Christopher—"

"Junior," Ethan corrects.

"Junior started school this year. Didn't you, buddy?"

Shakily, he answers. "Yes."

"He's doing really well."

His hand moves from Christopher's neck, and relief floods through me. "Is that so?"

I slice the cheese and place it on the buttered bread. "He's made lots of friends. Haven't you… Junior?"

His quiet voice shakes as he answers. "Yes, Mummy."

"Yes, Daddy," Ethan corrects.

I press the slices of bread together. My eyes linger on the knife I used to cut the slices of cheese.

"Yes, Daddy," Christopher says.

"Oh, look at you," Ethan says. "All snotty. Laura, pass me a tissue."

I pull off a sheet of kitchen roll and hand it to him. Ethan is momentarily distracted as he wipes Christopher's face. Gently, I place my hand on top of the knife, obscuring it, wondering if I can slip it into my jacket pocket.

"That's better," Ethan says. "Laura, open a beer for me. I need something to wash the sandwich down with."

"We don't have any beer."

He sighs. "What *do* you have, then?"

As I walk over to the fridge, I slip the knife from the kitchen counter and tuck it up the sleeve of my jacket. Then I open the fridge and peer in, positioning myself so that the fridge door blocks me from view. "Water, apple juice, milk." I slide the knife into my jacket pocket.

Ethan scoffs. "What kind of place is this?"

"Emily doesn't drink alcohol."

"Fine." He groans, eyes rolling up to the ceiling. "Milk, then."

I pour his milk into a glass.

"Back to the living room," he orders. "I want us to sit as a family on the sofa." He tugs Christopher's hand and leads him away from the kitchen.

I carry the drink and sandwich over to the sofa and place them on the coffee table. Christopher is resistant to get onto Ethan's lap this time, and I see the frustration on Ethan's face. As much as he wants *possession* of his son, actually caring for him is another matter. Finally, he picks Christopher up and places him on his knee, holding him still.

With his free hand, Ethan picks up the sandwich and makes a face. "What is this? Cheese? On white bread?"

"We're not in New York anymore," I say. "I can't pop to the deli for ham on rye."

He takes a bite and, thankfully, doesn't complain. But I can see him struggling to hold Christopher and eat at the same time.

"Maybe I could hold him for you?" I suggest.

"No!" he snaps.

He takes two bites and places the sandwich down. Then he bounces Christopher on his knee. "I lived and worked in Istanbul for a while. Beautiful city. You'd love it there. I went to the Hagia Sophia one day, and I was looking up at the beautiful ceilings, and all I could think about was taking my son to see such beauty." He glares at me. "You took him away from me."

I say nothing. He's goading me.

"If you ask me, it's a crime to keep a father from his son. Everything that has happened since Junior was born is all because of you. It's because you didn't do your duty. I would have provided everything for us. You know that, don't you? I had the means. Junior would go to the best school, you'd live in the best apartment in the city, and we'd have the perfect life. But you're such a cunt that you couldn't accept that."

I grab the knife from my pocket and thrust it forward, aiming for Ethan's thigh. He's on his feet in an instant, with me lurching into the sofa cushion instead. I let out a cry of frustration, but it's nothing compared to the squeal of pain coming from Christopher. Ethan has his hand on my son's hair, and he's tugging it hard. Poor Christopher scratches at his father's hands.

Christopher's screams chill me to the bone, and I freeze. It's enough time for Ethan to wrench the knife from my hand. Then he thrusts it close to Christopher's skinny neck.

"Stop! No. Please stop!" I scream. "I'll do anything you want. I swear. Please don't hurt him."

"Do I have your fucking attention now, Laura? Do you know where this will end if you don't do what I say?"

"Yes. I swear. I promise. I'll do everything you say. Just let him go. Please. Please, Ethan."

Satisfied by my contrition, Ethan gives Christopher's hair one more tug and then lets go. He puts the knife in his pocket and picks up his sandwich.

"You'll only make everything harder." He shakes his head.

Convulsions rattle through my body, teeth chattering together. There's no way out of this, not while Ethan is in control. I have to do whatever he wants.

CHAPTER 56

I bundle Christopher into my arms, stroking his back. He sobs against my shoulder. I'm shivering, my teeth chattering as I think about Ethan holding the knife against my son's precious flesh. One stab and he could have severed an artery. The top of his head is red and sore from where Ethan grabbed his hair. I notice a few strands scattered across his shoulders.

"Can you shut that damn kid up? All that racket is giving me a headache," Ethan says, shoving the sandwich into his face.

I wish I'd spat in it.

"Everything's going to be okay, buddy," I say. "It's all going to be fine."

"I want Em-em," he says between sobs.

"She's resting right now, but she'll be here soon." I glance up at Ethan. "I think Chris—Junior needs to go to bed now."

Ethan polishes off the milk in two large gulps then pops the remaining bite of sandwich into his mouth. Then he takes his arm and sweeps it across the table. The plate and cup topple from the edge and drop to the floor.

He turns to me with a smirk on his face. "Pick it up. You made a mess."

I don't want to let go of Christopher, so I ease him onto his feet and hold his hand. I crouch down and pick up the chipped plate. My heart skips a beat when I grab the glass. If it had shattered, I could have pocketed something sharp to use on Ethan. But it didn't break. After I've stacked the plate and glass on the coffee table, I lean back against the sofa cushions. I place Christopher down next to me, trying to think of my next move. There has to be something I can do.

Ethan shimmies closer until our hips and thighs are touching. He places one arm along the back of the sofa, casually grazing my shoulders. The smile on his face is devilish. It says everything. That he's won. He has all the control over me that he desired from the first day I met him. Ethan has me in the palm of his hand and can crush me at any moment.

I scan the room for makeshift weapons that I could use against him. I would have to break something. An ornament, maybe. Or there's a paperweight on the bookcase. I'm not sure if it's big enough, but I suppose I could try. But I think my best bet is getting out of this room completely. There's a landline phone in the study. If Ethan hasn't thought to cut the line, I can dial for help. But he's not going to let me out of his sight.

Christopher is still sniffling. His nose is red, and his eyelashes are damp. He blinks at Ethan, confused by all the tension in the room.

An idea pops into my mind. I play it out in my head for a practice run before I say it aloud, hoping I'll sound convincing enough for Ethan to comply.

As casually as I'm able, I turn my head towards Ethan. In my breeziest voice, I say, "Junior is tired, and he's had a long day. Can I go upstairs and give him a bath and put him to bed? Then perhaps we can talk about all this—alone. I don't want to scare him."

Ethan's eyes narrow. He cocks his head to one side, considering my proposition.

"You can see how scared he is," I say. "We don't want to traumatise him further. You want him to love you, don't you? You want him to love his daddy."

Something soft flickers in Ethan's eyes, but it's so brief, I find myself wondering if I even saw it at all or if my mind is trying to get me to believe in something that doesn't exist. That Ethan might, somewhere deep down, have empathy for someone other than himself.

"Fine." His jaw clenches. "But I'm going with you."

"Oh, you don't want to do that," I say, suddenly panicked. I had hoped that a parenting chore would be deemed too boring for him. "I don't think Junior will feel comfortable with you in the room."

"He'll be fine. Won't you, son?"

My heart sinks. "What if he needs the toilet? Do you need the toilet, Junior?"

Christopher's eyes fill with a watery panic. "I…"

"He doesn't need the toilet, Laura. Now, come on. Let's go bathe the little tyke. Hand him over." Ethan holds out his hands. "I don't want you trying anything. If you do, I'll strangle him."

"I get it, Ethan!" I snap.

"Watch it. I won't tolerate disobedience in this house."

I bow my head, pretending to be subservient. "I'm sorry."

Him coming with me is not what I wanted, but it's better than nothing. Maybe I can find a way to shove him down the stairs or at least see where he has Emily. My heart pounds as we stand up from the sofa. I make my way out of the room, constantly aware of his presence behind me, terrified by the fact I can't see my son as I move up the stairs.

There's a sigh behind me. "Hurry up, Laura. We don't have all day."

He knows I'm stalling as I try to think about my next move. I filter through the questions in my mind. What is the endgame for this man? Does he think he can keep my aunt tied up forever? That I'll play the dutiful wife for the rest of his life? Ethan is too smart for that. No, he knows this can't go on for long. He's dragging out my death. He's getting what he wants from me before he finishes off both me and Emily. And then he'll take my son somewhere, intent on turning him into a small version of himself.

As we make our way down the hallway, I search the bedroom doors for any sign of Emily. We pass Christopher's room with his superhero sign on the door. He'd picked it out at a local craft fair. I pull my eyes away, trying to concentrate.

"Is Emily up here?" I ask, trying to keep my voice gentle and submissive. "Can I see her?"

"Not yet," he replies.

"Okay."

We go into the small bathroom, and I pull the light switch cord. An image flashes into my mind of Ethan choking, the cord wrapped around his neck. Maybe once Christopher is in the bathwater. I wonder if I have the upper body strength to use a thin rope to kill a man. I doubt it. But it could be enough to distract him.

And then what? I still don't know where Emily is.

I start the water, and Ethan sits down on the toilet lid and watches, curiosity on his face. Christopher is at the age where I just supervise now. I don't properly bathe him. He can do that himself. But I notice Ethan's expression, as though he's drinking in this family moment.

"Did you bathe Chris—Junior—when you had him in Greece?" I ask, keeping my voice soft, still hoping he'll drop his guard.

"Mom did it," he says.

That doesn't surprise me. No wonder Alice wanted out. Ethan's desire to be a *good* dad is nonexistent. His desire to possess a mini-me, however… I pour soap into the bath to give Christopher some bubbles and also to keep my hands hidden, just in case I find a toy at the bottom I can use to strike Ethan in the face. God, I'm getting desperate. How much damage can a child's toy inflict?

"Can Junior come over to me now?" I gesture to where Ethan is still holding Christopher's hand.

Ethan nods and lets go. The terror on my son's face makes me want to burst into tears, but he's being a brave boy. There are no more tears now. He walks stiffly over to me and stands by my side.

"Okay, now get undressed, buddy," I say.

Christopher looks at me and then Ethan. "I don't want to, Mummy."

"It's okay, son. I won't look." Ethan turns his head away.

I glance at the door. I would have to get past Ethan to escape with Christopher. And at four, he's heavy on my hip. There's no way I could do it fast enough. Even if I wrapped the cord from the light switch around his neck, Ethan could cut it with the knife or simply overpower me. I close my eyes for a moment, hopelessness washing over me.

Christopher undresses, and I place him in the bathwater. He sits as still as a soldier. But I feel like I need to give Ethan a show for him to relax and have the experience of being a father like he desperately wants.

I crouch by the bath and scoop up a handful of bubbles. "Remember when you used to call these bub-bubs?"

I smile, but it fades from my face when Christopher's eyes widen, and his gaze rises to above my head. He opens his mouth as though to call out, but the sound is cut off when I feel pressure on the back of my head. The force makes me gasp, and soon, my mouth is filled with soapy water. I'm so startled that I start choking. I thrash, pushing against the side of the bath with scrabbling hands. The water splashes around us, and Christopher shrieks.

Ethan lets me go, and when I come up for air, I see him rubbing at a red mark on his hand. Quick as a flash, I grab Christopher and hold him against my body. Ethan grabs hold of my hair and pulls me forwards. My eyes water, and my nose burns, but I stay strong, keeping Christopher close to me.

"Your son just bit me," Ethan says. "Tell him not to do that again, or I will drown his mother."

"Don't do that again, Christopher," I say, forgetting to call him Junior. I twist my head to look Ethan in the eye. "You're a psycho."

He just smiles.

CHAPTER 57

"Don't drop him!" Ethan shouts as I help Christopher out of the bath and drain the water. "Be more careful. You're so stupid."

I do my best to ignore the insults and grab a towel from the rack. It's hard, but I focus all my concentration on Christopher and on keeping him relaxed. Water drips down my chest and back, but I ignore it. Instead, I wrap the soft towel around my son's small body and lift him up to my waist.

"Gosh, look at silly Mummy," I say. "Soaking wet." But Christopher doesn't even crack a smile. I turn to Ethan. "I'm going to take him to his bedroom now."

"Well, go on, then," Ethan says.

Aware of him behind me, I make my way through the hallway towards Christopher's bedroom. All the while, I wonder where Ethan has put Emily. I can't stand the thought of her tied up somewhere alone. Or worse. *What has he done to her?* Again, my mind drifts to the eventual outcome of what is happening here. And it's at that point I realise what I'll need to do to escape.

But I can't think about that now.

I switch on Christopher's bedside lamp. Warm yellow light splashes across the room, illuminating Christopher's pirate-ship bedsheets and matching curtains.

"God, what an awfully tacky room." Ethan wanders over to the curtains. "Did you pick these?"

"No, Christopher did." I lower my son into his bed and grab some pyjamas out of a drawer. They're his Superman pyjamas.

"Mother is right about you," he says. "You have no taste."

"Well, I slept with you, didn't I?" I say, too full of disgust to hide it. "Only the once, though. I wouldn't degrade myself a second time."

I brace myself, knowing I've gone too far. I expect him to hit me, and I stay very still, standing next to Christopher's bed, waiting for it to happen. But it never comes. Ethan walks over to the rocking chair in the corner of the room as I help Christopher into his pyjamas. He idly runs a finger along the books in the shelving unit next to the chair.

Once I'm done, Ethan snaps his fingers. "No, don't put him in bed." He pats his lap. "Come here, son.

I watch cautiously as Christopher climbs back out of bed. My heart is in my mouth. Christopher knows we're playing this game now, and he knows the consequences if he doesn't play along well.

"No," Ethan says, his frosty gaze set on me. "*Both* of you come here."

"You—you want us both to sit on your lap?"

Ethan smiles. "Yes. You on one hip, Christopher on the other."

I take Christopher's hand, and we walk across the room. It takes us only four steps, but the seconds drag on forever.

I hesitate as I slowly lower myself onto Ethan's waiting thigh. He lifts Christopher and snuggles his arm around him. My eyes drift to Ethan's neck, visualising myself strangling him to death. Do I have time to knee him in the crotch? Or bite his ear? Or push my fingers into his eyes?

While I'm considering every option, Ethan grabs a book and throws it at me. I catch it just before it hits me in the face.

"Read it," Ethan says. "Make sure the kid is sleepy."

I begin reading it in the most composed voice I can, forcing myself to do the voices like I do most nights. Usually, Christopher giggles with joy, but tonight, he stares at his father fearfully. As I read, Ethan boldly plants his hand around my waist. Careful not to flinch, I concentrate my efforts on reading. It's a chapter from *Winnie the Pooh.*

I quickly finish the chapter and get up. "Right. Let's get you into bed, mister. You must be tired." My voice sounds high-pitched and strange.

"Yes, Junior. You need your rest if you're going to grow into a strong man like your daddy." Ethan grins.

I tuck Christopher into bed and kiss him on the forehead like I always do. His eyes are drooping, which surprises me. But the stress of tonight must have taken a toll.

"Very good," Ethan says.

We step out of the room, and Ethan hesitates. He looks at Christopher's door and then at Emily's comfy reading chair she keeps by a window nook. He grabs the chair and jams it up against Christopher's door.

"No," I say. "You can't."

"Why?"

"What if there's a fire? Please, Ethan."

"I don't want him roaming around in the night." He jams the chair into place and then turns to me. "And now it's just you and me."

My stomach flips over. Just me and him. What is he going to want me to do? I know I'll do it. Anything to find myself in a position where I could harm him and get out.

He places a hand on my elbow as we walk to the lower floor, his fingers digging deep into my flesh. My heart flutters like a humming-bird caught in a cage. We're alone. At least Christopher is safe, but I can't stand the thought of being alone with this man.

"Ethan," I say, unsure where I'm going with this but sensing the need to say something. "I... I... We..."

He laughs as he makes his way over to a chair and flops down before placing both feet on Emily's coffee table. "Spit it out, won't you?" He takes the knife out of his pocket and begins playing with it, turning it over in his hands.

"This can't carry on," I say. "You can't just keep me here as a hostage."

His face is blank, unassuming. "I'm not holding you hostage. This is just a learning period. Once we're done, we're going to be a family."

"What do you mean by 'learning period'?" I ask.

"Well, I'm teaching you how to be a mother and a wife, of course."

I swallow disgust. "Okay. But the thing is, Ethan, you're wanted for kidnapping. How are we supposed to live as a family if you're a wanted man?"

"It's simple. Don't tell anyone I'm here." He shrugs.

It at least confirms to me that he has no plan beyond holding us hostage for as long as he can. He has no way to clear his name, and he has no idea how to keep this going. But of course he doesn't. His mother has been cleaning up his messes all his life.

"Oh, by the way, I have something for you." He digs into his pocket and produces a small, shiny object. Without another word, he tosses it to me.

My mother's emerald ring.

"Put it on," he says. "It's your engagement ring."

I slide the ring onto my ring finger, deciding not to ask any questions about how he got this. It's pretty obvious he was the one behind the burglary at my flat. Instead, I try changing the subject. I want to keep him talking, but I don't want the focus on me.

"Ethan, are you aware that your mother writes to me from prison?"

His face is a concrete slab, devoid of all emotion. I don't let this deter me.

"Anyway, her letters are desperate. She wants me to forgive her for what she's done. You see, she feels bad about abducting Christopher. Maybe if I read one of her letters to you, you might change your perspective."

"No. I'm not reading any of her letters," he says almost casually. "I don't care what she has to say. She doesn't know what's best for my family."

"She's appealing her sentencing. She might be leaving prison soon."

He nods. "I read about that." He pushes a finger against the tip of the blade, testing the sharpness. "Still, I don't see how it will affect us. She betrayed me. I want nothing to do with her."

"Okay, I understand that," I say. "But how can we restore what we had before, after all you've done? You've hurt me so many times, and now you're hurting Junior too. You held that knife to his throat."

Ethan's jaw clenches. "Seems like you're a hypocrite. Always waxing on about how everyone should spread kindness and peace, but here you are, unwilling to give us another chance."

"I've tried to give you thousands of chances, Ethan. You've torn them all to shreds."

"You could have made it easier on me," he says. "You've always been so cold to me. You barely let me see Christopher. You acted like I was a stranger who didn't deserve to be in his life."

I try not to laugh. The hurt in his voice, the puppy-dog eyes… he believes his words. He genuinely thinks this is all me and that I've somehow forced him to reach this point.

"Ethan," I say. "I'm only going to say this once. It's the truth of who you are. You are an empty space in this world. A void who will pull everyone and anyone into your darkness if they give you so much as an inch. Every time I allowed you into my life, you tried to pull me into your soul-sucking void. Every time. And now you want to do the same to Christopher. Listen to me, Ethan. I will kill or die to make sure that never happens. You will never have him. Never."

He's quiet for a moment, his chest rising and falling rapidly. Then he says, "Sit on the sofa, Laura."

"Why?" I take a step backwards, trying to position myself closer to the door.

"Because I said so." He points the knife at the sofa. "I don't want to fight with you. I just want to make things right. Help me make things right with you again." It's bizarre how he can ignore everything I say. He's like Teflon when it comes to criticism.

"I don't want to sit there," I insist. But there's a creeping sense of dread travelling up my body. He has a knife, and I have nothing. He wants me to obey him completely, and if I don't, I risk his temper. My hair is still wet from when he half drowned me.

"Do you want your aunt to die?" he asks.

I gaze out at the hallway then back at Ethan.

"You don't know where she is, and I do. Remember? Kill me, and you'll never find out."

"How do I know she isn't already dead?"

He rolls his eyes. "She isn't."

"If she's somewhere in the house, I can just find her after I kill you."

He leaps up from his seat in one terrifying quick motion. His wrist flicks, and he brings the tip of the blade under my chin. His other hand palms my damp hair.

He lowers his lips to my ear. "Sit. Down."

As I slowly lower myself to the sofa, he gently shifts the knife an inch away. And then he sits down next to me. There's a dot of blood on the knife's tip.

"Oops," he says, and then he leans into me, kissing under my chin where I'm bleeding. "There. That's better."

The feel of his lips on my skin will haunt me forever. I squirm away, tears streaming down my face. Ethan allows his finger to trail across my thigh. I can't bear it. I push him away. He pulls his body back. Penetrating, dark eyes roam over me. His mouth hangs open at my audacity in rejecting him. Then he lifts his arm and slams his fist into the side of my jaw. The searing sting makes the bones in my skull vibrate.

It knocks the breath out of me, and I lose my balance, tumbling to the carpet. My palms hit the threads with a flat slap, and I waste no time pushing myself up, feet scrambling underneath me. There are no thoughts in my head except for survival. This is flight—the need to get away from this man. My legs propel me forward, and I run. I don't know where. Somewhere he isn't.

I barrel towards the study. Maybe if I can get to the phone… But Ethan is too fast for me. He tackles me to the floor, and I slam into floorboards. When my wrist lands the wrong way under my weight, I yelp. The pain shoots up to my elbow.

I try to scramble forwards to get out from underneath Ethan's weight, but he has me pinned. He turns me over so that we're facing each other, him straddled across my waist. We're both panting hard, our clothes and hair askew. I taste blood from my busted lip. My wrist throbs.

"Laura, let me make one thing clear because I think you are misunderstanding me. You live under *my* rules now. There is no going back, and there is definitely no escape route."

CHAPTER 58

I blink against the sunlight as it filters in through the windows. There's a searing pain running along my skull. A tension headache, perhaps, or Ethan hurt me when he yanked my hair and half drowned me. Judging by the pale-yellow light, I'm guessing it's still early morning. It's quiet and peaceful.

Ethan. Christopher. Emily.

The events from the day before could be a dream, a nightmare. *God, I wish they were.*

Slowly, I open my eyes and check my surroundings. I'm still in the living room, leaning against the armrest of the sofa. The television is on, but the sound is low, and I can't make out what is being said between the characters on a show I don't recognise.

Ethan is awake, staring blankly at the TV screen. His eyes are bloodshot, his dark hair dishevelled. The collar of his shirt points up, scrunched slightly to the right.

He hasn't noticed that I'm awake yet. Slowly, I edge away from him, but Ethan is quick. His hand whips out to cuff my bad wrist. He digs his nails into my skin, watching me scream in pain.

"You're not going anywhere," he says.

"Ethan, please. That hurts."

He lets go but comes closer, his gaze focused on me.

"I need to use the toilet," I say.

He rolls his eyes. "Fine. Then I'm coming with you."

"Can you not give me thirty seconds of privacy?" I ask. "It's human decency."

"Human decency doesn't apply to women who try to keep a loving father from his son."

Ethan drags me up from the sofa by my wrist, and I smother a cry of pain. I don't want to wake up Christopher, not yet. Then Ethan gestures for me to walk. I make my way into the hallway and open the door to the downstairs toilet. He releases me but blocks the door with his shoulder when I attempt to close it for privacy. I'm forced to empty my bladder with him watching, a smirk stretched across his face. Power involves humiliation, doesn't it? He wants to know how much he can take from me. And this will continue until I stop him.

I quickly test my wrist while I'm in the toilet. It's injured but not broken. There's a slight swelling, and it hurts to use it, but I have mobility, and that's good.

Once I'm done and my hands are washed, he grabs hold of my top by its neck and steps into the toilet to use it himself. I turn my head away. The toilet flushes, and we head back into the hallway, still walking awkwardly together.

"You must be hungry," I say. "It's been a long night."

He seems impressed that I thought of him, but his expression is guarded. "What do you suggest we have for breakfast?"

"How about bacon and eggs? Emily gets them fresh from the local farm. They're delicious."

"No," he says. "Too risky. I don't want you anywhere near a flame. What about cereal?"

"I can do that," I say, forcing myself to smile.

We walk into the kitchen, and Ethan exchanges the knife from his pocket for a larger one. "You've been a bad girl recently. I'm not risking it."

My hands shake as I remove a box of cornflakes from a cupboard and grab some milk. And then I tell myself to calm down. Acting like a dutiful wife obviously works well with Ethan. All I have to do is fake it.

So I ask him how much milk he would like. I smile when I pass him the bowl. Then I watch him eat, forcing myself to smile.

"Would you like some coffee with that?" I ask.

He hesitates. "No."

He doesn't trust me around hot liquid. And he's right not to. I'd already fantasised about throwing boiling-hot coffee in his face.

Ethan slurps the milk from the cereal, his eyes always watching me. I glance over at the time on the oven. It's just after seven. Christopher will be awake soon. In fact, he's probably already awake, but he might be too scared to come downstairs. And I have no idea where Emily is. My poor aunt. I glance over at Ethan, wondering if he has softened just slightly.

I take a step towards him and place a hand on his arm. He seems alarmed at first, but then he lets it rest there.

"Can you please tell me where Emily is? I just want to know if she's okay." I make puppy-dog eyes at him, trying to come across as submissive.

"She's fine." He throws the spoon back into the empty bowl.

"Please, Ethan. Let me see her. It's just one minor request. You can do that for me, can't you? I made you breakfast." I squeeze his arm. "Perhaps in exchange for a kiss?"

He smiles. "I can see you're a quick learner, Laura. Maybe this is going to work after all."

He leans over, and I suppress the urge to vomit when his lips touch mine. It's a relatively chaste kiss. Ethan wants me that way. He wants me demure.

"Fine," he says. "I'll take you to Emily. She'll need feeding at some point anyway. Perhaps you can help with that."

"Thank you," I say, remembering at the last minute that he will want to be thanked.

It's remarkable how much fawning works with him. Even as he holds on to me up the stairs, his touch is lighter. He still has the knife in his other hand, but he isn't brandishing it towards me. He lets it hang by his side.

We make our way up two floors and walk past Christopher's room on the way. My heart skips a beat. The door is still jammed closed with the chair. Then we step into the converted attic, and Ethan turns on the light. I should have guessed she was here. Emily turned this attic space into a spare bedroom several years ago. It's a dark space with just one dormer window letting in light. The morning sun spills over the double bed in the centre of the room.

I lift a hand to my mouth, shocked. The room smells like urine.

Emily is tied to the bed, lying in her own filth. Her head lolls from one side to the other, and a low moan comes from her throat. She's trying to speak, but there's tape over her mouth. I try to run to her, but Ethan holds me back.

"Stay where you are."

"I need to check her over," I say. "She could have injuries. Ethan, what did you do? Is she drugged?"

Ethan pulls me back towards the stairs. "Come on. You got your wish. You saw her, and she's alive. Now move. I don't have time for this."

"W-wait," I stammer. "Can I at least give her some water? She's been up here so long—"

My pleas are short-lived when I hear Christopher calling me from his room.

"Your son wants you."

Ethan drags me back down the stairs, too hard and too fast, and I trip. I almost make us both fall.

"Be careful!" he snaps. He presses the knife against my back, reminding me he has the upper hand.

I pull the chair away from Christopher's door and let him out before scooping him into my arms.

"I need the toilet, Mummy," he says in between sobs.

Without even asking Ethan, I take my son's hand and lead him down to the bathroom. Potty training went smoothly recently, and I've grown brave enough to let him sleep without training pants. I didn't even think to give him some last night, and now I feel awful.

Ethan stops me from closing the door again, but Christopher's need is clearly too great for him to feel shy. Once he's finished, he washes his hands, and I settle him back into bed for a while longer. I need to plead with Ethan to let me do something about Emily up there alone in the attic. With a steadying breath, I decide how to approach it.

"Do you want to give your son a kiss good morning?" I ask, gesturing at Christopher lying back in his bed. "Right here, on the forehead. It's a morning tradition."

He glances at me first then steps forwards and leans over Christopher. "Good morning, Junior." He plants the kiss and then steps back.

I smile. "You're a good dad, Ethan."

"That's what I've been trying to tell you all this time," he says.

"I know. I'm so sorry I didn't listen." I sigh. "You're a good dad, and you're not a murderer. Which is why I think you should let me give Emily some water. If she doesn't have water and food soon, she'll die. You know that, don't you? You're smart enough to know that."

"Of course I am," he says. "All right. You can give her water. In a plastic cup."

When we head downstairs to get the water, I realise I'm sweating. Yesterday's clothing is sticky on me, and I'm sure I'm beginning to smell. It's the fear coming out of my pores.

I've never felt so alone. Every decision I make puts the lives of the two people I love the most in the world in jeopardy. It's so easy to fantasise about pushing Ethan down the stairs, or wrenching the knife from his hand and stabbing him with it, or the other fifty ways my mind has conjured how to kill him. Doing it is not the same. If I die, Emily dies, and Christopher is lost to a psychopath who will probably disappear with him somewhere and raise him in his twisted image.

I pour the cup of water, and the two of us walk back up the flights of stairs together again to the attic. As usual, he makes me walk first so that I can't push him. But this time, he lets me approach Emily. I sit on the edge of the bed, holding out one of Christopher's sippy cups.

She lifts her chin and blinks at me. Her eyes are cloudy, still unfocused. It could be the lack of water making her delirious, or else Ethan drugged her. I'm not sure which.

"Ah—" She croaks. Her lips are dry, and her hair is brittle. I've never once thought of my aunt as old or frail, and she certainly doesn't look like she's in her sixties. But today, she seems older. I can't stand it. Ethan came here determined to hurt not just me but also everyone around me.

"Shh." I stroke her cheek. It feels like paper under my fingertips. My heart batters against my rib cage. "It's okay, Em. I'm just going to give you some water. Can you part your lips? I'll hold the cup for you."

Emily parts her lips. A single tear slides out from the corner of her eye. A lump of grief and guilt swells in my throat, like an inflated balloon of anxiety.

I bring the cup to Emily's lips, but she struggles to drink from it. I take it back and remove the lid before pouring the water very slowly into her mouth. Some of the liquid dribbles down her chin, and I wipe it away. She swallows, the muscles in her parched throat contracting.

Emily's eyes keep rolling back in her head like loose marbles.

I look at Ethan, frowning. What did he do to her? And what do I need to do to keep her alive? Time is running out. I need to act before I lose her.

CHAPTER 59

I'm going to have to convince Ethan to let me help Emily more if I'm going to save her life. But I sense that if I push him too much too soon, he'll shut down and not allow me to see her at all. He follows me as I head back to Christopher's bedroom to get him dressed. Then we take him downstairs to make him some breakfast. I pour cereal into a bowl and add blueberries.

"Perhaps I could take Emily a slice of toast. What do you think?" I ask.

Ethan waves the knife around. "I'm not sure about that."

I stroke Christopher's hair, concerned he'll see the knife and be afraid. But he is staring down at his bowl. I'm worried about him. He's not doing well under these stressful circumstances. Every movement he makes is robotic, and he's extremely quiet.

"The thing is, there are clearly some drugs in her system, and she hasn't eaten. I think she'll need food to absorb the chemicals. I mean, you're not a murderer. Are you? You're a good dad, and you want to set an example for your son."

"Fine. Take her some toast. But make it quick. I don't have all day. You should be giving all your attention to me and Junior, not that dreadful woman up there."

"Thank you, Ethan. I can just take it up to her while you watch—"

"Are you *insane*?" His eyes are huge. "I'm not letting you out of my sight for one second. You'll untie her and make some ploy to get away from me."

"All right. Fine." I sigh.

"Oh, and clean your son. He has milk on his chin."

While the toast is in the toaster, I grab a damp cloth and wipe away the slight dribble.

"I'm sorry, Mummy," Christopher says.

It breaks my heart to hear his voice so defeated. I pull him into my chest and hug him tight. "Everything is going to be fine. I promise. Okay?" Ignoring Ethan watching me, I drop lower, to Christopher's line of sight. "Trust me. Everyone is going to be okay."

He nods. "Okay, Mummy."

The toast pops up. I grab butter and jam from the fridge and get to work. The whole while, Ethan's eyes bore into my back. I'm aware of him watching—with that knife—at every moment. I've made a promise to my son now. I never make him promises unless I know I can keep them. Today, I broke that rule.

Ethan takes Christopher's hand as we walk upstairs. I flinch as we step into the urine-scented attic, and Christopher places his fingers over his nose.

"Ethan, keep Christopher back, will you? He doesn't need to see Emily like this."

Ethan shakes his head.

I head over to the bed. Emily is half asleep. The skin around her wrists and ankles is raw from where the fibres of the rope have been digging in. But her lips aren't quite as dry as before.

"Emily," I whisper. "It's me, Laura."

"Just shut up and feed her the damn food," Ethan says.

I don't look at him. I sit on the edge of the bed and try to coax Emily to open her mouth. I give her some water first to make sure she won't have any trouble swallowing. She takes the water and gulps it down. There's more life in her today, I think. That gives me hope. She knows what to do with the sippy cup this time.

"I have some toast if you think you can chew it." I hold up a piece. I've cut it into tiny squares.

Emily nods. Her mouth opens and closes, but I can't make out her words.

I slide a piece of toast into her mouth and watch her carefully. After she swallows, I hand her another, and we repeat the process. I give her a bit of water in between bites to help wash it down. I stroke her hair and whisper to her, trying to soothe her and let her know everything will be all right. Emily moves her arm and winces in pain.

I look at Ethan, hoping that the pleading expression on my face will move him. He's more relaxed this time, sitting in the armchair next to the wardrobe. Christopher stands by his side, his face pale. This is so much more than any four-year-old should ever endure.

"Emily is in a lot of pain. Maybe we could untie her. She's too weak to try anything." I take a step towards Ethan, keeping my expression placid.

He shakes his head.

"What if we just loosen the ropes?" I suggest.

"Do you think I'm stupid?"

"No."

Christopher takes a step towards me, but Ethan grabs hold of my son's arm. He's losing patience. I need to keep my son safe, so I ask if we should go downstairs.

Ethan's eyes narrow. "Yes, we fucking should. You know, you're focusing too much on the wrong people. It's me you should be pleasing." He stands up from the chair, stretching his arms. As he moves, he trips into Christopher, knocking him to the ground.

I reach forwards and grab my son as he begins to cry.

"What a whiny baby. You've coddled him." He reaches out and ruffles Christopher's hair.

I shake my head, biting back the many cutting responses on the tip of my tongue. Then I grab the plate and walk towards the stairs. Ethan follows with his knife.

* * *

Ethan puts us both back on the sofa and paces the living room, still holding the knife. It's as I watch him trip over his feet that I realise he's getting tired. I look at Christopher, hoping he noticed too. If I get an opportunity to make a move, I need to know my son is on the same page. But right now, his expression is completely impassive. He's only a child, and I think he may have disassociated from this stressful situation. There's usually a glint of mischief in Christopher's eyes, but it's gone. Every spark of life my son usually exudes has been replaced by a flatness I've never seen before.

Ethan finally settles into the armchair facing the window. He places the knife on his knee and lifts his head back. The sunlight streams in, falling across his face. I wonder if he's worried we'll have visitors, but we rarely do. Aside from the postie and the occasional delivery from the local farm, Emily lives a quiet life. But I'm glad he chose that chair, because it's one of the warmest spots in the house. There he goes, sitting in the midmorning sun, absorbing the heat and letting himself drift off.

"Christopher, would you like to hear a story?" I ask softly.

He nods.

Moving very slowly, I take a book from Emily's cabinet. It's an adventure novel she used to read me when I was a child. Ethan watches beneath hooded eyes. I smile at Ethan before reading from the book, using my gentlest, most soothing voice. As Ethan's eyes begin to close, I ever so slightly adjust my accent to one similar to Alice's. And then I keep reading. Eventually, Ethan's eyelids flutter closed.

I keep reading in the same voice, but now I communicate with Christopher using my eyes. I look at Ethan, and then I look at the door. He nods. For the briefest of moments, I gaze at the knife. But it's not worth risking it before we leave the room.

Little by little, we inch out of the living room. I carry on reading, making my voice quiet. Ethan starts to snore—his head drops back. Step by step, Christopher and I slowly slide away from him. My heart hammers against my ribs. My hands are shaking so badly I can barely keep hold of my son's hand.

Sour sweat pours down my back. Is this going to work? Maybe, maybe not, but I'll never be able to rest until I try. I glance behind me, breathing out low and steady. We made it to the other side of the room. And then we're in the hallway. I move quickly now, running down to the study, pulling Christopher along with me. Gently, I inch open the door. It's noiseless, thank God. And I lift the phone and dial 999, but I don't wait to speak to an operator. Instead, I leave the phone on the table, knowing the call will be traced anyway. There's no time to spare. I need to get to Emily.

Back in the hall, I wait a beat, listening. Soft snores drift out from the living room, and now time is of the essence. There are three flights of stairs between me and Emily, and I need to be as quiet as a mouse.

I bend down to Christopher. "We need to be super silent. I'm going to carry you because I know the creakiest stairs. We're being superheroes now, buddy. We're rescuing Em-em. Do you understand?"

He nods.

"Good boy."

I hoist him onto my hip and hurry us up to the attic. I'm out of breath when we get there, but Ethan won't hear my panting from three floors away. I lower Christopher onto the carpet and scurry over to the bed.

Emily stirs as I work at the knots. Her arms drop to her sides like limp spaghetti. My heart aches when I see how red and raw her wrists are, but I don't have time to deal with that right now. I keep glancing over my shoulder, making sure Ethan isn't coming after us.

"Can you stand?" I ask.

She nods. But I see her wincing in pain as she lowers her feet to the floor. I kneel down and quickly massage her ankles where the ropes have chafed her skin. She lets out a moan.

"Can you take Christopher?" I ask.

She nods her head, and there's determination in her eyes. There's a glimpse of the Emily I know and love.

"Go into the bathroom with him and lock the door," I tell her. "Wait for me."

I hurry down the stairs before she can respond, careful about noise, adrenaline keeping me moving. I'm so close to freedom I can taste it.

There's movement below me. I dash for Christopher's bedroom to escape Ethan, but he sprints up the last few steps and grabs a fistful of my hair. I scream as he yanks me back towards him.

"Where do you think you're going?" He slams my head into the wall.

CHAPTER 60

There often comes a time when a person must take control of their own life. No one else is going to do it. Difficult decisions will be made, and those decisions will reveal the true mettle of the individual within.

When my skull collides with the wall, I know I'm facing that choice. I could give up and let it all go. There would be peace, at least. I hope so, anyway. Fighting means feeling the pain. Fighting means facing the fear and doing it anyway.

So which am I going to choose?

I'm going to fight.

Pain erupts from my forehead. I feel a trickle of warm blood seeping out from a wound. My hands grope the air, desperate to grab something, anything, but Ethan pulls me back. I lose my balance as he lets me go, falling onto my side.

He gets down low to the ground and brandishes the knife. "I warned you, didn't I? But you won't *listen*, Laura. You're so stupid."

The knife comes down, and I roll away, missing it by a few inches. It sticks into the floorboards, and he tries to yank it back out, but it won't budge.

I start crawling down the stairs, surprised by how fast I can make my bruised body move. I feel safer on all fours. It's harder for him to push me. I sense Ethan moving in my direction, but I have no idea if he has managed to prise the knife from the floorboard. I reach the hallway, and he stops. He shifts his weight, and his attention moves to the attic.

No, I think.

He barrels up the attic stairs, forcing me to follow him.

"Leave them alone!" I scream, sprinting back up the stairs as fast as I can.

He spins on his heel, the knife in his hand. I duck, and it almost unbalances me. But then I manage to throw my weight to the left, slamming his arm against the wall. The knife clatters to the ground, and we become locked in a tangle of limbs. I rake my nails across his forearms, leaving red tracks. Ethan wrenches his arm free, and his elbow cracks into my face, colliding with the bridge of my nose. The pain is short and sharp, an explosion. I manage to stay on my feet but barely.

Ethan bursts through the attic door to find the room empty. I use that moment to catch my breath, praying he doesn't try to knock down the door to the en suite bathroom.

He turns to me. "Where are they?"

He scans the room, and his eyes land on the closed bathroom door. My body stiffens.

"Open the goddamn door right now, you bitch," he hisses through clenched teeth. His cheeks are red with fury, and wrath dances behind his darkened eyes.

Ethan jogs across the room to me, then he turns. In one swoop, he starts racing in the opposite direction and collides his shoulder into the closed bathroom door, attempting to break it down. He growls with pain and frustration, rubs his shoulder, and repeats the same process a second time. His heavy footsteps rattle the trinkets on the built-in shelves on the front wall of the attic room. I consider searching the stairs for the knife, but there could be something closer. I glance at the shelf, looking for a weapon. My eyes rest on a chunk of agate. Emily bought it in Castleton after we explored the caves. I grab it, raise my arm over my head, and bring it down onto Ethan's skull, slamming it as hard as I can. Ethan's shoulders hunch, and his arms go limp as they fall to his sides. He wobbles on his feet before his knees buckle, and he drops to the floor.

"Emily!" I shout. "Open the door. I just hit Ethan, and he's knocked out, but I don't know how long it will last. Come out and go downstairs with Christopher."

A moment later, the lock unclicks and the knob twists. Emily emerges, taking one apprehensive step outside of the bathroom and across the threshold into the bedroom. Her eyes pan to the floor, where she spots Ethan lying like a crumpled piece of paper.

Christopher's eyes widen as he regards the man on the ground. "Is he dead?"

"I don't know," I say.

"I hope he is," Christopher says as Emily begins pulling him away from Ethan's unconscious body.

CHAPTER 61

O nce Christopher is out of sight, I whack Ethan one more time on the back of the skull. Then I hurry past Ethan's limp body and make my way to the ground floor. How long has it been since I called the emergency services? Fifteen minutes? Everything has happened so fast it's hard to tell. The police should be here by now, unless they decided it was a prank call and ignored it.

We need to get out of this house. Now. I have no idea if Ethan is even still alive, but I have no intention of going back to that attic room to check. On my way out of the door, I grab my car keys. Christopher is holding Emily's hand. His eyes are as wide as an owl's. Colour has returned to Emily's cheeks. Her eyes dart around, alarmed, frenzied.

"Let's go." I wave her towards the front door and unlock it with trembling fingers.

I wrench the door open, and a cool breeze hits my skin. It's a salve on sore skin. We're so close to leaving this nightmare.

"Come on," I urge, hurrying my aunt. I reach out to take Christopher's hand when I hear footsteps thundering along the hallway.

"What the fuck?" I mumble.

We hurry out of the house, but Emily is moving slowly. Christopher lets go of her hand and dashes towards the car, which I quickly unlock with my fob. I wait for Emily, holding out an arm for her to rest on. But just as she reaches me, Ethan stumbles out of the house.

"Get back here!" he yells.

Blood pours out from an open wound, mingling with the saliva spraying from his mouth. His eyes are bloodshot, his features twisted in rage. I watch in horror as he stretches out his hands, groping for Emily's hair. Christopher has the door open and has climbed into the back. I'm trying to push Ethan away from Emily, but his fingers lock around her neck. She winces in pain, her body crumpling.

I move behind Ethan and shove my hand into the open wound at the back of his skull. He almost faints, his hands dropping from her neck.

"Get in!" I yell.

Emily climbs into the car and closes the door, and I rush to the driver's side, watching Ethan try to stay upright. I can barely look at the wound he sports, the unnatural slope of his head where his skull is caved in. How is he still alive? He's right there as I close the door. His fingers are a centimetre away as I lock the doors. Then they make contact. Ethan grabs the handle. He jiggles it, trying to get in. I shove the gear into reverse and dig my foot into the accelerator. The engine roars to life. The wheels roll back a few feet, but Ethan now clutches hold of the wing mirror, refusing to let go. Emily screams when he throws himself onto the bonnet of the car.

"Fuck off!" I yell, slamming my foot down on the accelerator.

He slides from the bonnet, finally. I try to manoeuvre the car to get out of the driveway, but Ethan climbs to his feet, blocking the exit. His eyes are wild and sadistic. His chest heaves up and down. His fists are balled by his sides. I stare into the empty void of those evil, bloodshot eyes as I floor it and plough straight into my baby's father.

His body hits the bumper with a heavy *thud*. I hear him grunt. He drops down under the car. It's like running over a speedbump too fast. Emily shields Christopher's eyes with her hands.

I stop. I wait. Ethan doesn't move. He must finally be dead. I can hear the sound of traffic on the road. I wonder if the police are on their way. My hand rests on the gear stick. I check my mirror again. He still hasn't moved. But I thought he was dead the first time, didn't I? I put the car in reverse. I slam the pedal. Emily gasps. The car goes over his body, juddering us in our seats. And then I put the car into first gear and run over him one more time.

My fingers grip the steering wheel so hard that my knuckles are bone white. I glance up at the mirror one more time, satisfied by the smear of blood on the tarmac. Then I drive the car off down the street, not stopping, not looking back.

EPILOGUE

"Want a break? I can put the kettle on," Emily suggests.

There's sunlight on my face and a warm breeze gushing in through the open window. My new bedroom in this new house is light and airy. It's not quite as cosy as Emily's home—I'm determined not to allow the bad memories to erase the good when it comes to her house—but Christopher and I needed our own space, so we found a cottage to rent just a ten-minute drive from her.

"Thanks," I say, following Emily into the kitchen. In a moment of spontaneity, I wrap my arms around her waist. "Thank you for everything."

She pats my hands. "You don't need to thank me." She shakes her head slightly.

I unwrap my arms, knowing there are plenty of things I need to thank her for. And apologise for. Ethan tying her up, the terrible escape from her house, her statement to the police that convinced them what I did was self-defence when it was much more complex than that.

It's been a year since the nightmare unfolded at her house. Christopher is running around in the enclosed garden with our ten-week-old German shepherd puppy. Christopher is usually stuck to me like glue, but since we got the puppy, he's started to come out of his shell.

He's been through a lot. I can't help but frown as I watch him giggling as he kicks a small tennis ball for Louis the dog. A kidnapping, an imprisonment, witnessing unspeakable violence, and all because I thought I'd met a nice guy.

I nod towards Christopher as the kettle boils. "I think he's warming up to this place."

"He's going to love it here," Emily says. Then she notices my expression and leans closer. "Hey. Are you all right?"

I nod.

She rubs my upper arm. "He's gone. It's over."

I nod again and then touch my temple. There's no mistaking it this time. Ethan Hart is dead, and his mother is still in prison for the time being. Her appeal failed. But one day, she'll be released, and I'll have to deal with that. Until then, I'm free. I should feel light.

Emily hands me a cup of hot tea and stands with me at the window. I'm lucky to still have her here. The drugs Ethan gave her left her dehydrated and groggy but didn't have any lasting consequences. I know one of her wrists still aches in cold weather, but she never complains about it.

"Why don't you call Jessa and see if she wants to visit?" Emily suggests. "It's been so long since you both met up."

"I might just do that." I smile then wander over to one of the boxes on the kitchen table before idly pulling out kitchen utensils, the mug of tea still in one hand.

"And maybe Lucas?" She lifts an eyebrow. "I know you two still talk."

It's true. At first, it was just about Alice's appeal, but now, we Face-Time or Zoom at least once a week.

"I don't know about that. I think I like him as a friend more than anything." I glance at the clock. "How is it late afternoon already?"

"Time flies when you're having fun."

"Or when there's a million jobs to do."

"That too," she says. "Don't worry. It'll get done. Why don't you spend some time with Christopher and Louis? I'll finish up in here."

I shake my head. "No, I couldn't—"

"Ten minutes. Get some sun while you still can." She gives me a gentle shove towards the back door.

She's right, but then my aunt usually is. I step outside with my mug of tea and wave to Christopher.

He throws a ball to Louis, who immediately races across the yard to retrieve it.

"He likes the ball, Mummy." Christopher cackles and runs over to me. He sweeps his arms around my legs and squeezes me tight.

I ruffle his hair and smile. "I'm so glad you two are bonding."

Christopher peers up at me. His cheeks are pink, and his hair is chestnut brown, glowing under the rays of the sun.

"I love him," he says.

"I love *you*." I lean down to plant a soft kiss on the top of his little head.

Getting to experience this joy on my child's face makes it all worth it. Everything I did, everything I went through, it all comes full circle as I gaze into his eyes. His *father's* eyes, but I won't think about that.

"Do you think you're going to like it here in the new house?" I ask.

"Oh yes, Mummy," he says, hilariously sincere.

His eyes look up at me one more time, and I'm glad his father is dead. I'm glad I killed him. I'm glad my boy is free of that evil man. But what will Christopher remember when he grows up? The face of his terrified mother? His father's body smeared across the tarmac? I know the latter haunts me. I can't help but wonder what will become a core memory for my beautiful child.

And then there's the final thought, the one I've tried to lock away and never look at. The thought that there might be some of Ethan inside my son.

No, I think. He'll never be like Ethan. For one thing, I'll raise him right. I won't be another Alice. He'll have two strong women in his life to keep him on the right track. Me and Emily. Just like I had Mum and Emily to raise me.

I tilt my head to the sun, enjoying the final rays before twilight comes, soaking in the perfection of my small family, wondering what the future will bring.

ALSO BY THE AUTHORS

Sarah A. Denzil

Standalone Psychological Suspense

Saving April

The Broken Ones

Only Daughter

The Liar's Sister

Poison Orchids

Little One

The Housemaid

My Perfect Daughter

Find Her

The Stranger in Our House

The Nice Guy

The Silent Child Series

Silent Child, Book One

Stolen Girl, Book Two

Aiden's Story, a novella

Crime Fiction

One For Sorrow (Isabel Fielding book one)

Two For Joy (Isabel Fielding book two)

Three For A Girl (Isabel Fielding book three)

The Isabel Fielding Boxed Set

Supernatural Suspense

You Are Invited

Short suspenseful reads

They Are Liars: A novella

Aiden's Story (a SILENT CHILD short story)

Harborside Hatred (A Liars Island novella)

A Quiet Wife

SL Harker

Domestic Thrillers

The New Friend

The Work Retreat

ABOUT THE AUTHORS

Sarah A. Denzil

Sarah A. Denzil is a British suspense writer from Derbyshire. Her books include *Silent Child*, which has topped Kindle charts in the UK, US, and Australia. *Saving April* and *The Broken Ones* are both top-thirty bestsellers in the US and UK Amazon charts.

Combined, her self-published and published books—along with audiobooks and foreign translations—have sold over one million copies worldwide.

Sarah lives in Yorkshire with her husband, enjoying the scenic countryside and rather unpredictable weather. She loves to write moody, psychological books with plenty of twists and turns.

To stay updated, join the mailing list for new release announcements and special offers.

SL Harker

Even as a young child SL Harker would conjure up stories to share with her family. That love of books and storytelling never went away, but her skills have improved since then.

As a lover of twisty fiction, her books are fast-paced domestic thrillers with a little spice added in.

Keep up to date with her new releases by joining the mailing list.

Printed in Great Britain
by Amazon